A CHERRY BLOSSOM IN WINTER

A CHERRY BLOSSOM IN WINTER

BY

RON SINGERTON

www.Penmorepress.com

A Cherry Blossom in Winter by Ron Singerton

ISBN-13: 978-1-942756-92-7(Paperback)
ISBN 13: 978-1-942756-93-4 (e-book)

BISAC Subject Headings:
FIC014000FICTION / Historical
FIC032000FICTION / War & Military
FIC051000FICTION / Cultural Heritage

Editor: Chris Wozney
Cover Concept by Ron Singerton
Cover by Christine Horner

Address all correspondence to:
Michael James
Penmore Press LLC
920 N Javelina Pl
Tucson AZ 85748

In Appreciation

I wish to extend my deepest gratitude to my editor, Chris Wozney, for unstinting attention to detail and adroit suggestions that were of inestimable value. My thanks also to Michael James, my publisher, for his encouragement and insight in the development of this novel. Thanks to Christine Horner, for her design of the book cover, a compelling and thoughtful work. And always to Darla, my wife, for her questions, comments and remarkable willingness to listen and evaluate the writing and rewriting of each page of *A Cherry Blossom in Winter*.

Anguish and Longing
Bud of the Cherry Blossom
On Winter's Bare Branch.

CHAPTER 1

St. Petersburg, Russia
September, 1897

The invitational fencing competition was already in progress when Admiral Kochenkov, superintendent of the prestigious Nikolaevsky Naval Academy, mounted the platform to observe the saber matches. The admiral was a stout gentleman, with a flushed face partly hidden by a full white beard. His uniform was dark blue, adorned with three resplendent medals, the Order of St. Andrew, the Order of Alexander Nevsky, and the Imperial Order of St. Anna, all presented for military gallantry. An officer's jeweled sword hung at his side—a gift from Tsar Alexander III for bravery in the war against Turkey. He joined the two dozen other dignitaries gazing down at the sparring cadets in their distinctive white trousers and canvas jackets. After nodding his greetings to several of the elite, he turned his attention to a knot of fencers who were avidly watching one particular match.

"Daddy, you're here!" cried a lithe, lovely young woman. She broke away from a gaggle of girlfriends and ran up the steps to throw her arms about him, her gleaming red hair tousling against his uniform.

"Decorum, Svetlana, decorum," admonished the admiral, embarrassed by his daughter's exuberance.

"To hell with decorum," she said, disregarding the raised eyebrows of the assemblage. "You look positively handsome! Doesn't my admiral look devastating?" she called to her friends. Then, standing on her tiptoes, she whispered, "Boris has been doing well in the competition! You have to see him."

"Yes," the admiral said, "but he may meet his match today. And you know I do not approve of your flirting with him."

"Oh, Daddy, he is a little pompous, but he is a cadet, and he does like me."

Not wishing to argue with her, the admiral said, "Be a good girl and rejoin your friends. I must watch this competition."

Svetlana made a face and tossed her head, then clattered down the stairs to rejoin her friends.

"Who are those two?" asked Kochenkov, addressing Captain Isorovsky and gesturing towards the two masked fencers upon whom a dozen cadets were focused.

"The tall one is Cadet Sergei Ivanovich Vershinin. The other is Alexei Yevgenovich Brusilov," the captain replied.

A surprised look came to the admiral's face. Seeing it, Isorovsky explained, "Alexei has already eliminated two of our best. We are quite interested to see how he does against Sergei Ivanovich."

"Ah, yes, the champion of the épée team," remarked Kochenkov. "But saber is not his best weapon."

"True, but I'm told that he taught Alexei saber. They're good friends despite the age difference, and Alexei looks up to him. It's unfortunate that Alexei is only seventeen, a year too young for the Academy."

"He'll be here soon enough. I'll speak to his father; I know him well."

The match was for three points to win, and touches were

counted when the blade connected with the steel mask, a sleeve, or the torso of the opponent. Scoring with the point of the saber was legal but rarely done, since the saber was predominantly a slashing weapon. Though it had been decades since swords had been employed in naval combat, carrying the weapon and expertise in its use were considered the marks of an officer and a gentleman. Moreover, the saber was utilized by cavalry of all nations.

Sergei, tall and stocky, was better suited to the épée, for which a long reach is invaluable, since only the weapon's point connected with the target. Endurance was also essential; an épée match could last minutes, whereas a saber bout might be over in seconds. But Sergei's strength served him well with the saber, too, and he prided himself on his skill.

Members of the saber and épée teams spent hours in the gymnasium practicing parries and lunges under the uncompromising gaze of fencing masters. Decorum was studiously observed; jovial camaraderie had no place in competition, especially when cadets of the Naval Academy faced those of the Army. On rare occasions students of other universities were invited, or sons of the nobility, such as Alexei. Guests were unknown quantities, so it was with intense interest that the cadets watched the match, gauging the speed and agility of the rivals. Even an amateur could see these two young men were extraordinary.

Alexei had scored the first and fourth point, Sergei the second and third. The next touch would be the decisive one.

Sergei was wary. Ignoring the judges and breathless cadets, his eyes were fixed on Alexei. He took two steps back, so that Alexei would have to advance to keep up the pressure of his blade against Sergei's. A slight misstep, the saber's guard a fraction out of line, could be an opening for a lightning strike. Choosing an unusual attack, Sergei executed a slashing head cut to bring the saber down atop Alexei's mask. But a parry *in prime*, the blade held horizontal over the head, stopped the blade. Sergei had no time to recover to an *en garde* position; Alexei swept his saber down, striking Sergei's jacket with an audible slap.

"*Touché!*" called the two judges standing behind Alexei. The match concluded, cadets applauded as both fencers removed their masks, saluted one another, and shook hands.

Sergei grinned and said, "Another damn welt. A little softer with the blade would be greatly appreciated, Alexei. This is demoralizing. Challenge me in épée and I'd cut you to pieces and regain my honor."

"And I'd spend the day sewing up holes. No, thank you, I'll stick to saber. But I'll whack you more gently next time. Just remember the words of Danton: *'de l'audace, encore de l'audace, et toujour de l'audace'*."

"Audacity, and more audacity, always audacity," said Sergei. "*Now* you tell me!"

There was congenial laughter from the onlookers as the fencers stepped out of the circle to take a break. Slapping each other on the back, they had started for a table that held glasses of cold water when an insistent voice made them both stop and turn their heads.

"It's my turn," said a tall, lanky cadet with a pinched face and dark hair brushed over his forehead.

"Can't you wait a moment, Sokolov? *Mssr.* Brusilov has just finished three matches; I suspect he would like a moment to recover," said one of the fencing masters.

"I'm a cadet with responsibilities," Boris Sokolov said airily. "I don't have time to wait, and I doubt that one so young would need recovery time."

The fencing master looked from Boris, who imperiously couched his saber in the crook of his left arm, his mask tilted up on his head, to Alexei.

"I'm fine," said Alexei. "I would be honored to face him."

"In that case, you may both take your positions," said the instructor. "The winner must score three touches."

Two judges stood behind and on either side of Alexei and two behind Sokolov, each ready to raise a hand and call "*Touché*" when a point was scored. Both fencers raised the hilt of their saber to eye level, then swept it down in a smart salute.

"*En garde*; begin!" came the command from the fencing master.

As before, cadets stood to the side of the large chamber, whose walls rang with the clash of blades, their eyes taking in the forward and back movements and parries of the two fencers. Boris towered over Alexei, but each of his extensions was met by a parry and a *riposte,* causing Boris to rethink his next *sortie*. He was an adequate fencer, particularly with the foil; but he was known to be temperamental and surly if he lost a match, and more than one junior cadet had lost to him deliberately to avoid retribution. As a result, Boris had an inflated, and inflamed, opinion of his abilities.

Alexei, not having had any opportunity to observe Boris's technique, decided to start on the defensive. Sensing hesitation, Boris lunged, but Alexei disengaged, dropping the point of his weapon to the outside of Boris's saber, striking it and sending the blade far off target. Then with a flick of the wrist, the tip of Alexei's saber touched the glove of Boris's hand, and two judges abruptly called "*Touché*."

Boris was startled, but it was only the first victory of the match. He could acknowledge the touch with a quick salute without losing face. There was still time to humble this youth, and it would not do to incense the judges with blatant rudeness.

The second round took much longer, both participants making quick lunges and repartees. Tiring of the back and forth, and sensing fatigue in his opponent, Boris made a feint to the mask and a quick lunge to the torso, but he was late.

Alexei parried the blade and struck Boris's mask in a lightning move.

Again the judges called the touch, and Boris, mindful of his audience, haltingly saluted before resuming the *en garde* position. All eyes were on the duelists, so none of the observers noticed Admiral Kochenkov walk onto the gymnasium floor, followed by the captain.

I must reverse this, thought Boris. He would come from behind, even the score—with opinion against him—and drive home the point. He would humiliate this child! There must be no missteps, no vacillation.

All his attention was on his opponent. He did not see the cadets make way for the admiral. Boris advanced, his blade tapping Alexei's, forcing the youth back between the parallel lines of the court. Boris lunged, his saber, an extension of his arm, aimed directly at Alexei's midriff. Alexei leapt back; his blade swept in a half-circle to appear on the other side of his opponent's. A swift, decisive parry with a slight tap sent Boris's thrust into mid-air. Suddenly Alexei dropped to his left knee and shot his right arm forward. Boris, continuing his forward movement, was appalled to feel the point of Alexei's blade strike his fencing jacket. Enraged by the speed and daring of the move, Boris stopped, flung off his mask and threw his saber to the ground.

Alexei removed his mask and, alarmed, glanced at the amazed audience. Not knowing what else to do, he extended his hand to Boris for the customary handshake, but the cadet stormed off the court.

"Halt!" a deep voice commanded.

Abruptly Boris stopped, turned.

"You will show sportsmanship and respect. You will recover your weapon and shake his hand in accordance with the requirements of the Academy. And you will do it now!" barked Captain Isorovsky.

Boris, ashen-faced, took in the reproving looks of both the admiral and the captain. His eyes narrowed. Spinning on his heel, he returned and said in a brusque voice, “I am ordered to shake your hand.”

“You don’t have to,” said Alexei.

“Of course I do. It was an order.” Fury and disgust welled up in Boris as he barely touched Alexei’s extended hand.

***

Still seething, Boris stormed down the sidewalk, ignored the evening crowds as he and Svetlana walked along the illuminated Nevsky Prospekt.

“Humiliated, absolutely humiliated!” cried Boris.

“I thought you fenced very well. That boy is very quick but hardly has your experience. You would certainly beat him in foil. Maybe you should challenge him.”

“I will, but it won’t be in foil. I’ll get him, just like I did that Jewish kid.”

“The one who was enrolled in the Academy?”

“Yes, that one.”

“No one ever found out about that, did they? I mean, the way he simply disappeared?” asked Svetlana with a worried look.

“Of course not. And you must never say a word. You promised.”

“I will never say a thing. I adore you, Boris, and I know how to keep secrets.”

In a quieter voice she added, “I have some of my own.”

Boris, striding ahead, head hunched forward, did not hear.

***

“I have never seen such a lack of sportsmanship. It was despicable,” said the captain. “He should be dismissed from the Academy."

Admiral Grigory Kochenkov signaled for his glass to be refilled before replying. "Sokolov is a difficult young man, and I will not tolerate such conduct again, but perhaps he learned from the episode on the court. I believe in giving a second chance."

"But *is* it a second chance? Or is it an umpteenth? The lads are wary of him; his uncle, you know."

"His uncle doesn't concern me, but the honor of the Academy certainly does," replied the admiral, as a waiter brought him a glass of Scotch, a taste he'd acquired during his time in England.

"And Svetlana? Were she *my* daughter—" But what Captain Isorovsky would do were Svetlana his daughter went unstated, for their conversation was interrupted by a new arrival.

"There you are! I thought you would be here," said Count Brusilov, huffing his way past fashionably dressed gentlemen. The English Club was one of the finest in St. Petersburg.

"I am furious! I am absolutely beside myself! You can't imagine what those idiots have done," said the count, sitting heavily in a chair at Kochenkov's table.

"Furious, Yevgeny? About what? I'm sure you heard that your son whipped every saber fencer on the team. I would be proud, not angry," said the admiral, wondering what had riled Brusilov this time.

Waving off the praise for Alexei, Brusilov said, "No! I mean the Foreign Office and that toad, Witte."

"Count Witte, the Minister of Treasury?" inquired Captain Isorovsky.

"Who else? I spent my entire life in the service of the Tsar! Junior consul in every despicable country you can imagine, and just last week I was finally promoted. I was to be senior consul in Bavaria! It would have been an assignment worthy of all my efforts as an esteemed representative of Nicholas II."

"Indeed! So what happened?" asked Kochenkov, lighting a cigar and sitting back in his chair. He watched Brusilov closely through the veil of smoke.

"That damn Witte stuck his head in where it did not belong! Trod right into the foreign office and said, 'Oh no, that position is promised to Count Kiliovska. Brusilov should be sent to Japan!' Japan! Can you imagine? The Tsar hates those monkeys, and so do I. And the post is for three miserable years."

"Were you in the foreign office to protest?" asked Captain Isorovsky.

"No, I was detained," said the count, and he motioned for his vodka.

"Japan is an important posting, especially in today's political climate," the admiral pointed out. "Wilhelm is an ally; we have nothing to fear from Spain. But Japan...."

"Am I supposed to eat rice and raw fish and sleep on a straw mat? And what about my own business? I will be too far away from the decision-making. I am on the board, you know. The timing is preposterous!" declared the count vehemently. He swallowed half his drink, then set about extracting a cheroot from a monogrammed gold case.

"You can telegraph from Japan, just as you would from Bavaria," said the captain soothingly. "The mill will continue to function. Lumber will be cut."

"From Berlin I can get back here in two days. By ship from Tokyo it will take weeks," Brusilov countered morosely. He puffed furiously, then expelled a cloud of aromatic smoke.

"Speaking of *Mssr.* Witte, I hear that he's proposed a trans-Siberian railroad to go from here to Vladisvostok," said Kochenkov quietly.

Count Brusilov sipped from his drink and looked closely at the admiral. "So? How does that involve us?"

"If the Tsar approves the project, we're talking about the greatest building enterprise in the history of Russia and the longest railroad in the world. I have a major share in the St. Petersburg steel mill, and a railroad needs tracks," said Kochenkov.

"*And* railroad ties, bridges, telegraph poles, and train stations," interjected the captain. "Made of lumber."

Brusilov cocked his head, then said, "But if Witte is in charge...."

"He's simply proposing the construction. I doubt he will be awarding contracts, Yevgeny. I do have influence at court, and the Romanovs enjoy the company of my wife. She could charm a cobra. This venture could prove extremely profitable. Worth millions," said the admiral.

Brusilov leaned back and considered. "Very interesting. But I maintain that I am worthy of a higher office, and I'm sure the Tsar will agree. A little effort in the right direction could gain me an ambassadorship. Perhaps in Spain, a real plum," said the count.

"The railroad will be a few years in the planning. Perhaps the less you criticize Witte the better," suggested Captain Isorovsky with a smile.

"Now I do have a question," said the admiral. "I presume that you are going to Japan in the next few weeks, so let's settle this now: I want your son in my Academy. He would be invaluable on the saber team—you know how intense the competition is between the Navy and Army—and I can waive the matter of his age. He will be looked after, of that I can assure you. I assume he *is* staying in St. Petersburg with his mother?"

"I have no intention of taking him with me, if indeed I must go. He would only get in trouble there. I don't need an embarrassment."

"I hardly see how he would be an embarrassment," said the admiral.

"I don't want him to get any ideas about Japanese girls. God forbid! No, he stays here, and that concern will be off my shoulder," said the count. Just as abruptly as he'd come in, he finished his drink, excused himself and bustled out.

Captain Isorovsky watched him go and turned to Kochenkov. "He doesn't care much for his son, does he?"

"Unfortunately, no," agreed the admiral.

"The lad is a good boy. Any father would be proud to have such a son. So I would like to ask, since I may be one of his instructors, is there a problem I should know about?"

"There is a problem, but not one that should adversely effect the boy's progress at the Academy. Brusilov's anger with his son is misdirected. It's a rather complicated family problem."

"Involving his wife?"

"Something along those lines."

"And these are things that you know," said the captain, lighting a cheroot and giving the admiral a quizzical look.

The admiral flicked an ash from his cigar, considered for a moment, and replied, "Yes, Isorovsky, there are things I know that he does not."

"And you are not about to inform him, are you?"

"No, I will not 'inform' him, nor will I inform Alexei. Not that he doesn't deserve to know, but it will be for him to find out."

"I did not appreciate how complex you are, or should I say, how devious, Admiral. There are state secrets and family secrets, and both are magnificently intriguing."

"Indeed. And both must be guarded."

***

"I'm surprised that your father didn't come to the fencing competition. He would have enjoyed seeing you win," said Sergei.

"The competition was in the morning, and he's rarely sober before noon," said Alexei, trying to keep up with his friend as they hurried through a dingy part of the city consisting of windowless factories. It was cold; bundled workers, including young women and children, trudged through pathways of slush. Heavily laden carts pulled by horses in shaggy winter coats rumbled past. On occasion a three-horse troika with tinkling bells sped past, sending spray all about. Those invariably carried factory owners or wealthy investors, their passengers oblivious to those scrambling out of the way.

"Do you think we can get in?" asked Alexei, an anxious tone to his voice.

"*You're* not going anywhere near the door! It's too damn dangerous. If your father found out he'd kill both of us."

"But Tatiana will be inside. Won't it be dangerous for her?" asked Alexei.

"She lives for danger and for the revolution. It's in her blood. But you must not be seen."

"But you mustn't, either. If you're caught you'd be expelled, or worse."

"I'll only be inside for a few minutes. I promised her."

"You're in the same cell as she, aren't you?"

"Don't talk about it!" Sergei warned sharply. "The *Okhrana* has spies everywhere. Any opposition to the regime is dangerous."

They slipped away from the stream of workers and stood in an alcove of a boarded up and abandoned warehouse.

"She's in there," Sergei said, jerking his head in the direction the clothing factory across the street.

"Why did she choose that one?" said Alexei, his hands in his pockets to ward off the cold.

"She didn't. Her cell did. A delegation learned of our efforts to help workers. This was after they went to the owners and asked for a raise and better lighting around the machines; it's quite dark inside, and people get hurt."

"Did they get the raise or the lighting?"

"They got fired. So a second group of workers came and said that they need coordination and an agitator, because many of the women and children are afraid to protest working conditions."

"And that's when your girlfriend was sent?" asked Alexei, as he watched a huddled group of women in coats and shawls furtively glance up and down the street.

"We'll wait here," said Sergei as he pulled a hat low on his head and peered at the heavy door of the Number Four Goronska clothing factory.

***

Tatiana, wearing a brown woolen coat smeared with mud and a scarf over her head, carried a bundle of cloth to a shearing table. An elderly *babushka* with a round face and little piggish eyes glanced at her and said, "*Nyet, nyet*. I know what you do—and what follows. The police, the bully gangs, or the *Okhrana* will come. They will beat us. See my grand-daughter over there? She is only six; she may be hurt. I will not help you."

"I am here to help you," said Tatiana over the staccato rattling of five hundred sewing machines. "Your grand-daughter should not even be here. She has rickets, doesn't she? There's no sunlight here. We can change that."

The old woman shook her head, and her eyes darted towards a determined inspector checking stitching in army overcoats. Tatiana averted her face and looked at the inspector from the corner of her eye. Then she nodded and said, "Tomorrow at eleven."

Tatiana left several reams of cloth with the old woman, passed two children carrying bobbins of thread, then stood at a table where a man and his wife were trying to extract thread from a faulty machine. A pile of officers' coats and pants were stacked beside them. She spoke to them softly. The man glanced about. Then, looking down at his work, he murmured, "It will be too dangerous for the children. They should stay home."

"It's the children that the foreign journalists will photograph and write about! The demonstration must be peaceful, but the capitalists will only comply with our demands if condemned by the foreign press. English and French journalists have been told about the protest. They will be here."

"The owners won't care about European papers, and I think the journalists will alert the bosses."

"The reporters want a story. They won't tell."

"They want blood, and they'll get it. You'll see. The owners are only concerned about profits. I think the demonstration will be meaningless. The only thing that will change the system is revolution, and that must come from inside Russia itself," said the man, and his eyes bored into Tatiana like drills. "Tell your Mensheviks or Social Democrats or whoever you're with to stockpile guns. *That's* how things will change."

"Not war, not yet. The proletariat must be organized, and there must be leadership. We will only get support if a revolution starts without violence on our part. Just help me spread the word about tomorrow."

"Would you like me to tell the Tsar? Invite him perhaps?" the man said with a cynical grin. "Yes, yes, I'll help, but nothing goes according to plan. I hope you have lots of bandages and stretchers."

"You will be with us, won't you?" asked his wife.

"Of course I will," said Tatiana. "I intend to lead the demonstration. We will begin here and march past the steel mill, the ammunition factory, and onto the Admiralty building. There should be thousands."

"It should start earlier, before the factories open," said the man.

"No, it will have greater impact if workers put down their tools and simply walk out. A strike, even for a day, will get the attention we need," said Tatiana, worried that events might spin out of control.

"I just hope it stays peaceful. Not everybody is willing to be beaten without hitting back," said the woman, with worry in her eyes.

***

The next morning, the chanting of dozens of people could be heard even before Tatiana, Sergei and Alexei reached the factory. Sergei glanced at his pocket watch and said, "It's not even ten yet. They started early, and without you."

"Then who's leading?" asked Alexei, as they hurried through an alley to catch up with the procession of heavily bundled workers, some holding signs aloft. Others, led by a priest, were singing a song in praise of the Tsar. An Orthodox cross was held high, surrounded by icons.

From a block away, Alexei spied several men with large tripod cameras. "Journalists?" he asked Sergei.

"Perhaps, or *Okhrana*."

Turning their faces away, the three hurried past the photographers on their side of the street and shied away from those on the other.

"It's harder to break up a large demonstration that is attracting a lot of attention than a small one just starting," said Sergei. "If the *Okhrana* was tipped off ...."

The procession had come to a halt in front of a crowd of men with truncheons. Behind them, a squadron of cavalry filled the entire road. There was indecision amongst the marchers. The priest, upon seeing the armed men, walked forward through the marchers, holding high his cross.

"Brothers, servants of the Lord, we appeal to—"

There was a rasping scrape of steel as sabers were drawn from scabbards. Cavalry horses pawed nervously at the frozen ground. A child began to cry, and the crowd stirred anxiously. Sergei, Alexei and Tatiana were still a hundred yards from the front. In a low voice Sergei said, "Don't go any further." Grabbing Tatiana's hand, he pulled her behind a line of wagons as truncheon-wielding men rushed forward. Shouts and screams filled the street as people tried to flee; many slipped and fell on the icy pavement. Children and women were trampled underfoot, and the priest, holding tightly to his great wooden cross, was pummeled and beaten until he was immobile.

Sergei, Tatiana and Alexei tore down a back alley.

"It's over, it's finished," Sergei gasped, when the three finally came to a halt.

"Do you think we were photographed?" asked Alexei.

"I doubt it. Anybody moving is a blur, but somebody from the factory might have recognized me or Tatiana," Sergei replied. Catching his breath, he turned to Tatiana and said, "You'd better get out of St. Petersburg for a few months. Go to Sweden; that's where the cell has a meeting house. You'll be safe there."

"Will you come with me?" she asked, her voice shaky.

"I mustn't. I can only help if I remain useful, and anonymous. If I am accused, I will insist that one young man looks very like another, that I wasn't at the protest. If I leave the Academy now, *Okhrana* will know I was involved, and that could implicate Alexei."

"You should not have brought him," said Tatiana.

"It was my decision," Alexei spoke up. "I saw the condition of the workers and I was embarrassed about the way we live compared to them. No one that I know has to work. They all have servants. I wanted to do something, but I didn't think it was going to be like this."

"Well, now you know how one hundred and ten million people in this country are being treated by a few thousand aristocrats and capitalists!" Tatiana said bitterly. "The *Okhrana* must have an informer in the factory. We were betrayed, but this is just beginning."

***

"You are a cadet and will be a naval officer," said Alexei, as he and Sergei sat on a bench overlooking the frozen Neva River. "I wonder how you can be a defender of the Tsar and the state, and a revolutionary at the same time."

"I never started out to be a revolutionary, and I'm not as extreme as Tatiana. I don't think my sympathies conflict with my allegiance to the Tsar. I love the sea and I love fencing, and the Academy is the only place I can go to have both. And yes, I want to be an officer in the Russian Navy."

"But there had to be something that made you become involved," persisted Alexei.

"You ask a lot of difficult questions," said Sergei, lapsing into silence. Alexei said nothing as he watched skaters on the frozen river. After a long silence, Sergei spoke.

"Both my father and Tatiana's are minor nobles, hardly important enough to be invited to the Winter Palace or ever have an audience with the Tsar. I met Tatiana at church when we lived beside the Don River. She had two brothers, both older than she. The elder was Eugene. He was smart and funny, and the three of us used to go skating and ride her father's horses. Then he got involved in a labor strike. He was falsely accused of shooting at a policeman, and he was hanged on the spot."

"Wasn't there a trial?" demanded Alexei, aghast.

"Of a sort," Serge said grimly. "The defense lawyer was told what to say, and it was over in an hour. Tatiana virtually disintegrated. She spoke to no except me for over a year. When at last she emerged from her grief, she and I had become very close."

"Lovers?" asked Alexei, having only a vague awareness of what that might entail.

"Yes, lovers," said Sergei. "And she became a determined and bitter revolutionary. She's courageous and motivated, and she throws herself into any movement that will bring down the tyrants. So does her other brother, Vassily. She may speak of gradualism, but her final goal is the destruction of the Romanov dynasty and all it condones."

"And you feel the same?"

There was a sigh from Sergei and he said, "I do not, and she tolerates that. Tatiana assumes that someday I will be just as determined as she. But I won't risk my career, unless the regime does something completely intolerable, something absolutely requiring revolution."

"I think changes are needed, but I won't support the overthrow of the Tsar," said Alexei. "I think you're right. You don't just overthrow six hundred years of rule. Some of them, like Peter the Great and Catherine, were innovators who made Russia a great power."

"True, but that doesn't excuse the excesses, the brutal repression and a frozen class system," said Sergei. "But change will not come easy. I hope to work quietly within the system. But you, Alexei, must let matters take their course;

stay out of it. It's damn dangerous, and despite your lineage the authorities would not be kind to you."

"Are you afraid?" asked Alexei.

"Of course I am," Sergei said somberly, looking his friend straight in the eye. "It's all very frightening, Alexei. Now I think you should go home. You have seen enough. Now you know."

***

A cloud of cigar smoke wafted toward the parlor ceiling as Count Brusilov sat brooding in his favorite chair.

"I expect that I shall still have some money and this house when I get back," he said without preamble.

"What are you talking about?" asked his wife, as she watched a light snow fall on the garden's bare branches.

"I thought I already told you. The bastards in the Foreign Office are sending me off to Japan! I'll be gone for three years, so you and Alexei will have all the time you want to fool around, doing whatever it is you do."

"Three years?" exclaimed Olga, shocked by the abrupt announcement.

"Yes. I will have the admiral check on you while I'm gone. Now, where's my drink?" he demanded, oblivious to the stunned look on Olga's face. A servant appeared, carrying a tray and the day's paper. Olga continued to stare at her husband. After inhaling his drink he glanced at her and said, "What? Why are you just standing there? Surely you must be happy about my impending departure."

"You're announcing this with less concern for me or Alexei than you would have for one of your race horses."

Brusilov shrugged and said, "I'm being sent away, that's all there is to it. And it wasn't my choice. They decided without me."

"Maybe because you were too drunk to intercede," Olga said, with an edge of bitterness to her soft voice.

"You do not judge me," he said harshly, opening the day's paper with a slap. For a long moment he stared at the lead story, pointedly ignoring his wife's clenched jaw.

In a far corner of the room, Alexei was reading a book about the history of Japan while awaiting a visit from his tutor. Not having ventured out of the house that day, he had heard nothing about the previous day's events. He hoped that its volatility would be brushed off as a minor incident involving disgruntled workers.

The only potentially incriminating detail was that he had told his mother the previous morning that he would be with Sergei. Alexei was certain that she knew nothing about his friend's revolutionary thinking, but he had once mentioned that Sergei had a girlfriend named Tatiana who had revolutionary inclinations.

Suddenly Brusilov bellowed, "What the hell? Look at this! The bastards should be shot!"

"Whatever are you shouting about?" asked Olga, still disconcerted by her husband's abrupt announcement.

"This right here! Another strike. Peasants! Ignorant scum! Listen to this article!" He read aloud.

> *"Number Four Goronska Clothing Factory. A motley rabble threw down their tools and deserted their machines to illegally protest wages and working conditions yesterday. Numerous journalists, including those of the foreign press, reported that many workers were armed and numerous shots were fired, wounding those who valiantly stood up to the rampaging mob. Fortunately a squadron of the Tsar's Imperial Hussars stood in the way of any destruction. The owner of the St. Petersburg Clothing Factory, a Mr. Grigory Glavokov, said that wages at the factory were higher than anything the workers*

could have earned in their squalid villages and they should be happy to have work at all. In addition, extensive improvements have been made to ensure the comfort and safety of everyone in the work place."

Brusilov saw that his wife and Alexei were listening intently, so he continued.

"The factory produces uniforms for our military, and the government deplores the disruption of work by a few disgruntled and violent workers. All efforts are being made to locate and prosecute organizers of yesterday's unpatriotic act. Photographers were on the scene and the police have been provided with photos. Nevertheless, the public is requested to offer whatever information may lead to the arrest of those involved. Fortunately the injured officers are reported to have survived their wounds."

"The officers were *not* wounded, and the only shot was fired into the air," protested Alexei. "It was the workers who were trampled and maimed!"

"What? You were there? What in God's name were you doing with that damned rabble?" demanded Brusilov, getting up from his chair.

"I wasn't in any protest."

"But you were there! How else would you know about the shot? What the hell were you doing in that district anyway? Were you there alone, or with those revolutionary thugs you hang out with?"

"My friends are not thugs, and we took a short cut and ran into the demonstration, that is all."

"I don't believe you. In fact, I don't believe anything you say."

"I'm sure he didn't know that there would be a strike," said Olga, bristling at the condemnation.

"Look here, photographs. These three, who are they? You and your accomplices?" demanded the count.

"They're so grainy they could be anybody," said his wife.

"No!" said the count, turning to Alexei. "This is you; you are lying. Admiral Kochenkov told me that he wants you in the Naval Academy, but you will never be allowed in. You are unworthy of a naval commission! I have done everything for you, I have given you everything. You live in this mansion, you have private tutors and expensive clothes, and you embarrass me like this? You betray and disgrace your family? I am terrified of what trouble you will get into when I'm gone."

"Then take him with you," said Olga.

"That would be worse! No, he will stay here under the thumb of Kochenkov."

"I am appalled at how little you think of Alexei. What has he ever done to sully your name?" asked Olga. "You could not ask for a better son. Why are you acting this way?"

"You damn well know why," said the count, his face flushed with anger.

Alexei braced for the escalation that he knew would come: his father's ranting, his mother's pleading, the blows and the bruises that she would cover with a veil and thick crème. When he had been younger he would hide in his room and cower as Olga ran from room to room, her shrieks heard throughout the house. He would try to console her afterwards, wiping her tears as she sat disconsolate, her hands shaking with fear.

"I will not let it happen again. I will not let him hit you," Alexei had said after the beating a week ago.

"What can you possibly do to stop him? He will beat you, too. You are still small, Lyosha," his mother had said, using his childhood nickname. But Alexei no longer felt like a child.

"I have a rapier, Mother. It is very sharp."

Her eyes had widened and she'd clutched his wrist. "No, never! You would kill him, and that would be murder. Do you know what they would do to you?"

"It will be in self-defense. They will do nothing."

"No! You will have to run away, and I will never see you again. Alexei, there is adversity in the world and I will put up with it. But it is kind of you to come to my side on these terrible days."

"I will not let him hurt you again," Alexei had said softly, as his mother dried her tears and walked to her room. Half way down the hall she heard her son repeat his vow, "Never again, Mother. He will never do it again."

CHAPTER 2

"How dare you accuse me of ineptness!" shouted the count. A line of spittle dribbled down his silver goatee. The violence always began with cold deliberation. As he spoke, his anger would build until hateful words tumbled out: a litany of vituperation. His entire body would shake and his arms would flail about, then he would hurl anything at hand.

"They set their minds against me. The bastards would have done it whether I was there or not. Japan! The Antarctic would be more desirable. But you gloat! Yes! You will get rid of me; that's what you want, isn't it? I can see it in your eyes. You are despicable! And who are you?" he exclaimed, thrusting a finger at Olga. "A peasant, a whore who tricked me to get my money and my name. I am royalty! You knew that!" shouted Brusilov.

The man's mouth twisted with rage. Suddenly, he shoved Olga hard, and she fell. Alexei helped her to her feet, then dashed from the room, the sound of curses and insults hounding him. "It will not happen again," he said through gritted teeth. Enraged by the sight of his mother sprawled on the carpet, there was no question of what need be done.

On his bedroom wall were crossed rapiers, a gift from Sergei. He snatched one and bolted down the stairs and into the parlor, where his father was clutching his mother's wrist, shouting at her. She writhed in his grasp.

Whatever trepidation Alexei might have felt vanished. Blind with rage, he charged across the room, the weapon's grip clutched tightly in his right hand. Brusilov dropped Olga's wrist and, eyes wide, stepped back as Alexei aimed the rapier's point at the count's heart.

"No!" screamed Olga, throwing herself against Alexei. Stumbling, he crashed into the wall, the weapon spinning from his grasp. His father strode forward and a hard fist slammed into his face. Blood spurted from his nose and he reeled back, falling over an Ottoman. The rapier lay on the carpet by Olga's feet. Brusilov turned and reached for it, but Olga kicked it away.

"Damn you, I will thrash him!" he cried, lunging for it.

"No! He is my son, Yevgeny, no!"

"But he is not *my* son!" shouted Brusilov, grasping the sword.

"Excellency, you must stop," a voice shouted behind him. Turning, weapon in hand, Brusilov eyed his valet, a hulking form in the doorway. "I will inform the police. I swear it," the servant declared.

Everything stopped. Olga looked at the servant, now joined by two women of the staff.

"There was no need to strike the boy," said the valet.

"He was going to kill me. You have no right to interfere. This is not your business," said Count Brusilov hotly, his face livid. But the passion of his fury had left him. "Bastards," he hissed, tossing the rapier into a corner and stomping out, slamming the front door behind him.

***

"He said that I'm not his son," said Alexei, as he sat with Olga that night. Brusilov was not likely to be back until dawn, if he followed his usual routine of going to The English Club, and perhaps his mistress's home later on.

"You're not. Not his real son, I mean. But you are *my* son, Lyosha," said Olga.

"What?" Alexei was stunned. For a long interval, there was silence.

"So who is my real father?" Alexei asked, finally. His mother was so quiet he thought she would not answer, but then she said, "I will tell you all about it—someday."

"You don't think my real father would want me to know?" Alexei persisted.

Olga had dismissed the servants and lit a half-dozen candles. Electric lighting had been installed five years earlier, but she liked the soothing, dancing light of tapers. In the glow Alexei thought that she was still quite beautiful: her black hair braided on top of her head, a slender face, an elegant neck ensconced in a white lace Edwardian blouse. She sipped from a glass of Chardonnay and gazed at Alexei's face, the ugly bruise visible in the candlelight.

"Not now, Lyosha," she sighed. "Not when things are so complicated." But she knew it would always be complicated, very complicated indeed.

"Are there more secrets, Mother?"

"There are always more secrets, Alexei. Now I think I will go to bed."

***

Two days later Alexei sat on his bed, rereading a note that had been delivered that morning by a student from the Naval Academy. It was ridiculous, he thought; no, it was insane. No one did this anymore, not for half a century!

I require satisfaction from you and herewith do challenge you to a duel. We will meet on November Sixth at nine hundred hours in the copse of trees east of the Naval Academy. Failure to arrive will be

deemed an act of cowardice. Although you have the right to choose the weapon, I would prefer rapiers.
Cadet Boris Sokolov, Esq.

Alexei had had no reservations about using the rapier against his father, but that had been in defense of Olga. He had been powerfully motivated by anger and hatred, and had the weapon not been deflected there would have been death in the house. But this was different. Dueling to kill was unthinkable, but Sokolov's sense of sportsmanship was... unreliable. That business of no seconds sent a prickle of warning down his back.

What horrific complications would there be, he wondered, if he killed the cadet? He could only imagine his father's fury at the public outcry. "*Armed with a rapier, enraged boy wantonly kills a senior naval cadet in antiquated duel....*" But the newspaper article might have a very different story to tell, Alexei reflected; it might be reporting his own death. Boris was two years his senior, and much stronger. A rapier was hardened, inflexible steel, a weapon akin to épée or foil. Indeed, both were practice weapons for the rapier, and Alexei rarely practiced with either. Now he wished that Sergei, adept with both weapons, had schooled him more proficiently. But it was too late.

Glumly he stared at the wall. *So, what if I don't appear?* He was only seventeen; no one would expect him to fight a duel, not in this day and age. In fact, Boris would appear ludicrous if he bragged about challenging a boy on such a flimsy pretext. What had he done to deserve such a dangerous summons besides defeat an opponent in a fencing match? He'd beaten a half dozen other cadets, including Sergei. Each had shown proper sportsmanship, saluting and slapping him on the back, even laughing it off. But not Boris.

A shiver went through him. He had told Sergei about the challenge, shortly after the receipt of the note.

"The admiral or his staff should know of this," Sergei had insisted. "The whole thing is sheer nonsense. I can have Captain Isorovsky end it right now. He might even give Boris demerits for this stupidity."

"No, don't tell anybody yet. I have to decide what I'm going to do, and I don't want the captain to deal with my problem. Promise me that."

"Fine, but I don't know why he doesn't want a second. In the old days there was always a second in case the primary was wounded or killed."

"Because he expects to kill me. He doesn't think he'll need a second."

***

The morning of the sixth was terribly cold. A light snow fell on bare limbs as Alexei left the house, his sheathed rapier wrapped in a nondescript cloth. It would be a long walk, but it was still early. A week had passed, and he had heard nothing more concerning the duel. There had been no visit by an officer from the Academy, and nothing from his accuser. Alexei hoped that the entire matter had been forgotten. Perhaps Boris had come to his senses, maybe laughed the whole thing off, thinking a good scare would be sufficient to assuage his wounded pride and appease his honor. Alexei suspected that was not the case.

Alexei stopped to read Boris's note once more. *This is all so foolish and so dangerous,* he thought. This was not about his own pride. It was not he who desired revenge. What stupidity had kept him from alerting the Academy officers, or the count for that matter? Any of them would have condemned the duel and demanded that it be stopped. He should have listened to Sergei, but it was too late now. The duel would go on; the challenge would have to be met. He sighed deeply and, with a sickening feeling, continued on.

***

Boris Sokolov and a cadet friend strode through the copse of birch trees and came to a sudden halt. Standing in the clearing was Sergei, his rapier catching the dull light and making it flicker along the length of the exposed blade.

"My duel is not with you," called Boris from twenty feet away. He had stopped short.

"I'm afraid it is. My friend will be here momentarily, but I won't allow him to engage in a duel. He's far too young, and his father will prosecute if you continue your harassment. But since you insist on a duel, I will gladly stand in for him. Are you ready?"

"It is I whom he challenged," said Alexei, stepping into the glade.

"I will not permit it," said Sergei tersely. "You stand aside. That is not a request. You have shown courage by simply appearing. That is good enough; I insist upon accepting the challenge in your stead. So I repeat, *Mssr*. Sokolov, as a fellow cadet, are you ready to face the consequences of your challenge?"

Boris's eyes went from the gleaming rapier to Sergei, then to Alexei, who had drawn his weapon prior to entering the glade.

"This is not an arrangement *Mssr*. Sokolov is required to accept," said Boris's friend, attempting to quash the duel.

"He was never 'required' to issue the ultimatum in the first place," said Sergei. "But now his honor is at stake, as is mine. Should I assume that he wishes to extricate himself from a very dangerous situation?"

"I think we will terminate these proceedings," said the cadet with great formality.

"Then for the affront there must be an apology. Refusal will result in my challenge, here and now. And there will be blood," said Sergei.

The cadet whispered in Boris's ear. Sokolov shook his head vehemently. Clutching Boris's arm, the cadet remonstrated again. Boris, clenching his jaw and in a barely audible voice said, "I may have acted hastily. I retract my challenge."

"I accept," said Alexei.

"That is not an apology," said Sergei, the tip of his rapier menacingly raised two feet above the ground.

Sokolov eyed at the weapon and said, "I apologize, but on the condition that nothing further be said about this."

"On that you have my assurance," said Sergei.

With a quick about face, and followed by his friend, Boris stormed from the woods.

"You had no need to interfere," Boris said angrily to his friend.

"Of course not. But he would have killed you, and you know it."

"I am not done with him," Boris ground out.

"With Sergei Ivanovich?"

"With either of them," replied Boris, clenching the hilt of the rapier that he had not removed from its scabbard.

***

"How did you hear about it?" asked Count Brusilov, as smoke rose from his cigar. Seated in the opulent Yegorov Club, he swirled his drink and waited.

"From Svetlana," said Admiral Kochenkov. "She rarely confides in me, but she was quite worried. Almost frantic, I would say."

"Frantic? That doesn't sound like her."

"She was afraid Boris Sokolov might be killed in the duel, and she is quite attached to him," the admiral said with a sigh.

"Unlikely that Boris would be killed," said the count, brushing off the incident.

"I wouldn't be so sure. If Alexei would not kill him, Cadet Sergei Ivanovich would have. Regardless, it remains a dangerous situation, even though I told Boris that he must never do anything so egregious again."

"So it's settled, and there's nothing more to be concerned about," said Brusilov, sipping his cognac and impatient to get on with the business he hoped to push forward.

"I don't think it's settled at all," said the admiral. "I know this Sokolov type, and it's only a matter of time before it blows up. If he *had* drawn that rapier I would have had him expelled."

"Indeed, but let's put that aside for now. Have you heard from Count Witte about the Trans-Siberian railroad?" Brusilov asked testily.

Kochenkov placed his officer's dress sword across his lap and said, "Wait a moment, Yevgeny. I must tell you, I cannot accept Alexei in the Academy at this time. Of course I want him in when he's older, say in two or three years."

"But you said—"

"Yes, but matters are different now. In fact, I think it's imperative that you take him to Japan with you."

"That's hardly what I had in mind!"

"Think about it. He will gain enormous experience, which may be of great value in years to come. Intimate knowledge of Asia will be invaluable, in conjunction with a commission from the Naval Academy. You should think of his future. However, there are physical requirements for the Academy he cannot yet meet. And then there is the matter of Boris, who will be gone from the Academy by the time Alexei returns."

"And you are afraid for Alexei if he enrolls now."

There was a lapse of several seconds before Kochenkov said, "It is all too predictable. Where there is bad blood there is eventually spilt blood. I do not want that in my academy. Take him, Yevgeny. It's time to play the part of a father. Whether you had it in mind or not."

"That sounds like a requirement. The railroad deal is connected to this?"

"It may be," said the admiral quietly.

"Very well, if it must be. Now that you've beaten me over the head you can at least tell me about the railroad deal."

"Another glass of port or vodka?" offered Grigory Kochenkov, as he signaled to a waiter. They were in a sequestered nook of the room, surrounded by elegant furnishings, plush carpets and the ubiquitous ferns that complemented the dark paneling. The scent of cigar smoke mingled with that of fine spirits. Others of the aristocracy lingered over their meals of caviar, French wine, herring, and sturgeon from laden tables.

Now that the count had acceded to his suggestion, the admiral was ready to entertain Brusilov's interest. He could see the curiosity in the man's eyes.

"Yevgeny, I'm involved in a very special project; one of immense national interest. Ekaterina met Sergei Witte, the finance minister, at one of those horrendous parties, the type one would never expect him to attend. In my opinion the man would rather hide under a rock than be at a social event, but my wife hunted him down and actually got him to talk."

"About?"

"About the greatest single project this country ever embarked on."

"The railroad."

"Precisely. The Trans-Siberian. It was Witte's idea, and he got the backing of the Tsar. It is already underway; but the project, even with a single track, is consuming our resources very rapidly."

"Iron ore, steel and lumber," said Brusilov, nodding.

"Exactly," said the admiral. "Ekaterina mentioned my half-interest in the Smolensk steel mill. It's close to the Dnieper River and materials can easily be transported on the waterway. So Witte seems willing to use the mill to increase production. He has a timetable, so my wife invited him to the villa. I have agreed to his proposal and I assured him that the board will also approve."

"Splendid. How much of the track will come from your mill?"

"A length of four or five hundred miles toward Siberia, but there is a catch," said Kochenkov, taking another sip of his drink. "I will also be responsible for the construction of trestles, ties, and all wooden structures along the route."

"And for that you need lumber."

"I need what your mills produce. Timber, and lots of it. Your sites are close to the tracks, so transportation will be affordable."

"Excellent," said the count, warming to the idea. "But like you, I am not the sole owner, though I do have influence. Most of my money is in the mills. When will you need the lumber?"

"Immediately. If you weren't heading to Japan I would give you an axe. When can you have your men cut down more trees?"

Yevgeny Brusilov laughed and signaled for another drink. Then in a more serious vein he said, "So who will supervise my mills if I am in Japan?"

"I will appoint one of my men, a highly qualified engineer. Production will continue. There will be nothing for you to worry about," said the admiral.

"One thing does worry me," said the count. "The renewal of this damn revolutionary activity. It's an ill wind and may hinder production if the workers and peasants buy into it. Have you seen any disruption amongst the youth at the Academy?"

"There have been rumors of discontent, but nothing 'revolutionary'. I know some of the cadets think of changing the world, and sometimes that kind of initiative is valuable. We've all read Turgenev's *Fathers and Sons*. That generation also had its rebels, but little came of it."

"But there's no problem with real dissidents at the Academy, is there?" persisted Brusilov, lighting a cigar.

"Absolutely not. I wouldn't tolerate anything like that. No one denigrates the Tsar or the regime," said Kochenkov with finality.

"That's good to know. Sometimes I feel as though this country is a simmering kettle of water. If revolutionaries stoke the flames it may boil over. Men like you and I propel Russia into the industrial world. We must be on guard. The autocracy, for all its splendor, is a fragile thing. If we wish to enjoy its benefits and profits, we must defend it," said Brusilov adamantly.

"We must defend it with our labors, and with our lives."

"Indeed. And with the lives of our sons, if need be."

CHAPTER 3

Ekaterina was never like this before. Brusilov, surprised and alarmed, watched as the lady approached. She was, as always, stately and elegant; but this time her usual warmth and intense sexuality were banked. All he received was a cool smile, not even a kiss on the cheek. Hardly what he expected, having been her lover for nearly ten years. She prepared a drink for herself and sat down at a distance from him, slowly stirring her drink. Brusilov glanced about the apartment he rented for their trysts, searching for some clue to her mood. True, on some occasions she seemed preoccupied, but that always changed in bed: there she was demanding and virtually insatiable. Her insistence upon repeated orgasms was exhilarating, and Brusilov swam in the current of her lust.

He stood before her, arms out, palms up in supplication. "I thought you wanted to see me. I received your note and came as quickly as I could," he said, a perplexed look on his face.

"Yes, I did send for you, Yevgeny, but not for what you think. I am terribly distressed."

"I had the furnishings completely changed, just as you wanted."

"That's not what distresses me. I spoke with Olga after you—"

"What happens between me and my wife is hardly your concern," he interrupted loftily. "And my actions were justified. Moreover, I was attacked."

"Not by her. I saw the bruises. She was hit very hard and her wrist was sprained terribly. I adore you, but I cannot, will not, tolerate that sort of behavior toward my friend. It is a sign of a brutal man. Are you a brutal man, Yevgeny?"

"Never toward you. I love you and always have."

"I know that you love my body. It is a narcotic to you, just like your vodka and Scotch. But you disappoint me. In fact, sometimes you repel me."

He sat in a love seat across from her and stared at the lights of St. Petersburg. So it had come to this. He said nothing while the antique clock on the mantle ticked away the time.

"I will be leaving soon for Japan," he finally said, breaking the silence.

"She told me. You will be taking your son." Ekaterina said it as a statement of fact.

"Yes, he will come with me. It's part of an arrangement," said Brusilov, not caring to elaborate. *This is going nowhere.*

"But you're not taking Olga," said the woman, raising a hand to touch the silver hair just visible below an enormous hat, elegant with ostrich plumes.

"No, I don't think she'd be comfortable in Japan. It would not be easy for a Russian woman. She wouldn't know anyone and doesn't speak the language. There are places men can go for entertainment and socializing that are not available to women," Brusilov said, trying to make conversation; anything to break this damnable coolness.

"Entertainment for men, yes," she said, repeating his phrase woodenly. "And I suspect that you will find another mistress there. What do they call them, *geishas*?"

"I doubt that I will have time or interest in Japanese women. I detest the Japanese."

"Of course. You detest just about everyone, Yevgeny. And if you are going for three years, and if my husband and I don't reconcile, I suppose I shall have to find a new lover."

"I imagine you will find someone rather quickly," he said, exasperated by her imperious posturing. He wanted this over; nothing was going to please him tonight. "Would you like me to leave, or shall I escort you to your carriage?"

"Neither, really."

"By that you mean?" said Brusilov, impatiently.

"I mean that I'm not leaving, and neither are you." With that she removed her hat and went into the bedroom. "Believe it or not, I am quite famished. Are you coming, Yevgeny, or are you going to pout all night?"

How delicious it would be to simply walk out and leave her, he thought. Would she run after him, begging to be satiated? Of course not; she was as stubborn as he. Brusilov sighed, went into the bedroom, and closed the door.

***

Like wine not quite properly aged, the evening lacked the intense passion he was accustomed to. Perhaps, Brusilov mused, Ekaterina had chosen to go to bed with him simply out of habit, or because she hoped that an orgasm would take her mind off whatever it was that was bothering her. It could not simply be her disdain for his violence toward Olga! For his part, her criticism left him in a funk. They lay in silence for a long while, listening to falling snowflakes kiss the window pane.

"I think my husband wants me back," she finally said, her face turned away from him.

"As his lover?"

"It's possible. He has been quite attentive lately."

"Would you want that?"

"I am not sure. It has been so long, and of course he has had mistresses over the years," she said tonelessly.

"Does that bother you?" asked Brusilov, breathing in the scent of her exotic perfume.

She sighed and said, "All men of our class have mistresses, and all the women have lovers. That's just the way it is, Yevgeny. No, that doesn't bother me. I don't expect him to give up his mistresses, either."

"Does he know about me, about us?"

"He knows that I have a lover and suspects that it is you. But he's never asked me. It's an understood thing, and I think he's afraid that bringing it up would have unpleasant repercussions. So it lies, like the spines of thistle. Water it and one might not like the thorns."

She sighed again and said, "You should make up with Alexei. He is a fine boy and a very brave one."

"Brave?" said the count, hardly wanting the subject to intrude upon his evening.

"He is extremely brave. How many boys his age would confront a father as he did? You are much bigger and stronger than Alexei, yet he challenged you, knowing the consequences. That shows real courage. He will be a fine man someday. He will go places, Yevgeny."

"You like him, don't you?"

"I do. In fact, I was just thinking, and this is an amazing thought. He may be a wonderful husband for my daughter. She will need someone strong like Alexei, someone to keep her out of trouble. I do worry about her. I think she is becoming promiscuous, and I don't approve of the young men she sees."

"Maybe she'll be a nymphomaniac like you," said Brusilov, his hand touching her nipple.

"That's not funny, Yevgeny. And I'm not a nymph. I just like...." Her voice drifted off.

"What made you the way you are, Yevgeny? You can be gracious, but you anger so easily, and you can be terrible. Was your father like that? Was he strong? Did he beat you?"

"He was weak, timid, and I despised him. He once took a mistress, but my mother found out and she nearly killed him. He never tried it again, but he took his weakness out on me. I think all men beat their sons."

"Not all, and I do not recommend it. Sons can become their father's nightmare. Next time he will kill you. That would make me unhappy, Yevgeny."

The silence that followed was strained. Finally Brusilov said, "I think it's time to go."

"Not quite yet. You always listen to me because you know I'm right."

"But what transpires between me and Alexei is my business, Ekaterina, not yours."

"It will be when he marries my daughter."

Now she's angry, thought Brusilov. *But when has she ever been wrong? Never. And the woman gets everything she wants.* If she divorced the admiral, he could have her. She knew that, but she wouldn't divorce; her life was too comfortable.

Changing the subject, she said, "My husband has been spending more time at Court and speaking to important ministers lately. They respect him and want his advice."

"Who has he spoken to?"

"Witte, for one. You already know that."

"But he's Treasury."

"Treasury and everything else. He has a lot of sway with the Interior Minister and even the Tsar."

Interior, thought Brusilov, wondering if there was any connection. *The man wants his wife back, so he conspires with Witte.*

"I know what you are thinking, Yevgeny," said Ekaterina, her hand touching his face with a gentleness he hardly expected.

"And that is?"

"That my exalted husband, the admiral, wants you sent far, far away."

***

"But you are in love with Boris, aren't you?" asked Elena Vanova, as she and Svetlana left the church.

"Of course I am! But this is so exciting! Did you see how he was looking at me all through the service?"

"Father Rozinski looks at a lot of women." Elena rolled her eyes. "He even appraises me. But yes, he did have an eye for you today. I guess he likes young women. I heard that he was originally from a Siberian village and all the priests there belong to the Khlysty, the Flagellants."

Svetlana shivered, more from the idea than the cold. "I've heard of that cult. It's ancient and very wild. They believe that the way to God and salvation is through love-making."

"Orgies?" asked Elena, her eyes wide.

"They take all their clothes off and have sex until they are completely exhausted. Every man can have any woman and every woman can have any man, and it lasts for hours. It's supposed to be spiritually enlightening—a catharsis," explained Svetlana.

"So if the priest was a member of that sect and enjoyed it, why did he come to St. Petersburg? I mean, he had to have taken a vow of celibacy, because no one here would condone that kind of activity."

"I think he might have been running away," said Svetlana.

"Do you think he killed someone?"

The two girls pulled their shawls tighter against the chill as they hurried to their favorite tea shop on the Nevsky Prospeckt.

"No, not at all. I think he made someone," Svetlana said with a grin. "You know, got some girl in what they call 'a family way'. But it had nothing to do with family." They entered the tea shop and paused to admire the elegant samovar. In a whisper she added, "And I bet he never stopped doing girls."

"What do you mean?" asked Elena excitedly.

"I know that many women like him, and there are all kinds of secret places in the church."

"Has he taken you to any?"

"Once, in a room behind the iconostasis when no one was there. I think he wanted to see how I would react. We didn't really do anything. He made it sound like I was to receive some special instruction. But I knew what he was thinking."

"Did he know what *you* were thinking?"

"He might have thought I was just naïve, but I did kiss him. Just once."

"What did he do then?"

"He was very surprised. I wanted him to know that I wasn't a child. Then he put his hands on my backside and said, 'You are too young now. But later, when you're older, then come see me, but say nothing about it.'"

The two girls sat at a table in the rear of the shop. Elena leaned forward and in a conspiratorial voice said, "I know that you want him, but he is so much older than you! I think it's very daring but terribly dangerous. I mean, what if you are found out? Can you just imagine the scandal? He would be thrown out of the church, and you—well, what would everyone say?"

"Elena, I'm not going to do anything with him now. No, I'll wait; but I will keep seeing him. It will make him anxious, and that's half the fun. For now it's just a tease."

"Someday he may not want to simply play. What if he...."

"Has me?" said Svetlana, sipping her tea through a sugar cube.

"He is very handsome in those vestments with his red beard and those dark eyes. Any girl would want him, whether he's a priest or not. So when are you going to see him again?" asked Elena.

"Maybe in two or three weeks. I want him to wonder if I'm coming back."

"So he'll be more excited to see you?"

"Exactly. But in the meantime I have Boris, and we've been doing some exciting things that unmarried people are not supposed to do."

"You mean... touching?"

"That, and kissing in very special places," said Svetlana just loud enough for others to glance her way.

Elena sucked in her breath and said, "You have to tell me all about it. Everything."

"I'll tell you when we do more. It won't be too long from now. He wants more. And so do I!"

***

"I had a long talk with your father, and he wants to speak with you," said Olga.

"My real father?" asked Alexei. He sat with his mother in a room adorned with icons of St. Nicholas and paintings by Russian masters.

"No, I mean Count Brusilov. I will continue to speak of him as your father, since he's the only one you know."

"He said that I'm not his son, so I won't call him father any more."

"What will you call him?" Olga asked, wondering if more strife was on the way.

"I'm not sure yet, but I don't want to talk to him."

"You must, Alexei. It's very important and involves your future. He's in the smoking room, and he wants me to come with you."

"Oh, another one of those 'family councils' where he assumes an official role. Fine, I can't wait to hear what he has to say," Alexei said disgustedly.

"I know he hurt you, and he hurt me, but he is still the head of this household, and you have to listen to him. Please do so, for me."

She turned to go, and Alexei followed, wordlessly.

Brusilov looked up from the newspaper and removed a monocle when Alexei and Olga entered. He stood and gestured for them to be seated. Olga sat, but Alexei said, "I'd rather stand, Count Brusilov."

Raised eyebrows were followed by an inquisitive look and he said, "'Count Brusilov'? How interesting. Not 'Excellency' or perhaps 'Father'?"

"You're not my father; you said so. I will call you Excellency, if you wish, or Count Brusilov," said Alexei, having just made this decision.

Brusilov said nothing for a moment. He appeared to take no offense at Alexei's impertinence. He cupped his right elbow with his left hand and the fingers of his right tapped his lips as he considered the statement. "Very well," he finally said. "You may call me Count Brusilov, except when we are in the company of others. Questions might be raised, which I do not care to answer, and," he said meaningfully, "they would not reflect well on your mother. At such times I will refer to you as my son. Do I make myself clear?"

"Yes, Count Brusilov," said Alexei. "But I don't want to be with you in the company of others."

"That is not a matter of choice. There are obligations of state for which you will be required to accompany me. In fact, I may even require your assistance at times," he said with a conciliatory smile.

"Yes, that would be nice," said Olga, hoping the comment might smooth the way for what was coming. "There is something Yevgeny wishes to tell you; something we thought best for you," she said in a soft voice.

"Yes, it was something we agreed upon," said Brusilov, laying emphasis on the word 'agreed'. "I have been informed of troubling developments in which you were obliquely involved. That is not to say that you instigated the event or were guilty in any way. I refer to the almost-duel. It was an amazingly stupid thing for a naval cadet to orchestrate. This individual, I've been informed, is pernicious and vindictive, so this may not be over. I have also been told that you were willing to engage this person in combat; very brave, considering the differences in age," said the count with a courteous nod to Alexei. "But the danger persists; therefore you will accompany me to my next posting. We are going to Japan."

"Japan?" said Alexei, looking from Brusilov to Olga. "I don't want to go to Japan with you."

"I will not have you stay here and become a problem for me or your mother. I cannot run back for a family emergency. It's as simple as that. However, I have arranged for you to be enrolled in the Naval Academy when we return. You said that you want to be a naval officer, and with that I concur. In fact, I have already given my approval to the superintendent of the school, Admiral Kochenkov."

Alexei stared at his mother and said, "You agreed to this? How could you? I don't want to go anywhere with him," he said, pointing to the count.

Olga Brusilov stood. She put her arms around Alexei and said, "I will miss you terribly, but it is for the best. You will have many new experiences, and when you come back you will be a grown man and will wear the uniform of a naval cadet."

"True," said Brusilov. "I will find you an accommodation of your own, a room in what the Japanese call a *ryokan*. And you shall have an allowance as well."

"Is Japan an assignment for which you asked?" inquired Alexei.

"No, but I am a servant of the Tsar and I go where required," Brusilov said stiffly. "I do not particularly favor the Japanese, and I do not expect you to emulate their values. You are Russian; I expect you to remain that way."

"Yes, Count Brusilov," said Alexei, privately vowing to become as Japanese as he could.

CHAPTER 4

"Do you still hate your life?" Svetlana asked Boris, as she lightly played her fingers over his chest.

"Hate my life?" he said as he kissed the nape of her neck, still warm and damp with perspiration after their exertions. "No, I haven't for a long while."

"You used to, after the fire."

"That was eight years ago, and I was only twelve."

"But I think you still have nightmares. Last time, you fell asleep and were saying horrible things."

"It was a horrible time, but I don't regret what I did. I used to be sorry about my father, but he deserved what he got. His wife certainly did."

It was the academy's winter vacation and most students were drunk and carousing along the Neva. A classmate of Boris had a flat, and Boris had cajoled him into handing over the key.

"You were lucky; you could have died. Then who would I have to make me happy?" said Svetlana. By way of answer, Boris slipped his hands to her breasts. A lock of her luxuriant red hair fell over his forehead; he breathed in the scent of the sensuous, tantalizing girl.

"I think you have several other lovers," Boris whispered in her ear.

"Have you been stalking me?" she demanded, her eyes wide.

“What if I am? I’m practicing. Someday I might be a spy and follow beautiful women,” he said with a lascivious smile.

He lay back, luxuriating in the warmth of her touch. He would not tell her that the nightmares still came, always accompanied by the sound of his stepmother’s shrill screams. Nor had he forgotten the scorn and contempt she had heaped upon him.

He had been eleven years old when his mother died. Boris remembered her as forgiving and saintly, and he’d loved her very much. His father’s new wife considered her husband’s son an unnecessary appendage. The woman had been impossible to please, and she bristled at every comparison or perceived slight. She’d dismissed their wonderful cook and insisted on preparing endless servings of *borsht*, beet soup as red as her round face. She’d only married his father, Boris reasoned, because he had money and a tenuous connection to power.

They’d all repaired to his father’s *dacha* for the summer. The vacation cabin had only two rooms, and Boris was assigned the smaller one, a storage room. He did not mind that; he enjoyed the privacy, even though he had no bed; he slept on the floor beside the wall. But he could hear everything. Inquisitive, like most youth, he stayed awake at night listening to his stepmother’s moans and squeals. It became an intoxicant, and simply listening was not enough.

As if sensing how his thoughts had strayed back to that time, Svetlana asked, almost dreamily, “When you could hear them doing it, did you ever touch yourself?”

“What do you think?” he answered, his mind straying back to those hot nights when the couple vigorously pleasured themselves, oblivious to the boy staring through a peephole he had bored through the wall. During the day he plugged it up with a chink of wood, and they suspected nothing. Each night he removed it when he heard the first stirrings in the adjoining room. One night, however, he forgot to extinguish his kerosene lamp, and his stepmother, less than three feet away, spied the glow and immediately knew what it meant.

Retribution came upon him swiftly. Naked, the woman shot out of bed and grabbed a length of twisted rope. Screaming, she hauled the boy from his room and threw him against the wall, then began to whip him. His father half-heartedly tried to restrain her, but to no avail. The beating went on and on until the woman, exhausted, stomped back to her room. Shaking his head, but without saying a word, his father closed the door and joined his wife in bed. They shoved a bookcase against the wall to cover the peep hole. For an hour their voices rose and fell: scornful words countered by conciliatory ones. Then they resumed their prior activity.

"I hated them both," Boris said in a low, thick voice, remembering.

"Did you resolve to do what you did that very night?" Svetlana asked softly, drinking in the contorted visage of her lover.

"Yes, but I waited, and I said nothing. At first I could hardly move, and I thought the bleeding would never stop. Except for disgusted looks, they ignored me. I spent hours making my plans. It was exciting, especially since they had no idea that I wasn't cowed or broken."

"You did the deed at night didn't you?" she said, her eyes wide with curiosity.

"Yes, two nights later, when they were at it again. The whole *dacha* was filled with her squeals and wails of delight, like a pig rutting. I'd resolved there would soon be a different kind of wailing. I had made a vow and I would not turn back. I was still in pain from the beating, but I got up and went out to the shed behind the *dacha*. It was never locked; nobody lived within a mile of the house. The kerosene was kept in the shed."

"Did you spill it on you when you poured it?" asked Svetlana, remembering an accident of her own in childhood.

"Only a little. I was very quiet as I splashed it on the walls, especially around the doors. Then I lit the match."

The sounds of the revelers seemed further away as Boris lapsed into silence.

"And they screamed," said Svetlana. He could feel her shudder. He knew that the anticipation of horror was titillating for her. His right hand tightened in her hair, and he stroked her back with the fingers of his slowly descending left hand. She quivered with excitement.

He resumed the tale, enjoying her reactions. "It took a while for them to see what was happening. The flames roared up the walls to the roof. Then the screaming, the real screaming, began. I think they could see me looking in. The dacha was old and the flames were very hot. A spark ignited my pants. I rolled in the dirt to put the flames out; still, the burn hurt. But it was good that I was burned; it made my story convincing.

"They pleaded—just like I had pleaded when she was whipping me. The windows were too small for them to get through, and the only door was a sheet of flame. I watched their horror as flames consumed them. They begged and pleaded! I couldn't hear them over the roar of the fire, I saw their agony, and I gloated. I sat and watched until the last embers died. Nothing was left of them. People came by the next day and felt sorry for me. I was still in pain from the beating and the burn. They crossed themselves when I told them of the accidental fire and the death of my father and his wife. They gave me a dozen kopeks, took me to a train station, and sent me to my uncle. I had done what I had to do, and that was the end of it."

"And you turned into another person, because you did something like that again," said Svetlana.

"I did that for a very different reason. Are you scared of me now? I think it excites you," said Boris.

"It makes me feel strange being with you. And, dear Boris, regardless of your reason, you are still a murderer."

"But it thrills you, doesn't it? Doing something scandalous and forbidden, like tonight. I'm sure your father would be in a rage if he knew what we are doing. I know how much he dislikes me. No, he detests me."

"He doesn't know you as I do. I think you're brave, and you're not afraid to let people know what you think. You have strong opinions, like you're hatred of Jews. Most people in Russia don't like them either. You are just very, very... focused," she said, trying to find exactly the right word.

"Focused, yes, I guess that's a good word for it," Boris said with a smirk.

"Did you learn to hate them in church?" she asked, as his hand slipped between her thighs.

"Not so much at church. When I went to live with my uncle."

"The policeman?" she said, the words coming unevenly as his probing touch sent a spasm of current through her.

"Yes, my Uncle Plehve. But now he's much more than just a policeman. He will soon be the head of all internal security for Russia. He's very important; and I, his nephew, will be feared as he is." Plehve was not actually his uncle; the kinship was less direct, but Boris did not see any need to explain that in detail.

"That's what you want, being feared, isn't it?" she said with sudden insight, and she shivered—but not with fear.

"Power inspires fear, and power is what it's all about."

"Not love? You do love me, don't you?"

"Of course I do. But even love is power, especially when it's denied," said Boris. "There are many things one can hate. It's a sort of motivation. There are people, revolutionaries, who hate the Tsar and the state. They must be purged. There is no place for them in Russia. I hate them, and that is a kind of joy."

"I think you are obsessed. I wish you were not always so intense," said Svetlana, putting her arms around him.

"Those who are not obsessed are pointless. But I'm not pointless, and Uncle Plehve isn't either. He sees what has to be done with the Jews, and he hates them. I read reports of their plots and schemes to overthrow the Tsar. They're vile, Svetlana. Plehve wants to ship them out of the country. *I* want to execute them."

"Because they are smart? Because they make us look like fools?"

"What?" he said, astounded by her observation. She'd said it so softly, so innocently. He stiffened; this was blasphemy.

She removed his hand and remained pensive for a long moment. He could only see her silhouette in the faint light. What did she really think of him, he suddenly wondered? He didn't care what others thought, but her opinion mattered. Her sudden silence made him feel uneasy. Perhaps he had made a crucial mistake in revealing his innermost thoughts. He sensed a divide: a chasm. She had no sense of reality, and she was not committed to his cause. In fact, she was oblivious to the whole crisis facing the nation.

Then he wondered if she knew any Jews, perhaps even had friends who were? If so, would she warn and protect them? He needed to find out. He would ask her sometime in an offhand way. But not tonight. He was glad when she changed the subject.

"Did your uncle believe you about the fire and your escape?"

"You mean, did he think I started the fire? He had his suspicions. In fact, he went to the site where his brother and my stepmother died. I showed him where my room was and explained how I ran from the flames. But he's an investigator, and he found pieces of metal that still smelled of kerosene."

"Did he accuse you?" Svetlana asked in far away voice.

"Not exactly, but he looked at me very strangely, especially after he saw the red and purple welts on my back and arms and legs. I stared back at him and showed him my own burn. I told him I'd nearly died. He nodded, but he hardly spoke to me after that. I've tried to befriend him, especially by talking about Jews and saying I wanted to help him, but we've never became close. He's a hard man. It was strange that he insisted I go to church more often."

"It might have been to make you feel better, I mean calmer. They say the Mother Church is the soul of Russia," said Svetlana.

"Maybe for some, but for me it's a distraction. Of course, the church is against Jews, too."

He thought for a moment then said, "You go to church, don't you? I don't think it's because you particularly care for Gregorian chants or scriptures."

"Whatever do you mean?" said Svetlana, propping herself on her elbow.

"I've seen you cross that bridge, the Bankovsky Most, and go into the Kazan Cathedral. I've followed you. I even saw you join the queue to kiss the icon of Our Lady of Kazan. But that's not why you go there, is it?"

"You *are* a spy, aren't you, Boris!" she exclaimed.

"I even saw you talking to an acolyte, then hurrying off with him," he said, evading her question.

"Are you jealous?"

"Of a boy who wants to be a celibate monk? Of course not," he said, as if it were a ridiculous idea. "But you can tell me what it was all about."

"A spy keeps secrets, and I have secrets of my own. But I will tell you this: I needed a very special spy, and the boy was perfect."

"Why did you need a spy? You have one."

"But you're not in the church, and Theodosis Rakunin is. He is my age, and he knows everyone and everything about all the priests. He's made it his business. You see," said Svetlana, warming to her subject, "I have gone to Kazan Cathedral since I was a child. There is a lady there, one who assists the priests with baptisms of women, who always smiles and looks at me kindly. I don't know who she is, and I really want to know. My parents seem to know her, but they never speak to her. It was as if they know something—something that I shouldn't."

"But you found something out, didn't you?" probed Boris, hoping to learn all the details.

"A little, but it was by accident. A few weeks ago, my mother asked me to fetch a necklace from her room. I was upset because I was already late for a skating party. I yanked on the drawer and it fell to the carpet. Jewelry everywhere! I had to pick it all up. As I shoved the drawer back in, it jammed on something at the back: an old piece of paper, a sort of document with a seal from the Kazan Cathedral. The writing was faint, and I was about to put it back when I saw that it mentioned a baby girl. Because of the date, sixteen years ago, I'm sure that the baby was none other than me, but I didn't have time to examine it, for my mother was coming into the room."

"Probably a baptismal record," said Boris dismissively. "Were there any names on the document?"

"There were several, but the only one I could make out was my father's. The others were illegible. I'm sure it's important and very secret. And they've kept it hidden all these years."

"So you had to know what it was about, didn't you?" said Boris.

"Of course. I was sure that the lady in the Cathedral, the one who always watched me, would know. But she became very sick recently and was sent to a church hospice. I thought I would never see her again, never get answers to my questions. I didn't even know her name or where she was sent, but I suspected the acolyte knew. He always smiles at me, so I approached him. He was very excited and said he would tell me if I did him a favor—a very special one."

"You had sex with him?" Boris attempted once again to slip his hand between her thighs.

"No, not really. Are you listening?" she said, pushing his hand away.

The thought of her with the church boy angered him, but he said, "Of course I am. This is very interesting."

"He told me he was enrolled in the choir when he was very young and thought that the church would be his lifelong passion. His love, he said, was Christ and Christ alone. But as he got older he wanted to know about girls and said that he had never seen one. Naked, I mean. He would tell me anything I wanted to know if he could just once see what a girl looks like. I think he hates the idea of a celibate life and regrets his commitment but can do nothing about it now. "

"So you showed yourself to him?"

"I did. We went into a little room, and I undressed and let him touch me. I could have had him easily! He was on his knees and actually shaking. He had tears in his eyes. Can you imagine that? Afterwards he was thankful, profusely so."

"I'm surprised he doesn't want to see you naked again," said Boris sourly.

"Oh, he did ask, but I said no, it would only lead him into temptation and ruin him. I thought it a rather silly remark, but he crossed himself and said that he would sin no more.

Then he told me the woman's name, Eudoxia, and where she was."

"And you went there right away?"

"Yes, that same day. I bought flowers, and a nurse took me to her room. I was told that I could only stay a few minutes; that it would not be long before she would see our Savior."

"Did she tell you what you wanted to know?" Boris asked impatiently.

"Not exactly. I asked her many questions, but she merely gazed at me and put a finger to her lips. I was very disappointed. I put the flowers on a nightstand and was about to go when she took my wrist with her bony fingers. Her hand felt terribly cold. I looked at her, thinking she would answer my questions after all, but instead she said, 'Stay away from the priest. You must, he is unholy.'

"'Father Rozinski?'" I asked, astonished that she would say such a thing. Her voice was very faint, but her eyes became large and she admonished me with that skinny finger. 'Father Rozinski is—' but just then the nurse came back in. I was frantic. 'Father Rozinski is what?' I asked, almost shouting. But the horrid nurse ordered me out. She pulled me away and fairly shoved me out the door! I heard from the acolyte that Eudoxia died that night."

"So you never learned about the adoption, or Father Rozinski," said Boris.

"No."

"Priests violate their vows by having sex," commented Boris.

"I'm sure Father Rozinski has plenty of girls; he's very handsome. But I think she meant something else."

"Such as?"

"I don't know. But the acolyte can find out anything."

"Even if it takes another... favor?"

"You said it, my dear Boris: it's all about power, isn't it?" Then she laughed and rolled on top of her eager lover.

***

Admiral Kochenkov glanced up at the gilded spire of the Admiralty building, the headquarters of the Russian Navy since 1711. By the gate, frolicking bronze nymphs held aloft a globe, and marble columns fronted the imposing structure. Olga Brusilov, walking at his side, said, "Someday you will be in charge of all this."

"That's sweet of you, but I want modernity, and the antique battlewagons that run that building would never allow drastic changes in the Navy. It would threaten the status quo and the bureaucrats' indolent complacency."

"But if you could, what would you do?" she asked, as they strolled from their viewing place on Voznesensky Prospekt through the open gates and into the splendid Mikhailovsky Gardens. The wide vistas allowed the constricted soul to expand; the avenues of trees, even this late in the year, exuded calm; and the classical structures seemed assured that Russia would endure in all her dignity and majesty.

A winter breeze chilled the air and Olga buttoned the top of her sable coat. It was still early, and bright sun splashed over the trees, turning the few remaining leaves into shades of russet and gold, and the curving branches into bowls of light.

"Ah! First of all, I would insist upon educating every bluejacket in the Navy. Scarcely any enlisted man can read, and reading a manual is absolutely essential. Sailors in every other European navy can read. And training would be a yearly endeavor, not a rushed thing only done when the fleet sail past the Baltic ice. Then I would bring in the best engineers from England, France and Germany. We haven't much time to prepare."

"Prepare for what?"

"Japan, and I pray that we don't go to war with them. Their navy is far superior to ours, even though the Admiralty won't dare admit it."

After the gardens, their walk took them past the Church of the Spilled Blood, named for the spot on which Alexander II was assassinated. Olga shivered and the admiral said, "I will hire a carriage and we will be on Kamenny Island before dark. Then tomorrow, if it's warmer, we can meander through the woods." Olga turned to him and smiled gratefully.

The *dachas* were vacation cabins dotting the island. All were hideaways for the wealthy: places to find quietude beyond the bustle of the city. It was here that Grigory enjoyed *umilenie*, the very soul of Russia, a combination of tenderness, exaltation, and the ever-present sense of sadness. Snow fell on birch trees and on the simple wooden dwelling, from which he and Olga could hear strains of accordion or balalaika. Enjoying her company, he could breathe in the cold air and think only of the present.

The last rays of sun illuminated dust motes that languidly rose as she cleaned the chairs and table. A bed and nightstand stood against one wall, a couch against another.

They had packed a basket of meats and fruit, along with a bottle of French Sauvignon. Grigory poured two glasses, from which they sipped as they watched the sun go down behind the birches.

The light from two oil lamps made a warm glow as the two settled on the couch. On a table were several dishes and a *kovsh*, a common two-handled vessel. Olga said that she would prepare *kvas*, a concoction of honey, salt, and barley. Ice was added to keep the drink cold. Now, relaxing after their long carriage ride, she said, "When were you last here?"

"Three years ago, when Ekaterina and I were still together, or pretending to be. We stayed for only one night. It did not go well."

"Would she be surprised if she knew that I am here with you now?"

"No, she would expect it. She knows about us."

Olga leaned back against him, letting his white beard brush her face. He was no longer the slim youth she had known in her childhood. He had thickened, but not so much as to be considered obese.

He sighed and said, "We tried to put things back together. I really wanted to, at least for the sake of Svetlana. We are concerned about her."

"Does Ekaterina have a new lover?" asked Olga as she sipped wine and nibbled on cheese.

"If she does she hasn't told me. I did take her to a Naval Academy ball and she stayed with me long enough for people to see us together. Then I saw her with a German admiral before the two disappeared. But I don't think he's her real lover."

Olga sighed and said, "We've come full circle, haven't we, Grigory? And it has taken so many years. You should have married me back then."

"I should have, but there were difficulties. Then I met and fell in love with Ekaterina, and we were happy for a while. But I don't think she ever really loved me. I was a good catch, you know," he said, pinching her cheek.

She laughed and said, "You were very popular! A military hero recognized by the Tsar."

He smiled and said, "Have you heard from Alexei lately? It has been over two months since he left."

"I received a letter yesterday. I brought it with me." She rose and slipped an envelope from her coat pocket. "I'll read it to you, if you wish."

"Of course. Is he doing well?"

"He's fascinated with Japan, but he has concerns."

"He had concerns in his last letter too. The boy is perceptive for his age."

"So were you, but you were naughty," said Olga giving him a smile. She again sat beside him and unfolded the letter, reading it aloud.

"My dear Mother,

The count required me to attend a function at the Imperial Hotel in Tokyo. It's a magnificent structure in European style in a district called Kojimachi. The hotel is a three-storey building, popular with wealthy foreigners as well as higher-ups of the many embassies.

I didn't think I would enjoy being there, having to smile and lie about how fortunate I was to be in the company of the count, but in fact it turned out to be a most educational evening.

I had another chance to meet my friend Itomo Karamatsu, the Japanese naval officer. He is five years older than I am and is a bit reserved, but he appreciates the fact that I am studying Japanese. He speaks English; he has even been sent to Portsmouth to study naval tactics. I have been teaching him fencing, and he invited me to join him in karate classes. I will never be as proficient as he, but I am doing well.

Itomo's father is a high ranking military officer, and he has a sister, but I have never seen her. When I asked if I might meet her (I haven't met any Japanese girls), he said that she is studying nursing in a hospital and is very busy, and he doubts that I will ever meet her. These people are very insular, and it's hard to penetrate their formal disposition. Getting to meet a Japanese girl is virtually impossible. They have a saying here, Ware, ware Nihonjin, *meaning they are Japanese and anybody else is a geijin, or outside person. But fortunately Itomo gives me a window into their way of thinking, something few foreigners get to experience.*

I love exploring this city and have found areas where foreigners do not venture. Itomo says that some places are quite dangerous (there is a feared underworld society here), but being a geijin I am such an oddity that nobody bothers me.

I have also met a British journalist named William-Stuart Jones. He speaks many languages and is an international traveler, since he works for the London Times. *He has met Admiral Kochenkov and sends his regards.*

The count arranged for me to live in a ryokan in an area called the low city, as opposed to the wealthier district known as Yamanote, the high city. That's fine with me. Shitimachi, the low city, is where all the shops and geisha houses are."

"Does he say anything more about Count Brusilov?" asked Kochenkov.

Olga held up her hand and said, "Wait, I'm getting to it." Finding her place she continued:

"The count has me run errands for him and expects me to attend the official banquets and ceremonies. In such places he makes an effort to treat me well enough, though his flattery is very condescending. Aside from those occasions I rarely see him. I do understand that he is frequently out until very late. Since we don't speak beyond absolute

necessity, I have no idea where he goes. It's quite mysterious, but I will not ask him about it.

I love you and miss you. Give my best wishes to Admiral Kochenkov and tell him that I have not forgotten how to fence.

You son,
Alexei

P.S. There is an undercurrent of tension here over Russia's aims in Korea and Manchuria. Itomo thinks there will eventually be hostilities."

"His friend may be right on that score," said Kochenkov. "But the real mystery is your husband. I wonder what he's up to?"

"I'm sure we'll find out someday," Olga said. She put down the letter and smiled up at the admiral, who took her hand and led her to the bed.

CHAPTER 5

Tokyo
April, 1897

"Kimi-san, I can't tell you how excited I am," said Noruko Toshikawa. The two girls were walking slowly to allow the *one-san*, Noruko's "Elder Sister", to catch up. She had stopped to talk with an acquaintance. "It's so wonderful to be able to get out of the *Yukaku* after being cooped up for two years. You know I could not leave until the debt for me was paid off."

"How many girls are still kept there?" asked Kimi-san. She was not associated with the "Flower and Willow" world of the *geisha*, but she was happy for her friend, who had finally advanced from the lowly status of a *skikomi* to a *maiko*, the next level on the way to being a full *geisha*. Proudly Noruko raised her bright, long-sleeve kimono with her left hand as she had been taught, while she delicately walked in her four-inch high black clogs.

"There are five. The *geisha* house paid their fathers a lot of money when they were bought, so it will be a long time before they can leave," said Noruko. "But I have to tell you about last night. One of the *geishas* had her *mizuage* ceremony."

"Is that when she's given to the man who bids highest for her?" asked Kimi-san.

"Yes, then she can be de-flowered, and the buyer, the *danna,* must take care of her and pay for everything she needs. She's still a *geisha* and can entertain others, but she will not give her body to other men. Anyway, a lot of saki was drunk, and it was all very exciting. Afterwards our housemother, our *Okasan,* noticed a man watching me. He was a foreigner and had come in for the last three nights. I was playing my *shamisen,* but I don't think he particularly liked the sound of it."

"But he must have liked the *geisha* house," said Kimi-san.

"Yes. The *geijin* was sitting alone and drinking saki—a great deal of it. *Okasan* came to me and whispered that the man was watching me and I should go to him. I thought he looked unhappy and very uncomfortable, kneeling as we do. He ignored all the revelry and wasn't laughing. I was surprised he even stayed."

"I suppose he wouldn't laugh if he didn't understand Japanese," said Kimi-san, as they waited for a horse-drawn trolley to cross the road. This gave the *one-san* a chance to catch up.

"But he was looking at you," Kimi-san continued. "You are very pretty, so he must like you."

"Perhaps. I sat beside him, as *Okasan* ordered, and gave him a little smile. I began to play my *shami.* He watched me play and nodded when I finished. Then he gave me an envelope with five yen."

"That's a lot! What did he say when you finished playing?"

"Nothing. I told him my name and I think he understood, but he didn't give me his. I was quite surprised. I thought it was rude of him, but maybe he had a reason. I was hoping that he would say something so I would know where he came from, but he didn't," said Noruko.

"I think he's rich," interjected the *one-san,* who had listened to the last exchange. "He was wearing expensive clothes and a top hat, and it takes a lot of money to be entertained in a *geisha* house."

"Was he handsome and young?" asked Kimi-san.

"Distinguished, like a long-nose *geijin,* but not young. He is certainly more than twice my age."

"Do you think he'll come back to see you again?" asked the *one-san.*

"I have no idea. I'm pleased that he gave me the money, and of course I gave most of it to *Okasan.*"

Noruko fell silent, then added, "He made me nervous. I don't know what he was thinking, and I really don't care to play for him again, even if he does give me money."

"But I'm almost certain he'll come in again," said the Elder Sister.

"Then I hope he finds somebody else to stare at," said Noruko.

They spent the day peeking into *kabuki* theaters and tea shops in the *Asakusa* district of the Low City. There were enormous crowds through which the occasional rickshaw runners had to navigate, their shouts warning pedestrians out of their way.

From time to time, as part of her training, every *maiko* was escorted by a more experienced, older woman to places where she could observe the artful ways of highly respected *geishas*. The training was meticulous, with each ceremonial step practiced rigorously. How to use the fan to cover her face when she laughed, how to engage in titillating and discreet repartee with guests, how to listen indulgently to men who poured out their problems, were all part of the *geisha*'s accomplishments, and all was woven into an art form appreciated by the wealthiest men in society. Indeed, the highest caste of *geisha*, the *tayu*, was even favored by royalty.

They began their climb up the steps of Atago Hill toward the strange looking red brick building called the Twelve Storeys, which could be seen from anywhere in Tokyo. Many considered it a disgusting structure. It was certainly very un-Japanese, but it had the first elevator in the country.

"This is the most popular place I've been to," said Kimi-san, as the three entered the octagonal "cloud scraper" to browse goods from almost every continent. Then they ascended to the top floor to peer through telescopes into distant parts of the city. Almost two hours passed before they finally left the building.

"Is Doctor Kazuma still your teacher?" Noruko asked Kimi-san, as they made their way to Ueno Park a short distance away.

"Yes, he has me go around to all the wards with him, and last week I was allowed to watch him do an amputation. It was awful, and I almost got sick, but he was very understanding. He sat and talked to me about how much less pain the patient felt now compared to earlier days. I am very fortunate to have him as a teacher."

"I think he likes you," said the Elder Sister. "You said that he took you to the Ginza to look at all the art work. He wouldn't do that for just any girl."

"He had just discharged his last patient that morning, and it was a beautiful day. He said that we should get away from the hospital and the smells of ether and disinfectant. I know he likes me, but like the man you entertained, Noruko-san, the doctor is twenty years older than I am."

"But just think," said Noruko, "he is wealthy and very prestigious, working at St. Luke's Hospital in the foreign quarter. He would be a wonderful catch."

"I'm not interested in a man just because he has money, Noruko-san. Besides, my father is just as important, and I doubt that my father would allow me to marry the doctor."

"Why not?" asked the Elder Sister. "I would certainly marry him. I think you're just being overly romantic, reading all those English novels about love."

"There's nothing wrong with that," sniffed Kimi-san. "But I do *not* love him, though I respect him very much."

"But why would your father object? Has the doctor ever met your father?" asked Noruko.

"No, though I'm sure he would like to. But Ise-san—"

"Oh, how intimate! You two are on a first name basis! Not Doctor Kazuma, but Ise-san!" chimed in the Elder Sister.

"There's nothing intimate about it," said Kimi-san dismissively. "We are friends on a professional basis. Now if you don't keep interrupting me I'll tell you what's important. Doctor Kazuma is a pacifist. He deplores the military build-up. He uses the English word 'jingoism' and says that it's all propaganda for the Army and Navy. He believes that war will be a disaster for Japan, especially against a European nation."

"And your father wouldn't approve of his views?" asked Noruko.

"Absolutely not. My father is a great patriot. So you can see why I don't encourage a meeting. Besides, I overheard my father tell my mother that he thinks he found a man for me."

"Who? Did he tell you?" asked Elder Sister.

"Not yet. I have no idea who it might be. Perhaps a military officer or someone in the foreign office. My father knows many important men."

"Then you must be very excited," said Noruko.

"Excited is not the word, Noruko-san. I am terrified."

***

Alexei spent the day wandering through the Ginza, practicing his Japanese while stiffly bowing to merchants who bowed back in appreciation of his efforts. Unlike many other parts of the city, the streets of the Ginza were wide, and the thousand stores were built of red brick in accordance with the alderman's decision following a disastrous fire that had obliterated the district. There was much to see, and the ways of manufacture were completely different from those in Russia. Nobody at home squatted when working, but here it was the most common thing in the world.

Another curiosity was the mixture of traditional and modern clothing. Some Japanese women wore western dresses with bustles and hats from Paris or London. Many men wore suits, but others, more traditional, might wear a western jacket with a long *yukata* and open *getas* instead of European shoes.

He listened to passing conversations and sampled teas from outside stands. At one point he stepped aside for three women, one of them a *maiko*. Staring was considered highly improper, but one of the girls was so strikingly beautiful that he simply stopped.

The girl glanced at him, her eyes widened, and she continued on. Later, he wondered if he'd said "*Konichiwa*", good afternoon, or some such thing; he had been too stunned to remember anything clearly but her face. He wondered if he had appeared silly; worse, his behavior might have been misconstrued as improper.

He waved down a rickshaw and returned to his *ryokan*. The old *obasan*, a grandmother, bowed and handed him two letters. He bowed in return and said "*Arigato*", then went to his room. He took his *futon* from its shelf, laid it down on the woven straw *tatami* mat, stretched out, and opened the first envelope. He smiled when he saw that it was from Sergei, but curiously, it appeared to have been opened and resealed. Picking up the second envelope, he recognized his mother's handwriting. He laid that one down, extracted Sergei's one page letter, and began to read.

Hello Alexei,

I hope that you are having a wonderful time in Japan. It seems so far away, and we know so little about that mysterious place. My friend and I can't wait to hear all about your adventures. Have you met any girls there? I'm sure it would not be difficult since, in your last letter, you said that your Japanese is rapidly improving. I am curious about those baths you mentioned, the ofuru*. Do men and women bathe together? If so, that must be VERY interesting!*

Tatiana and I will marry after I graduate next year. She has been spending a lot of time in church, restoring old manuscripts whose ancient pages are a marvel when held up to the luminous rays of the Almighty. We have both become quite devout. We have even attended mass with Boris, if you can believe that. Tatiana has also devoted time to orphanages, with a religious passion of nearly revolutionary intensity.

All is going well at the Academy, but the fencing squad desperately needs your talent; we were defeated by the Army's saber team.

On another note, we cadets cruised on the Navy's training ship, the Verny*, a three-mast relic. Sailing around the Baltic gave us a chance to experience life on the ocean. We encountered a storm, and that tested our training.*

We all look forward to seeing you again. Take care of yourself and enjoy the girls.

Your friend,
Sergei

P.S. I hope that it is nice and sunny in Tokyo so you can read this outside. I have heard that most houses in Japan still do not have electricity.

This is bizarre, thought Alexei. Certainly Sergei's news of the fencing team, the cruise, and his future marriage was worth writing about, but the rest made little sense. Sergei was well read; he knew all about Japanese culture, from daily baths to the improbability of foreigners, especially Russian, meeting girls in Japan. And what 'friend' did he mean if not Tatiana? And her going to church and devoting time to ancient manuscripts was pure fantasy. Tatiana was Jewish, for one thing, and only the most skilled monks would be allowed to touch the precious vellum. Then there were the words "revolutionary intensity." What bizarre wording.

He reread the letter. "The luminous rays of the Almighty," was the strangest departure from Sergei's customary speech. Could he have had an epiphany and Tatiana a conversion to Orthodoxy? She had never mentioned religion, and Alexei doubted she was much of a believer, even in her own faith. Then there was the weird postscript about reading outside in sunny Tokyo.

Alexei poured himself *ocha*, green tea, from a cast iron pot and, taking both letters, went into the tiny garden behind the *ryokan*. He sat on a stone bench, Sergei's letter illuminated by the rays of the late afternoon sun. A possible explanation for Sergei's odd phrasing came suddenly to mind, and he held the paper up to the sun. He didn't notice anything at first, then something was there: something very faint between the lines.

The envelope had been opened and somebody had read the letter. Had that person not seen the secret intelligence, the hidden letter? Or had they read it and allowed the letter to continue on? He had no idea. Holding it up to the warmth of the sun the secret writing darkened. *It might be milk, or a citrus*, thought Alexei.

> *Hello, Alexei. I hope all is well with you. I wish I could say that life here is getting better but that would be a lie. The country is still reeling from famine and the cholera epidemic. The peasantry falls into ever worsening poverty, and the Tsar has encouraged the Okhrana to arrest anyone considered suspicious. Worse, a pseudo revolutionary group has been set up, led by the police. Only last month the Tsar called constitutional monarchy a 'senseless dream.'*
>
> *T had a narrow escape. The cell she belonged to is part of the Social Democrats, a Marxist entity led by Georgy Plekhanov. He wants to gather delegates for a national organization but T thinks it will be raided. Instead she's now following the ideas of a Russian revolutionary living in England. His name is Lenin and believes that destroying the Tsar requires a small but dedicated group of professionals. They don't shy away from violence. I have very mixed feelings about remaining in the Academy but T says the revolution will need military leaders. I'll write again later. Stay safe, come back and join us. Sergei.*

Join what? wondered Alexei. *Join the Academy, or violent revolutionaries? What makes him think that I will align with extremists to be ferreted out and hanged?* He feared for his friend, and for Tatiana. He wanted to write a warning letter, but the one Sergei wrote had been opened and read by either the Japanese or the Russians; who might read a letter from him? The Japanese might let Sergei's letter through, thinking that he could be cultivated as a future spy, but the *Okhrana* would want to know if he had an accomplice.

Alexei pondered the options. He could caution Sergei, but how effective would that really be? His friend was influenced by Tatiana, a young woman willing to die for the cause. *No,* he reasoned, *my warning would be ignored.*

Examining the envelope, Alexei wondered why the secret reader didn't simply put the letter into a fresh one with the proper posting and send it on. Had he done so, Alexei would never have known that the letter had been read, and a serious reply could have been intercepted. Future communication between Alexei and the revolutionaries could have been tracked, with potentially serious consequences. The whole thing seemed bizarre, and Alexei wished that he could have a meaningful talk with his friend, but there was little he could do. Events and calamities would have to take their course.

Alexei looked closely at the second envelope and saw that it had not been opened. The dainty Cyrillic writing was distinctive. Somebody would have had to practice diligently to copy it, and he doubted that was the case. The letter was short, which was unusual, since her earlier missives went into detail about her garden, a place in which she found solace.

Dear Alexei,

The admiral and I hope that you are comfortable in the little ryokan you described. It sounds quaint, yet serene, and close to nature.

There have been rumors surrounding Grigory's daughter, Svetlana. I know she must seem quite frivolous to you, always wanting to be glamorous and popular. But recently she has been going to church regularly, to The Lady of Kazan.

Ordinarily, such signs of devotion would be all to the good, but it seems that Svetlana was seen in rather intimate company with a young man at the cathedral named Theodosis, who is studying for the priesthood. As you probably know, she also has some sort of relationship with a cadet at the Academy, the Boris Sokolov who once challenged you to a duel.

The matter with the acolyte is only gossip and may be false; but her fondness for the cadet is widely observed. I am concerned that he may be pursuing this friendship with the admiral's daughter for advancement. More aggravating is that Cadet Sokolov frequently invokes the name of Vyacheslav Konstantinovich von Plehve in his attempts to gain favors at the Academy.

Anyway, by the time you return in two years Sokolov will have graduated; you will never have to see him, and hopefully Svetlana will have got over her infatuation.

I am curious about the count. You alluded to his strange behavior and I wonder if you know any more about it? I'm also wondering if he has treated you well and introduced you to others. Of course I'm extremely curious to know if you have met any young ladies, European or Japanese. Please write, and do not worry about me.

Your loving mother,
Olga

P.S. The admiral has been very kind to me, but I do miss you.

Everything his mother described felt utterly far away. Alexei had only met Svetlana once before and had not been impressed. Rumors about her abounded, but he was not interested in the shallow girl. His mother would have given the incident with the acolyte scant attention if Svetlana were not the admiral's daughter. Svetlana, he knew, was not high up on Olga's list of notable women in St. Petersburg.

Then there was the matter of Boris Sokolov. Again there were rumors. Sergei had said that Boris bragged about "taking care of" a naval cadet who'd mysteriously disappeared. Many at the Academy were wary of him. No, Alexei thought, he would not regret missing cadet Boris Sokolov when he entered the school two years hence.

Alexei had nothing more to tell his mother about the count's after-hours activities. The man never confided in him. The only thing the count ever repeated were his warnings to not embarrass him and to never make any advances to a Japanese girl. That, he said was "*Verboten!*"—the count enjoyed using German when it suited him. And so, with the exception of a few formal occasions, he was neglected by the count and virtually forgotten.

It also occurred to Alexei that the count may have communicated with the admiral regarding the Trans-Siberian Railroad; he wrote few if any letters to Olga. She never mentioned receiving any, nor did she express any longing to hear from him.

Dusk stealthily snuck into the garden, and with nothing to do he returned to his room and put on his long *yukata*. He lit a lamp and picked up a book about great Samurai warriors, but his mind wandered and he put the volume aside.

A sense of loneliness came over him and he thought of the girl he had seen in the Ginza. She seemed serene, almost floating in the teeming street. It was just his imagination, he told himself; nevertheless, he wondered what she thought of him—if, indeed, she had noticed him at all. But she was unapproachable. Alexei breathed in the scent of the night and slowly drifted off to sleep.

CHAPTER 6

The first time Alexei had met Itomo-san was at a fencing demonstration on the grounds of the British Embassy, not long after his arrival in Japan. The demonstration had been open to the public: one of the few occasions in which Westerners and their culture could be seen by the local population. Alexei had scored well against numerous fencers of European nations, all of whom were much older than he. At the conclusion of the final match, a young Japanese man in a starched white uniform and wearing an officer's sword caught Alexei's eye and stiffly bowed. Alexei returned the courtesy, arms at his side. The man approached and said in English, "I enjoyed watching your strategy. My name is Lieutenant Itomo Karamatsu of the Japanese Imperial Navy."

"I am Alexei Brusilov, a student and an assistant to my father, a consul with the Russian delegation," he replied. "I am honored to meet you, but as a fencer I still have much to learn." It was self-deprecation, which was good manners in Japan.

In Japan never raise your voice, never directly contradict, never flaunt importance, and never slap any Japanese on the back, a guide book had warned. *Decorum is everything. Remember, you are an outside person, a* geijin. *There is an expression in Japan: 'Talented eagles hide their claws.' Never boast, and be reserved and formal until a comfortable relationship has been established.*

Itomo studied Alexei for a moment then said, "Your pronunciation is quite good. It is unusual for an outsider to speak more than a few words. I have received English lessons, but it is a difficult language to master. There are sounds in English that we don't have. But that aside, I'm interested in becoming a fencer in foil and saber. In fact, a number of our officers would like to form a team and enter competitions. I grew up with the Japanese fencing method, *kendo*, but that is for a two handed-weapon."

"With the bamboo sword, a very fast sport."

"It was a practice weapon for the samurai."

"Was your family samurai?" asked Alexei.

"Yes, but we are samurai now only in the spirit of *bushido*, the way of the warrior. My father, Colonel Karamatsu, was samurai when he was young. All samurai had to find other kinds of employment after the Meiji Restoration."

As the two men left the building Alexei said, "I would be quite pleased to teach you fencing."

"And how might I reciprocate?"

"Do you practice martial arts?"

"Karate, yes. Perhaps you would like to learn. It would be a trade of skills; equitable."

"Excellent. I would like to have a *tomadachi*, a friend. I have not had the honor of a Japanese acquaintance and there is much for me to learn. Japan, for a foreigner, can be a mysterious place. And there are ceremonies that very few westerners ever get to see."

"Such as?"

"Well, the tea ceremony, for one. I hear it is most serene, but I doubt that I will ever experience it."

Itomo thought a moment and studied Alexei. "What you call the tea ceremony we call *cha no yu*. It is an ancient and usually private ceremony, rarely available to a *geijin,* but I think you would appreciate its beauty. I will bear your request in mind. But you must be prepared to sit with your knees beneath you for hours and follow a prescribed etiquette."

"I enjoy a challenge," said Alexei with a grin.

"It will be that," Itomo said, with a flicker of a smile.

"I have been to England, but only as part of a skeleton crew to sail a naval vessel back to Japan," Itomo continued. "The British build many of our ships. I have been advised that I should expect more foreign travel. It would be valuable to understand western customs, and in that you may be of some assistance. With your permission, I shall call upon you, perhaps at the Russian Embassy tomorrow morning?"

"Excellent. And that is when we shall start your fencing lessons," said Alexei.

And so their friendship had begun.

***

"I'm amazed that Doctor Kazuma actually visited your house," said Noruko Toshikawa. She and Kimi-san were walking in Asakusa Park, a place of cherry trees and sublime beauty. Graceful, tiered pagodas provided rest and shade for the visitors who tired of walking beside the water, and the trees breathed a delicate freshness into the air. It was the *maiko's* day off and the two girls had arranged to meet, since both had startling events to relate.

"No less amazed than I was. Father was at home entertaining an army colonel when the doctor came. When the doctor saw that he was interrupting he offered to come back at another time, but father asked him to stay. It was the only polite thing to do, and mother served tea and cucumbers. Doctor Kazuma brought a beautiful gift-wrapped box. Father accepted it and put it aside. They all exchanged small talk about the renovation of the *torii* at the Meiji Jingu

Shrine, the one dedicated to the spirits of Emperor Meiji and his consort Empress Shoken. The conversation seemed quite agreeable."

"The doctor came to talk about you, didn't he?" asked Noruko-san.

"Yes, but he was circumspect. There was a great deal of polite silence, then he said that he wanted my father to consider him as a candidate for my hand in marriage. Father said that the idea was new to him, then asked me to leave the room, since it would be a conversation for men only."

The two girls found a bench and Kimi-san, in a low voice said, "I went to my room, but I sat near the wall and was able to hear everything." Noruko nodded. Privacy was an act of will in homes where the inner walls were sliding frames of opaque paper. If one sat close, it was easy to hear a conversation spoken on the other side. "Doctor Kazuma praised my medical abilities and said that he greatly enjoyed being my mentor. Then he said that although he was only a staff physician, he could offer me comfort and a fine home. My father asked about what sort of patients he treats, and Doctor Kazuma spoke too quietly for me to hear. But then he lamented the fact that Japan seemed to be intent on war again. He said that he had worked as a doctor in the same war against China my father fought in, and thought it a sad commentary for Japan that, even in victory, there was such terrible loss of life. He said that politicians make the final decisions, no matter how much blood is spilled."

"Did your father respond?" asked Noruko-san.

"He said war is an honorable and noble demonstration of Japan's new power, and what the nation did was a matter to be decided by the Emperor, not a doctor, despite Kazuma's humane considerations. Then father said that war might still be years away, but Japan must be prepared for western aggression. The doctor did not agree or disagree, but said that he would consider it an honor to be considered as a suitable husband.

"Then father suggested that Doctor Kazuma might consider a woman closer to his own age and hinted that he had already discussed my betrothal to a naval officer, though nothing formal had been decided. They drank more tea, and the doctor thanked my father for allowing him to speak and left."

Noruko-san looked thoughtful. "Did your father at least open the gift? Did you get to see what it was?"

"Yes. It was an exquisite statue of Kwannon, but I think my father was displeased. It is a wise custom to open a gift only when the one who gives is not present. The look on my father's face!"

"And your mother, what did she say?" asked Noruko-san.

"Afterwards she confided in me that father was offended by the doctor's pacifism, and he saw the gift as an offensive reminder of it. She thought the doctor was disappointed by my father's coolness toward him. When I arrived at the hospital the next day, Doctor Kazuma was very correct and professional towards me, and I thought he would have me transferred; the sadness on his face showed. But instead I could see that he wanted me more than ever and would simply hope and bear the unbearable."

The girls entered a tea shop and ordered *ocha*. Then they sat close together and watched the crowds idly, their minds filled with their own thoughts.

After taking a delicate sip of her tea, Noruko-san said, "The mysterious man I told you about came into the *geisha* house again last night, and I was told to sit with him and play my *shami*."

"How did he behave?" asked Kimi-san.

"He was much friendlier this time. He had a French-Japanese dictionary and referred to it many times. We drank many cups of saki. He said that his name was Jean-Louis

Remanche and that he was a wine merchant from southern France. He even gave me a business card. I don't know if he was unaware of our customs or if it was the amount he drank, but he seemed to like touching my hand. I think he would have touched more given the chance."

"Did he stay late?"

"Very late, and he asked *Okasan* if I could go with him; but she said no, it would be improper until she knew him better. He kept saying, '*Hai, hai*', while bowing. He finally left, very drunk, and *Okasan* and I laughed about it afterwards. But he must be very rich, and I was told to always entertain him."

"He may want to spend special time, private time, with you," said Kimi-san.

"That won't be for a while, if at all. Anyway, he may tire of me and find another girl, maybe a prostitute in the Ginza. Then I will have no concerns."

***

It had been several months since Itomo had begun fencing with Alexei; and, to Alexei's way of thinking, a friendship had developed.

The spring weather had turned quite warm. After an hour of saber practice both men found a bench and removed their masks. "Itomo-san, you have a fine balance between aggressiveness and patience, and you are fast," said Alexei.

"Thank you, but I am not fast enough," replied the naval officer with a rare smile.

"But I am seventeen and you are twenty-three. That makes a difference," said Alexei.

"It's kind of you to invent an excuse. I am not as proficient as I would like to be with the western style weapon. But I do enjoy the sport, and the training is valuable. Officers carry swords."

"True, but bullets are faster than swords," Alexei quipped.

From their vantage point they saw two men walk out of the Russian Embassy. Alexei said, "Itomo-san, the man on the left is my father, and the other is a British journalist. His name is William Stuart Jones. I will introduce you."

Itomo stood and bowed; the two men approached and did the same. After Alexei made introductions, Jones appraised Itomo and said, "I have interviewed Baron Ichiro Karamatsu; might you be his son?"

"I have that honor," said Itomo. "I am pleased that you know of him."

"He made a name for himself defending the Emperor during the last war. But he is Army and you are Navy! Considering the rivalry, I'm surprised that you did not follow your father into the Army."

"I have always been fascinated by ships and the sea. When I was a boy I read all about your Admiral Nelson and was determined to become a naval officer."

"Ah yes, the crossing of the T at Trafalgar; an effective tactic. His flagship, the *Victory*, is still afloat at Portsmouth. You might enjoy seeing it."

"I may have that chance. I'm told I will be sent to England soon to study torpedoes and attend the naval college. I will also be tasked with attending the construction of warships for the Japanese navy. So my stay in Britain may be lengthy."

"I invite you to visit me. I will show you around London. Then I will be off again, another assignment."

"Where to this time?" asked Yevgeny Brusilov.

"The Yukon. Haven't you heard? Gold has been discovered there, and the *Times* wants full reports. I think it will be positively thrilling, like California in forty-eight, eh. Just think, the Americans paid Russia only seven million for the Alaskan territory, over five-hundred eighty-six *thousand* square miles! Even so, the expenditure was so unpopular it was called 'Seward's Folly', in mockery of the Secretary of State who advocated the purchase. Now it's worth a fortune!"

"We have plenty of gold in the Urals," countered Count Brusilov testily. "A few miners in Alaska may get rich, but most will go home penniless."

"If only some of it would waft our way, eh?" Jones replied cheerfully, and the two men moved off.

"I didn't know that you were going to England," said Alexei.

"Not right away. Perhaps in a year, when construction is further along." Their attention was drawn by a *geisha* in a rickshaw, then Itomo said, "I will visit my father in Sasebo in a few days. If you accompany me you will see a different part of Japan."

***

A light rain had begun to fall, but Alexei focused his attention on a Japanese dictionary as he walked, shielding the pages from the drops of water with one hand. Oblivious to his surroundings, he rounded the corner of a flower shop and collided with a young woman carrying an *ikebana* arrangement in a lacquered vase. The impact propelled his book skyward, but the girl was sent tumbling into the puddled street. The vase spun away and struck the ground, shattering and scattering the blossoms.

Alexei was stunned. What had he done? The girl's expensive *kimono* was soaked and stained with mud.

On her hands and knees she looked up at him, seeing a tall *geijin*, his mouth open, eyes wide.

Alexei gasped, recognizing the girl he had seen in the Ginza a week before. Reflexively he reached down to help her, but she avoided his hand and struggled to her feet. A flicker of recognition showed in her eyes, but it was quickly suppressed.

"*Sumimasen*, I'm sorry, it's my fault," Alexei said, stooping to pick up pieces of ceramic. She waved her hands back and forth, admonishing him not to bother. It would be impossible to reassemble the vase. A middle-aged woman appeared at the doorway, her eyes going from her student to the pieces of the broken *ikebana* vase, then to Alexei. Horrified by what he had done, he bowed and again apologized profusely.

"Excuse me for my *busui yabo*, my clumsiness," he stammered. The woman, too shocked to bow in return, simply stared.

"I will pay for the flower arrangement and the ruined clothing. I am *wabi-sabi*, imperfect," he said, bowing again.

"No, it is not necessary to pay for anything," said the girl in a hushed voice. Then, not wishing to hear any more apologies, she turned and, dripping wet, scurried into the shop.

In a last desperate attempt to remedy the catastrophe, he called after her, "Please, what is your name so I may make amends?"

The elderly woman waved a hand across her face. She followed the girl into the shop and closed the door. Alexei picked up his book, brushed himself off, and ashamedly hurried on.

That night, sleep did not come easily. Images of the girl flooded his mind. He had seen Japanese women at the receptions held at the foreign delegations. In attendance with their husbands, they were extremely deferential and never mixed with the men folk. Others were the daughters of distinguished Japanese officials or military officers in attendance, but he never spoke to them. Those who saw him would cover the lower part of their face with the ubiquitous fan. Always in a group, they would giggle like school children.

Somehow, Alexei thought, the girl he'd bowled over outside the *ikebana* shop was different, perhaps more mature. He could only surmise; after all, the circumstances had not been exactly cordial. Still, there had been that look of recognition, more surprise than anger. Perhaps it was sympathy. Or was it sadness? She seemed fragile, like a porcelain doll, but then there was something else, something indefinable. How amazing that in a city as large as Tokyo he had actually encountered her again! He could hardly believe it. He laughed, wondering whether it was coincidence or fate.

He had to see her again, he had to know her name. Surely something could be done to compensate her loss. He wondered if she had been a student or a customer. Would she be in the shop again? Would the elderly lady know her name? Would she tell him? The cold reality of the situation chilled his hopes and he wondered what could possibly come of it, even if he did see her again. This was not, he chided himself, St. Petersburg, where a young man could meet a young lady, introduce himself, and spend a spring day in a park or take a troika ride in winter.

No, this was Japan: formal, reserved; where everything, including courtship, was orchestrated. The culture was a ritualized web of rules and ceremonies. Every response to every action was a matter of protocol. The customs and rules, he thought, were like train tracks, carrying everyone along an unvarying, predetermined route. Certainly no Japanese girl would even consider going to a tea shop with a strange man. Even if she were escorted by a relative, she would have to have her father's consent, and what father would allow his unwed daughter to be in the company of a foreigner?

Yet... if only he could see her again. Finally drifting off to sleep, his last conscious thoughts were of the girl's oval face and deep, searching eyes.

***

He spent much of the next morning in the information salon attached to the Russian embassy, which featured a small library. He was thumbing through Turgenev's *Fathers and Sons* when an idea occurred to him. He set the book down and left the embassy as quickly as good manners, both Russian and Japanese, allowed. Back at the *ryokan*, he pulled open a drawer and grabbed a handful of coins. Then he sprinted to the densely packed neighborhood where he thought the *Ikebana* shop was. Abruptly he stopped. He was lost.

A morning rain had further dampened the already muddied roads. He searched through a labyrinth of cramped streets. Merchants gawked at the blond *geijin* who anxiously peered into one shop after another. Finally he decided to retrace his steps to his tutor's house and start from there. It took a full hour, but eventually he turned a corner and recognized a flower arrangement in the window.

He stood numbly before the shop, wondering what he might say if she was there. Taking a deep breath to calm himself, then leaving his shoes on the step, he entered quietly. Exquisite floral arrangements were on display on a shelf, and two women were selecting leaves from a table while, in a very soft voice, the *sensei* made suggestions. The elderly teacher's greying coiffure was as elegantly arranged as the *ikebana*. She looked up when Alexei entered. Seeing her bewildered expression he bowed low, and she bowed as well.

The girl wasn't there, an anxious glance informed him. The teacher looked at him quizzically but said nothing. There was an awkward moment, then Alexei took an envelope from his coat pocket. The woman knitted her brows.

"I have come to pay for the vase I broke yesterday and to again apologize to the young lady." He proffered the envelope with both hands, as was the custom. "Certainly it is insufficient for the cost of the beautiful arrangement, but I humbly ask that you accept it," he said, knowing how one must belittle a gift before one offered it. Hesitantly the *sensei* accepted the envelope and said, "I will give this to the young lady if I see her again."

"I hope she was not injured. Would it be possible to learn her name?"

The *sensei* looked from Alexei to her students and back to him. There was an agonizing pause, then she said, "Her name is Kimi-san."

Alexei waited for a family name, but none was forthcoming. "Does she come here often?" he ventured.

"On occasion," the woman said haltingly, looking down at the envelope as if to say, "No other questions will be answered."

She does not want me here any longer; I am an intrusion, an oddity, thought Alexei. He was silent, then said, "My name is Alexei Brusilov. I would be very pleased if, when you see Kimi-san, tell her that I would again like to apologize in person. I thank you and I regret any unpleasantness I may have caused." Once again they exchanged bows, and he closed the door behind him.

Alexei walked down the street, oblivious to the stares. He had done all that was possible. Of course he could wait on the street day after day for a chance encounter, but he would appear foolish, and possibly attract unwanted attention from the shopkeepers who watched everyone, especially a *geijin.* That the *sensei* refused to give the girl's family name ended everything; there would be no way to meet her through official channels. Somberly, her returned to his room.

He told himself that he was not a fatalist, that not everything was preordained. Perhaps he might see her by chance; but logic argued that his efforts would terminate like wind-swept pathways in a wasteland.

But logic, his mother had once said, rarely makes sense when it comes to infatuation, or, for that matter, genuine love. So once again Alexei had difficulty falling asleep, as he lay on the hard *tatami* mat. Images of Kimi-san flitted through his mind. At last he slept, and dreamed of chasing her through a copse of trees as she moved from one to another, but he could never catch her. A fog drifted in and she became mist, then nothing at all.

***

"You seem tired," said the sensei the next afternoon, handing Kimi-san a cup of green tea. She knelt across from the girl on the straw *tatami*, studying the enchanting oval face with the strange, green eyes.

"*Hai, sensei.* I did not sleep well last night."

From her kimono, sensei Hiroku-san took an envelope tied with an elegant ribbon and placed it before the girl. "This is from the young man, the *geijin*, with whom you had the terrible accident. He came back and insisted on giving me this. He said it was for you, for the ruined vase. He was profusely apologetic, and his Japanese was good. How unusual. I think he really wanted to see you again."

Kimi-san looked at the envelope but did not touch it. "It was an accident; he did not have to give me anything," she said in a hushed voice. After a moment she said, "Please, *sensei*, you open it."

Hiroku-san untied the ribbon, slid open the envelope and extracted a twenty-yen note. Kimi-san's hands flew to her face and she said, "No, it's far too much! That would buy twenty vases."

"It's a small fortune," said the teacher, her hand covering her mouth. "He must be very rich."

Kimi-san shook her head. "He did not seem to be." Then she became silent.

"He asked for your name."

Kimi-san looked up expectantly.

"Yes, I told him, but only that it is Kimi-san. He knows nothing more, and you will never have to see him again."

"But I want to see him again," Kimi-san said in barely a whisper.

The *sensei* sat bolt upright and said, "He's *geijin*! Your father would never approve."

"I must thank him for the gift, *sensei*."

"Only if you accept it. You may leave it at my shop and I will return it, if he ever comes back. That is the sensible thing to do."

There was a long pause, and Kimi-san seemed quite distant. "You don't understand," she finally said, looking down at her cup of *ocha*.

"Oh," said Hiroku-san, "I think I do."

Kimi-san sipped her tea and for a brief moment relived the previous evening's thoughts as if they were a silent *kabuki* play. It had been another nearly sleepless night as she lay on her *futon*. The sudden collision, the horrific sprawl into the mud, and the crash of the vase had happened so unexpectedly. Then the young man, tall, with a mop of wavy blond hair and deep blue eyes, begging her forgiveness. So startled had she been that, for an excruciating moment, she could only make a sound of shock as she stared at him. She remembered again the proffered hand she'd refused to take.

It had all happened so quickly, yet his whole being was present in her mind. Who was he? The only name *sensei* remembered was Alexei. Where did he come from, and how was it that he spoke fluent Japanese?

She had seen woodcuts of *geijin* with their long noses and strange faces. Illustrated books with photographs her father owned showed old bearded men from distant countries; none of them looked at all appealing. On several occasions she had seen European business men sweeping past in rickshaws, but never had she spoken to one, nor ever really looked at them except out of mild curiosity. But she had seen the youth who stared at her.

What would she say to him if they ever met, she wondered? How would she explain that her discomfiture demanded no gift? Surely his embarrassment was payment enough. Was it his demeanor, his earnest apology, or was it something else about him that played upon her mind so persistently?

She had seen her brother's classmates, all military and overbearing. Would any of them have been as humble in similar circumstances? She doubted it. At best there would have been a curt apology. Surely the imperious friend of Itomo, of whom her father had spoken, would have overlooked the incident altogether.

She had read popular novels that extolled the virtue of marriage and reverence to family and emperor. They made much of filial piety and even devotion, but little was said about love or romance. Such fanciful emotions were not encouraged. Marriage was hardly about love, nor the pleasure of a man's company, nor even of his touch, she'd surmised.

It was not a woman's place to show discomfiture or register a slight. Conformity, obedience, and docility were required; but she had her own ideas, which were not properly Japanese. On occasion her father berated her for her boldness and unseemly independence. What would he say if he could read her thoughts now?

She looked wistfully beyond the *shoji* screen to the tiny garden behind the flower shop.

"I might be able to arrange something," *sensei* said, her gaze following Kimi-san's as it lighted on a single flower in the garden. "But it will be under the strictest circumstances. Your meeting will only be with your eyes."

"Yes, only with our eyes," said Kimi-san, wondering what her *sensei* could possibly do.

***

The next morning Alexei awoke and, half dozing on the *tatami* mat, considered his situation. He'd had little experience with girls in St. Petersburg beyond an exchanged smile or a few words. He knew almost nothing about females.

He would say nothing to the count about this girl. Why should he? He would never see her again, and he didn't need the rebuke. "Don't be foolish," the count would say; "you are Russian; these girls will have nothing to do with you. They regard us as barbarians and they fear our power. You will never understand what they are really thinking. In their world there is the public face and the private, *honne*, a face you will never see. They will never allow it."

Once Alexei had asked, "You are a diplomat; don't diplomats have understandings and make trustworthy agreements?"

With undisguised contempt Brusilov had replied, "Agreements are a matter of interpretation, and languages have subtle nuances. Our dealings with European nations are concrete and above board, in part because we have languages in common. In the Orient everything is hidden. You look, but you only see shadows.

"We Europeans are basically from similar cultures," his father had continued airily. "There may be hypocrisy, but it is detectable. Here they say *ware ware nijonjin:* 'We Japanese'. Only they know what they are truly thinking. They are a mystery, and damn little they say is believable. As for socializing, do not even consider Japanese girls. It is a waste of time. You will embarrass them and degrade yourself. I encouraged you to learn Japanese only for political and military reasons, not for social purposes."

Alexei realized that no matter how much of the language and customs he learned, and however much he wanted to ignore the remonstration, the count was right.

But he still wanted to learn all he could, and Itomo Karamatsu would be the key, his own *sensei.*

He had read a book of Japanese *haiku*, the beautiful poems of nature and love. Suddenly he sat up and decided to write his own. He had read that a *haiku* poem was characterized by brevity; the most highly regarded ones ended with a surprising or unattainable possibility. Lighting an oil lamp he sat cross-legged with pen and paper. A dozen cross-outs later, he finally completed his *haiku.*

Anguish and Longing
Bud of the Cherry Blossom
On Winter's Bare Branch.

CHAPTER 7

Alexei peered out the window of the train as black smoke rolled past, staining the summer sky. Itomo, beside him, sat ramrod straight in his naval uniform, disregarding the shy glances of young women. The crowded train swayed back and forth as it moved along the tracks at twenty-five miles an hour.

They had left Tokyo behind; Alexei turned his attention to the fields where workers in conical straw hats and black knee-length pants bent over rice shoots. Dotted amongst the fields were humble dwellings with thatched roofs.

The train rumbled through a village and Alexei strained to read signs touting both Japanese and foreign products, but the most flamboyant signs were not commercial. Brightly painted, they proudly displayed the Japanese flag: a red sun on a white field, signifying a nation at the center of the universe. Other signage proclaimed the Emperor to be a direct descendant of the sacred sun deity Amaterasu. On wall after wall, the citizenry was reminded that the nation's success was due to Emperor Mutsuhito.

Other signs announced Japan's determination to become a great power. Bold characters shouted, "Modernize! Industrialize! Build Big Guns!" while still others rallied the villagers with "Western technology, Japanese genius!"

Alexei sat back and considered their significance. It had only been a little over thirty years since Japan and the Meiji dynasty had erupted from its feudal past. What really motivated this jingoistic display? Perhaps, he thought, it was because all the great powers were intent on territorial expansion and Japan could become a colony of one of them if it did not assert itself.

The train stopped for passengers at a small village and Alexei read another sign: "Every man must serve the Army of the Rising Sun!"

"That sign sounds like war, Itomo-san. Is every man to be in the army?"

"Starting this year, every male over eighteen must be available for the military. We intend to have an army second to none. The world is in upheaval and Japan must be prepared. We will not suffer any more insults from European powers."

"Insults? Do you mean the old treaties? The ones Japan said were unequal?"

"Not just those," said Itomo. "I mean a recent one which particularly angers my father. Two years ago he was a battalion commander in the war against China and was cited for bravery. The war was fought in Korea, a very strategic place, since any invasion of Japan would likely originate there."

"It was a decisive conflict. China was no match for Japan."

"True, and the world was amazed by how quickly Japan won. But the Europeans became fearful. At the war's end Japan took control of Korea, until we were forced, at sword point, to abandon the peninsula. It was an embarrassment and a great dishonor. The European powers interfered with Japan's security. Later, England realized that it needs Japan as a bulwark against Russia, so it concluded a treaty with us."

"Does Japan expect a Russian invasion?"

"Why not? Most of Asia is controlled by Europeans, and Russia is a very real threat. I hope this does not upset you, Alexi-san, but it is *real politic*."

"I understand. I hope that my presence will not upset your father."

"You are my guest, and my father is a very traditional gentleman. You have nothing to worry about."

They lapsed into silence as the countryside slid past. Finally Alexei said, "I had an extraordinary encounter a few days ago. I want to ask you if my actions were appropriate."

"Was it a distressing encounter?"

"Extremely, and not just for me. I was returning from a tutorial session when I rounded a corner and literally ran into a young lady. She was coming out of a flower shop carrying an *ikebana* arrangement, and our collision left her in the mud. I tried to apologize, and I even went back to the flower shop and gave money to the *sensei* for the destroyed art work. I was hoping to see the girl so I could present the payment in person, but she wasn't there. I quite felt that I had lost face."

"Did you learn her name?"

"The *sensei* told me her name was Kimi-san, but nothing more. I'm afraid I will never see her again."

Itomo sat quietly and perfectly straight for a moment before asking, "And were you hoping to?"

"Wouldn't you, if she were the most beautiful girl you ever saw?"

Alexei thought Itomo gave him an odd look, but the naval officer said nothing.

Alexei decided to change the subject, since his friend made no further comment. "I heard that there is to be a new civil code coming out this year. One about families."

"I've heard that, too. It just puts into law what custom has always dictated. The father of each family has supreme authority and will be able to disallow the marriage of a daughter up to the age of twenty-five."

"But why must it become law?" asked Alexei.

"So there can be no argument. Japanese society attempts to refrain from discord. But there is also another law that says divorce is allowed for men whose wives commit adultery."

"But not for women if husbands commit adultery?"

"Certainly not. They are to be submissive and do their duty for home and the Emperor. The whole country is devoted to him. Women as well as men must honor His Majesty."

A few minutes later, the train stopped at the port of Sasebo. Alexei's eyes wandered to the massive warships floating offshore.

"Those two are the *Fuji* and the *Yashima*, the most modern battleships in the world," said Itomo, a note of pride in his voice. "They have guns that fire shells twelve inches in diameter and nearly four feet long. They are the biggest ever made, and their hulls are protected by nickel-steel armor. They're virtually invincible."

"And you'd like to be the captain of one of them," said Alexei with a grin.

"Of course. But I'd be pleased with a destroyer."

Alexei studied the twelve-thousand ton ships with their ominous guns and tall masts and said, "Were they built in Japan?"

"No. They were built at the Thames Iron Works in England, but ideas from Japan have been incorporated to improve the design. The ships are expensive, but necessary."

"Where did the money come from?"

"China. It was from the indemnity they owed us. Since we cannot have Korea we have battleships instead. And with ships like those we will get Korea back when the time comes." Itomo gave a short, resolute nod of his head. His eyes lingered on the warships, and Alexei wondered whether his friend was envisaging himself on the deck of one.

From the Sasebo station it was a short walk to the docks. A group of army and navy officers exited a building and Itomo said, "The colonel with the medals is my father. He is a baron and a division commander in Japan's Second Army."

Itomo and Alexei bowed deeply, to show the deference due an elder of superior rank, and the colonel gave a short, crisp bow. "So this is the young fencing instructor my son mentioned," he said.

"It is an honor to meet you. Itomo-san is a quick learner and very fast. Any fencing team would be pleased to have him," responded Alexei.

"Your Japanese is quite accomplished. That is good."

"Besides being an army officer, my father is a noted scholar of art, both Japanese and western," said Itomo.

"I particularly like the Impressionist artists. It's refreshing to see that some of them now have a following in Europe," said the baron.

"I also like the Impressionists; especially Monet and Renoir," said Alexei, warming to this rather intimidating man. He could not help comparing the colonel's almost ferocious alertness to the quiet regard of Admiral Kochenkov. *What must it be like to have a father like this?* he wondered.

"That is the sign of a cultured man. A worthy attribute." Then, turning to Itomo, the colonel said, "We shall take the train back to Tokyo, but I wish to stop and pray at the Grand Shrine of *Ise*."

***

A quiet reverence, a sense of serenity lay over the shrine. Before entering, Alexei, Itomo and his father washed their hands with water spouting from a stone demon into a small pot, then they passed beneath an opulent red *tori* gate. Baron Karamatsu bowed to a priest, who recited a prayer and rang a bell. Inside the ornate shrine, Alexei's eyes took in carvings of animals and a sand-raked garden of extreme simplicity. In its center was a large rock, and several trees festooned with white strips of paper.

"What are those?" asked Alexei.

"*Omikuji*," said Itomo. "People buy envelopes containing a slip of paper on which is written a fortune. Put it on the branch and it may come true."

"Can I buy one?"

"Of course, but not all the *omikuji* are lucky. It may be better to make a prayer to the *kami*, the gods, and ring the bell to announce your wish."

"I have never been in a Shinto shrine before. It's so peaceful. Is it always like this?"

"This is Japan's most famous shrine. For fifteen hundred years Japanese have gained inspiration from nature and *kami*, a spirit of purity and the essence of life. Our gods are not like the Christian one. Shintoism has nothing to do with the afterlife; it's about the joy of this realm. As you can see, we celebrate nature. The closer to nature the closer you are to the spirit, to what you may call the gods."

"I visited a Buddhist shrine once. Is Buddhism as important as Shintoism in Japan?"

"It has many believers, and it is not considered alien, even though it came from China. Shintoism is a purely Japanese religion. About twenty years ago the Emperor established a Ministry of Divine Rituals with Shintoism at its core. Its purpose is to use religion to further the national spirit."

"So like the signs we saw from the train, it's all about the nation."

"Yes," said Itomo. "The nation, our indomitable spirit, the military and the Emperor."

They were silent for a few moments when Itomo said, "Since you are so interested in Japanese culture, I shall take you somewhere special and you will see the essence of this land."

They were about to leave when Alexei stood by the gate, wrote a wish, and rang the bell. It had nothing to do with the Emperor.

***

Two days later Alexei sat with Itomo in a teahouse in Shinjuku Gyoen Park. The teahouse was small and rustic, with bamboo floors covered with *tatami* mats. Imitating the seven other guests, he knelt and awaited the start of the ancient rite.

"The *chanoyu* ceremony is very old. Coming from China, it has Buddhist roots," said Itomo in a quiet voice. "We will be drinking green tea, but that's a ritual, an activity, not the central purpose of the building or the ceremony."

Alexei nodded and said, "It's very quiet, like the shrine we visited last week."

"Yes. This tea house, this *soan* with its grass roof, is the embodiment of nature, like a shrine. If one identifies with nature the spirit sheds all impurities. That was the teaching of a Zen priest, Rikyu, four hundred years ago. It's still a core belief today."

Outside Alexei could hear the sound of a brook as water flowed past ferns, over rock falls and into a pool, giving sanctuary to colorful *nishikigoi*, the ornamental carp that represented longevity. A delicate scent wafted into the teahouse.

On one side of him knelt Itomo, and on the other, Itomo's father. Across from him was a naval officer sitting stiffly, his eyes telling Alexei that this was a Japanese ceremony and no *geijin* could possibly understand its intricate symbolism or appreciate the truth it embodied.

"This is Lieutenant Atsugi Yoshiharu, captain of a naval transport," Itomo had said, introducing the man. There had been a curt bow from the taciturn officer, but not a word spoken. Alexei had returned the bow and taken his place. Now he glanced at the three other men who sat formally, all dressed in simple but expensive *yukatas* that exemplified the Japanese aesthetic of *shibusa*, a concept of rarified simplicity that Alexei found soothing to the senses. In a corner behind Itomo a young woman plucked soft music from the *koto*, the stringed instrument on her lap.

An elegantly kimonoed woman slipped into the teahouse to prepare the lengthy ceremony. Attending to a teapot, she was completely focused on the procedure, although she had performed it numerous times throughout her life. Only when she turned did Alexei recognize her as the *sensei* of the flower shop. The woman's eyes found his and she stopped for the briefest moment, then silently left.

Alexei drew in his breath and was about to say something to Itomo when the officer shook his head.

"This is a time for reflection," he murmured.

The teacher, thought Alexei, must have been astonished to see him in the company of Japanese officers. She must have wondered why he was here, and whether his presence had any connection to the misadventure in her *ikebana* shop. Several moments passed, and a young woman entered and observed that the teacups were set out in exactly the proper manner. She departed, and Alexei turned his head toward the musician as the strains of *koto* permeated the room with a haunting, faraway sound. He felt as if he were walking on the bottom of the sea. He turned back, his mind still far away.

She was standing there, a long-handled wooden ladle in her hand, staring at him. Stunned, Alexei made a short bow and half whispered her name, "Kimi-san." She also bowed, but it was to Lieutenant Yoshiharu and Itomo's father. Again her eyes met Alexei's but quickly shifted back to Lieutenant Yoshiharu. It was a look of apprehension, as though something ominous had entered the confines of the close room with its rice paper windows. Deadening stillness permeated the room.

Had the elderly woman warned her of his presence? Alexei wondered. For a moment Alexei thought Kimi-san might put down the ladle, excuse herself and not return. But that would not be proper etiquette. She had no choice, and once again Alexei felt that he had made a terrible mistake; he had brought her unimaginable distress.

There was tension in the room, and that was a travesty, thought Alexei. The entire ceremony of holding and turning the stoneware cups, the pouring of the hot green tea, the serenity of nature had been violated. There were looks of concern and barely masked disapproval, and they were directed at him. He wanted to flee but sat as immobile as the rocks in the garden.

In spite of his discomfort, Alexei could not help but be aware that Kimi-san's eyes sought his time and again as she went through the lengthy tea ritual. It was, Alexei thought, as if he were having a hypnotic effect upon her. They had only spoken to each other once, and for only a few distressing moments. So why, he wondered, was she constantly looking at him?

The colonel also noticed his daughter's discomfort and her glances at Alexei. That Kimi-san was not paying proper attention to the requirements of the ceremony could be an embarrassment upon the family and an affront to her *sensei*.

Lieutenant Atsugi gave Itomo a questioning look, then leveled his eyes like a trained gun at Alexei. The man's lips were compressed into a thin line. Alexei knew that, had Atsugi been a samurai in an earlier age, *geijin* would have stained the ground.

***

"You knew that the girl I mentioned to you was your sister, didn't you?" Alexei said.

"She told me of a strange encounter with a *geijin*."

"And you still invited me to the tea ceremony."

"I made a commitment; little did I think she would behave as she did," said Itomo.

"If I had known that she would be there I would have saved everyone the embarrassment. I apologize for the unpleasantness I created," said Alexei, genuinely distressed.

Itomo had come to the Russian consulate the morning after the tea ceremony and was walking the grounds with Alexei.

"It was my fault," said Itomo. "I should have given you the opportunity to beg off, but I was conflicted. I knew how badly you wanted to see her again and didn't realize that she...."

"She what?" said Alexei stopping on the tree lined path.

Itomo looked away and said, "Apparently she took an interest in you but said nothing about that to me. I was quite surprised by her conduct at the tea ceremony."

Alexei couldn't help but smile. "So you think she likes me?"

Itomo turned to him and said, "My friend, whether she likes you or not is of no consequence. And to be truthful, any further attention you give her could be problematic. It is not very Japanese for me to put it in such terms, but she is not allowed to speak to you. My father asked me to tell you this, and that's why I'm here."

Alexei was silent for a long moment, then said, "I once mentioned my interest in Japanese girls and my father berated me, saying that no Japanese girl would even want attention from a *geijin*, especially a Russian one."

"You are still young and will have many girlfriends. I think we've all had first loves and unfulfilled longings, *tomodachi*. Besides, there is something I haven't told you."

Alexei stood stock still, as if a sentence was about to be handed down.

"Do you remember the naval lieutenant I introduced you to, Atsugi Yosihara, the man who gave you the awful look?"

"Of course. I think he wanted to kill me."

"He probably did. My sister has been promised to him. He will be her husband when my father thinks she's ready. The lieutenant's grandfather was a great warrior and my father was his student. The colonel feels indebted to the old samurai and agreed when Atsugi requested a union with Kimi-san."

"Does he love her?"

"I don't know if he loves her, but that is not of importance. Atsugi is a fine officer and will rise quickly in the navy. My father will be proud of that. One more thing, Alexei: he is a dangerous man."

CHAPTER 8

St. Petersburg, Russia
July, 1897

The tap on the door was soft but insistent. It was answered by the footman, who ushered in two men. One was a tall, dour policeman with a pinched face; the other a bearded, rotund priest wearing a cassock adorned with a heavy cross.

"We are here to speak with Admiral Kochenkov and his daughter. Are they available? asked the priest.

The footman nodded warily and returned moments later, accompanied by the admiral and Svetlana. With a slight bow the policeman said, "Excellency, I am Chief Detective Vassily Lebedev, and this if Father Isador Glinka."

The priest inclined his head, and in a nearly inaudible wheeze said, "If you will kindly indulge us, we would appreciate a few minutes of your time. It is in regards to a rather delicate but important matter."

"Of course," replied the admiral. He knitted his brows and gave his daughter a curious look. The footman took his leave and Kochenkov said, "Let's proceed to the parlor, and you can acquaint us with the purpose of your visit." He indicated two over-stuffed Queen Anne chairs and said, "Would you care for a cup of tea?"

The detective shook his gaunt head, which appeared to be supported by a neck so spindly that the whole assemblage would topple over if not held upright by a tight starched collar. The priest glanced at Lebedev with a flicker of displeasure, as though he would have enjoyed the tea and whatever delicacies might have accompanied it. He eased his mastodonic posterior in the antique chair with a glacial descent like a penguin about to cover her eggs.

"Are we being investigated for something?" Svetlana demanded curtly, as the detective meticulously extracted a pencil and a thin notebook from the breast pocket of his coat.

The admiral raised a finger and gave his daughter a stern look. "These gentlemen are here to ask questions, and we are to answer them," he admonished Svetlana. She gave an exasperated sigh, which the detective chose to ignore.

Lebedev studiously turned several pages, looked up, and with sudden diffidence said, "Excellency, you should understand that we have just begun our investigation and neither you nor your daughter are considered suspects in any sense. But there has been an unfortunate incident, the death of a young man, a church acolyte named Theodosis. We are wondering if perhaps you or your daughter may have been acquainted with him?"

"You may have seen him in the Kazan Cathedral," Father Glinka volunteered with an ingratiating smile.

The admiral frowned and said, "Death. Do you mean of natural causes, or something else?"

"We are speaking of murder," said the detective in a very quiet voice.

"How terrible. But I, and I'm quite certain my daughter, have no knowledge of this. What makes you think that either of us would?"

"Both the church and the police made inquiries at the Cathedral," said the priest. "And, please excuse the unpleasant insinuation, but it has been suggested that your daughter may have known the acolyte. That... she might have had some contact with him."

"And not exactly in the spirit or to the approval of Our Savior, if you understand the implication," said Lebedev.

"No, I don't understand your implication," retorted Kochenkov. "And who might have made this suggestion?"

"Excellency, at this point I am not at liberty to divulge his name, though I assure you that you will learn of it if necessary," said the policeman.

"I most certainly will." Turning to his daughter he said, "Do you know anything about this?"

"Not really. There was a young man, an acolyte, who did smile at me on several occasions. Of course, many men smile at me," she said, coquettishly tilting her head. "I might have exchanged a few words with him, mere pleasantries, nothing else. I most certainly know nothing of a murder. How very sad!" Her eyes were downcast and her voice prim.

"But you were familiar with him," the detective said, a little more brusquely than he intended.

Svetlana shrugged, stared into his eyes and said, "Hardly 'familiar.' I mean, how could I be? He never left the Cathedral, and who would do anything inappropriate there?"

"The detective is not accusing you of anything," said Kochenkov, taking his daughter's hand. "The officer is merely carrying out an investigation and asking questions, as he should. The murder of the young acolyte is a most serious matter." Then, addressing the officer, he said, "I assure you that my daughter is a very proper young lady. And though she is innocent of any unsubstantiated and unholy act, I will be available if the investigation requires it. Now is there anything more you wish to ask?"

The detective glanced at his notes, then at the priest, who upon examining Svetlana's posture, merely smiled and said,

"No, not at this time. Perhaps later, if that is necessary. But, of course, we pray that it is not."

The admiral pensively accompanied the detective and the priest to the door. There was a quiet exchange of pleasantries. After their departure Kochenkov turned to Svetlana and said, "My dear, I am not naïve, nor am I unaware of your proclivities. I suspect that there is far more to this matter than you care to admit. Both I and your mother require the unvarnished truth. Our reputation and, should I say, your innocence demand it."

"I had nothing to do with that boy's murder!" Svetlana flared, and she stormed up the stairs. "Did you see how that priest was gawking at me? It made me sick! And that ferret, that hideous inquisitor? Now I am very tired and very distressed. I am going to bed and do not wish to be disturbed."

"Svetlana, you are not dismissed!" retorted Kochenkov.

"Dismissed? I am not one of your obsequious servants. I repeat, I do not want to be disturbed!"

Her bedroom door slammed and a bolt shot in place.

Not long after, a servant was sent off with a note to deliver, and Svetlana, bundled warmly in furs, slipped out of the house to meet Boris.

"What did you tell them?" Boris demanded. He was agitated, striding along with both hands thrust into his pockets. They hurried past the ungainly buildings of the Academy. Cold wind tore at their coats and scarfs and swept dead leaves into gutters.

"I didn't say anything that would incriminate you," said Svetlana.

"Do they suspect me?" cried Boris.

"They have no reason to."

"But an investigation! Why so much fuss for a mere acolyte?"

"I don't know. A priest was found murdered last week. Maybe they think there's a connection," Svetlana speculated.

"Was Theodosis a revolutionary?" asked Boris intently. "Perhaps they are investigating the Church's support for revolutionaries."

"He never said anything about politics. He was very devout, but starved for knowledge about girls. I showed him what he wanted to see, and he gave me some of the information I needed."

"Some? What more do you need?"

"Something even more important."

"What? And what more would you have done to learn what you want?"

"Anything. Everything. I told you, he was my spy."

"So you would have had sex with him," said Boris peevishly.

Svetlana didn't answer, and they walked in silence until he finally said, "But who would want to kill an acolyte?"

"Besides you?" said Svetlana, half in jest.

"I told you, I did not kill him!"

"But you would have, wouldn't you?"

He stopped and took her by the shoulders. "You are everything to me, and I am a jealous person. I admit it. I'm sure that other men have desired you, and I haven't done anything to them. But maybe someone else at the Kazan Cathedral was aware of how Theodosis spent his time. Maybe he had an enemy there; perhaps someone jealous, someone who saw him with you."

"Nobody saw us!"

"Churches are worlds all to themselves where things are sacred but not secret. Maybe his death was due to something no one is thinking about."

"What do you mean?" Svetlana asked.

"Theodosis wanted to have sex with you, it's obvious. That's what he was after. But that doesn't mean he wasn't having sex with somebody else, somebody in the church who was very jealous of his intimacy with you."

"Somebody else? You mean...?"

"A man. Perhaps a priest or bishop. Somebody who used him or even loved him, then saw him with a girl. Things like that happen in churches. They take vows of celibacy, but they are still men. For some priests God is simply not enough."

Svetlana thought about it and said, "But then why would the church bring in the police? It could only lead to scandal."

"I don't know. But I don't think the police are done with either of us."

***

"You will never slam a door in my face again, you will not leave the house without informing us, and you will tell us everything that transpired between you and that acolyte! What the detective and the priest said this morning is extremely disturbing, and I want the truth."

The admiral spoke to Svetlana with unwonted sternness. She had just returned, to find both her parents waiting for her at the door. There were no servants in sight. It was exactly ten o'clock; she could hear the chimes of the great standing clock in the parlor. Her father stood before her straight as a pillar, with an imperious resolve she had rarely seen in him, and never before directed at herself.

"We expected you home earlier. This is no time of night for a young girl to be walking alone," said Ekaterina.

"I am not a girl, and I am quite capable of walking alone," replied Svetlana tensely, her eyes darting from the admiral to Ekaterina. She was about to step past them when Ekaterina, grabbing her wrist, said, "You are not going anywhere until we have answers."

Svetlana pulled away and hissed, "I already told you, there was nothing more than a little flirtation. It was all completely innocent. *He* was completely innocent. He just wanted to kiss me."

"Kiss you?" shot Ekaterina. "And you let him? He was to be taking church vows and you tempted him, as I'm sure you do others. Dare you deny it?"

"It was nothing!" Svetlana shouted. The admiral's eyes bored in to her and she let out a long sigh. "I met him, yes, we spoke after Mass, but I swear I had nothing to do with his death. You must believe me. And I did not have sex with him. Not real sex."

"What do you mean, not real sex? What did you do, take off your clothes?" barked the admiral.

"Of course not! I let him kiss me, that's all. He wanted to so badly. He said that he had never kissed a girl before and he just had to before he became a priest. So yes, I let him."

"And had he not died, it would have happened again and again," said Ekaterina, her words rushing in a torrent. "Oh yes, your flirtations, to put it mildly, are hardly a secret. It is becoming scandalous. And just who were you with tonight?"

"With a friend, and who that might be is my concern, not yours," retorted Svetlana.

There was a hard silence, then the admiral said, "These matters *are* our concern, daughter. There is something else that requires explanation. Something rather puzzling that arrived this afternoon." Nodding to his wife, he said, "I would like you to show it to her."

Ekaterina slipped an envelope from a vanity drawer and handed it to Svetlana.

"It is addressed to you," she said tersely. "A nurse from a hospice brought it. I took the liberty of opening it, since events here have become so unpredictable."

Svetlana snatched the envelope angrily. "You have no right to open my mail!" Glancing at the enclosed card she said, "There's nothing mysterious about this. I delivered flowers to a woman who was very sick. I saw her in the cathedral every once in a while. I heard that she died."

"But the card says that someone there, some undisclosed person, wishes to see you. Why?"

"I have no idea."

Grigory Kochenkov exchanged a long look with his wife and said, "Svetlana will not leave this house without my permission."

"Pyotr," Svetlana called to the head footman, who had stuck his head around the door and was staring at the unusual scene, "bring heavy chains and locks. My father wishes to imprison me. Do hurry, before I escape."

"What rubbish! This girl is impossible!" sputtered the admiral. Then turning to Ekaterina he said, "You deal with her. She is scandalous."

Grigory Kochenkov threw up his hands, brushed past the footman and stalked out of the room. The servant, still incredulous, asked timorously, "The chains and locks, madam?"

"No! Just leave us," said Ekaterina petulantly. "You just love a scandal, don't you?" she said, turning to her daughter.

Svetlana shrugged and said, "I am not doing anything so different from what other women in the aristocracy do. Oh, they all pretend to be wholesome and demure, without a blush of scandal. It's a sham, a façade. Tell me what woman does not have a secret lover? I am not deceiving anybody, because I am not married. And, Mother, who is *your* lover this month?"

The slap spun Svetlana's head, and her cheek turned crimson.

"How dare you insult me! You are a tramp and everyone knows it. Father and I have had enough. I am your mother and I'm telling you—"

"You are *not* my mother. You cannot deny it. I found that paper from the church, and I'm going to find out more."

"Think what you want, but you may not like what you find. And as for *affairs*, dear child, discretion is everything. Failure to be discreet is the end of life. And there is no resurrection."

"But mother, a juicy scandal is so much fun," said Svetlana, and she stormed from the room. She slammed the door behind her.

***

The next morning, Svetlana waited impatiently until her father departed for the Admiralty building and Ekaterina drove off in the carriage before slipping out of the house and joining her friend Elena Vanova. After a twenty-minute walk they arrive at the hospice.

"I hear footsteps," said Elena in a near whisper.

The door was opened by a diminutive nun, and the two girls were led through a narrow corridor to a small, sunlit room. "Someone will be with you shortly," said the nun, before she closed the door and soundlessly departed.

Elena looked curiously at Svetlana and said, "Why do you think somebody asked you to come here?"

"I have no idea. The lady from the cathedral died the night after she spoke to me. She had something she wanted to tell me, but the nurse shooed me out. Maybe she left a message."

"To tell you more about the priest?"

"Perhaps."

The determination that had propelled Svetlana began to melt as she sat in the hard-backed chair, staring at an icon of Saint Nicholas flanked by a painting of Mary and the Christ child. Whispers and the creaking of a wheelchair were heard in the hallway. Elena fidgeted.

There was a tap on the door and a matronly woman stepped in.

"My name is Sister Vishnaya," she said authoritatively to Svetlana. "I was hoping that you would come alone, but..." she glanced at Elena then concluded, "it matters not. I have much to do, so I'll be brief. Eudoxia, the sick lady you visited here, left you a letter. She told me that it was very important and confidential, and I must be the one to hand it to you. She always watched you, yes?"

Svetlana nodded and Vishnaya said, "Well, she had reason to. Did she ever tell you why?"

"No. I always saw her, but she never spoke to me. I didn't even know her name."

"Under the circumstances she could not tell you, though she desperately wanted to."

"What circumstances? I don't understand. I wanted to speak to her, but if I approached she would always walk away. But she seemed very kind. Sister, who was she?"

The nun was silent for a moment, then looked at Svetlana with more compassion and a little less impatience. "Here, Child, I'm sure it's all in this letter. Sister Eudoxia only mentioned you to me on a few occasions, and I promised her that I would remain silent. So there is nothing more I can tell you."

"She was trying to tell me about a priest. Did she explain that to you?"

Again the nun was silent. Finally she said, "Whatever I know I cannot say. Now please, take this and read it at home." She handed Svetlana an envelope, then opened the door to usher out the two girls.

***

Elena and Svetlana settled in a tea shop on Inzhernaya street, a block from the Pushkin statue. "What does it say?"

Elena urged her friend. She was practically bouncing on her seat with excitement.

Svetlana read and reread the handwriting, a shaky script that filled less than a single page. "Oh my God," she murmured. "No wonder."

"No wonder *what*?" demanded an impatient Elena.

Svetlana looked around the crowded tea room, then passed the letter to her friend, who read it in turn, pausing now and then to puzzle out the handwriting.

To my dear, dear Svetlana,

How many times I gazed upon you as you grew into such a beautiful young woman. How many times I wanted to hold you and ask about your dreams and aspirations. I adored you from afar, and I saw how you wanted to know who I was and why I cared. Night after night I cried myself to sleep after looking into your eyes. I endeavored to hear every word you uttered. I would turn them over in my mind, thinking of answers or cautionary remarks. I saw your wandering eyes and the stares of boys and men as you grew older, and I feared for you. Once I nearly took you by the hand, breaking my promise, to warn you of danger. But I dreaded what you might ask me and how my answers (for I would be truthful) would effect the harmony of your family.

But now I am about to gaze upon the Lord and, come what may, I think you should know.

Perhaps, my dear child, you have already guessed. If I am doing wrong, I most assuredly will have to answer for it, but hopefully God will forgive me. I long to see you one more time. I want so badly to hold your hand and share our tears. But I will be with you forever and ever. Be careful, especially of the priests. I will pray for you, my child, with everything I have,

Sister Eudoxia,
Your loving mother

The two girls were speechless. Finally Elena said, "All those years, the poor lady. And Ekaterina never said a word about it. But... if Sister Eudoxia was really your mother, who is your real father? I mean, is it the admiral, or someone else? Would there have been any reason for an adoption if the admiral was your real father? If he accepted you as his daughter, no document would have been needed. The Sister would have handed you to your father and that would have ended the matter."

"Yes, and it would all have been hushed up. No one would have wanted any record kept."

"But Ekaterina would have known all about it," said Elena pensively.

Irrelevantly she added, "No wonder her figure is so good. She never gave birth." Then she lowered her voice and asked, "Are you going to tell them that you know about your real mother?"

Svetlana shook her head and said, "That's my secret. I won't mention it unless I have to. It's a weapon."

"Scandal, you mean?"

"Exactly."

"Just one other thing perplexes me," said Elena. "Sister Eudoxia used the word 'priests'; plural. Isn't that strange? You don't think she meant the acolyte, do you?"

"I don't know what she meant," said Svetlana, tossing her head.

"Maybe she was just warning you about churchmen in general. But you've talked about that one priest, often. Do you think *he* is dangerous?"

"I think all men are dangerous. That's the fun of it, Elena."

***

There had been no questions, and no one had approached him. The acolyte had been buried in the hallowed grounds of a monastery outside St. Petersburg, where his family lived. The priests of the Kazan Cathedral had accompanied the coffin and attended the internment. Mass had been held and condolences given to the youth's parents.

Of course the body should never have been found. It had been hidden in the forest; but a passer-by, following his dog, had found it and called police. Now it mattered little: an unsolved mystery that would be forgotten. There were many murders in the city, though this one, involving an acolyte, was unusual.

But it had had to be done. The young fool had been seen with the girl, and he'd had the temerity to brag that he would soon have a conquest of his own to rival any of those enjoyed by older priests.

The lascivious boy's transgression had made his death inevitable. The murder with the steel letter opener had not been difficult. Now it was over, thought the priest, and he would bide his time. The girl would come like a hungry fish to the hook. He smiled to himself, for she was a true beauty.

Then he remembered of Eudoxia, and a worrisome thought came to mind. He did not sleep well for many nights thereafter.

CHAPTER 9

St. Petersburg
August, 1897

It was late in the summer and a full month had passed since the murder of the acolyte. There had been no further visits by the detective or the priest, and Svetlana brazenly defied her father's restrictions and left the house whenever she wished. The admiral chose to ignore her transgressions, and she did not reply when Ekaterina would sharply say, "And just where are you going? You know what your father said, Svetlana!"

Exhausted by the marathon session, Svetlana lay with an arm draped over her lover. "I want to do that every day, maybe two or three times a day."

"Then you will kill me, but it will be an enjoyable death," said Boris Sokolov. Lifting himself on one elbow he kissed the admiral's daughter, his hand cupping a breast. She sighed, ran her hands through his black hair, and gazed at him with hauntingly beautiful eyes. A pale light penetrated leaden clouds, illuminating the bedroom of the rustic *dacha*.

"Marry me, Svetlana Kochenkova."

"I will not. Not unless...."

"Unless I am rich. I know, I know."

"Oh Boris, I'm having too much fun to marry anyone! I love flirting with men, especially important ones."

"What if *I* were important, like my uncle Plehve?"

"The uncle who got you into the Naval Academy?"

"Exactly. He'll be chief of *Okhrana's* internal department, the police force going after Jews, revolutionaries and other criminals. Everybody is afraid of him. Except me. I'm his favorite nephew."

"So how did he get you in? It's so expensive! You never told me."

"Simple, really. I learned that Stephan Zorin, who attended the gymnasium with me, had enrolled in the Academy. His family is very rich, so even though they attend St. Isaac's Cathedral I had my suspicions. There was just something about him, maybe those eyelids, or that nose. Anyway, I heard rumors that Stephan's family has Jews in it. My uncle showed his father the documents, made a few threats, and I had all the money I needed. Then Stephan was expelled from the Academy his second year, and, strangely, he disappeared," said Boris smugly. "With Plehve's backing I am invincible. Absolutely invincible!"

"You are incorrigible!" said Svetlana.

"When I am commissioned I'll work with my uncle; undercover, you know. Perhaps he'll station me with the secret police to protect the Tsar, or I'll help Plehve expel Jews. Did you know that Grand Duke Sergei Alexandrovich, the Tsar's uncle, said that he wouldn't go to Moscow until all the Jews were driven out? It's true. He said that they should all be crucified."

"Oh Boris, sometimes you bore me with such talk."

"I am no less conniving than you. So tell me about the priest. What have you done for him lately?"

"That is my secret and mine alone. Don't ask me about that," Svetlana said petulantly. She saw Boris stiffen. *Yes,* she thought, *the priest is his only real competition.* None of the others mattered—they were just conquests, and only of interest to her if someone else wanted them first. They were wealthy and fun to be with, for carriage rides and expensive luncheons. Sex, however, with them was dull, tedious; of all her lovers, only Boris excited her. But surely the man of the cloth had imagined devious plots and sexual escapades in dark, dank chambers hidden from prying eyes: sinister, delectable, and lustful.

Svetlana saw her lover brooding and she suddenly pitied him. She knew him so well: knew when his thoughts turned to despair, knew when the façade of confidence crumbled like ancient sandstone pillars into a bottomless abyss. Then he would contemplate vengeance. Perhaps he enjoyed being hated; some people found that thrilling. A dark self-loathing —lust of a different sort—must course through him, she thought.

The silence hung heavy until she said, a bit too cheerfully, "By the way, I thought you were supposed to be on some battleship today."

"Oh, the training cruise? It is hardly a battleship. I wanted to be with you, so I told the physician that I was sick. They can sail that old tub without me. I hate being at sea."

"I thought you liked the navy. Battles would be very romantic, especially if you were in command of some great ship."

"Only if you're winning. Our ships are floating coffins and I'm not taken with the idea of romantically perishing at sea. I've seen photographs of modern navies—the British, the American. The United States has a brand new navy, big battleships all painted white. And the British are building battleships for Japan. It gives me chills. I hate the Japanese. Did you know the Tsar was almost assassinated when he visited Japan?"

"Boris, is there anybody you don't hate?"

"I don't hate you."

"My father would be very angry if he knew you were in his dacha with me instead of training to defend the Motherland." But then she giggled, slipped beneath the sheets, and said, "I like undercover. I think I will stay under here a while."

She was quiet for a moment; then, with a sigh, she said, "I do love you, Boris and I will never marry anybody else, no matter what my father wants, but it will not be for a very long time." Excitedly she sat up and said, "My father has a mistress, but I don't know who she is."

Boris eyes lit up with pleasure and said, "I can find out. Do you think she's pretty and fun?"

"You mean good in bed? She must be. What man would want an ugly mistress who doesn't like sex? So, my darling, do you want to find out? I'm really angry with my father."

Boris laughed pulled the sheet back to nuzzle between Svetlana's thighs.

"It sounds like you want to blackmail him. Why would I antagonize him when I want to marry his daughter? He did put me on the fencing team. Besides, what important man doesn't have a mistress? The Tsar's brother, Grand Duke Mikhailovich, had an affair with Mathilde Kschessinska, the most famous ballerina in Russia. So who would I report the admiral to? Uncle Plehve? I'm sure *he* has a mistress, too."

They lapsed into silence, then she said, "I'm upset with him, but I don't really want to see my father hurt. He does spoil me, and I haven't been very kind to him. I do love him, though. I'm probably the only one who does."

"Doesn't your mother? I always see them together."

Svetlana ran her fingers along Boris's arm and said, "I suppose she did at one time, but now they sleep in separate bedrooms. It's very sad. My father was very dashing and quite brave in the war against Turkey. He was just a young lieutenant, but women swooned over him. He could have had any of them, but my mother was charming and pretty, and she thought he would become important, so she chose him for herself."

"He is the commandant of the Naval Academy. That's important; and he is very rich."

Svetlana sniffed. "Boris, my mother is royalty, a countess. She expected him to command the entire Baltic Fleet or be the supreme advisor to the Tsar. She wanted to be the favorite of the Tsarina and flit about the Court, not be the wife of an administrator of a stuffy old school. And she expected to be fabulously rich, much wealthier than we are now. She hungered for a palace like the Yusupovs', the diamond magnates, and live beside the *Fontanka* Canal with the richest people in Russia. She's a social climber. She's encouraged my father to invest in all kinds of money-making schemes. I know she wants me to marry someone connected to the Court or high up in government, someone of great promise."

"I have great promise."

"But you don't have money, Boris. You are poor and you are from Tartar stock, not that your pedigree bothers me."

"You don't need money when you have power over people," argued Boris. "Fear is more powerful than money. It makes people do whatever you want; it humbles them. And that's all I need, it's all I really want—that and you. I want you forever, and you know what?"

"What, Boris?"

"I will kill anybody who gets in the way."

"Don't be so dramatic," Svetlana said as she languidly held up a crystal necklace between her delicate fingers. Colors floated across the ceiling of the dacha as light caught the prism. The spectrum of color intrigued her, and dreamily she said, "My mother left her lover. I know she'll be looking for another one. She tried going back to my father, but I don't think it worked out very well. I saw her at a cotillion with the German attaché."

"How many lovers has she had?"

"At least four or five. Perhaps more. But they tired of her. She's very demanding."

"In bed?"

"There too, most likely. And I'm sure they were afraid of scandal hurting their social or political standing."

Boris grinned and said, "What rich family in this city is free of scandal? Does your father know about her affairs?"

"I'm sure he does, but he won't mention them. He knows he disappointed her, so he lets her do as she pleases. But I know things that she doesn't think I know."

"Like what?"

"That she is not my real mother," Svetlana said matter-of-factly.

"That's astounding! How did you find out?"

"I told you I have spies. But I won't say any more, at least not now."

"You must! This is intriguing, the stuff of scandal. What power you have over her! Will you tell her you know?"

"When it suits me. I've come to hate her, you know."

"Why?"

"Because she's deceitful."

Boris appeared to consider the revelation, then surprised Svetlana by saying, "I saw you coming out of the Kazan Cathedral the other day. You go there often, don't you?"

Svetlana nuzzled close to his ear and whispered, "It's very delicious, but I simply can't tell you."

"Why do you tease me? Why can't you tell me these things?"

"I will when I know everything. Just don't ask so many questions."

"You said that church is delicious. I wouldn't think so. And you're not really religious. It's about the priest, isn't it? So tell me, I like delicious. You're delicious."

"I said it's a secret," she reiterated before lapsing into silence.

Boris slipped a hand between Svetlana's legs again and said, "You'll let me do anything I please, don't you?"

"Wait," she said suddenly pushing his hand away. "I have to tell you this, it's so strange. I'm almost certain that my mother invited Count Witte to our house."

"I've heard of him and I despise the ogre; he likes Jews. I hope he's not your mother's new lover."

"Of course not! He's shaped like a plum and hasn't the slightest bit of social charm. In fact he's a complete bore. But he *is* a confidant of the Tsar. I heard that Witte controls the Treasury. "

"So what? Why in the world would your mother invite him? Why would he even come?"

"Because of a scheme my father got into, the one about steel and the railroad."

"Railroad? What railroad?"

"Witte wants to build the Trans-Siberian Railroad all the way to the Pacific, and my father's company makes rails. Witte said that the government wants the company to turn out thousands of miles of rails, but at a very special price."

"And your father agreed to a bad deal?"

"It's not a bad deal if you have a monopoly."

CHAPTER 10

Tokyo, 1898

Alexei and Count Brusilov received an invitation to an elaborate reception held at the British embassy, and at the count's insistence, they both attended, dressed in their finest.

A dozen chandeliers glittered overhead, dignitaries and their wives sipped champagne, chatted, and joined clusters of animated guests. A string quartet played the music of Sir Edward Elgar, as well as Liszt, Chopin, Brahms and Tchaikovsky. Military men wore uniforms emblazoned with medals, and women in silks and satins traded the latest gossip. A few Asian women present wore the latest Western fashions, but most of the Japanese wives adorned themselves in traditional kimonos.

"Taking it all in?" A familiar Scottish voice drew Alexei's attention away from the crowd.

Alexei turned to William-Stuart Jones and said, "It's quite a display. I never attended anything this grand, or with so many important people."

"Quite so. They all look splendid, don't they? But the thing to remember is everyone here has his own agenda. Everyone is trying to sell or buy something. Consider the French ambassador yonder, whose interests are all focused on extending the French presence in Indochina. I dare say he's 'false of heart, light of ear, bloody of hand', what?"

"Where did you get that?" asked Alexei with a perplexed grin.

"Shakespeare, my boy. A classical education does that for you. Eton and Cambridge, in my case."

Alexei spied the rotund Hapsburg ambassador and said, "What about him? Have you a quote to describe him?"

"Ah, 'veriest vartlet that ever chewed with a tooth,' a true 'lump of foul deformity.' And that one, the Italian, 'an anointed sovereign of sighs and groans'; the Spaniard, 'a beetle-headed flap-ear'd knave.'"

"I guess Shakespeare is quite useful," said Alexei wondering what invective might come next. "So are you here as a spy or a journalist?" he asked, studying Jones' tweed jacket, his round face and bristling blond moustache.

"A spy, you say?" Jones pretended to be shocked. "Well, in a sense, yes. We journalists must get to the raw meat of the matter, ask the uncomfortable questions, rip away the deceit and get the hard facts. That, my lad, is what's important. The rest is fluff and façade."

"So how do you get the truth?" Alexei asked, his eyes seeking out Colonel Karamatsu and Itomo in earnest conversation with a stiff, unsmiling little man in top hat and tails.

"You watch, you listen and piece together the machinations. You lift the boards of half-truths and look at the termites underneath. Little can be taken as solid fact, and there is usually a scheme afoot."

"That sounds very cynical," said Alexei.

"Youth has the pleasure of idealism. But there are dark forces and they can have dire effects. Take the man speaking to Colonel Karamatsu and your friend Itomo. His name is Yamagata and he's an ultra-nationalist. Ice water runs thru his veins. He established the *kempeitai*, the secret police, and they strictly enforce every edict of the *gumbatsu*, the militarists.

"You make it sound like a police state."

"It most certainly is! There is no dissent, no opposition; at least none that survives. There are only patriotic societies with unswerving allegiance. See that fellow over there, the one talking up the Russian princess? He's Ito Hirobumi. Spent years in London. 'Wild as a hawk' the papers said, always in one woman's bed or another. He's the Emperor's chief advisor and almost single-handedly created the sacred god myth, the divinity of Mutsuhito. He also wrote the Japanese constitution: very authoritative and hardly an instrument of democracy. Look around, Alexei. Rooms like this is where a significant portion of the Great Game is played."

"What Great Game?"

"That's what we in the U.K. call it. Specifically, the rivalry between your country and mine. The British want to keep the Russian fleet bottled up in the Baltic and Black Sea. And there's always competition for the new markets."

"If we are on opposite sides," Alexei said a bit stiffly, "should you be talking to me in this way?"

Jones snorted, as if suppressing a guffaw. "Ah, but I am not a player of the Game, young man, and neither are you! But both of us need to know how to read a room, and the people in it. For myself, it is how I get a story. For you, it might be more... personal."

"How do you mean?"

The journalist seemed to ignore the question, for he said, "Look at that Frenchy attempting to sell battleships to the Japanese procurement minister. The Nip is trying to avoid saying 'no' as a matter of etiquette; but the truth is, the Japanese buy our ships because they are better. Then there's the German ambassador with your father, and I would put ten guineas on the probability that he's talking about Japan's threat to Russia and how Germany and the Tsar should sign a mutual defense treaty. It's like a chess game, but every piece is a different nation with different goals and different threats. Think of a whirlwind—with bombs."

Alexei did not see how he should be concerned about *real politic* over which he had no control. Then he saw Kimi-san standing beside a woman, her mother he guessed, near a table laden with English cookies and tea. His attention was instantly riveted.

"She's been looking at you all evening," said Jones, seeing the interest in Alexei's eyes. "She's absolutely intoxicating."

"And someone I'm not allowed to speak to. Her father said—"

"Yes, yes, I know. She's probably promised to some Japanese mucky-muck."

"Do you know her?"

"She attended the exclusive Peer's school for upper class girls. I did a story on the English style school, and she was the star pupil. That was a few years ago."

Alexei's eyes met Kimi-san's and held her gaze for a long moment. Then he heard the Scotsman say, "I want to speak to his father. Are you coming?"

"Do you think it would be appropriate?"

"You want to see the girl, don't you? Show some fortitude, lad."

Where was Atsugi? Alexei wondered. Then he realized that Kimi-san's suitor might be at sea. Only senior officers had been extended invitations. In fact, Itomo would not be present were it not for his father.

Alexei followed the journalist and stood to the side as Jones bowed to Colonel Ichiro Karamatsu. The officer returned the bow. Turning to Alexei, Jones said, "Come here, young man. Don't be shy."

Alexei, bowed deeply, feeling very uneasy.

The Colonel gave a very slight bow to indicate his disfavor, then gesturing he said, "My daughter, Miss Kimi Karamatsu, and my wife, Mrs. Kyoko Karamatsu."

A formal introduction, thought Alexei, *in the European style*. Again he bowed, and the two women did the same. Then he heard Jones say, "Miss Karamatsu, I heard you play the *shamisen* at Peer's." Then to the baron, "Your daughter is a fine musician. Perhaps she might play for the British embassy. I do have some influence and I might be able to arrange it."

"It's a possibility," said Karamatsu, not wanting to make a commitment.

Alexei tried not to stare at Kimi-san. He knew that Itomo was watching him. *Say nothing*, Alexei warned himself; meeting her again was enough for now. How or when he might see her again was beyond his imagination.

Standing behind her mother, she looked at him, lowered her fan briefly, and gave a flicker of a smile. For just an instant he smiled back, hoping that her father did not notice.

There was a pause in the conversation, then the journalist said, "I am doing a piece for the *Times* regarding Japanese strategy in the war against China. I would be honored if you could offer some insight, since you were there. Most western readers have little awareness of the conflict. Could we set up a meeting?"

"Certainly," said the Colonel, "but now I'm afraid we must leave. It has been a pleasure seeing you again."

All very formal and abrupt, thought Alexei. Perhaps Karamatsu had seen him smile at his daughter and wanted to show his displeasure. All bowed; the Colonel departed, followed by his son and his wife. Their daughter trailed behind. Just as they disappeared into the crowd, Kimi-san looked back and smiled again.

Alexei was yanked back from his distraction when Jones said, "By the by, I was at the Russian embassy yesterday to speak to your father regarding trade. He seemed a bit agitated. He said that he really didn't have time to speak but I might come back next week. I asked him if he was well, and he said that he wasn't and might have to leave Japan."

"Leave?" said Alexei. "He told me nothing about that."

"He said that there were problems at Lake Baikal with the railroad and he might have to stop there."

"Did he say that I would be going as well?" asked Alexei, suddenly anxious.

"No, but I assume you will. So, unfortunately, your infatuation with the young lady will have to be put on hold."

The disappointment on Alexei's face could not be hidden. "Sorry to deliver the unpleasant news," said Jones, observing the young man's reaction keenly.

Unpleasant indeed, thought Alexei, bitterly. He knew how much the count hated Japan. The chance of returning was virtually nil.

***

"You don't look well," Kimi-san said to Noruko Toshikawa. They sat on a bench in Shinjuku Gyoen Park beside a gently arching bridge. It had been two weeks since she had seen her friend. Noruko appeared anemic and pale and seemed to have shrunk in her kimono. She held her hands to her face and emitted a plaintive sob.

Drying a tear, Noruko said, "It's about the man who comes to the *geisha* house, *Mssr*. Jean Remanche. He said that he wanted to take me to nice places when I wasn't working. He gave *Okasan* expensive gifts, which she really didn't want, because she would have to give gifts in return. But she eventually relented and allowed me to go with the *geijin*. He asked me to quit my work at the *geisha* house so I could be his woman, his own *geisha*. But I said no and told him that I would have nothing once he left Japan. He was disappointed but seemed to understand. At first he took me to parks, then to *kabuki* plays and nice restaurants in Kyoto. He seemed very pleasant and accommodating, always using his dictionary and even teaching me words in French."

"But something happened, something awful," said Kimi-san seeing her friends tears well up again.

"Two months ago, we were in Ginza and there was a terrible rain. We were soaked," she said haltingly. "Jean-san said that we should go someplace warm and I suggested a teahouse, but he said that a *ryokan* would be better because we could still have tea and dry off. He insisted in helping me out of my kimono, and then he was kissing me and...." Her voice drifted off. She hung her head and said, "Now I'm with child, and I don't know what to do."

"Does he know?"

"Yes, I told him and he was very surprised. At first he denied that it was his, but he knows that I was with no one else. Then he said that he did not want a child and I must not have it."

"Does *Okasan* know you are pregnant?"

"Not yet. But she will know soon. Then she will be angry because I will have to leave the *geisha* house."

"Do you want the child?" asked Kimi-san.

Noruko shook her head and said, "No, absolutely not. He told me to go to a doctor and get rid of it. I said that I had no money for a doctor and he gave me some, but it's not enough. There is someone I can go to, but he's not a real doctor."

"I can get money for you," said Kimi-san. "You must go to a good doctor."

Noruko shook her head and said, "I will tell *Okasan*. I'm sure she will help me. I think it has happened to other *maiko* and *geishas*."

"It sounds dangerous," said Kimi-san worriedly. "You can come to the clinic where I work. I'm sure doctor Kazuma can do the procedure. He's a very fine physician."

Again Noruko her head. "*Mssr*. Remanche said that, because of his company's sensitivity, he would not want it recorded, as it would be if it were done in a hospital."

"I think that's very unkind of him to say. Publicity is of little consequence when dealing with something so serious, and you need not give his name. I am truly worried."

***

The heavy knock on the door of the *ryokan* startled Alexei. Nobody, except the mama-san, disturbed his solitude, and her tapping was barely audible.

"Get packed," said Count Brusilov, abruptly, appearing in the doorway. "I'm being transferred and the embassy expects me to leave tonight. A ship will be waiting. I will return at six; be ready, or I leave you behind."

"They aren't giving you a two or three day notice?" asked Alexei, surprised.

"I don't argue with St. Petersburg. I'm required to inspect the railroad, so we will take ship to Vladivostok. Six o'clock, or you find your own way home."

The door slammed and he was gone. Alexei consulted his pocket watch. It was already two, and the first thought that came to mind was to stay behind. Surely there would be something he could do to support himself in Japan. He could teach French or Russian, or even English. Staying here, he envisioned, would allow him to see Kimi-san. But remaining in what might become a hostile nation could have dire consequences. Furthermore, not returning to Russia would signify the end of his education and any future career.

Traveling to Siberia with the count was a hideous prospect, but there was little choice. And, he lamented, there would be no reason to remain if Kimi-san was forbidden to see him.

Still, there was one thing that had to be done. Snatching paper, pen and an envelope he wrote a letter, scurried out and bolted to the *ikebana* shop, praying that Kimi-san or her *sensei* would be there.

Breathless, he tapped on the door, and when it was opened he bowed to the elderly woman. A quick glance showed him that the girl was not there. Extending the envelope with both hands he said, "I am terribly sorry to disturb you, but I ask you to give this to Kimi-san. It's very important, *sensei*."

She hesitated for a several worrisome seconds, then said, "*Hai*, I will make sure she receives it. But she might not be here for several days."

"I will be leaving Japan tonight, in a few hours. I was hoping to see Kimi-san one last time, but...."

The *sensei* gave him a sad smile and said, "I will make sure that she receives your letter. I think she also would have liked to see you. She thinks you are a very nice young man. And so do I."

***

After a frigid, three-week stay at Lake Baikal, Alexei and the count continued on to St. Petersburg and home. Five days later, a letter was delivered to Alexei. Looking at the envelope he was surprised to see that it was from Itomo Karamatsu. Curious, Alexei repaired to his room and, opening the envelope, extracted three sheets written in English.

To my friend, Alexei, it began.

My sister, Kimi, would have liked to say good-bye, but your sudden departure made that impossible. She asked me to write this letter to you because she is quite distressed by recent events and the communication is of a delicate nature. Much of what follows is based on my personal investigation, as well as that of the geisha house mother.

I am gratified that you were able to leave Japan without difficulty because, unbeknownst to you, your lives were in danger. I am tending you the following information so that you might understand how dangerous it would be to ever return to my country. But you should know that I am no threat to you, and I still regard you as my tomodachi.

What in the world is he talking about? wondered Alexei. "In danger? Why would there have been any threat at all? And what investigation? Perplexed, he read on.

My sister had a friend named Noruko, a young woman who was employed as a maiko at a geisha house in Tokyo. It is one that, on occasion, I have visited with other naval officers. Apparently, Noruko became quite familiar with a geijin who went by the name Jean Remanche, a man claiming to be a French salesman.

This particular gentleman engaged in sexual relations with Noruko and the girl became pregnant. When the maiko did not come to work, the okasan tried unsuccessfully to find her. Then the man came to the geisha house to find Noruko. According to okasan, he became quite belligerent when she condemned him for what he had done and had to be escorted out of the house.

I have met your father and the description the okasan gave me fits him perfectly. My suspicion aroused, I went to the Russian embassy and learned that your father had left quite hastily—and was **not** *required to do so by the ambassador.*

Three days before his departure, the maiko went to an inept individual who attempted an abortion. Regretfully, it was poorly done and the girl bled to death.

Here is the danger: Noruko's brother is a member of a criminal organization. He was incensed and vengeful, and it was fortunate that you had a police escort to the ship. Had he and his compatriots found you, your father would have been held accountable for his transgressions, and you might have been regarded as sharing in his guilt.

The incident involving Noruko has been reported in newspapers, intensifying the hostility toward foreigners, particularly Russians. The populace is enraged, and there may be repercussions. I hope that you are not personally affected by them.

I am sorry to have found it necessary to inform you of these terrible events, but I and my sister thought you should know.

Lt. Itomo Karamatsu

CHAPTER 11

St. Petersburg, Russia

Olga Brusilov sat in the dimly lit parlor, reading Itomo's letter. Her hands shook. When she finished, she stared disbelievingly at Alexei and said, "I wondered why he returned so soon. Did you ever meet this girl, Noruko?"

"No, I only learned of her through my friend's letter."

And who is this... Kimi-san?" she asked, consulting to the letter before saying the name.

"I did meet Itomo's sister, Kimi-san, and hoped to see her again during our stay, but now all that has changed. I liked her." Alexei's voice was bleak with unspoken longing.

Olga nodded and said, "I am sorry for your loss, but I'm shocked, absolutely shocked that Yevgeny virtually raped this poor girl and then let her die. But I had an intimation something was wrong."

She rose from the settee and thumbed through several newspapers beside the fireplace. "I was going to burn these; they are three days old, but for some reason I kept this issue of *L'Écho de Paris*. I usually just browse through it for the latest French fashions, but I came upon this article."

She handed the paper to Alexei and, standing with her arms folded, said, "It's rather lengthy and starts on page three."

Alexei turned the pages carefully and skimmed the columns until he found the relevant article.

Two days ago our reporter began the investigation of a curious incident presumably involving a Russian consular official residing in Tokyo. According to the spokesman of the French embassy, a high-ranking member of the Japanese government visited our embassy seeking information regarding the violation and subsequent death of a young Japanese woman studying to be a geisha.

Based on testimony of the okasan, the head geisha of the establishment in which she worked, the gentleman in question claimed to be one Mssr. Jean Remanche, a French citizen from Normandy. Our embassy in Tokyo categorically states that they have no knowledge of any such individual in Japan and that all French citizens are instructed to contact the embassy upon arriving in that country.

In addition, our journalist was told that the company Mssr. Remanche claimed to represent does not exist. The Russian embassy in Tokyo would not comment on the matter, but it has been learned that one of their diplomats, yet unnamed, departed Japan quite suddenly, ostensibly to investigate problems with the Trans-Siberian Railroad.

In light of the death of the girl, the Japanese government is demanding that Russia contribute one hundred thousand rubles for the bereaved family. It is said that failure to do so will result in the publication of the name of the Russian official.

***

At five in the morning, two hours after Count Brusilov returned from his debaucheries, Olga opened the bedroom door and lit the lamps. Then she roughly shook her husband awake and said, "Are you sober?"

"What? What time is it? And why in Christ's name are you waking me? You have no right—"

"I'm afraid I do, *Mssr. Jean Remanche.* Now sit up and read this." She slapped the paper down on her husband's stomach.

"Your monocle," said Alexei, emerging from the shadow and tossing it to the torpid count.

"It's too early for this nonsense, this stupidity," Brusilov protested, waving away the paper.

"I suggest you read it," said Alexei. "You, we, are about to be ruined."

Brusilov snatched the paper and fitted the monocle to his eye. He squinted and snapped, "Exactly what the hell am I supposed to look at?"

"Third column, my dear," said Olga. "It's in French."

"I damn well see that it's in French!"

Twenty seconds passed as he read, then Yevgeny Brusilov exploded. "One hundred thousand rubles? They demand a hundred thousand rubles? Their entire village could live on ten rubles. I will not pay a single kopek, and neither will the Tsar's government! Not a kopek, do you hear?"

"I'm gratified that you show so much concern for the girl you raped and condemned to death," said Olga bitterly. "You, with all your consular privilege, could not extend the girl enough to have an abortion in a reputable clinic? You are a murderer! No wonder you fled Japan in the middle of the night."

"I did not flee in the middle of the night," he said huffily. "The Japanese are antiquated and bestial people. The girl was a seductress. She was ordered to please me. Those people still cut off people's heads, for God's sake!"

"Perhaps you would like to read this," said Alexei thrusting Itomo's letter at the count.

"A letter from a Jap? Why would he write a letter? And to you?"

"Yes, to me. It seems that we barely escaped with our lives."

"Why is so much of this blacked out?" demanded the count.

"Because it doesn't pertain to you. It's private, 'father.' It's written in English. I think you can manage that."

Brusilov read the letter, then tossed it aside and sat fuming, his arms crossed.

"So what are you going to do, my cheating count?" demanded Olga.

"Don't accuse me of cheating. I'm sure you've been in bed with our illustrious admiral."

"I did not kill anyone!" Olga screamed as she hurled a vase against the headboard.

"Not a kopek! You hear? Not a damn kopek!" the count shouted as Olga slammed the door behind her.

***

Three days later the telephone jangled. The head footman listened closely and said, "Yes, absolutely. I will inform him immediately."

He sought out Count Brusilov in the parlor and said, "Excellency, the call was from the aide to Grand Duke Vladimir Alexandrovich. He requires your appearance at his office the day after tomorrow at nine-o'clock in the morning. At the Kremlin."

"Moscow? Are you sure of Vladimir Alexandrovich?" said Brusilov, startled and suddenly apprehensive.

"Indeed, Excellency. It sounded imperative and quite brusque."

Count Brusilov had only met the Tsar's feared and overbearing uncle on one occasion at his Vladimir Palace. It was even grander than the Tsar's Winter Palace, its opulence intended to show up his despised nephew. Alexandrovich, the third son of Alexander II, was eternally petulant over the throne going to the naïve and timid Nicholas.

"He's an arrogant bastard," said Count Brusilov to his wife. "I once heard him say that he was drunk every night and the only cure was to get drunk in the morning."

"You two have much in common," said Olga, looking to see if anything more was said in *L'Écho de Paris*.

Brusilov gave her a disdainful glance and said, "I can't imagine what that monster has to say to me. And now I have to take the train to Moscow."

"Then I suggest you arrive sober," she said, tossing the paper aside.

***

The count bowed and extended his hand, but Vladimir Alexandrovich ignored it and pointed to a chair.

"I'm sure you've seen this," said the Grand Duke, holding up the French paper.

"I can explain everything, your Excellency. It's a lie, a—"

"Please spare me the slavish, grubbing whining. I am in no mood for it. The Tsar detests the Japanese but is not interested in overtly hostile relations. Now those relations are being imperiled by your stupidity and one hundred thousand rubles."

"Surely it can be raised; it's a matter of—"

"Are you mad? The Tsar's government will not pay the Japanese! *You* will! You will pay every fucking ruble and it will be done this week!" screamed the Grand Duke.

Stunned, Count Brusilov stared at Alexandrovich, and an intense jab of *torschiusspanik* swept through him. The Grand Duke continued angrily. "The Tsar will not budge on this, and neither will I. This is all your doing; your stupidity and your pettiness. Had the girl died at the hands of a proper physician, it might have been a different matter. It would have been the doctor's fault. *This,"* he slapped the paper, "is all yours." Apoplectic, the man stopped to catch his breath. "You must do what is required or be disgraced in the eyes of the Tsar."

***

"So you will lose the mills, all of them." Admiral Kochenkov leaned back in his armchair and watched the flames dance in the fireplace. Snow blanketed the grounds of his estate, but Brusilov had overcome the elements to call on him.

"I have no choice. That or exile. I will have to sell the timber land in the Urals and my holdings in Ukraine and Siberia. All of it," said Brusilov grumpily.

"And what of Alexei?" asked Kochenkov, lighting a cigar.

"What about him?" said the count dismissively. "I certainly won't have money to send him to the Naval Academy, if that's what you're thinking. I will hardly be able to pay for a tutor. In time he may wrangle a post in the government."

"I think he should attend the Academy," said Kochenkov. "I can get him in."

"Exactly how will you do that?" asked Brusilov, staring numbly into the fire.

"Because *I'm* going to buy all your properties, including the mills."

Brusilov's head shot up and he said, "You will? At what price?"

"You need one hundred thousand rubles. That's what I will pay."

"They're worth more."

"I am doing you a favor, Yevgeny. Who else will give you that much in a week's time?"

"Yes, yes, you're right of course. I could do worse."

"Much worse. But there's something else I'm going to require."

"What's that? I have nothing else to give. You already have my wife."

"And you had Ekaterina. You thought I didn't know? What I will unequivocally demand is something I shall mention at a later date," said the admiral, taking a puff on his cigar and watching the smoke rise to the ceiling.

"So secretive?" said Brusilov. "I'm supposed to agree to something you will demand at a later date?"

"It will be mutually beneficial. You've had enough of a shock for the last few days." Kochenkov watched the falling snow, then said, "Why a Japanese girl, Yevgeny? You don't like those people. Why not a European one? Surely there must have been some at the embassy balls?"

"Not many; perhaps twenty, twenty-five. It was not like the capitals in Europe with hundreds of bored, married women. An affair in Tokyo would have been too easy to spot; far too messy." He laughed ruefully. "I might have been shot by a jealous husband, but it would not have cost me one hundred thousand rubles."

He settled into a melancholy state, then said, "Cold, lonely nights, Grigory. Nothing to do most of the time. I went into the Ginza, the entertainment area of Tokyo, and looked at the brothels. They were hardly appetizing. Then I heard about the *geisha* houses. The women there are not exactly prostitutes, but—"

"So you seduced one. She became pregnant, and because you thought she was a plaything, a trollop who would disappear into the night, you assumed you could simply walk away. But *geishas* are not trollops, and if you'd done your research you'd have known they are a world apart, no matter how demure and obliging they seem. She had friends in high places. So who is this Itomo, the Japanese lieutenant you mentioned?"

Brusilov shrugged his heavy shoulders and said, "I assume he's someone Alexei met; I really have no idea, nor do I care. Alexei and I didn't talk much. I have nothing to say to him. He knows nothing about the adult world."

"He knows more than you think. Too bad you didn't talk to him when you were there."

"He doesn't know anything about women."

"You should give him more credit. He's quite smart. If nothing else, he learned enough of the language to communicate."

"I was able to communicate!"

"Only with sperm, Yevgeny."

***

The admiral entered the Kazan Cathedral and was ushered into a private chamber adorned with icons and orthodox crosses. The air was rich with the lingering scent of the frankincense used in the service, and the admiral felt a sense of abiding peace in the church that was very much at odds with his mission.

The ancient Patriarch, his shoulders weighted down by his embroidered robes, steepled his fingers and listened intently as Admiral Kochenkov explained the looming catastrophe. Stroking his beard, the churchman nodded sagaciously and, narrowing his eyes, said, "If what you say is true, and of that I have little doubt, the priest will be removed at once."

"But not excommunicated or exiled?"

"I do not have that authority. But I can certainly recommend it. In the meantime, I will have him transferred to a monastery outside Moscow. He will learn how to beg forgiveness for his sins. Yes, he will leave in the morning. I am saddened and sorry for your daughter, but thankfully the relationship did not result in anything worse. You know what I mean. I will pray for the soul of our fallen priest."

The admiral was pensive for a moment, then said, "Under the circumstances and considering his transgression, I would think that his crime warrants a greater penitence than a mere transfer."

"Excellency, his punishment will be nothing less than internal exile. It will not be pleasant."

"Very well, but I am not trustful of the man. Perhaps somebody should make certain that he actually arrives at the monastery."

"And you wish to be that person?" inquired the Patriarch.

"Perhaps," replied the admiral.

"As you wish." The Patriarch looked at the admiral through his milky cataracts and said, "Years ago such transgressions were dealt with quite harshly. But that hasn't happened for a very long time."

***

His protestations of innocence had been ignored, and remonstrate as he might the decision had been absolute and irrevocable. How could they simply order him away to a hovel of an ancient monastery? He, who had given twenty years of his life to the church! They had no evidence, and surely no one had ever seen him with one of the girls. He had always kept the door shut, and the chanting of the choir had been enough to drown out the sounds of lust.

But someone had said something so damning that the expulsion had been venomous. As the train rattled toward Moscow, he wondered what Eudoxia, prematurely aged by illness, might have said before passing from this world. He should have spoken to her; but she had shunned him, and to be truthful, he had been content to be done with her. She had always been hovering over that girl; what had she told Svetlana in her last, fading hours? But the old woman had died long ago, and nothing had been said to him then. There had been no incriminations, no inquisition. Besides, his transgressions were practiced by hundreds of priests and women of the church. It had been that way for a thousand years. In hushed tones and furtive glances, the clergy whispered that dozens of fetuses were entombed beneath cathedral floors. Demands of the flesh, he rationalized, revolted against the blind, impossible intolerance of celibacy. Those who throw stones, he rationalized, had done as much themselves. How dare they point an accusing finger at him? Purgatory, thought the priest. No, not purgatory, the monastic life would be absolute Hell.

What possible pleasure could there be in the stifling catacomb-like world of silent and austere monks bent over fading vellum? How long could he possibly endure that? Perhaps he should leave the priesthood. The one-time grandeur and ethereal wonder of it all no longer appealed to him. There were days he wondered if he was still a believer, as he stood before the iconostasis and evaluated the comeliness of wealthy women. God's judgment of him would be no worse than for the majority of most men. We are all sinners in one way or another, he reflected. His way was just more enjoyable than most.

Svetlana came to his mind again. She was more enticing than of all of them. He wondered how he could see her again.

Then, like an epiphany, it struck him. He would resign from the priesthood. Yes! Incognito, and devoid of beard and church trappings, he would secrete himself amongst the worshippers at the church and stand behind her. How thrilled she would be to see him again, so close and so available.

His mind bolted forward like an antelope bounding joyfully in the morning's light. Why subject himself to the disdainful contempt of a superior at the monastery? Once there he would be watched, and any absence would be duly noticed. No, the Holy Church in its hypocrisy condemned him to a withering existence. He would not do their bidding. He would not supplicate himself to a life of misery and imprisonment.

The train sidled up to a dilapidated station in a wooded region two versts from the monastery. He had traveled the route years before and knew of a store that sold clothing, much of it second hand. He would buy civilian clothes and wait in the woods for the train back to St. Petersburg.

Five other passengers also disembarked at the station, but he paid them no attention. The walk on the snow-covered path was soundless and he stared at the late afternoon sky emblazoned with streaks of gold and crimson. Birch trees with their black splotches flanked the narrow way, their bare branches a filigree of snow-laden fingers. He already felt elated and unchained from strict and tedious ritual. His life was starting over: fresh and unfettered by relentless dogma.

The faint sound hardly registered, but with peripheral vision he saw the flash of metal as the shovel's turned edge slammed into his windpipe, instantly breaking his neck. He heard his own voice emit a gurgled scream. There was a second slashing, merciless whack. He was falling, the trees seemed to spin in a darkening sky, and then there was nothing.

The assailant dragged the body into the woods and covered it with snow, rocks, and branches. The shovel was deposited behind the station amongst a collection of maintenance equipment. The train to St. Petersburg arrived twenty minutes later, and nobody took notice of the woman in the shabby clothes who boarded the last car. A plume of black smoke smudged the sky as the engine laboriously rolled forward. Satisfied but tired, the woman looked forward to the lights of St. Petersburg.

CHAPTER 12

Winter, 1898

"If the count has lost all his commercial assets, how can he afford to send you to the Academy?" asked Sergei Ivanovich, as he and Alexei hurried along the rutted road towards the old church.

"I don't know, but I was welcomed when I arrived," Alexei replied, his exhaled breath mingling with the fog that swirled about them.

"And Admiral Kochenkov put you on the saber team right away." Sergei blew warm breath on his hands and rubbed them together. He looked about, making sure they were alone, and asked, "Do you miss Japan and that girl?"

"Very much. I had hoped to stay for at least two years. It was serene there. And Kimi-san, well, I fell in love with her."

"But as you said, getting anywhere with her would be impossible. Different culture, different world. You'll find somebody else right here. It's bound to happen," said Sergei. "Girls will be all over you when you're commissioned."

Other girls were not what Alexei cared to think about, so he said, "Isn't this dangerous? The *Okhrana* is everywhere. If they even suspect we're doing something provocative it's the end of the Academy—or worse."

"You needn't worry. The people in the congregation are very docile; not a revolutionary amongst them. Well, there's a sympathizer, but he won't say anything."

"I said that I would go with you, but I'm not getting involved in any attempt to overthrow the government. I saw what happened with the demonstration at that factory, remember?"

"But you agree with the movement, the reason behind it," Sergei said, wondering if bringing Alexei had been the right thing to do.

"I see the inequality, the helplessness of the peasants, but if you continue to agitate you'll get yourself killed, and a lot of them will die with you."

"Isn't it the same in Japan? They have unhappy workers and peasants there, too."

"Yes, but they are committed to the national goals. There's no revolutionary movement in Japan."

"You mean none are tolerated. Okay, no more talk," said Sergei as they entered the small church.

The scent of wet coats, shawls and muddied boots mingled with the fragrance from censers. The flickering glow of candles, muted by the smoke from incense, and the sonorous Russian Orthodox chant seemed to bathe the worshippers in wonder and holiness. Icons in luminous colors hung on the walls; paintings of the Savior and saints peered down at the commoners who crossed themselves with absolute devotion.

Alexei stood with Sergei at the rear of the assemblage. His eyes lingered on the fervently pleading *babushkas*, aged women bent from years of toil. He peered at the exhausted children who came from peasant villages to work for a few *kopeks* in the capitol's factories. Fathomless reverence for the Church and the Tsar was etched deeply upon weathered faces gazing with hope into the mystical light. These were the soul of Russia: timeless in their toil, limitless in their faith, and trusting in Nicholas II. He was, after all, the "Little Father" of all Russia who would right eternal wrongs.

Sergei and Alexei stood with the parishioners for an hour, then they slipped out the heavy door. A freezing sleet enveloped them as they crunched through snow to the rear of the ancient church. Glancing up, Alexei could see the snow-encrusted cross atop the onion dome. But for the whisper of flakes all was quiet; in the distance the birch forest was a blur. He felt anxious and vulnerable, as if he were being watched. Turning, he spied a small door partially hidden by barren shrubs.

"In here," said Sergei, pulling him in and quickly closing the door behind them.

"We only do this on the Sabbath," he said, as they descended narrow wooden stairs that had cracked and slumped over the centuries. "I came to this church as a child, when I was a believer." They ducked under low overhead beams. "Now they see me going through all the ritual and say, 'Praise God, he's come back.' They can vouch for me if I'm ever questioned."

"It's still dangerous," said Alexei. "People in the church above might hear the noise when you're working."

"No, we only operate the press while there is chanting, and that will go on for another hour. Then we wait until dark before leaving, and we never leave together. Tatiana has a disguise; no one will recognize her."

"Does the priest know what you're doing?"

"He may suspect we're down here, but he's never seen what we do. The acolyte knows, but he is the only one. No one in my cell knows where the leaflets are printed."

The stairs led steeply downward to a multi-chambered basement. The pale light of oil lamps cast shadows as Alexei stepped into a tight, dank room. It was permeated by the acrid smell of cheap paper, tobacco and printer's ink.

Tatiana, in a blackened smock, looked up and gave a bleak smile. Her hair was covered by a kerchief and her face was streaked with ink.

"Sergei told me you'd come back," she said, taking her eyes off a thin sheet of newsprint.

"Three days ago," said Alexei.

"And now you're enrolled in the Academy," she said dispassionately.

"Yes, I'm on the fencing team with Sergei."

"But you'll be joining us," said Tatiana, glancing back at the words on the sheet.

"I didn't say that. I've just started at the Academy and I'm expected to defend the Tsar and the state."

A man with thick glasses entered the room in time to hear this exchange. He plopped down a bundle of pamphlets and glared at Alexei. "That worries me," he said.

"This is my brother, Vassily," said Tatiana.

Vassily turned to Sergei and demanded, "Why did you bring him here? We're in enough danger as it is. One word from him and it's the firing squad."

"Don't worry, I'll keep your secret," said Alexei. "But what do you really expect to accomplish? Those peasants upstairs won't support a revolution even if they favored one. And they certainly can't read anything you print."

"We're not expecting anything from the peasants. Not yet," said Tatiana. "It's the skilled workers, the educated we need. They're suffering as much as the peasants, and things are getting worse. No dissent is allowed; the Tsar himself said that any thought of reform is a senseless dream. He believes that everything he does is sanctioned by God. That's why he can be a tyrant; he's not accountable for anything. We toil so they can have balls and feasts and countless ceremonies. They honestly believe that everybody exists to support their personal fortunes."

"She's right," said Sergei. "The aristocracy and the bourgeois capitalists must be overthrown. There's no other way. The Tsar won't compromise and neither will we. Have you read Karl Marx's *Das Capital*? There will be revolution, and it's we who must make it happen. Russia will be a dictatorship of the workers and peasants."

"But according to you we already have a dictatorship," said Alexei.

"This will be different," said Tatiana. "Dictatorship is just a term. It will be a worker's paradise."

"And if the pamphlets don't stir the pot, there is another way," said Vassily, pointing to a pistol hidden beneath his coat. "What happened to the Tsar's grandfather will happen to Nicholas."

"Assassination will get thousands of people killed, including all of you," said Alexei.

"This is not a game, and yes, many will die. But it's for the survival of Russia," said Tatiana. "We've been a slave state for too long. We're going to change that, no matter what it takes."

"As I said, I will keep you're secret, but you are playing with fire," said Alexei, as he scanned the inflammatory broadside calling upon all loyal comrades to assemble and march in support of the Duma.

"Not a word," repeated Vassily. Alexei looked at the pistol and said, "You don't frighten me. I will keep your secret, but I am afraid for all of you. This will not end well."

***

"I told you in confidence that I was working to change the system," said Sergei angrily, as he and Alexei left the church. "You said that you agree and wanted to see what I was doing. Now you've seen it. I should not have taken you there. I don't think you are with us."

"I am in spirit. But you are putting your career in jeopardy. You know what happened in ninety-two during the famine when the revolts took place. Thousands were killed. What can you hope to accomplish? You are so few."

"It's not numbers, it's having the right people: those who are totally dedicated to the cause. Five years ago the liberals, the intelligentsia, expected the starving peasants to rise up. It was delusional. The only salvation they saw was through God and the Tsar, and they thought those were one and the same. Sooner or later, Alexei, God will come in the shape of artillery."

"Well, you keep your head down and be careful of whom you trust."

"I expect I can trust you."

"Of course. But think about it, Sergei, if Tatiana doesn't get you in trouble her brother will. I would distance myself from both of them. They're zealots, and zealots have short lives."

"A short life struggling for freedom is better than a long one under oppression, Alexei."

The concept of freedom was not a subject Alexei had seriously thought about. On his way home he began to consider the plight of his own freedom under the control of a man he regarded as a wife-beating bully and a tyrant.

Tatiana, Vassily and even Sergei were confronting the power of a merciless regime that would not hesitate to imprison or even execute them for treason. What would be his own penalty for defiance against a man who was not his father but still controlled his destiny? How foolish, he wondered, would rebellion be? What price freedom?

He was amazed that his mother had tolerated the count's tyranny for so long. Would he have done so? But how would she have survived without his money, and indeed, how could he on his own? The very concept of rebellion was fraught with peril; it was a conundrum that he would put off for another day.

***

Following the morning class on propulsion systems for the coal driven fleet, Alexei joined Sergei on a walk across the Academy grounds.

"So why are you staying in the barracks during *Maslenitsa*?" asked Sergei. "Everyone will be celebrating before Lent. There will be circuses and dances all over the city."

"I don't feel like going to dances or circuses," said Alexei. "The count will take to the bottle and his clubs, or he will be home and berate me. And my mother will be visiting her friends, ones who don't know that we are penniless. But *Maslenitsa* doesn't take place for another week yet. Will you be visiting Tatiana during the holiday?"

"No, she'll be at another one of those interminable meetings and won't be paying any attention to me."

"With all your anger against the system, I'm surprised that you're not more involved."

"I might court the revolution, but I'm not married to it," said Sergei. "I'm not a fanatic like Tatiana. She's a zealot and feeds on the polemics and vision of class warfare. It's a raging heat within her, but lucky for me that rapture doesn't end when the meetings are over or the lamps are turned low."

"I don't understand what you're talking about. What makes you so lucky?" asked Alexei, noting a cluster of cadets observing them both.

"You're pretty naïve, aren't you? That girl's revolutionary heat turns her into an animal at night. She can't wait to rip off my clothes, and I have her naked in seconds."

"You mean in bed?" exclaimed Alexei, his eyes wide.

"Of course in bed, you idiot! We are at it for hours. I can show you the claw marks on my back, for God's sake. Tatiana's better than any I've had, even the married ones."

"You've had *married* women?" gasped Alexei.

"Eight, to be exact. Most women in this city are just praying for it. They're neglected by their husbands who are hunting for something new and exciting."

Sergei followed Alexei's eyes to the cadets, who still watched them, and said, "You should begin hunting deprived married women. There are thousands here. Of course, you have to be discreet. You can do anything as long as it's never talked about in public. Yes, married women," said Sergei, nodding his head emphatically as they distanced themselves from the cadets.

"And you think I can do as well as you?" said Alexei, attentive to his would-be mentor.

"Well, perhaps, in time. But you have to understand that the great misconception in society is that women don't enjoy sex. That's absolute rubbish. Do you know what men have done?" Sergei said expansively. "They have concocted the illusion that women are devoid of lust and are supposed to be virtually chaste. For women, sex is considered sinful, an affliction. Married women have been fashioned into white marble busts and set on golden alters."

"What's the logic of that?" asked Alexei, never having considered any of this before.

"Simple. It's believed that men need to stay healthy by having sex, while married women do not. That assumption gives married men the liberty to find women outside of marriage. It's common practice all over Europe."

"So you are doing a great service for women by countering bourgeois hypocrisy," said Alexei, trying to keep a straight face.

"It's all about a socialist sense of equality. I have proudly done my part, you ass."

"I'm sure the revolution will endorse your efforts," said Alexei.

"Don't mock me. You just haven't experienced the joy of carnal lust. Now I'll tell you something more about married women, since I can see how inquisitive you are. They're extremely understanding and appreciative. They will teach you everything, but you must learn how to satisfy them, bring them to a red hot heat, as I have always done."

"I don't know any women," said Alexei, glancing over his shoulder.

"I can introduce you to a few I used to bed. As I said, I know all about women."

"But what about Academy regulations? We're not supposed to...."

"Grow up, Alexei! No one pays attention to that rule. Give me some time and I'll see what I can do for you."

Alexei gave Sergei a look of awe, then punched him hard on the shoulder. "You're lying!" he laughed. "You won't do anything of the kind."

"Of course not. You find your own women, that's how you learn the game," said Sergei, suddenly pushing Alexei into an alley beyond the sight of the cadets.

The ribald talk and the bragging of conquests abruptly ceased as Sergei said, "They can't see us here. Now listen, this is serious and it involves you. The hazing of plebes starts after dark."

"Are you in on it?"

"No. In fact, they didn't want me to know that it's tonight. They probably guessed I would alert you. I found out anyway."

"Will you be around?" asked Alexei.

"I'll be around, but I'm not supposed to interfere. I'm sure you've heard of the hazing, it's a tradition. They did it to me, but I got off light since I was a star on the épée team. But it's not always that way. Last year an unpopular boy was beaten so badly that he had to quit the Academy."

"What happened to his assailants?" asked Alexei, the thought of women banished from his mind.

"Not a damn thing. There was an inquiry, but there were no confessions and none were expected. That's the way it is."

"Do you think I will be beaten that badly?"

"I hope not, but Boris Sokolov might have something planned. He has had it in for you since that saber match last year. And he won't be alone."

"So what do I do?" asked Alexei, a shiver inching up his spine.

"Roll up in a ball, don't scream for help, and don't try to run. Most of the cadets will quit after a few punches. Just enough so they can say that they did their part. Don't incite them and it will probably be okay."

***

There were two other cadets in the barracks. Both were second year students who had endured the previous year's hazing with little more than bruises, unpleasant memories, and the prestige that came from surviving the harrowing rite of passage. Grateful that they themselves were no longer targets, they waited on their bunks for the forthcoming assault, of which they had been apprised. There had been talk that this would be a severe hazing.

Alexei pulled his thin blanket tighter about himself and listened. Every sound seemed a threat, a sickening portent of what was to come. The pot-bellied stove at the end of the barracks held nothing but embers, but he was sweaty despite the cold. A shrill wind shook the bare trees outside and a skeletal branch tapped like bony fingers against frosted panes.

The door opened a crack and a sliver of moonlight streaked across the floor. There was a whisper and a muted cough, followed by other voices. Suddenly they burst in, with Boris leading the assault. Raising a stout cudgel, he slammed it against the bunk frame—a prelude of what was to come.

Alexei rolled into a ball as Sergei instructed. His hope for light treatment evaporated as two upper classmen grabbed the bed and threw it against the wall. Alexei sprawled on the floor as one boot, then another, thudded into his ribs.

The youths were shouting, encouraging one another as the blows and the excitement increased. The intensity of the attack, Alexei realized, would have no parameters. There would be no restraint.

His ribs throbbed but he managed to get to his knees, only to feel Boris's staff slam into his back, knocking him again to the floor so hard his teeth nearly met through his tongue. He felt a wave of dizziness and he tasted blood. In the pale light he could see the cudgel raised again and he twisted away as the weapon cracked loudly on the ground, missing him by inches.

They intend to kill me, Alexei realized with shock. One of the cadets grabbed his hair and yanked him up so another could punch him hard in the face, then he was dropped to the ground. Blood spurt from his nose as they circled him, each determining the moment to deliver a distinctive blow.

Spitting out a broken tooth, he wretched as another kick caught him in the chest. Gasping for air, he knew that a well-placed blow to his head would finish him. Eyes blurred, he heard the jubilant sounds around him.

Then, strangely, a vision of the count, leering and gleeful, appeared before him. The man was screaming epithets as if spurring the assault to its final conclusion. As the face became clear, a fathomless hatred welled up in Alexei. An unquenchable resolve emerged—he would not die, not here, not now.

The taste of blood forged itself into an iron-tipped spear of vengeance. The seniors didn't expected retaliation. The bloodied, helpless form staring into the abyss of death had submitted, he was waiting for the end. Gloating, cheering each other on, eyes watering from their exertion, they were caught off guard when Alexei surged to his feet and, with a straight arm and knuckles down, rammed his fist into the face of Boris.

Dropping the cudgel, he screamed, hands reaching for a gushing, broken nose. Stunned by the unexpected assault, the others stared at their leader, who wailed and sank to his knees. Sensing their confusion, Alexei drove his heel into the chest of another, knocking him head first into a metal pillar. The connection of skull and iron had the deep sound of a bell in a Japanese shrine. The cadet, unconscious and with eyes rolling back, slumped to the ground.

Astonished by the violence, the two second-year cadets sprung from their bunks and ran to the door as Alexei placed a well-aimed kick to another assailant's groin. As he doubled over in pain, his jaw was met by Alexei's rising fist, and several of his teeth were knocked loose. The fourth of the senior cadets bolted, but ran into Sergei, whose blow sent him staggering into the night.

With unbridled hatred, Boris glared at Alexei, and then at Sergei, as he lurched for the door, followed by the weeping youth cupping his bruised testicles. Sergei peered down at the cadet at the base of the pillar whose eyes seemed unable to focus.

"Hurts a bit, yes? Here let me assist you," said Sergei, grabbing the cadet's collar and hauling him across the floor. With one violent push the youth was propelled out the barrack's door.

The pain flooded back as Alexei attempted to right his bunk. Sergei nudged him aside and with one heave put the bed onto it legs. Alexei collapsed on the bunk, not knowing what part of his body hurt less.

"Most interesting. I guess you did learn something in Japan. Apparently you know more about fighting than you do about women. But those impaired seniors won't forget your impertinence," said Sergei, looking at the pool of blood donated by Boris.

Clutching his ribs, Alexei said, "They wanted to kill me, I'm sure of it." The words came as an indistinct mumble through bloody and swollen lips.

"If they didn't before, they certainly do now. Of course, they won't say a word about what happened to them, that they were pulverized by a plebe. But no, they won't forget." Sergei was silent for a moment, then said, "I didn't think they would attempt murder, even if they could have gotten away with it."

"Would that have been possible, I mean not getting caught?" asked Alexei, probing the space with his tongue where his front tooth had been.

"If you hadn't bested them, and if I hadn't come along at the end, they may have rolled you up in a blanket and tossed you in the Neva. Your body might never have been found, and the two junior classmen would not have said a word. I know it must hurt, but just sleep it off. The pain will eventually go away. Then you can strut about knowing that you beat the shit out of all of them. The word will get around."

In the stillness Alexei heard the insistent tap of the twig against the window. He said, "It was Boris. He would have been the killer."

"He's got it in for me as well," said Sergei. "I've made a mockery of him in class and on the fencing court. And he suspects my politics. I have expressed some opinions regarding a lack of charity by the ruling class. He reminded me about his uncle and the power the man wields."

Sergei went to the barrack door, then turned and said, "Oh, I should have mentioned it earlier. I think we were followed that day we went to the church."

"By whom?"

"By the same ones who have followed us everywhere. The ones who were here tonight."

"Boris and friends."

"Of course."

CHAPTER 13

"It must have been something I ate. It hit me all at once."

The doctor put away his stethoscope, gave Boris a doubtful look and said, "More likely something you drank."

Boris grinned sheepishly.

"Go back to the barracks and rest. Whatever it is might still be in your system. Too bad, they could have used you on board today."

Leaving the clinic, Boris donned a heavy overcoat and hurried out the Academy's unguarded back gate. Passing the wall, he removed a brick and extracted a letter. He then replaced the brick, making sure it appeared untouched.

Minutes later he pulled the scented envelope from his pocket and sniffed. Rose. She always wore that exquisite perfume. Svetlana told him that it was extraordinarily expensive, imported from Persia. Each year a small bottle was her birthday present from her father. Carefully he broke the seal on the envelope and read the note.

His steps quickened as he imagined her waiting for him, already seeing her naked. She was a visual treat, a rapturous delicacy, an intoxicant.

He read the note again. Even the elegant Cyrillic letters were daintily written in a sensuous hand; the invitation bore the fragrance of lust.

Dearest Boris,
Meet me at the dacha on the third. Noon.
Kisses, kisses, kisses
Your Beloved
S

***

"Does it still hurt?" Svetlana asked as she examined the damage. They were lying side by side on the bed. Boris delicately touched his nose and said, "Of course it does. The bastard did it intentionally. It will never be the same again." He glanced at a mirror beside the bed and said, "It will remind me of how much I hate him."

"Hate whom?"

"The new kid at the Academy, the one who came back from Japan, the one whose hand I was forced to shake at the fencing competition. He must have learned some peasant ways of fighting there. Damn bestial. And his son-of-a-bitch friend, Sergei, was there too. It was just a hazing. I'm going to get both of them, you'll see."

Svetlana sighed and said, "I don't care about that. Spring is coming, Boris. There will be dances and parties. You will take me to them, won't you?"

"If you're nice to me," he said, unbuttoning her blouse and admiring her milk-white breasts and crimson nipples.

"I'm always nice to you, especially when my father is away." She rolled on top of him, so that her loosened hair formed a curtain about both their faces and said, "The other day, Ekaterina—I call her Ekaterina, now that I know she isn't my real mother—practically demanded that I get married."

"How can she demand if she's not your real mother?"

"Because my father agrees with her. I hate that woman, Boris."

Of course you do. I would too after all the deceit. But who would you marry if you had to?"

"I told you. I don't want to marry anybody. Well, maybe I'd marry you, if—"

"If I were rich. Yes, you told me that. Eventually I'll do something that will really impress your father, like saving the Tsar. Then he will have no choice but to let me marry you." Boris gently squeezed her buttocks. "I know how to impress people."

"Mmm," said Svetlana dreamily.

"Look," Boris said glancing at the table beside the bed, "I have your note. I love the scent."

"Did it make you want me?"

"More than you can imagine. I read it over and over. It made me very... excited."

"That sounds yummy. I'm glad that you came. But I overheard Papa say that there was supposed to be a training voyage, now that some of the ice has melted. Were you supposed to be there? Maybe I should have put off our time until later."

"Absolutely not! You think I would rather be on that miserable tub than here?"

"But you want to be a naval officer! Don't you have to go on ships and shoot guns and give orders?" she asked, toying with his thick, black moustache.

"I want a commission because it will get me into high places. But I hate the sea, and our ships are hideous junk."

"But think of all the medals you'll get! That will impress my father."

"You are ridiculously romantic. At sea, if you don't win you drown, and that's not romantic."

"Oh, I didn't think of that," she said, quickly dismissing the entire idea. Then, between kisses, she said, "Do you know something?"

"Not unless you tell me, my silly girl."

"I went to the Kazan Cathedral twice last week. I always go on the same days, and—"

"Oh, you are so devout!" said Boris, his hand seeking her most intimate place.

"Listen for a minute! I was looking for the priest; you know, the one I tease."

"Are you trying to make me jealous? I don't like that man. He's a hypocrite and someone will deal with him. You'll see."

"Shush. I don't want him hurt. But he wasn't there."

"So? Maybe somebody cut him up in tiny little pieces," said Boris with a Machiavellian grin.

"Did you?" Svetlana demanded, alarmed. "Did you kill him?"

Boris playfully shrugged. "No, my sweet. But, I think you will tire of him. He is so much older than you, and he's all about church. That's so terribly boring."

"I like older men. I just hope that nothing bad happened to him. He was always so nice to all the girls."

"I'm nice to you, but I'm not nice to everybody; especially Sergei and his Jap-Jew friend."

Svetlana screwed up her face and said, "I really don't like it when you talk that way."

"Well, I do talk that way, and I mean what I say. There will be blood, and next time it won't be mine."

***

"For you," said a cadet, handing Alexei a sealed envelope. In precise bold letters was written, *Alexei Brusilov, naval student.*

"Who is it from?" asked Alexei.

The cadet shrugged. "It was stuck on the gate when I reported for guard duty. No one saw who put it there. Mysterious, huh?" The youth grinned and walked out of the barracks. Moments later, Sergei entered. Alexei, having opened the envelope, showed him a card embossed with gold letters.

M. Hiroshi
Silver Petals Silk Company
Nevsky Prospekt

On the back was inscribed

Please come to the Hotel d' France, Bolshaya Morskaya Street at your earliest convenience.

"Do you know him?" asked Sergei, handing back the card.

"I never heard of him, and I've never been to that hotel."

"It's a very posh place; mostly French and Britishers, and it has a very fancy restaurant. Too bourgeoisie for my blood."

"Nonsense, you've been to fancy places. Your family has money."

"Not as much as you think, and the place embarrasses me. Its opulence is obscene."

"Well, do you want to come along?"

"Of course not. You're the one invited to see this fellow. Besides, I have an épée match. Maybe I can poke holes in some jackets."

"Like Sokolov's?"

"What an amazing idea."

***

Alexei entered the elegant hotel and his booted feet sank into its deep carpets. The high ceiling, adorned with classical frescoes of nymphs and satyrs in resplendent hues, was a nod to the architecture of the Eighteenth Century. Crystal chandeliers hung from gilt chains and glistened with newly installed electric lights; polished teak railing spiraled upward to private rooms above.

"I believe a Mr. Hiroshi is expecting me," he said to an attendant behind the desk. The man studied Alexei in his blue cadet uniform, then located a box containing an envelope.

"Mr. Hiroshi left this for you. He said that he had to go to Moscow but will return shortly."

Alexei left the hotel and found a bench facing the Neva River. With great curiosity he extracted two sheets of lined rice paper. The script was unlike the bold print on the envelope. The sentences were in a delicate hand.

Dear Alexei-san,

I hope I am not too bold in addressing you as such, and please excuse any mistakes I make; I am still learning to write and speak in English.

I hope you still remember me, since it has been many weeks since we last saw each other. I am the young lady you encountered at the ikebana shop, at the tea ceremony, and again at the embassy. You may consider it presumptuous of me to write, since I was so terribly rude, but I hope you will read this. I am writing to you for several reasons. The first is to say that I regret asking my brother to write regarding your father's presumed involvement in the death of my friend, Noruko. I was very upset and acted out of anger. I am embarrassed, particularly because you may think that I was somehow implicating you, and I meant no such thing. Please accept my most humble and heartfelt apology.

I also want to ask your forgiveness for my unseemly indifference toward you at the tea ceremony, but tradition requires that I say nothing to any young man unless my father allows it. Nor would I have dared to do so in the presence of Lieutenant Atsugi Yoshiharu.

I want you to know that I was greatly impressed by your kindness, particularly in your attempt to pay for the ikebana vase. Now that I think of it, the whole scene of me in the mud seems quite comical, as if it were something out of a kabuki play! I was also taken by your noble effort to speak Japanese.

I would be very pleased to receive communication from you, if you are inclined to write. Of course I will completely understand if you feel that such an effort would be meaningless, or perhaps you have given attention to a young lady in your homeland. But I do think of you often and I believe that we could be friends. In my current circumstances it would be most pleasing.

With most sincere regards,
Kimi Karamatsu

P.S. Mr. Hiroshi is a cousin of my sensei, Hiroku-san, and he is the European representative for a Japanese silk company. Hiroku-san was gracious enough to ask Mr. Hiroshi to carry my letter in his personal effects, since sensei suggested I not send a letter to Russia through regular mail. Please regard any correspondence as very private, for there is some risk involved. Mr. Hiroshi said that he is willing to carry correspondence if it is done with utmost discretion. Again, I thank you for all your consideration.

For a brief moment Alexei's eyes strayed to the Neva. The cracking of ice sounded like rifle shots.

Alexei read the letter three more times. Perplexed yet elated, a flood of emotions welled up. The vision of Kimi-san had played upon his mind since his return from Siberia, but the image of her had grown fainter with the dark realization that he would never see her again. That conviction had left him with an emptiness nothing could fill, not even pride in being a member of the prestigious naval academy.

Now, suddenly, her letter. Not only had she remembered him, she wanted to be his friend and correspond. More astonishing was that she would reply despite the disapproval of her father and lieutenant Atsugi. They would not know about her secret; nevertheless, it was very bold and very un-Japanese.

There seemed to be so many layers to the letter. So much was said, and so much only alluded to. Seemingly it was a reflection of Japan itself: a mystery inside an enigma. The mention of the lieutenant was perplexing. Was he not her intended? If so, she was virtually married to him. In what "circumstances" did she find herself that prompted her to write?

Corresponding, Alexei mused, would be pleasurable, but it was distressing to think that nothing could come of it beyond mere friendship. Indeed, how much longing could he devote to a girl, even as beautiful as Kimi-san, with whom he could only engage in words and dreams?

He sighed, put the letter in his pocket and, deep in thought, walked to the Academy.

***

It was a blustery afternoon during an unseasonable thaw when Alexei sat with Sergei in the Academy library pondering the hazing of the previous week. The swelling to his face had subsided, though it was still turning subtle hues that an artist would have admired. Though he had seen Boris and his other assailants, no words had been exchanged, yet the looks he'd received had been venomous.

"I was followed again this morning," said Alexei.

"So was I," replied Sergei, flipping the pages of an engineering manual. "I told you, they will not attack, but they will not let it go."

"But we could report the stalking and the harassment. It is against Academy rules."

"It would show weakness. But perhaps I might do some stalking of my own." He stopped when a plebe entered, came to attention before Sergei and said, "Sir, there's a young monk outside the main gate asking for you, and he looks quite desperate."

With a shrug and a look in Alexei's direction, Sergei followed the messenger. Alexei, alarmed, accompanied him.

"What's this about?" asked Sergei, when he met the acolyte.

"We mustn't talk here," said the youth in a half-whisper.

"It's Tatiana, isn't it?" demanded Sergei, as he and Alexei walked briskly beyond the Academy, the acolyte by their side.

"She's sick, terribly sick," said the young clergyman, looking back at a half-dozen classmen. "There's nobody else at the church," he said. "The priest left for the convocation, and there are no parishioners. She won't let me summon a doctor, so I came here. With my bad leg I can't carry her, and she can barely walk."

It was near dusk and foreboding clouds hung over the city. The monk pulled his robe closer about him and limped behind the striding cadets, trying to keep up.

Furtively, they squeezed through the concealed door behind the church. At the bottom of the stairs they pushed open a second door. Tatiana was lying on the floor. A sallow light from oil lamps cast shadows about the room. The musty smell was overpowering.

"You finally came. You have to help me. The committee needs those tonight." She painfully waved her hand toward a jumble of broadsides on a sagging shelf. "Just help me stand, I have work to do," she gasped.

"No, you're sick and you need a physician," said Sergei, wrapping her in his naval coat.

"I don't want a doctor," she insisted, trying to push him away. "There's nothing a doctor can do for me."

"We mustn't stay long," said the monk anxiously.

"Are we in danger now?" asked Alexei.

"We might be. I saw Father Glinka talking to some men two days ago, government officials of some sort. They were definitely strangers, and they stormed into the church. They didn't cross themselves before the iconostasis, and they don't belong to the congregation."

"Were they police?" asked Alexei.

"I suspect so. Who else would act that way? They were very stern and they weren't interested in the icon of Saint Nicholas that Father Glinka is so proud of."

"If they're police or *Okhrana,* they'll be back," warned Sergei.

"Maybe soon. I saw someone running when we left the Academy," said the monk.

"Alexei, get Tatiana out of here. I know it's cold, but go into the forest. That's the best escape route. Then take her to my aunt's house; you know where it is. I'll bundle up these papers and get them to the committee," said Sergei.

"I'll stay behind and hide everything I can," said the monk. "Now go, all of you. There isn't much time."

"Do you think the priest was forced to tell about us?" asked Tatiana, as Alexei prepared to carry her up the stairs.

"I fear so," said the acolyte. "Father Glinka has sympathy for the peasants, but he's no revolutionary. He warned me to stay away from agitators. He's never come down here before, but with those men coming to the church, who knows?"

"But if he did come down here, he's seen the papers," said Sergei.

"In which case we're guilty of revolutionary activity—treason," said Alexei.

"Not you. Only me, Tatiana, her brother and the monk. You are completely innocent," replied Sergei.

"But they've seen me with you," said Alexei, unconvinced.

"Enough! Take Tatiana and go as fast as you can," said the acolyte.

Alexei turned to Sergei and said, "You better forget about the revolution for a very long time."

***

A freezing rain, pushed by gusts of wind, came in waves, drenching them as they reached the forest. Exhausted from carrying Tatiana, Alexei laid her down and peered into the field behind him. In the fading light he saw Sergei hurrying from the church. A dozen men were racing to catch up. There was a muffled yell, then the splashing of hoofs in puddles. A figure in a naval coat was among the persuers. A pistol shot ripped through the air and Sergei fell to his knees, causing the papers to scatter with the wind.

Tatiana rose and screamed as Sergei was surrounded and pummeled. One of them looked about, but seeing no one through the driving rain, turned back to their captive.

"We can't stay here, we have to go," Alexei urged.

"Where will they take him?" she cried, straining to see through the torrents.

"Prison, most likely, if he's still alive."

"They don't release revolutionaries, they kill them," sobbed Tatiana. "Oh my God, Sergei is going to hang!"

Moments later, smoke and flame erupted from within the church. Despite the rain the conflagration spread rapidly. The onion dome became an inferno; it tilted then rolled down the roof, bursting into a pile of flaming shingles and timbers. The monk ran from the church, his vestments and hair on fire. Pirouetting as the flames enveloped him, he stumbled toward the riders before collapsing. The rain gradually extinguished the engulfing flames, leaving a charred lump where there had been a young man.

***

"How fucking stupid could you be?" Shouted Count Brusilov as Alexei bolted through the door. "How dare you accuse *me* of anything when *you* do this? An accusation is tantamount to guilt! What are you trying to do, destroy us?"

"I didn't do anything. I sure as hell didn't cause someone to die!" shouted Alexei, surprised that the count already knew of the disaster at the church.

"Guilt by association! They caught your accomplice with incriminating evidence, and you were seen leaving the Academy with him!"

"Is Sergei hurt?"

"He was shot, wounded, but he'll live long enough to be executed," the count said viciously. "He damn well deserves it!"

"He's my best friend. Is he in prison?"

"Not yet, but he should be. Admiral Kochenkov heard about it from the *Okhrana* and used his influence. The traitor was taken to the infirmary at the Academy. Without Kochenkov's intercession you, too, would be in prison! Now there will be a full investigation of this family, and that could be the end of us."

"Worse than what you fled in Japan?" said Alexei, angered by the count's hypocrisy.

"That was of minor consequence, only money."

Alexei gave him a disdainful look. Brusilov tried to grasp his arm, but Alexei pulled away.

"Come with me," said the count. "There are things, critical things about this family that you should know, but I dare not trust you with them. I'll only say this: you must never do anything that would bring the *Okhrana* here. And it matters little what position I have in the government."

"Why don't you trust me? Do you think I'm so irresponsible?"

"Absolutely irresponsible. Now there may be charges against you. If the admiral gets them dropped I will be even more indebted to him."

"How are you indebted?" asked Alexei.

"It's none of your business. We'll have to see where all this goes. But without question, you will do whatever I and the admiral require."

"Meaning?"

"You'll find out when the time comes."

CHAPTER 14

"And just where are you going at this hour?" Ekaterina demanded, as Svetlana crossed the parlor, swaying her hips, gesturing for the servant to open the door.

"To holy services at the Kazan Cathedral. I heard that they have a new icon of Saint Andrew," she said nonchalantly, tossing her head, knowing that nothing infuriated Ekaterina more.

"Services will be finished by the time you get there. Why don't you sit down, so we can have a nice mother-daughter talk?"

Ekaterina poured herself a glass of sherry and sat self-assuredly on a winged back chair. Svetlana turned away from the door and looked at her with a bemused smile. As if preparing to go out, Ekaterina was elegantly dressed, her silver hair arranged in a perfect coiffure, the enormous hat with ostrich feathers by her side.

"What have we to talk about, 'Mother'?"

"What about a priest you are intending to visit? A Father Rozinski, I believe?"

"Rozinski? I never heard of that name," said Svetlana, standing quite still.

"He never told his name? Pity. And Sister Eudoxia didn't either?"

"You knew Eudoxia?"

"Of course, silly girl. I knew her from the day you were given to us. I was willing to let her befriend you, she being your real mother, but she declined. So she lovingly watched you for almost eighteen years. We would exchange looks from time to time, but she cared not to complicate things."

Ekaterina pointed to the sofa opposite and said, "So perhaps you would like to hear what I have to say. It will determine the rest of your life."

With reluctance Svetlana sat across from Ekaterina, her demeanor guarded.

"The rest of my life? Are you going to tell me, for instance, whom I should marry?"

"I most certainly shall in due time."

Anxious to change the subject, Svetlana asked, "What about Father Rozinski?"

Ekaterina laughed, nearly spilling her sherry. "My dear..."

"Stop calling me that! I am not 'your dear' and you are certainly not mine."

"Tish," said Ekaterina. "Why, he is the man who murdered your young friend Theodosis, the one with whom you played 'show me yours and I'll show you mine.' He didn't tell you?"

Svetlana stared at Ekaterina in horror.

"Oh, yes," said Ekaterina lightly. "The good priest wanted him out of the way so he could have you all to himself. Are you pregnant yet?"

"Pregnant? Of course not!" Svetlana said indignantly. "We never—I mean..."

"I know what you mean. He was just biding his time; playing you like a harpsichord. Each melody a little more lustful, until it swelled to a climactic strain. And then a full blown finale."

Svetlana slowly shook her head. "It wasn't going to be that way. I was teasing him, but—"

"No you weren't. It was the other way around. Even tonight you were going to the Cathedral hoping that he would do you. Don't bother denying it, Svetlana. But alas," she said archly, "he hasn't been there lately, has he?"

"They must have sent him away."

"Indeed they did. Yes, he is away answering for his sins, I presume. We all have sins, of course, but his were rather substantial."

"Where did they send him?"

"To some old monastery beyond Moscow. But you won't find him there. Or anywhere."

Svetlana gave the woman a hard look and said, "What happened to him?"

"What do you think?" Ekaterina raised her eyebrows.

"He's dead. You killed him! Oh my God, you murdered him, didn't you?"

"I did, yes," Ekaterina said matter-of-factly. "So, will you go to the authorities? Will you drag the police here and have them arrest me? Will they demand to know where his body parts are strewn? I doubt it."

"I will, I'll do just that," Svetlana said in a nearly inaudible voice.

"No, you won't."

"Why not? You admitted that you killed him. You said 'body parts'. You cut up Father—"

"Father? Yes. You were going to have sex with Father Rozinski. Child, you have no idea who he really was. But he knew who you are. He most certainly did. *He* was your father!"

"*What?*"

"You didn't know, did you? Rozinski was watching from behind a door when you were handed to me. He was holding a taper and dropped it. He reached down to pick it up and I saw him. Within a week, a month from now, you would have been impregnated by your own father. I saved you!"

Svetlana had both hands on her face as tears streaked down.

"I hope the tears are not for him," said Ekaterina.

"Does Father, I mean, the admiral know?"

"About Rozinski's sudden encounter with the beyond? Not yet, but he insisted that Rozinski be banished from St. Petersburg."

"And he told you?"

"Yes. And I followed Rozinski. The whole thing was a most satisfying experience. I don't know how many girls that man violated, and what I did should have been done years ago. Now it's over. And you are eternally indebted to me and the admiral. So to protect you from your own promiscuity you shall marry, and the admiral and I shall determine who will be the happy groom."

"You wouldn't dare!" Svetlana screamed hysterically. "I'll refuse! In front of everyone, I'll refuse!"

"Very well," said Ekaterina, rising and walking to the door. "Then you will be banished from this house, deprived of any inheritance, and be penniless on the street. And that will happen this very moment."

Svetlana sat frozen and stared at the indomitable woman who opened the door with seeming indifference. "Yes or no? What is your choice?" Ekaterina said to the shaking, petrified girl.

***

Alexei read his letter again. He was sure it had the right tone, neither sentimental nor expectant. It could hardly be the love letter he yearned to write. No, he thought, this must be conceived as pleasant communication, nothing alarming or impulsive that would make her wary of future correspondence, but still enticing enough for her to want to write again.

Hello, Kimi-san,

I am greatly pleased that you would remember me without rancor and take time to write. Of course I have thought about you, and I only wish that circumstances had allowed us to speak to one another when I was in Japan

Though we may never see each other again, I enjoy writing to you. I am glad that you learned to read and write English. Here educated people speak English, French and German more often than they converse in Russian!

I do miss the beautiful shrines and gardens of Japan, and I also miss conversation with your brother. He is a fine fellow and I wish him well. I enjoyed the tea ceremony in which you so expertly participated. I fervently hope that no foolish geijin will collide with you at the Ikebana shop!

I am now a student at the Naval Academy in St. Petersburg and hope to graduate in two years. Then, like Itomo, I will also be a lieutenant.

I do wish to be your friend and I hope you will continue to correspond. And I do thank the sensei and the silk merchant, Mr. Hiroshi, for their kindness.

Your everlasting friend,
Alexei

***

Grigory Kochenkov and Olga Brusilov met at the edge of the city, and together they took a carriage to the dacha. The driver was given his kopeks, and with a flick of the reins quickly sped away. Kochenkov put his arm around his beloved's waist and ushered her in. She kissed him deeply, as if she had found a pool of fresh water after a drought.

Their love-making, though passionate, was not rushed. They lay together and savored each touch, for moments like these were hardly daily occurrences. Olga was not whimsical, nor was there anything frivolous about her. Every decision was given deliberation.

Their desire satiated, they listened to the soft wind wafting through the early spring leaves and watched squirrels scamper up elms.

"Grigory, I have an idea and I think it makes perfect sense."

"I know your mind, my sweet, and I'm sure it involves my favorite cadet, does it not?"

She brushed his lips with hers and said, "You are so perceptive. Brusilov and I are indebted to you."

"That was business, and what you are thinking has nothing to do with money. Ekaterina and I discussed the situation of Svetlana, and there is no one else I would entrust the girl to. She is capricious and flirtatious, to say the least. There have been some very frightening developments and she must be married as quickly as possible."

"Will Svetlana agree to it?" asked Olga.

"She has no choice, and she knows it."

"Something has happened?"

"Yes. Something she did, or was about to do."

"Promiscuous?"

The admiral nodded and said, "But we must think of Alexei. He has a mind of his own."

"I will talk to him," said Olga. He listens to me and he will see the logic in it. If you and I decide to make it happen, it will happen."

"You and Ekaterina have one thing in common," said Kochenkov, nuzzling Olga's neck. "You both get what you want. It would mean stability for Svetlana. She needs that."

"Yes, women her age require direction. I just hope we're doing the right thing."

"They may not think so at first. They are opposites, but sometimes that works quite well," said Olga, smiling at her lover.

The sun was nearly down when she finally dressed. She made a sensuous display of it, and the admiral admired her, as he always had. He reached for a stocking that had fallen between the bed and the vanity table. His fingers touched the cotton material, then brushed against something else. Olga, her back to him, was attending to her hair when he lifted an envelope. Examining it, he noted its scent and slipped it into a pocket of his nightshirt. He ushered Olga into the carriage that arrived at the appointed hour. It was time to go.

***

Boris and Svetlana met for a hurried tea together, when she had ostensibly gone for an outing with her friends. Seated at a small table by the window, their chairs close together, they had a clear view of the street outside.

"Your mother? Ekaterina?" I can't believe that she would actually do such a thing. Murder the priest?" said Boris, amazed that Ekaterina would be so bold.

"But she did, and she buried him. But who knows where? He must have been far away when she did it. I don't know how no one recognized her."

"Disguised, I would guess," said Boris. "It's just that she seems so poised, so..."

"Proper and refined," said Svetlana.

"Amazing. You say that she shows no remorse, no sentiment at all?"

"None. She was quite pleased with herself," said Svetlana looking past the window of the tea shop to the golden spire of the Admiralty building.

"And you say that nobody knows she did this except you and me," said Boris.

"My father, I mean the admiral, doesn't even know. At least that's what she said."

Perplexed, Boris asked, "But isn't she afraid that you might report her to the police, or the church? Surely the people at the monastery are wondering what happened to him."

"What proof would anyone have? She could deny everything." Svetlana did not meet his eyes. She twisted her fingers tightly, dreading what she still had to say.

So the priest was gone, thought Boris, too pleased to notice that Svetlana was distraught. *Good riddance*. Killing him was something he had been contemplating himself, and now Ekaterina had done it for him. How fortuitous. He could not bear to have Svetlana dallying with anyone else. What now could possibly prevent him from having Svetlana for himself? Certainly not Ekaterina. And the admiral? He would do anything to keep the murder secret. The mere hint of his wife being a murderess would destroy him.

Svetlana had handed him a magnificent weapon, thought Boris excitedly. Despite what she'd said, he was sure could use Ekaterina's admission if she dared oppose him. He could even lead a search; after all, the murder had to have occurred somewhere between the train station and the monastery. Come summer, there would be evidence of a grave: an unusual depression in the ground, perhaps even skeletal remains dug up by animals.

How grateful the church would be to know what happened to their priest, Boris mused. Would he not be in the papers, honored as the young detective, the exalted naval cadet who found the defiled body of the holy man? To the worshipping masses he would be a hero.

Boris looked into Svetlana's eyes and saw something he had not seen before. Was it regret for the death of the priest, a man she was unable to resist? Or was it fear? Something was still unsaid.

And then there was the unfinished business with the traitor, Sergei Ivanovich. Certainly the *Okhrana* would heap praise upon him for leading them to his capture, and most assuredly the revolutionary would be imprisoned or executed. Boris was surprised that he had not yet heard from his uncle Plehve, but it was only a matter of time. He might even be promoted to full captain upon graduation at the insistence of the secret police.

His reverie was broken when Svetlana said, "There is something else I have to tell you."

"Yes?" said Boris. What other gift could she possibly give him?

"I won't be able to marry you. At least, not for a long time."

Boris froze. After a moment he said, "Why not? Is there somebody you're in love with? Someone you haven't told me about?"

"No, no one. I'm not seeing anybody else."

"Is it because I'm not rich?" he demanded hotly. "You said that you would marry me if I became rich."

"Yes, I said that. But that doesn't matter now, and believe it or not, I am indebted to Ekaterina. I admit it; I *would* have had sex with the priest. Boris, I was stunned to find this out."

"What are you talking about? Stunned?"

"The priest, Father Rozinski... he was my father," she said haltingly. "He was my real father, and I didn't know it. If I had become pregnant...."

Boris stared at her and said, "That's astounding! Thank God the man is dead. Svetlana, you told me you love me, and I want you. I will do anything to have you. Ekaterina may have prevented something horrible, but she can't dictate your entire future. She's not your real mother, and even if she was—"

Svetlana held up her hand and said, "You don't understand, my dearest. I must do what she asks, what she and the admiral require. I must marry somebody of their choosing. If I refuse I will be turned out of the house without so much as a kopek. I will be disinherited, and even lose my title. I will have nothing, and I cannot live on our desires alone. I cannot, I will not," she said, shaking her head emphatically.

"But I can find a way! I'm certain I can work undercover for my uncle while at the Academy. There are surely revolutionaries, and I can ferret them out. He'll pay for the information, I know it. Then I can find a place for you. I will be getting a regular lieutenant's salary when I'm commissioned. We can live on that."

Svetlana sighed and said, "It's not the same. I know that sounds petty, and I'm terrified of who she will find for me, but I'm too selfish, to—"

"Yes, I understand. You were raised as an aristocrat with everything money could buy. I survive by my wits and a bit of guile. I admit it. But Svetlana, this isn't over. I will marry you. I promise."

CHAPTER 15

The envelope, like the one before, was addressed in Mr. Hiroshi's bold hand. Alexei closed the door to his room, opened the letter and extracted a single piece of paper folded around a photograph.

Dear Alexei-san,

I was delighted to receive your wonderful letter. I think of you often and remember your kindness and understanding. It is good to have a friend with whom I can communicate, particularly outside Japan. I would love to know more about the city of St. Petersburg and how you spend your day.

I am continuing my study of English and I find it useful, since I am still taking nursing courses.

As I may have mentioned before, my father has been speaking to the family of Atsugi Yoshiharu about a possible marriage. I'm sure the lieutenant is a fine gentleman. But I suspect that he is of a severe nature and will be a very traditional husband. Women in Japan are required to be subservient, but (to my father's regret) I often have a mind of my own. I doubt that Mr. Yoshiharu will ever really love me. I pray that my marriage to him will not be soon, but I've heard that the lieutenant wants to marry before hostilities break out.

Enclosed is a photograph of me taken when mother and I visited Mitsukoshi Department store in the Ginza. I only wish that photographs were in color, as I am wearing my new green kimono. If you have an opportunity perhaps you might send me a picture of you, if you still care to write to me.

I certainly wish to continue our letters and will do so as long as I can.

Please give my regards to Mr. Hiroshi when you see him. I must end this letter; sensei is waiting and will give it to Mr. Hiroshi, who is departing for Europe tonight.

I do look forward to your next letter, and I miss you.

Your friend,
Kimi.

Alexei looked at the photograph and saw the face of a lovely girl who stared wistfully into the camera. He read the letter again and was dismayed by the prospect of her marriage to a man who would never make her happy. He frowned when he again saw the words "hostilities ensue." What hostilities? Japan's war with China was over, and though there had been tensions between Japan and Korea, he had read of no major cause for war.

Of course, Japan was chaffing at Russian troops still in Manchuria. Their presence was contrary to the treaty agreement that stipulated their removal. But the mere soldiers' presence could hardly lead to hostilities.

He again looked at the photo and dismissed the prospect of war. Yes, he thought, he would certainly write and hope that someday he might see her again.

Feeling buoyant, he walked into the bright sitting room where his mother was gazing out the window. The first flowers had erupted with the spring thaw. She smiled at him and accepted the photograph he handed her.

"So this is the girl you told me about. Yes, she is very attractive. But she is very far away, my dear."

Olga handed back the photo and Alexei was about to go out when she said, "Alexei, there is something I must discuss with you, and it's rather important; so please stay and listen to me."

"Of course, but I hope it's not too distressing," replied Alexei, settling himself on the divan across from her.

"There are some aspects about our family's circumstances that you should be aware of, for they will determine our future." She fell silent. This was harder to say than she'd expected. "As you know, my husband, due to his atrocious behavior in Japan, was required to pay an enormous sum in restitution. You may wonder where he came up with all that money."

"The count rarely spoke to me about his money or any other assets, except to boast. I assumed he was wealthy enough to buy his way out of anything."

"He had property and stocks, yes. And he had money, but now he is virtually bankrupt."

"Bankrupt?" exclaimed Alexei.

"Yes, Alexei. He, or should I say, we are penniless. It was the admiral who saved us by purchasing all his investments: mills, lands and stock. Yevgeny has graciously allowed us to remain in this house, although he actually owns it. All we have left are our titles. No one in society knows any of this, and it will remain secret."

"I had no idea we are in such desperate straits," said Alexei, genuinely startled and concerned.

"I was sure you did not," said Olga, again staring out the window.

"But I am a student at the naval academy, and that must be quite expensive," said Alexei, intruding on his mother's reverie.

"Indeed it is. Only the wealthiest families can afford it, but Admiral Kochenkov insisted that you be enrolled. He's the one who sponsored you, and he is paying your entire tuition. You would not be there without him; and your future prospects, even with a title, are dependent upon the good will of others."

"I must extend my gratitude and live up to his expectations."

"I know you will. He considers you his star pupil. But there is something else, a way in which we can help him." She fell silent, and again she gazed out the window with a distant, melancholy look as if something in her own life had gone awry. To Alexei the wait seemed interminable and a harbinger of regret.

Alexei waited, not knowing what more he could do besides striving for academic honors.

"Yes," Olga continued, folding her gloved hands. "He and Ekaterina have had to contend with an extremely difficult situation, one that has caused them a great deal of *angst* and disappointment. And like it or not, we are the only ones who can save them from ostracism and disaster."

"What could be so—"

"Please let me finish," interrupted Olga, reaching for his hand. "It involves their daughter, Svetlana. She is beautiful, vivacious and very popular, but she has an inclination toward, well...." Olga stopped and tried to find the right word. "Of being flirtatious with the wrong sort of people. Dangerously flirtatious. The admiral is concerned, I should say terrified, that she will get into real trouble and, to put it bluntly, destroy the family. We can't allow that to happen. We are indebted to him for our very existence."

"Of course we must help, but I don't see how we can help. I barely know Svetlana. I have seen her with a cadet—Boris Sokolov, a horrible choice. There are rumors about her, not exactly complimentary. She is, I heard, rather promiscuous."

"It's apparently true. You can see the crisis facing the admiral and Ekaterina. The girl must marry before any real damage is done, and there is only one person they can rely on."

Alexei leaned forward, his face darkening. "Mother, you're not suggesting..."

"No. I am not suggesting. I'm telling you. You are to marry Svetlana."

***

"It is insane! Can you believe it?" Alexei hissed. He and Sergei stood in a room of the Admiralty building, and Alexei had told his friend of the impending nuptials. Two armed guards looked on, waiting to escort Sergei into the office of the investigative commission.

"Is that why you accompanied me here, to tell me that you have to marry Svetlana? I'm about to be sentenced, Alexei, and that's what you are pestering me with?"

"I'm sorry. It's just that—"

Sergei glanced at the bayoneted rifles of the guards and said, "From what you told me, you and your family owe the admiral your entire existence. So marry the girl. You could do much worse; she's beautiful and probably a pistol in bed. And who knows? The marriage may be short."

"But I don't like her; she's mindless. I detest her type, and she cares not a whit for me. We have not even spoken and have nothing in common. And she's—"

"Not scholarly enough?" Sergei said, exasperated. "She's an aristocrat, titled. Damn few of those women have ever read a book or have an intelligent thought in their head. Just enjoy fucking her and get your commission."

There was a knock on the door and a soldier looked in, motioned, and the somber guards led Sergei into the court chamber.

The examination of evidence and the sentencing lasted twenty minutes. Alexei paced the floor until a guard glared at him, then he stood still.

"What did they say?" asked Alexei when Sergei was marched out of the chamber.

"Expulsion from the Academy, and five years in a Siberian prison," he said, his voice choked with disbelief.

As Sergei was marched down the hall, Alexi walked alongside and asked anxiously, "But you will be free after that, won't you?"

"Of course not. I am also sentenced to twenty years in the navy as a common seaman. Can you believe those bastards? I, a senior cadet, one of the very best they had. Do they think they can get a brilliant engineer by snapping their fingers? Exactly what did I do to deserve five fucking years? I had a hand full of papers, that's all! They think I'm a revolutionary, well, they have no idea of what kind of revolutionary I can be. But they will find out. God damn right, they will! And, it was Boris, that ass. Yes, Boris sent the executioners. I should have run that rapier through him when I had the chance. But I'll get him. Vengeance will keep me alive in that Siberian sink hole. I don't care if it's forty below, I'll come back, and there will be hell to pay, common sailor or not."

The courtroom door closed thirty paces away and the chief interrogator glared at Sergei with contempt said, "What was that about hell to pay? A traitor to the Tsar, a rotten thug who disgraces the uniform? One more word and I haul you back to court and double your sentence! I should have ordered you shot!" Then turning his attention to Alexei, the officer said, "I strongly suggest that you get the hell out of here. Maybe I should have you interrogated, since you are so chummy with this criminal."

Then to the guards he said, "Get this filth out of this building."

With a bayonet pricking his back, Sergei was marched down the corridor. He turned and shouted, "Alexei, marry the bitch, make the admiral happy. You'll have a lot more fun than I will."

Alexei called back, "Take care of yourself, Sergei! I'll see you again!"

***

Shaken and fearful, Alexei paced beside the Neva. *Dear God,* he thought, *my best friend in a Siberian prison.* Regardless of the boast, most men did not last more than three years toiling in subzero conditions at hard labor.

But God knows, I warned him. He knew he was playing with fire. Sergei, Sergei, why didn't you listen to me, thought Alexei. But then there was Tatiana, a magnet of revolutionary zeal who pulled Sergei into her senseless web. *Now what will she do?*

She is a zealot and will redouble her efforts to overthrow the regime. Of course she will, Alexei told himself. *But who will tell her of Sergei's fate?* Should he? And if so, how could he even find her? And what if he was caught in the process? So many questions assailed him, and there were so few answers. Stricken, he realized he would probably never see Sergei again.

***

"Why here?" asked Alexei, as the carriage halted in front of the *Hotel d' France* and the coachman opened the door for him, Olga and Count Brusilov.

"We are meeting some people," replied the count shortly. They were escorted into the hotel's fashionable restaurant, with its precious art work, sparkling chandeliers and elegantly dressed patrons. A tremor surged through Alexei.

He damn well knew why they had been summoned to the hotel. It was all too soon, and spiraling out of his control. This first faltering step would be the beginning of the end. He envisioned a tremulous march to the guillotine and wondered if the French nobility felt much the same a hundred years before. He was hardly surprised to see Admiral Kochenkov, his wife, and Svetlana sitting at a formal dining table.

They rose, and the admiral and his wife kissed Alexei, Olga and the count on both cheeks. "Welcome, welcome," said the admiral expansively, beaming at his guests. "Please sit. For this special occasion I have ordered the finest vodka in all Mother Russia."

A tuxedoed waiter arrived, filled the glasses, and silently departed. "A toast," proclaimed the admiral, "To family, and to a glorious future!"

"Indeed," responded Count Brusilov. "To family and success. We are delighted and honored to be in your company."

Yes, the count should be delighted to be in anybody's company, thought Alexei.

"Svetlana, dear, you look absolutely lovely," said Olga. "Isn't she the most beautiful young lady in all of St. Petersburg?"

"Beautiful, yes," said Alexi haltingly, glancing first at the admiral, then at Count Brusilov, who issued a warning look.

Olga smiled and said, "We, that is, my son has been waiting for an opportune moment to say something to you, admiral. Haven't you, Alexei?"

"Sir, I most certainly do. I am grateful for your magnanimous assistance and your trust in me. I hope to excel at the Academy, so I might honorably serve Russia and the Tsar."

"Most noble of you. I appreciate and accept your gratitude." Kochenkov looked closely at Alexei and said, "You are still a young man, but men of my experience recognize character and the capacity for loyalty. You have that capacity, and I honor such qualities. You will make a fine officer, and I'll do all I can to promote you. I expect that someday you will be an admiral on the bridge of our finest battleship. As such, you will have the responsibility to commit your ships. The American Admiral Farragut in a Civil War battle said, 'Damn the torpedoes, full speed ahead!' Think of the positive, Alexei, and all will be well." Waving a finger, he said, "This you will do for Holy Mother Russia."

The admiral looked around the table and added, "Yes, we will be proud to consider him family."

"Thank you, I shall do my best," Alexei said quietly, all eyes upon him.

"But even admirals are often asked to do unexpected things for the benefit of all concerned." Again he gave Alexei a penetrating look.

"Yes, there are many ways to show appreciation," said Brusilov, nodding pontifically.

The admiral gazed at Alexei with an indulgent smile and said, "Having said all that, I, my wife, and your parents believe it will be a splendid thing when you and my beautiful daughter..." the admiral rose and placed Svetlana's hand on that of Alexei, "when you two are joined in holy matrimony."

Olga, the count and Ekaterina clapped as the admiral raised a glass and said, "Let us drink to their good fortune!"

"Yes," said Brusilov, "and the good fortune of our families!"

Slowly and as stealthily as possible Alexei withdrew his hand from beneath that of Svetlana, and then, with Olga nodding to him, raised his glass and took a sip. A cold tremor invaded him. For the first time, he met Svetlana's eyes. Unsmiling, she dully stared into his.

"I know that you two have not had much opportunity to engage in congenial conversation," said Ekaterina, dabbing her napkin to her lips and glancing at the menu, "but we're planning many such occasions. We will have parties galore at our houses, and all your friends shall be invited. As for right now, I'm sure that you both have questions for one another. So Alexei, dear, what might you wish to ask the young lady who will be your bride?"

Olga smiled and inclined her head, an invitation for a pleasant beginning. Alexei glanced at the admiral, who raised his palms as if saying, "Let the games begin."

Very well, thought Alexei, *I'll put my cards on the table and let her show her hand. At least all will know what I must contend with.*

He looked thoughtful; then, with an innocent smile addressed Svetlana and said, "I'm sure you read a great deal and have picked up a copy of *Anna Karenina*. Was there a special character or event that particularly excited you?"

A moment passed, then she said, "Oh, I read most of it, but I get bored by Turgenev. I much prefer verbal exchange; I think that's so much more enlightening, don't you?"

Alexei flashed a smile and nodded as Ekaterina placed her hand on Svetlana's and said, "I'm sure you meant Tolstoy. But there *is* something to be said for the social exchange of ideas, isn't there, Alexei?"

***

"Can you believe it?" demanded Svetlana petulantly. She and Boris were sitting in a tea shop in view of the Admiralty building's golden spire. "Of all people they insist I marry, he's a complete bore! Do you know what he asked me? Some idiotic question about a book I would never read."

Boris reflexively ran his finger over his nose and contemptuously said, "That ass will never make you happy. Not like I can. And you know what I mean."

"I bet he's still a virgin. I'm sure he knows nothing about women," said Svetlana disdainfully. "Oh, Boris, I can't stand being anywhere near him! Do you know, the admiral practically married us in front of everybody."

"But you might not have to marry him."

"What do you mean? I have no choice."

"But you do; it's very simple. Make it impossible for him to stay with you. You don't have to divorce him; he will divorce you."

Svetlana glanced up from her tightly folded hands, her eyes wide.

"Yes! I understand. An affair with you."

"Not just with me. With some well placed person in Court: an outrageous scandal, a big splash that can't be ignored. Alexei will be shamed and will demand a divorce."

"It would hurt the admiral," she said thoughtfully, "but he already knows that the marriage will be a sham, something I was forced into against my will. Yes, I will play the marriage game to appease them, and then—"

"And that is not all," said Sokolov, interrupting her. "As I said, you might not have to marry him at all. I have an idea, Svetlana."

CHAPTER 16

With an impudent air, Boris Sokolov strode into Admiral Kochenkov's office, saluted, cleared his throat and said, "Sir, I have been granted special permission to carry out an investigation at this institution by my uncle, the head of internal security."

"Is that so?" said Kochenkov, looking up from a sheath of papers. "I have heard nothing about it."

"It is quite confidential. There has been sedition and traitorous activity in this academy, as proven by the expulsion and imprisonment of cadet Sergei Vershinin. He had an accomplice: one who as yet has not been expelled."

"And who might that be?"

"Junior cadet Alexei Brusilov. Together the two planned acts against the Tsar. They and Jewish miscreants intend to destroy the Russia we know, the Russia to which we have pledged our lives and our allegiance. I demand that cadet Brusilov be turned over to the office of the *Okhrana*."

"You demand? You demand nothing!"

"Sir, you are protecting a traitor, and by so doing you harbor the same guilt. I can write to the Admiralty and they will require your resignation."

The admiral leaned back in his chair and appraised Sokolov, who, suddenly realizing his impudence, appeared anxious.

"No," said Kochenkov. "In the first place, you have absolutely no evidence against cadet Brusilov. Secondly, you dare not insult me or question my integrity. And thirdly, I intend to have you expelled."

"That will not happen!" said Boris, his voice carrying into the hall.

"Moreover,' the admiral continued implacably, 'I have the right to demand satisfaction on the field of honor."

"Satisfaction? You mean—"

"Exactly, *former* cadet Sokolov." The admiral walked to the door and, seeing an instructor, called out, "Captain Isorovsky, please come in. I need a witness."

"You see, Sokolov, I happened to find *this*," Kochenkov said, extracting an envelope from his drawer and tossing it onto his desk. "You will read the note inside and you will read it aloud."

Recognizing it, Boris's eyes widened.

"Pick it up. I insist!" shouted the admiral.

His hands unsteady, Boris slid the note from the scented envelope. He scanned the writing and hesitated.

"The admiral commanded that you read it, Cadet. You will do so immediately," ordered the captain.

"'Dearest Boris, meet me if you can get away. Noon. Kisses, kisses, kisses. S.'" Boris read in a low voice.

"You skipped a critical part. Read it!" commanded Kochenkov.

"Yes sir. 'At the dacha on the third.'"

"And in whose dacha did I find it?"

His head bowed, Boris again hesitated.

"Answer the admiral," said the captain.

"In your dacha, sir."

"The 'S' is for Svetlana. The perfume, rose, is what she wears. You invaded my private dacha to have an illicit affair with my daughter. That is a criminal offense. No unmarried cadet is to have sexual relations until after graduation. And no cadet *dare* do so with my daughter!"

"Admiral," said Captain Isorovsky, "the third was the day all students were to report for training at sea. I actually inquired why cadet Sokolov was absent. The doctor said that he was ill and had been told to return to his barracks and recover. The cadet lied to the physician. He had no intention of going to the barracks."

Pointing at Boris, the captain said, "Honor is everything here, and prevarications are grounds for immediate dismissal."

"So what is it, Cadet?" said the admiral. "I am an expert shot and a master with a rapier. A duel to the death, or expulsion?"

Silence hung in the air while the enormity of it all sank in. "Is there anything I can—"

"There is nothing you can do. You are dismissed from this institution, and on pain of death you will stay away from my daughter."

***

Olga Brusilov gave the servants the day off with pay, as she always did on Fridays. They thanked her profusely and were allowed to take the carriage to shops catering to the working class. Assuming that nobody was left in the house, Olga went to her room.

Alexei entered the mansion quietly, went to his own room and stretched out on his bed, invitation in his hand. The RSVP note was for the Academy's masked ball, and like all other cadets he had been looking forward to it—until he'd been informed of his forthcoming marriage. The horror was only compounded when fellow cadets, hearing of the coming nuptials, congratulated him.

Now he thought of the girl who, in a few short months, would become his wife. What would life be like with

Svetlana? She was ravishing but vapid, a temptress who'd flit about, dangling men like charms on a second-hand bracelet. He had to assume that, with their mutual antipathy, their love life would be non-existent. How empty it would be, he mused, to have all the responsibilities of marriage with nothing but a platonic relationship. Everything about it would be a sham, one he could not escape.

He had only spoken to her a half-dozen times since the dinner, and only when, for the sake of their parents and presumed conviviality, he was forced to do so. Never did either share any intimate thoughts. Only indifferent banalities passed between them.

It was not that sex with her would be something to avoid, he thought. It was just that coupling would be devoid of any warmth or caring. *And she is no doubt more experienced than I am*, he thought ruefully.

At best a union with the beautiful Svetlana would be an embarrassment. He doubted that marriage would cause the impulsive girl to change her flirtatious ways. Perhaps, as Sergei had said, in time he might find reason to divorce her. The trouble was, while mistresses were tolerated, expected even, divorce was a stain on one's family honor.

The image of Kimi-san came to mind, and for a brief moment he wondered how different love with her might be. The fact that she had not written back left him with an empty feeling. Perhaps she had already married Atsugi Yoshiharu and feared sending any correspondence. Moreover, it might have become inconvenient for Mr. Hiroshi to carry her letters. There was nothing Alexei could do to alter his fate. The beautiful face of the girl would eventually fade and leave but a ghost in his mind.

The light footsteps of Olga Brusilov passed in the hallway. It was less than a half hour before sunset and there was a scent of smoke. For a moment Alexei wondered if the smell came from a log smoldering in a fireplace. Rousing himself, he entered the richly paneled corridor and walked toward his mother's door at the end of the hall. It was ajar and emitted a soft flickering light. He nudged the door open and was stunned by the scene in front of him.

Olga had covered her eyes and in a hushed voice was intoning the words, *"Barukh atah Adonai Eloheinu, Melekh ha'olam, asher kid'shanu b'mitzvotav v'tzivanu l'hadlik ner shel Shabbat."*

Somewhere Alexei had heard the words before. Yes, he remembered the narrow winding street in Kiev when he had strayed from his father and stood outside a synagogue. Count Brusilov had found him listening to the Jewish blessing and, disapproving, had quickly hustled Alexei away. Now the sacred words came back to him.

"Blessed are you, Lord, our God, sovereign of the universe, who has sanctified us with his commandments and commanded us to light the lights of Shabbot."

How strange that his mother was saying this! Only last Sunday she had fervently prayed and solemnly crossed herself in church. Crosses and icons were conspicuously displayed in nearly every room of the mansion, and every Easter she joined the congregation as the priests walked three times around the church joyously proclaiming, "Christ has risen!"

In astonished silence he watched as she continued with the *Kiddush*. Taking a crystal glass in her right hand she took a sip of wine and said, "And there was an evening and there was morning, a sixth day, the heavens and the earth were finished, the whole host of them, and on the seventh day God completed the work that He had done and He rested on the seventh day and—"

The door, pushed by a draft, opened with a tiny squeak. Countess Olga Brusilov froze, then slowly turned about.

"Alexei, I didn't know you were—"

No words came for a very long moment. He gazed at her in the soft light of the candles. She still held the crystal goblet.

"Please, Mother, finish the prayer. I will reveal nothing, I promise."

She inhaled deeply, slowly shook her head, and sat on a hard-backed chair. "Perhaps another time. Another *Shabbot*. You understand *Shabbot*, Sabbath, it's in—"

"Hebrew, yes I've heard it before, long ago."

"But now you know. I mean about me, us." There was a mellow quality about her that he had rarely seen. It struck him as quite foreign, considering the decisiveness with which she had helped orchestrate his marriage.

"One time the count said that there was something unsettling about the family. There was apparently a secret he would not divulge. He said that he would not trust me with it."

"Yes, he would say that. He hated me, once he learned of my faith; and he feared that with a slip of the tongue you would put us in great jeopardy. You know that he is devoutly Russian Orthodox, a true believer in Christ. He detests Jews."

"And you are—"

She gave a wan smile; her eyebrows raised, and said, "A Jewess, Alexei. I am a Jewess. And that is the secret. Apart from being a bomb thrower, it is the worst possible thing in the *mir*, the world of the Tsar."

"So it's not just Svetlana's sexual drive compelling this marriage. You want us allied to a man, an admiral, honored by church and state."

"In part, yes. My union with Count Brusilov is and has been quite strained. I do believe that he is looking for a reason to divorce me."

"And I, married to Svetlana, am the essential link to our survival."

Olga looked at him and said, "It is far more complicated than you can imagine."

Alexei grinned and said, "I don't see how that could possibly be. But tell me, if you dare divulge it, why in the world, you being Jewish, did the count marry you? If people knew he would be ostracized, if not excommunicated."

"You forgot banished," she said, a sudden sparkle in her dark eyes. "Yes, it would be a terrible disgrace if anyone knew. But only one other person does, and he won't say a word."

Alexei was about to ask, but Olga shook her head. "Not now. Maybe some day."

Olga put the candles, wine and crystal in a wall compartment behind an icon of St. Nicholas.

"There are some things I can tell you, though. That is, if you want to know."

Alexei nodded, and she led him onto the porch. Summer weather had warmed the air, and but for a half-moon the night was quite dark. The servants, now into their third or fourth bottle of vodka, would not return for many hours.

"It was during the Crimean War, 1856, when my father, a colonel and an Orthodox Christian, was ordered to Sevastopol. Apparently he was handsome and had many mistresses, although, from what I learned, he was terribly inept as an officer. He met my mother, a seamstress, seduced her, and she bore me."

"And she was Jewish?"

"Yes, and he knew it. But war was war, and she was attractive. Unfortunately, she died a week after giving birth. He, being in the army, could not raise me, even had he wanted to. But he was friends with the Kochenkov family, and they agreed to raise me. Knowing nothing of my mother's faith, they brought me up in the Russian Orthodox Church. The colonel was killed two months later, so I never met either of my parents.

"I had no idea that I had a Jewish mother until I visited her friends when I was seventeen. I was a rebellious teenager and took an avid liking to my late mother's faith. Of course I had to keep up the pretense of Russian Orthodoxy, and it was easy to do because I hardly look Jewish. I once saw a photograph of my father and I look much like him: Scandinavian, with high cheekbones."

Alexei had never considered that before and said, "You were raised by the Kochenkov family. So you must have known Grigory Kochenkov when you were growing up."

"I certainly did. I was raised as his sister and I didn't know that I was adopted until I was ten. It was a stunning surprise. I never let his parents learn that I knew."

"Did the admiral know?"

"I told him. He realized it was a great secret and swore to keep it that way. He said that he'd never thought we were really brother and sister."

"He was not upset that you had inherited a title and were pretending to be Orthodox but were really Jewish?"

"Grigory is extremely caring and always has been. Certainly me being Jewish presented a situation he had to come to terms with. I'm sure it required an adjustment on his part and considerable tolerance, since he had been indoctrinated against Jews like so many other Christians in Russia. But we were in love, and that superseded faith, especially when I reminded him that Christ was a Jew—and a rabbi, moreover."

She sighed and said, "So you see, Alexei, the admiral and I have always been in love. And yes, my dear son, I am still his lover. But that is not for public knowledge." She was pensive for a moment, then said, "We must go to the church tomorrow and start making plans for your wedding."

"But I do have one question. Does the count know? I mean, about you and Admiral Kochenkov?"

"What do you think, my dear?"

It had become very dark, the moon having slipped behind heavy clouds. Alexei heard his mother's laugh and could imagine the fleeting smile on her lips.

Alexei poured himself a glass of wine and, after taking a sip, said, "Do you remember the argument you had with the count when I picked up that rapier and was about to use it against him? He said something that I have wondered about. He said that you had fooled him. I presume that it had to do with your marriage. Would I be right?"

"I didn't try to fool him, though he would never believe it. I was introduced to him at a court ball. He was quite enamored with me and assumed that I was an aristocrat. We had a whirlwind courtship and he seemed like a charming gentleman. I was attracted to him, though I can't say I ever loved him.

"What I didn't know was that I was already pregnant when I married the count. You were born seven and a half months later."

"And the count realized that he wasn't my father," said Alexei. "So I'm surprised that he didn't divorce you when he learned that I was not his son."

Olga said, "I'm glad you're not his son. You have none of his avarice or guile. No, Lyosha, it was I who wanted the divorce, especially after a particularly terrible argument. But he said, 'No, I will not grant you a divorce. Your punishment will be to remain my possession for as long as you live!'"

***

The Shuvalov Palace glittered as hundreds of guests in fanciful costumes filled its grand hall. Alexei stood stiffly beside Svetlana as her eyes avidly roamed across the room, taking in the enormous mirrors, decorative potted plants, and tables laden with silver trays of exotic pastries, meats and cheeses. Excitedly she said, “Isn’t that Countess Repolovich? I wonder if she’s going to put on her mask? I think she just wants everybody to see that she’s here. Oh, I see your mother! Doesn’t she look grand?” Then Svetlana’s eyes alighted on dashing men in recreations of clothing worn by Venetian princes or oriental potentates, with aigrettes of exotic plumes. Others of the elite were dressed as boyars of medieval Muscovy in long embroidered robes and high fur hats.

“I can’t wait for the dancing to begin,” she cried. Then in a doubtful voice she added, “I don’t imagine you like to dance, do you, Alexei? Well, I’ll only require that you do one waltz with me, just for show. Then you can dance with any lady you care to.”

“I appreciate your consideration, but in fact I dance very well. But as you wish: one waltz, or perhaps a quadrille, would be acceptable.”

Svetlana sniffed and took a glass of champagne from a passing waiter. Alexei turned about as a man in the uniform of Russian Cossack tapped him on the shoulder and said, “A message for you.”

He handed Alexei a folded card, then disappeared into the crowd.

“What’s that?” inquired Svetlana.

Alexei scanned the note and said, “You’ll have to excuse me for a few minutes. This looks important.”

“The Master of Ceremonies is starting the dance. We should do the first one, so don’t be long,” said Svetlana.

“I don’t know how long this will take, but I’m sure somebody will dance with you before I get back.”

At least I hope someone does, he thought, glancing again at the card.

A vital message from a friend of a friend.

Come alone to the garden on the west side of the Palace.

The gate is unlocked. Do hurry.

The cryptic note was unsigned. *"A friend of a friend,"* thought Alexei. Could it possibly be Sergei's girlfriend Tatiana? If so, did she have news of him? What if he needed money to sustain himself? Or perhaps he'd escaped and needed help?

He wended his way through the crowd and hurried around the side of the building. In the near darkness he pushed the gate open. The garden with its heavy foliage was all shadows, the only light coming from gas lamps in windows high above.

"Come in, the gate is unlocked. Remain silent."

A man's voice, he thought, as he took three steps beyond the gate. Then there was nothing but terrible pain.

***

"So, you've come back," said Svetlana tartly. "I did have one dance while you were gone. I simply had no desire to wait." Then looking him up and down she said, "Did you change? Those are not the same breeches you had on before."

"That's because I was not with you before."

For the briefest moment Boris lifted his mask. Svetlana gasped and, putting her hand to her mouth said, "You're here! How did you—"

"I'll explain later. We don't have much time. Come with me."

"Where are we going?" she asked, looking closely to verify that he was indeed wearing Alexei's mask and hat.

"This way, there's a room," he said, as they darted between couples and scurried down an empty hallway and up a flight of stairs.

"Where have you been? I was looking for you. I heard that my father had you expelled."

"He did. I was in Moscow until I heard about the ball. I came back three days ago."

"Where is Alexei? He was given a note and left me just standing there!"

"Don't concern yourself with him. Here," Boris said, pushing open a door.

"What's here?" Svetlana asked, looking around at the disheveled room.

"It's being renovated. I hired on as a carpenter a few days ago and worked in this room." Closing and locking the door he said, "No one will know we're here."

"But won't Alexei be looking for me? What will I tell him?"

"That you were dancing on the other side of the hall; tell him anything. He'll be indisposed for a while. Now hurry, take all this off," said Boris, nudging her to the wall.

Their hands feverishly tore at buttons and sashes until clothing littered the floor. "Take me," demanded Svetlana, and Boris caressed and sucked her breasts, then his hands pulled her against him. She moaned, starved for his passionate love-making. Smothering him with kisses, she said, "I can't do without this, without you. You must promise me..."

"Yes, whatever happens, I promise."

He snatched a bundle of painter's sheets and laid them on the rough-hewn floor. Lying upon them, she offered herself. The scent of the rose perfume reached his nostrils, stirring unquenchable desire, as well as the ghastly memory of the admiral thrusting before him Svetlana's rose-perfumed letter. Shoving the latter thought aside, his hands slid beneath her, gripping her flesh, and with a famished moan he penetrated what he had dreamt about for months.

She pleaded that he not stop, that he bring her to the summit of passion. Her thighs wrapped tightly about him as she groaned, "Boris, dear Boris, I will die without you being in me."

When they had satiated their lust, he told her, "I can kill him, make him disappear. Nobody will know."

She shook her head. "They will, Boris. And you will have to run and hide for the rest of your life. I thought about it, I truly did."

"I have some money. We can get out of Russia, go up to Norway and take a ship to America. There's land out there, huge empty spaces where no one asks questions, no one will know us. Let's just run away. Let's do it tonight."

"They will hunt for us. My father will have all the trains and the borders checked. You know what will happen to you if he finds us. And I will lose my inheritance. Besides, he is old and may not live long. Then I will be free."

"Don't marry Alexei. I won't let you. I'll put him in prison."

"No more, please, no more. It's too late!" Her horror of being poor, of being *nobody*, surged through her. She had seen how poverty aged the women who attended church; they walked, thin-lipped, worn and pale, wearing the drabbest of clothes, along the avenue as she rode by in a carriage. She could never, ever be one of them. Better, she thought frantically, to marry the silly puppy her parents had chosen; surely she could fool him to be with Boris whenever she chose!

Murmuring endearments, Svetlana vowed she would find a way for them to be together. Marriage had been no impediment to Ekaterina's pleasures; why should it be for her?

***

"Where have you been? Almost everybody's gone," said Olga to Alexei. He had just rejoined them. It was quite late, and carriages were driving away into the starry night. Olga looked more closely and saw that Alexei looked very pale, almost sick. She led him to a chair and helped him sit down; the others gathered around. Alexei brought his hand up to the back of his head and winced.

"I woke up in the garden. Somebody hit me and I was robbed."

"What was taken?" asked Admiral Kochenkov, with a curious glance at his daughter.

"I had five rubles, and they're gone," said Alexei as he gingerly probed the lump on his head.

"Do you know who attacked you?" asked Svetlana, bending over to examine the wound. It was not bloody, but the lump was pronounced.

"I have no idea. It was very sudden and it was dark."

"But where were you, and why did you leave the dance?" demanded his mother.

"I was handed a note that instructed me to go to the palace garden. I thought it might be from... a friend," Alexei explained.

"Do you still have it?" asked Olga.

Alexei shook his head, then regretted doing so. "No. Whoever hit me must have taken it. The whole thing was very strange."

"That person must have taken your mask and hat too," commented Svetlana. Then to Olga she said, "He was gone for a long time. I tried to find him, but I had no idea that he was in the garden."

"I noticed you were both missing; I thought perhaps you were out walking together. But Alexei, the gate to the garden is kept locked. Sometimes there is a guard, too," said Kochenkov.

Still dazed, Alexei tried to focus and said, "Somebody said that the gate was unlocked and I should remain silent. I don't remember anything after that."

"I will call the police," said the admiral. "It must have been riffraff, hooligans. But you said that you received a note. Who gave it to you?"

"I saw a man in a Cossack costume give him the note," volunteered Svetlana.

"I don't know who he was, but he was young," said Alexei.

"Possibly a cadet?" asked the admiral.

Alexei put his hands to his temple and said, "Sir, I have no idea."

"Alexei," said Svetlana solicitously, "You need to rest. I would be so sad if you were hurt any worse."

"I'm sure you would be," said Olga. With a supreme effort she kept her voice neutral.

Looking at his mother, Alexei said, "I just want to lie down. Let's go home."

CHAPTER 17

The previous night's rain lay in puddles as Alexei, the count, and his mother waited with the bridesmaids on the steps of the majestic St. Isaac's Cathedral. The golden dome of the magnificent structure towered three hundred and thirty feet into the sky. Red granite columns with Corinthian capitals were part of its imposing front. The edifice lent solemnity to religious occasions; it was here that the elite of St. Petersburg paid their respects to God and Holy Mother Russia.

It was traditional for the groom to appear first, to show the bride's family his sense of responsibility. Alexei, Count Brusilov and Olga stood waiting for the carriage bringing Svetlana, the admiral and Ekaterina. Alexei prayed that she would not come, that she would realize how incompatible they truly were and refuse to go along with the wedding. But it was Kochenkov's insistence that they marry, and nothing would alter that.

Alexei shivered in the pallid rays of the morning sun. Eventually a carriage arrived, and the admiral's family ascended the cathedral steps. The men greeted each other with hugs; Olga kissed Ekaterina and Svetlana on each cheek and was bussed in turn.

Alexei stood apart from Svetlana, and after an awkward attempt to meet her eyes, he looked around and was astonished to see Boris across the street, hands balled into fists. Svetlana glanced at her groom and followed his eyes.

Seeing Boris, she offered the slightest wave and looked into his pale face. Ekaterina, following this exchange, shook her head and whispered, "That's over, dear. Now pay attention; you will be married within the hour. And do remember: if there is the slightest hint of scandal involving you and that disgraced young man, you will be the one to suffer."

Svetlana looked anguished. For the last few days, Ekaterina and the admiral had warned her repeatedly of dire consequences should she have anything to do with Boris, but their threats and admonishments had only made her more determined to find a way. The idea of spending all her nights with Alexei, after the sensual pleasures she'd found with Boris, was too horrible! And yet, here was this charade, thrust upon her! Almost whimpering with fear, Svetlana steeled herself to play the part demanded of her.

Two little girls appeared on the steps holding eight-inch high icons, which the bride and groom kissed. More bridesmaids assembled, and the entire party entered the opulent cathedral through richly decorated doors.

Alexei wore his dark blue uniform with gold braid and held at his side the engraved scabbard of his dress sword. Svetlana's head was covered by a thin veil and her gown was of the finest white satin embroidered with antique lace, brocade, and flecks of silver tissue. Her trembling fingers gripped the material.

How elegant, how regal they looked; an exquisite rendering from a mystical fairy tale by Pushkin. Their entrance garnered glowing admiration, for surely they were the epitome of the elite: cultivated, romantic and devout. Blond, handsome Alexei and ravishingly beautiful Svetlana reflected the splendor and perfection of the aristocracy's vision of Russia, and it would be the children of such couples that would insure the preservation and continuance of the privileged world—a world clung to with a death grip by those living in terror of revolution.

The eyes of the nobility, high-ranking military officers, and dozens of the crème of St. Petersburg, all in their immaculate uniforms and Parisian gowns, gave Alexei and Svetlana their rapt attention.

As they proceeded down the nave, Alexei knew that this union was a sickening corruption of what he'd hoped marriage would be.

He felt small, like a lead toy soldier, as his eyes stared into the interior of the great cathedral. He glanced at Svetlana, then quickly looked away. She was precisely what he had always thought her: an immature girl who embodied nothing but banality and narcissism.

As he approached the massive iconostasis adorned with images of saints and illuminated by the undulating light of hundreds of candles, all became a blur.

The ethereal voices of the choir surrounded him, but it was not holiness that resonated through him, it was terror. And now there was a sense of anxiety in the air. It was as if the congregation was breathlessly awaiting something rash, something unexpected. They came to the city's greatest house of worship, but for what? Theater? A *comedie pathetique*?

How many knew the real Svetlana? Did they believe the rumors of promiscuity that surrounded the unpredictable and flamboyant beauty? Of course they did, thought Alexei. They knew, they all knew. And they were certain that the proceedings were a sham, a prelude to disaster.

Through the wafting incense Alexei could see expressions of barely restrained mirth and hear muted whispers. He involuntarily shivered at the sight of the priests, the rings and the prepared cups of wine, all sacred elements of the coming apocalypse.

He glanced at his bride nervously. She was dazzling and held everybody's attention. But she seemed distant and unresponsive, distracted and far away. In front of the iconostasis she refused to make eye contact with Alexei, and he felt like a cardboard cutout, or a mannequin from a shop window. For a brief moment she turned and glanced toward the great doors that had been shut, as though they were a portal closing on a life she did not want to end.

The vision of Kimi-san with her tender smile and enchanting eyes came to Alexei. If only he were marrying her instead! He imagined standing beside her in a simple Buddhist temple surrounded by lush green hills: joyous, idyllic and serene. But that would never be.

Two Witnesses held red, regal crowns above Svetlana and Alexei's head as they stood before a senior priest. Each crown was topped by a small gold icon. A second priest carried a tray before them with two wedding rings. Alexei and his bride were handed tall candles that they were to hold throughout the ceremony.

Svetlana nervously glanced at Ekaterina, then her face drained of color and she stared straight ahead. Now the priest was uttering instructions to the couple. Three times they were to remove and replace the rings on the tray, a ritual to signify that husband and wife would be equal, generous, and together in every endeavor. Then, upon the clergyman's urging, Alexei slipped the ring on Svetlana's finger. The priest slowed for a moment and took in her far away, unfocused look. It was certainly not one of joy or expectation.

The crown held above Alexei's head was placed before the priest, who kissed its cross. Then he did the same with Svetlana's, its icon depicting Our Lady. The two crowns were placed on their heads, symbolically designating them as Tsar and Tsarina. In this way, each wedding was seen to strengthen the country; for a moment, each couple felt themselves responsible for the good of Mother Russia.

The clergyman waved a golden cross before them and asked the couple to clasp each other's hands. Then, taking hold of his robe, they followed him around a candle-festooned table three times, symbolizing the Trinity. As his sonorous prayer continued, he handed each a crystal goblet of Cahors wine from which they were to sip.

Abruptly, as if emerging from a trance, Svetlana turned and looked wildly about. Her eyes fell on Alexei and she blurted, "No, no, this is a terrible mistake. I can't do this! I won't do this!"

Spinning, she faced her mother and scornfully shouted, "I don't want him! I detest him! This is not happening!" Emitting a terrifying shriek she hurled the glass of wine. Its dark contents splattered the priest's vestments. With one swift move she tore the veil from her face.

For the first time that day she stared at Alexei and screamed, "No, never! Never! I want Boris, my dear Boris!" Avoiding the admiral's outstretched arms she turned and fled through the nave and past the astonished parishioners.

A gasp rose from the guests as Svetlana, waving her arms, ran for the great doors that had already been opened for the exiting procession.

Alexei looked at the astounded priest, then at his mother as she watched her daughter-in-law run into the street.

Those who craned their necks saw the panicked girl trip over her heavy dress and sprawl into a puddle beneath the wheels of a fast-moving carriage, whose driver desperately yanked on the reins to slow the horses. The conveyance skidded and flipped, pulling the four horses crashing to the ground. Several of the occupants were thrown from the vehicle amid cries and screams. Two of the four horses struggled to their feet, the others lay flailing with broken legs.

Guests bolting from the cathedral were joined by a crowd of pedestrians. Some stared or pointed or wrung their hands, while others pulled victims from the wreckage. A dozen people managed to upright the carriage, revealing the broken body of Svetlana.

Boris, from his vantage point across the street, stood transfixed. He had seen her bolt from the church, had shouted to the hysterical girl and watched the collision with horror. With sudden fury he charged at Alexei, fists swinging. Alexei, startled, lost his footing and fell backwards into the muddy street. Standing over him Boris shouted, "You bastard! You killed my Svetlana! I will destroy you!" He reached for Alexei, but grasping hands tore him away. Wailing, Boris put his hands to his head and stumbled away from the crowd.

Parents and priests, ignoring him, pushed their way forward. Upon seeing Svetlana, the admiral knelt and lifted her broken body into his arms. Alexei rose, his uniform soaked and muddied, and stared at Svetlana as Boris screamed obscenities. Turning away, Alexei followed Kochenkov, the priest, and his family into the cathedral as police restrained those who hoped to follow.

A bishop appeared and, recognizing the admiral, ordered a sturdy monk to carry Svetlana's body past the iconostasis and into a private chapel. The sweet fragrance from censors still wafted in the cathedral and votive candles glowed like dozens of eyes, while the sad expressions of icons gazed mournfully down on the little procession.

Empty of all guests, the cathedral was eerily silent. Svetlana's body was placed on a table and, except for her face, covered with a sheet. Her eyes with their startled expression had been closed. Ekaterina wept, and the admiral and Olga kissed her forehead. Alexei approached and handed Ekaterina a handkerchief for the tears that streaked her face.

"My sweet daughter," moaned Ekaterina. "You could have had anything and everything. Was this Boris, this nothing, so dreadfully important?"

There was no answer, and the question hung in the air. They gazed at the beautiful face, then Olga Brusilov took Alexei's hand and said, "It might have been a good marriage if there had been time. Oh, Svetlana, had you only given it a chance!"

Alexei looked into the eyes of the admiral and Ekaterina and thought he should say, Yes, Svetlana would have been a wonderful wife; I will miss her terribly." Instead, he slowly nodded. He could not say the words. The lie would have been too terribly obvious.

"It is my fault," said Admiral Kochenkov heavily. "I should have spoken to her. There were things I might have said. But would she have listened? She was a spirit unto herself, and short of sending her away, there was nothing I, or we, could have done to change her."

Alexei stared ahead, numbed by the horrific events. "Maybe Boris would have been good for her," he said, his voice just above a whisper. "She loved him, and she would have hated me every day. And sooner or later, Boris would have taken her."

"And killed you if you got in the way," said the admiral, remembering the ugly look in Boris's eye the day he'd confronted him.

"He still may. He will always blame me for her death."

The world seemed to stand still. Alexei had been peering at Svetlana; raising his head, he looked at the grieving admiral and his wife. What could be said that would ring true? What comfort could he give them? They knew about the girl. Her escapades and promiscuity were an open secret —an open sore that marriage was supposed to make right. He could not bring himself to feel loss. But he did feel great sadness for the Kochenkovs.

"I would never have wanted this to happen," said Alexei. There was silence, then he added, "She was truly a beautiful girl. She would have made somebody very happy."

"But not you," said the admiral.

"No, Excellency. Not me."

***

The funeral service ended late in the afternoon. Mourners offered condolences to the Kochenkovs as they stood at the gravesite. In small groups they gradually departed, leaving only the grieving families. Once the assemblage was gone, the admiral motioned for Alexei to follow him, leaving Olga, the count and Ekaterina to their own thoughts.

"I suspect that you are wondering where the death of Svetlana leaves you, especially in regard to the Academy," said the admiral, as they slowly walked the cemetery path.

The lush foliage of summer surrounded them and Alexei said, "It is too soon; I haven't given it much thought. I didn't think it would be proper to bring it up. But I am aware of the obligation I had to her and to you."

"It was a *quid pro quo*, was it not? And now, you are free to marry whomever you wish."

Alexei remained silent, wanting to choose his words carefully. Whatever relief, whatever elation he might feel was darkened by the tragedy that had befallen the admiral and his wife. "Sir, I know that the count's financial straits makes it impossible for me to continue at the Academy. I also know that you were assuming the considerable expense of my attendance. There is no need to continue doing so."

"It's honorable for you to say so, releasing me from any obligation. But I do not release myself. You will continue at the Academy, and nothing will be said about your tuition. You may so assure your mother. I know that she is extremely concerned for your future."

"Then I thank you." Alexei thought for a moment then said, "As you probably know, the count and I have little to say to one another, and with this tragedy we will speak even less. I'm wondering, after his misadventure in Japan, will he be allowed to remain in the consular ministry?"

"I have heard nothing to the contrary. He is still on the staff, though he will never be assigned to Japan again. Why do you ask?"

"Because his employment will be the only income my mother and I will have. At least until I receive a commission."

"Well, even though you are still a cadet, there may be some employment for you. The construction of the Trans-Siberian railway needs inspection from someone I trust. But we'll talk about that later."

Count Brusilov, the admiral, and Ekaterina left the gravesite and walked together, while Alexei and his mother followed some distance behind.

"He told you?“ said Olga.

"You know? About the Academy, my continuation there?"

"We have few secrets."

A light summer rain began to fall and she said, "You must be relieved."

Alexei shrugged and said, "In a sense, yes. But I feel guilty. I am still indebted to the admiral and can do nothing to compensate him."

"You cannot blame yourself. You did everything expected of you. I was thinking last night and came to the realization that her marriage to you would have eventually become scandalous. That would have been devastating for us all, but especially Grigory. Tragic as it is, she him a favor by dying."

Yes, thought Alexei. *She did me one too.*

In the silence that followed, a sharp report sounded and something tore past Alexei's head. Recognizing the sound of a shot fired, he turned to see a figure dash behind thick shrub then turn and take aim. A second shot nicked an epaulet on his shoulder. The third was followed by a piercing scream, and Olga fell to the ground, blood spraying from her left arm. Fearing still another round, Alexei pulled her behind a tree. Tearing cloth from his shirt, he attempted to staunch the bleeding. Hearing the shots, the admiral and Count Brusilov ordered Ekaterina to summon the doctor who had attended the funeral, then hurried back.

As people gathered, Alexei dashed between tombstones, searching for the assailant. He saw a movement, little more than a blur, sprinting into a copse of trees before disappearing. Calls for help brought police, but no one was found.

"Your mother was not the target," said the admiral heavily, when Alexei returned.

"I know. Boris is hunting me."

"None of this is your fault. Svetlana would have been horrified by his actions."

"I'm sure she would have," said Alexei, but he did not believe it.

CHAPTER 18

Even before hearing a tap on the door, Vyacheslav Konstantinovich Plehve had looked up from his files. He was a solid man who had not allowed himself to go soft sitting at a desk. His thick hair and full moustache were indicative of vigor, and he was well muscled. But it was his preternatural alertness that truly set him apart from most bureaucrats. He had not survived the Polish uprising and several assassination attempts by being careless.

"Excellency," said his aide, Fyodor Voronov, standing in the doorway, "There is a young man, a Boris Sokolov, at the security desk, who claims to be your nephew. He asks to see you. He appears desperate and is quite disheveled. "

"He is a distant relative. Bring him to the interrogation room. I'll speak with him when I'm done with these. Don't let him depart."

For all his talk about his close relationship with the powerful Minister, Boris had not spoken to his uncle for a number of years. He fidgeted nervously, uneasy at how he might be received. Sitting on a hard bench and scanning stark walls, he turned over in his mind what he would say to the nation's most feared policeman and head of the *Okhrana*. He glanced at the guard, who stood expressionless inside the door. The man had seen many enter this room, and they never were pleased to be there.

It had been three days since Boris had fired the rounds from his revolver, three nights since he had fled from one hiding place to another. He had slept in an alley, an abandoned factory amidst rusting machinery, and a worker's shack on the outskirts of St. Petersburg. Incessant rain and muddied earth had left his clothes stained and odorous. He felt unclean and anxious. Before, in uniform, he'd felt superior and could proudly go anywhere he wanted. Now everyplace seemed a trap waiting to snare him.

Only two months before he had been a senior-grade cadet on the cusp of graduation. He would have received an ensign's uniform, a commission and assignment in the service of the Tsar. Now, filthy and miserable, he hunched over, like a fugitive awaiting sentence.

Rage had gripped him in a vice of mindless hatred. The only woman, his woman, was dead. Surely she'd loved him, craved him enough to run from the cathedral to rush into his arms. What passion she must have had for him, he thought, to bolt past hundreds of the elite and turn her back on a man who might escort her to the heights of power. The pain of never holding her again, never having her madly wrapped about him, never hearing her moans and cries, was death itself.

He should have killed Alexei in the Palace when he'd had the chance. One more strike would have done it; nobody would have known. Svetlana would have kept their secret. Yes, one more well-directed blow and it would have been over. Despite her protestations they could have fled; she would have gone anywhere with him and he would have had her. Boris sighed deeply. Now it was all over.

There must be another interrogation room in the building, he thought. He could hear a man's sobs and then a groan of unfathomable anguish. Yet that man's physical pain could be no worse than his own emotional despair.

He had thrown the gun into the Neva where it would never be found. The police, he hoped, had given up looking for him. He was certain that he had not been followed. Yet upon reflection, he realized that he would be the only suspect. Had they notified the *Okhrana*? Did his uncle know of the attack? In the frantic moments of the shooting he could not see who had fallen, but he'd heard a woman's scream. Had he missed his target and struck another, or was the scream one of anguish over the death of Alexei?

His thoughts were interrupted when he heard the guard say, "His Excellency will see you now. Follow me, remain standing and remain silent unless you are asked a question."

"Uncle!" Boris blurted the moment he entered the opulent office.

"Silence!" hissed the guard.

Plehve looked up, then back to the files. "Dismissed," he said, waving off the guard. The man saluted and left as Plehve's aide stuck his head in the door.

"Excellency, there is something else I think would interest you. I will bring it. I believe it's important," said the aide.

"Yes, as soon as you can," said the Minister, leaning back in his swivel chair and twirling a pencil through his slender fingers. It was a long evaluating moment before he said, "You are a disgrace. Look at yourself."

"Uncle, Excellency, I—"

"Stop! You sneak in here like a scared rabbit. Do you think I don't know? We saw you. We see everything. We knew exactly where you were hiding; we knew when and where you ran. Oh yes, you are hunted, in case you were wondering. Attempted murder would be the charge. And I knew that you would come here."

"Will you arrest me?" Boris asked, his voice tremulous.

"I have every reason to. It's not the first time you have been involved in murder. You think I don't know what really happened those years ago?" There was a steady eviscerating stare before Plehve said, "A countess, the wife of a consul and advisor to the Tsar. That is whom you shot! Are you stupid, or just mad?"

Boris looked down and said, "It was rage, I admit it, but she was not my target. I'm sorry that I—"

"Sorry? What do you expect me to do with you? Just let you walk the streets? Give you a greeter's job in the front office? You are an embarrassment, a liability. You are a common murderer."

Boris felt that his mouth was filled with sand and nothing came out. His hands were clammy and he looked at his uncle with an empty, sickening feeling. The Minister of Interior could so easily throw him into a cell and forget him. He would become a non-person to be shipped off to some labor camp. Or shot. And Alexei still lived.

Coming here, Boris realized, had been a terrible mistake. What made him think that a man he hardly knew would give him sanctuary? It was another error, a sign of ineptness, such as had plagued him ever since the 'Jap' kid had entered the Academy.

There was a discreet tap on the door and the aide entered with a manila file. "This is what I was speaking of, Excellency. It involves suspicious activity in the—"

He stopped when Plehve's eyes shot toward Boris. The Minister took the file, opened it, scanned the report and said, "Has the activity spread to all of them?"

"The Retvizan, Tsarevitch, Pallada, perhaps several others," said the aide. It's still small, but it will spread like a cancer unless extinguished."

"I think exterminated is a better word, but why are they turning to us? Don't they have their own people?"

"Everybody is known and nothing is secret. They need someone from here, but not just anyone. He has to have the requisite skills."

"And preferably an officer."

"That would allow for greater access. But a junior officer, not one who would receive special attention," said the aide.

"Let me think about it."

Boris, ignored, was indifferent to the conversation. He stared out the double paned window and prayed that his uncle would simply dismiss him so that he could disappear. That would be best. He would board a train and scuttle to France or the United States. It would be new start. If only he could get out.

"Oh, I almost forgot, Excellency. Svetlana too," said the aide.

Plehve nodded as the man took his leave and closed the door behind him.

"Svetlana?" said Boris, suddenly alert.

Plehve said nothing. He sat back in his chair, finger tips touching, and evaluated his nephew. In a barely audible voice he said, "I will require absolute obedience and exemplary conduct. Nothing else will be tolerated."

A threat for sure, but also... a way out? Boris wondered.

"You will be given all necessary papers and only the highest ranking individuals will be informed of your assignment. You reveal nothing. You report only to me or those I authorize. You will await instructions."

"Uncle, are you really going to help me?" asked Boris, amazed at the turn of events.

"I'm not doing this for you. Right now I think of you as scum, but I need something. Carry out the assignment to my satisfaction you may lift yourself out of the gutter. Fail and, well... family ties will be of no help to you. There is no nepotism here and I do not accept failure."

"Will I remain in St. Petersburg?"

"Absolutely not."

There was silence and Boris said, "I appreciate anything you can do for me and—"

"You will remain in this building until all is prepared. Then you will be escorted to your assignment. That is all."

CHAPTER 19

St. Petersburg

Nearly two years had passed before William-Stuart Jones saw Alexei again. They met outside the Admiralty building.

Surprised, Alexei said, "I didn't know you were in St. Petersburg. What brings you here?"

"I'm sent wherever the *Times* think's there's a good story. Peripatetic, what? Boxer Rebellion in China, gold rush in Alaska, and back to Russia. But not for long. I'll be heading to London again. But, I say, you are now a lieutenant, congratulations," Jones said in his rushed, ebullient manner. With his rakish moustache sun-bleached to a paler shade of blond than Alexei remembered, his bowler hat and khaki jacket, he looked like he had just come back from safari in Kenya.

"I've been assigned to a consular mission in London as an observer for the navy," said Alexei.

"Indeed. Well, I met with an old acquaintance when I was there last month. A Mr. Hiroshi, who professes to be a dealer in Japanese silks."

"I know of him."

"Quite so. We all know a little about him, but he's an enigma. The bloke's into all sorts of things, maybe even espionage! You never know, eh? In any case, I have something for you: a letter. Perhaps a secret code," he said, looking at Alexei with a lopsided grin. "He said that I could bring him a reply when I return to London in a few days. So here it is," said the journalist, handing Alexei an envelope.

Alexei stared at the writing and said, "I appreciate your efforts, and Mr. Hiroshi's. I will compose a reply before you leave."

"Excellent. I have a meeting with a very unusual man. Very hush hush. You may wish to come along. Let's say we meet here at six. But remember, not a word."

With a nod and a half-wave, the journalist sauntered off.

Alexei found a bench behind the Admiralty building and slipped a single page from the envelope. The English writing was in a practiced hand, not the hesitant script of the previous letter Kimi-san had sent.

Tomodachi Alexei-san,

It has been a long time since we have written to each other, and much has happened. I hope you will not think me impertinent to write once more. I would love to hear from you and learn how your life is proceeding.

I have been married to Lieutenant First Class Atsugi-san, but as of yet we have no children. He has been awarded command of a large naval transport, the Kinshu Maru, *and spends almost all his time at sea or at the naval base at Yokohama. I rarely see him, but I recognize how important his duty is to the Emperor.*

As I mentioned earlier, I have been enrolled in nursing courses. Some of us who have studied English may be allowed to do advanced work in the United States or in England. I am one of those and have heard that I will likely be sent to the Women's Nursing College in London. The classes last two years. Mr. Hiroshi, the silk representative, may be reporting on our progress for the government. I am quite excited about the possibility of travel. I thought I might mention that my brother is also in England, observing construction of warships for Japan.

I would enjoy hearing from you, though you may be perplexed to have received a letter from me.

I do wish you great happiness and remember you fondly.

Kimi-san.

How strange to hear from her, thought Alexei. He was saddened that she had married Atsugi, and he wondered if Lieutenant Atsugi's long absences were a blessing for Kimi-san. Perhaps loneliness motivated her to write. It was still a bold thing for her to do, something that would result in certain punishment if Atsugi learned of it. Was there desperation in her letter? As in the past, he thought he would never hear from her again. He was puzzled; she was so specific about the college in England, as if he might meet her there. It seemed strange that she again mentioned Mr. Hiroshi. Was it just an off-handed comment? Perhaps it had some special meaning, something she particularly wanted him to know.

What was it that William-Stuart Jones had said? "The bloke's into all sorts of things, maybe even espionage." What Japanese merchant or industrialist would not have connections to the regime? Alexei wondered. And for what reason would an alleged silk merchant be writing a report on the progress of Japanese women in nursing study?

The elusive Mr. Hiroshi must have tentacles in many seas, since he apparently knew Jones and knew him well enough to entrust him with a letter from Japan. A letter from a married Japanese woman to a Russian in such a tense time would have to be delivered circumspectly. The man was taking a great risk, since he presumably didn't have diplomatic immunity—what he was really into made that irrelevant. Yet the delivery hardly mattered, thought Alexei. The letter did.

Kimi-san's letter expressed friendship, if not longing. She was honest about being married, and she did not allude to the danger of writing as she had done in the past. Was somebody directing her to write? Alexei considered the idea, then thought it improbable. No, the letter was heartfelt and sounded as though she still cared for him.

He put the letter into his pocket and began to think of a reply. He wondered how much he should tell, what was truly relevant and what might she really want to know about his life.

Should he even say that he had nearly been murdered? No, he thought, that would unnecessarily frighten her, and he would have to address the circumstances leading up to it. More to the point, she might be fearful that there would be another such attempt.

And what of Svetlana and his close encounter with a life of unhappiness? Again, it would be senseless to go into detail about the girl and her subsequent death. How painful would it be for Kimi-san to know that the horrific mismatch between Svetlana and himself might be a reflection of her own marriage. But she did not go into detail about her own misfortune, and he would not allude to it.

Nor could he imply that she might be so unhappy that she would long for considerate words from a foreigner who she might never see again. But then, he thought, maybe that's what made her letter possible. They would never again see each other, and that made everything safe. Safe, perhaps, as long as the letters were not intercepted by her husband.

He would write, but his reply would be a careful one, a pleasant missive devoid of unattainable longing. Yes, he mused, it would be convivial, light and perhaps entertaining.

Nothing in it would suggest hope beyond a casual reunion in the distant future. He would encourage her to write again and he would wait. Nothing, he thought, ever remained the same.

***

Extremely tall, muscled, and very dark, Jim Hercules sat across from Alexei and Jones in the off-beat restaurant Jones had selected and savored imported Scotch. He fingered the rubles Jones had handed him, and in a French-accented drawl said, "Do not use my name or even mention the word 'Abyssinian.' I don't want to lose my job. I've seen scary places, but this city is crawling with secret police. Mr. Jones, I can tell you things that no one else dare say about the people who run this country. I'm in the Winter Palace and see royalty every day."

"How did you get a job like that? It seems impossible," asked Alexei. The novelty of meeting this unusual person had diverted him from worrying about the letter he'd given Jones earlier.

"I was a boxer, and a damn good one. I toured Europe, and one day the wife of the Tsar, the last Tsar, Alexander III, saw me box and offered me a job right here in St. Petersburg. It wasn't because she wanted a fighter; it was for show, for what is more unusual than a Negro in Russia? The money was better than anything I could make in the ring, and I go where the money is. I come from the U.S.A., but the other Negroes come from Ethiopia. I wear a fez, a fancy costume with red baggy pants, and I open and close palace doors all day. The other 'Abyssinians,' as they call us, only know a little French, just enough to do what they're told."

"Do you speak Russian?" asked Jones.

"Enough to find women. Now here's the thing: the language of the court is French, even though officers' titles are in German. My boss, for instance, is called the *ober-*

gofmarschal, very big words," Hercules said, tilting his head back and using a finger to push up his nose.

"Now my mama is Creole; speaks only French and I learned it from her. So I understand everything said, but because I keep my mouth shut damn few know it."

"I'm particularly interested in the political situation. So what can you tell me?" asked William-Stuart Jones.

"Ah, there is so much, I could write a book about it when I get back to the States," said Hercules. "The families are all related, and they live on gossip. I stand like a statue but I hear it all; who's bedding who, power, money and where it goes."

"Money for weapons, the military?" asked Alexei.

"That, too. They think their peasant army can handle anything. And they brag about the navy, but just between us, they can't do shit against a European power or the United States."

"What about Japan?" asked Jones.

"The Ruskies call Japanese little monkeys, but I'll tell you something," said the boxer leaning forward conspiratorially, "I've met those little people, and they ain't no one to fool with. I never underestimated a man in the ring, and you don't scoff at people fixin' to bash your head in. And that's a fact."

He downed his Scotch, motioned for another and said, "I got it pretty good here. I'm an oddity, if you know what I mean. But if you want some gossip, get this. There are a few American women who married rich Russians, and one of them is named Julia, now a princess. She's the granddaughter of Sam Grant—Ulysses S. Grant, President of the U.S. Everybody's trying to tear her apart but they can't get a chisel in. She's quite a lady. Then there's Felix Yusupov, a real weird one. Richest family in Russia, old Tartars that did evil stuff to get power. The guy's married, but he does women *and* men, and likes to 'dress up.' Yep, in ladies' stuff. And he gets away with it."

"And the Tsar," said the journalist. "Do you ever get to see him?"

Hercules looked from side to side then in a hushed voice said, "Sure, the 'Little Father.' He's never criticized, and from what I hear, only answers to God."

"That's just it," said Jones. "He assumes no personal responsibility. You know the Russian saying, *sud' ba*; fate. Everything is predetermined. God and mysticism control it all, yet he alone makes the decisions of state. He wants everybody to love him, agrees with everyone, and pleases no one."

Hercules ordered another glass of Scotch and whispered, "His wife hates the Winter Palace. There's so much pomp, so much food; everything's so lavish. I've seen poverty down South where I come from, but here," he said, "those peasants are what we call 'po,' real 'po.' And the rich folks don't want to think about it. They's in a different universe, and someday it's gonna collide with something real nasty. Then I don't want to be in this town."

CHAPTER 20

November, 1901

Frigid air and leaden clouds hung over St. Petersburg as Alexei walked on icy paths from the tram to Admiral Kochenkov's estate. He wasn't certain why he had been invited; only on a few occasions, during the Byzantine courtship of Svetlana, had he been in the elegant residence.

A footman led him into a parlor where the scent of expensive cigars, brandy and cognac hung in the air. The effect, with its dark paneled walls, overstuffed chairs and nautical paintings, gave the impression of an English gentlemen's club. He was surprised to see the count and the admiral in conversation with William-Stuart Jones. In addition, there was Captain Isorovsky, whom he recognized from the naval college.

"When were you there last?" Count Brusilov asked the captain, ignoring Alexei.

"Port Arthur? Last year. The entire Pacific fleet was in port: battleships, cruisers, destroyers, all milling about. Nothing but torpedo nets giving any protection," said the captain.

"Isn't that enough?" asked Count Brusilov.

"Not against the Whitehead torpedo, the one the British sell to the Japanese. The damn thing can cut nets. If a flotilla of destroyers gets in the harbor there will be pandemonium," said Isorovsky.

Alexei was standing when the admiral pointed to a decanter and said, "Pour something, Lieutenant, and sit down. This isn't a board of inquiry."

Alexei grinned and obeyed the command.

"I haven't been to Vladivostok since I was his age," said Kochenkov, tipping his glass toward Alexei. "Of course, there was no railroad then. Little did I know that in ninety-three I would have half ownership in a steel company forging rails. I'm sure it's easier getting there now."

"If you don't mind walking," said Isorovsky. "The train stops at Lake Baikal and it's a hundred versts to the next railhead. And there's still only one track, so strategic *materiel* gets priority and you wait on a siding. And then there's Japanese sabotage."

Count Brusilov sat up and demanded, "With fifty thousand troops guarding the tracks? How is that possible?"

"Sabotage is stealthy work," said Isorovsky. "We've been trying to capture a Japanese spy named Ishimitsa Makiyo who was sent to Vladivostok. Reputedly, he often travels disguised as a monk. We think he's a member of the Black Dragon society, a secret group. He enlists Japanese in Manchuria, women as well as men. They're assigned to destroy tracks, lumber mills, anything to create havoc."

"I heard of some destruction, but I didn't think it was widespread." Brusilov sounded indignant.

"It's very serious, and the volunteers are fanatical. There are reports that those not chosen for missions have committed suicide. How many of *our* peasant soldiers are so dedicated that they would die if not chosen to destroy a Japanese railroad?" Captain Isorovsky replied.

"So that's the mentality we're up against," rumbled Admiral Kochenkov.

"Yes," said Count Brusilov, "But it's imperative that Russia hold onto Manchuria and our bases in Korea. It's all about resources and Russian power in the Far East. The Tsar insists upon maintaining it. I firmly believe that the Japanese are sub-humans, and the Tsar said the same. Their military must be destroyed, annihilated, and one or two battles will do it."

"I'm certain that we can beat them," agreed the captain. "One of our finest admirals, Makarov, is in charge of the Pacific fleet at Port Arthur. He is indefatigable, brilliant, and the men will follow him anywhere."

"But Japanese self-confidence is boundless," interjected Alexei, breaking his silence. "They are a monolithic entity. I have seen it. Their indoctrination is absolute; worship of the emperor is a religion with them. They obey him with total dedication. The emperor, the whole nation is on a single-minded crusade." He considered pointing out that they also had a modernized navy, but decided it was not his place to do so. These men were considerably his seniors in every way.

"But still, what can they do against Russia?" retorted the admiral. "We have an army of four million men, and three great fleets. The Japanese might get in a few punches, but then what? Two months into a war they will sue for peace. And we will dictate terms. In fact, Japan may become our colony, just like Manchuria."

"That's what worries them," said Alexei. "They look at the map: the Philippines in American hands, France controls Indochina, us in Manchuria, Poland, Ukraine. And every European power is in China. They will fight us as ferociously as they fought the Mongols. It will be more difficult than any of us think."

"I hope I do not detect defeatism," said Captain Isorovsky severely. "Because we will be going to war and you will be required to encourage our men, despite any setback. Anything else is reprehensible!"

A hard moment of silence engulfed them before the admiral turned to the captain and said, "What's your impression of Port Arthur, the city itself? It must become an unyielding bastion if we go to war."

Isorovsky raised his eyes to the ceiling, crossed himself, then let out a cynical laugh. "I wish it were so. It's a shambles, a hopeless slum of bars, prostitutes, rickshaws and a babble of languages. There is too much vodka and too much fighting between sailors and soldiers. There's one street and one hotel, the Effiemov. You wouldn't want to stay there a single night. The majority of buildings are warehouses. It is, after all, a connecting point for the Chinese railroad and the Trans-Siberian." His voice trailed off, then with vehemence he said, "The problem is that the place is run by Admiral Alexeiff. He's a monster and everyone fears him. He's destroyed morale, and in my opinion he's an arrogant idiot. It's not that it can't be improved, and don't think me too pessimistic," said the captain glancing at Alexei, "it's just that we may have little time, and for now Port Arthur is virtually uninhabitable."

"But what of its defenses?" pressed the count.

"They might have been sufficient fifty years ago, but there is little effective deterrent now. The guns don't have enough range. The Japanese fleet can easily destroy them."

"That is harsh reality," said the journalist. "I believe Alexei is right; Japan is arming very quickly, and they're going to fight."

"And I hear that they're angling for a treaty with England," said Kochenkov.

"So it seems," admitted Isorovsky. "Japan needs Port Arthur; it's ice-free and they want us out of Manchuria and Korea. They see it as a launching place for a Russian invasion."

"They do have British support; we were supposed to withdraw fifty thousand troops and reneged," said Alexei. "Apparently our military either perceived a Japanese threat to the region or we were building our forces in preparation for war. If that's so, there would be little reason to transport them back to St. Petersburg."

"The British want a counter-weight to Russia in the Pacific, and Japan fills the need. It's as simple as that," Kochenkov asserted.

The men sipped their drinks and stared into the blazing hearth.

Kochenkov sighed and in a melancholy voice added, "And the British are happy to build ships like the *Mikasa* for Japan. Biggest battleship in the world."

Alexei said nothing and thought of Itomo, now in England supervising the construction of a warship destined for the Japanese navy. The very thought of going to war against a nation of temples and tea ceremonies seemed incongruous.

"But certainly Britain, even if it has a treaty with Japan, will not go to war against us," argued Brusilov.

"No," Kochenkov replied, "they will not. But what they can do is deny us the Suez. It's eighteen thousand miles to send reinforcements from the Baltic to Port Arthur if the fleet has to go around Africa, across the Indian Ocean and the South China Sea."

"Eighteen thousand miles, and then fight the Japanese? That's a lot to ask," remarked Brusilov.

"Worse," said Isorovsky, "Unlike the British and the French, we have no coaling stations, whereas the Japanese don't have to worry, since they're only a few hundred miles away from Port Arthur and Vladivostok. Without coal the fleet can't go anywhere."

"So what do you think?" Count Brusilov said, turning to Jones.

The Scotsman was pensive, then said, "You Russians are in a damn precarious position, a sticky wicket, as we say. Your supply lines are too long and your fleets too dispersed.

Your sailors are land peasants unfamiliar with ships and the sea. But most significantly, they see no reason to fight the Japanese. There's no fire in their belly. They know nothing about the Japanese; consequently, they underestimate them, and they care nothing about profits from Korea or Manchuria."

Jones cocked his head to one side. "If I were the Tsar, I would do some compromising in Asia. The Japanese, for all their fervor, would rather negotiate than fight. They're a small nation and can't sustain a long war. But they will fight if they are forced to it, and fight using British-made battleships."

The glumness was broken by a servant who said, "Admiral, a telephone call for you."

"I detest those damn things, forever interrupting one's privacy," Kochenkov said irritably, putting down his glass. He rose and walked to the parlor.

"Well," said Jones, "I suspect that the *Times* will be ordering me back to London."

"The Queen?" asked Count Brusilov.

"She's in failing health. Has been for a year now, worked herself to death. She insists upon approving the commission of every officer in the army and navy. Think about it. She's been on the throne since 1837. The lady's outlived a dozen viceroys of India and steered Britain's rise to power. Indeed, an entire age has been named after her."

"She wields limitless power, much like the Tsar," said Isorovsky.

"Not exactly. We do have Parliament; Lords and Commons carry great weight. It's different in England," said Jones, choosing his words judiciously. "We have an aristocracy, but it has a duty to the people. Oh you may question that, but during the last half century there has arisen an understanding that philanthropy is a social if not moral responsibility to the lesser classes. There have been important legal reforms, as well as the establishment of charitable institutions. To be sure, there is poverty; but there will be no revolution."

"And you think Russia will have a revolution?" asked Isorovsky.

Jones stared into his drink, sighed and said, "What was it that King Louis XV said? '*Apres moi, le déluge.*'"

"After me, the flood," said Alexei, poking at the coals.

Count Brusilov glared at him and said, "It will not happen in Russia. Not in a thousand years."

"New orders!" said the admiral as he sauntered in, looking ten years younger. "I'm ordered to the fleet. I'll have to find my sea legs, but give me the high seas, a battleship or even a destroyer, and I'm a happy man."

"And a war," said Isorovsky.

"If need be. That's what we in the Navy do: we fight for the Motherland, for the *Rodina*. So let's toast the Imperial Navy, Russia, and Her Majesty the Queen," he said as he raised his glass.

"To the Navy, the Motherland, and Victoria, the Queen," they solemnly said, and downed their drinks.

The servant entered the room again and, in a very quiet voice, said, "I'm sorry to intrude, Excellency, but there is another telephone call."

"Can it not wait?" said the admiral.

"I can tell him to call back later. But it is from a Duke Pavlovich Mossolovsky. He says it's quite urgent, a matter of state."

"And it's for me?"

"No, it's for Count Brusilov."

"Really?" said the count. "Official calls to me usually come from the Interior Ministry."

Count Brusilov excused himself, and Jones said, "I once met Mossolovsky. Speaks decent English, but quite arrogant. He's despicable toward women, dissolute, and from what I gather a habitual drunk. But he's also involved with the *Okhrana* and is a close friend of Plehve. A dangerous man—with international connections."

"He speaks only of French cuisine and art, but he did support Sergei Diaghile. He likes the Modernists, not our traditional painters," said Isorovsky.

"I heard that he was involved in an orgy of drunkenness and fist fighting in a swank restaurant," said the admiral.

"It was a delicious scandal. The police had to call up reinforcements and he even accosted them. All for the mistress of a French actor! The Tsar sent him into exile for six months," said Count Brusilov.

"We do love our scandals, don't we, Admiral?" said Isorovsky.

"As long as they involve someone else," Kochenkov replied.

"We're off to London," said Count Brusilov as he returned from the phone call.

"Who?" asked Alexei.

"I am." Then with distaste, "And you will come with me, a directive from the Foreign Office and the Admiralty."

"Is it about Victoria?" asked the admiral.

"In part. The Tsar's uncle will represent him if the Queen passes and we—that is, Mussolovsky and I—will also attend the coronation of her son, the heir apparent."

"But only 'in part'?" the admiral said.

"The aide in the Foreign Office didn't go into detail but mumbled something about Alexei and the Japanese." The count looked at Alexei and said, "Perhaps you know something I don't. You were so enamored with those people."

"Enamored yes, but also concerned by the threat they pose."

The admiral stood and said, "So one last time let's raise our glasses with good Russian vodka, and toast Her Majesty and the Tsar."

"God save the Queen, God save the Tsar!" intoned voices.

And God save me, thought Alexei. *There is something very unsettling about this convergence,* he mused, draining his glass.

CHAPTER 21

London, February, 1901

"It's the end of an era," said William-Stuart Jones. It was late afternoon, and he and Alexei were gazing at the tremendous naval display. Warships and yachts from many nations stretched to the horizon, all honoring the Queen. Victoria's coffin, attended by soldiers of the Royal Horse Artillery, had been escorted from Osborne House, the place of her death, to the seaside town of Cowes. From there the coffin had been placed aboard the little *Alberta*, which steamed between the international armada. British destroyers accompanied the royal flotilla, the Union Jack at half -mast.

Throughout the United Kingdom all ordinary business had stopped. Thousands of mourners wearing severe black had assembled along the nine-mile coastline to Portsmouth harbor, the terminus of the Queen's final voyage. A great silence settled as their monarch, the only one most had ever known, proceeded on the glassy sea toward her final resting place. The quietude was broken when cannon on every warship fired salutes as seamen stood to attention lining the rails. In the windless air, smoke from the guns rose high into the brilliant sunset sky.

"We'll never see a sight like this again," said Alexei, motioning toward the steel behemoths just offshore.

Five British battleships, accompanied by the French *Dupuy de Lôme* and the Kaiser's towering *Hohenzollern,* thundered away, their salvos rattling buildings and creating tremors along the coast.

Jones scribbled notes, then pointed to the most impressive ship, which belched smoke from its main battery as the *Alberta* slipped past. "That's the *Hatuse*, the Japanese battleship. Built right here in the U.K."

"Damn impressive," said Alexei, surprised that no Russian ships had sailed for the historic event. Now he wondered how even the *Suvoroff*, one of their greatest battleships, would fare against the faster, newer and more heavily armed Japanese vessel. He hoped he would never have to find out.

"You know that your friend Itomo is here, don't you?" said the journalist.

"So I've heard. I would like to meet him again," said Alexei, thinking of renewing their friendship and acquiring any news about Kimi-san. He wondered how the journalist knew.

"His destroyer-torpedo boat is almost finished. I saw it a week ago. A devilish thing with its new torpedoes!" exclaimed Jones. "Of course, he can't leave the ship with all the work being done, but he's looking forward to seeing you."

The great crowd began to surge from the esplanade after the passing of the royal yacht.

"I will be covering the funeral of the Queen. Then I'll be going up to Scotland for a day or two. I have a flat here in London on Wych Street near St. Clement Dames Church. It's a bit run down, but cozy. You can stay there while I'm gone, if you want to whisk away from all the official stuff. You get in through the alley in back. Quite private and nobody pays any attention. It's a working class neighborhood but generally safe," Jones added, handing Alexei a key.

"Thank you, though I doubt that I will have reason to use it." Then he asked, "Will you be interviewing the new monarch?"

"If I can. The entire world wants to read about him. Everything else will be pushed onto the back page."

"I imagine there will be celebrations after the coronation."

"Indeed," said Jones. "In fact, I will be throwing a party at the tavern below my flat."

"What's the name of it?" Alexei asked, as a short man in a bowler brushed against him.

"The Rising Sun. Built around 1670 or so." Jones laughed and said, "Not too many Russians go there. The name, you know. But I've seen a Japanese or two. Of course you are invited."

"I'm not sure I can get away, but I appreciate the invitation."

"There will be a whirlwind of activity over the next few days. Over thirty-thousand troops will be in London, foreign dignitaries by the boatload, and hundreds of thousands will be brought in from the countryside by special trains. Standing room only, and more pomp and circumstance than one can imagine." Meditatively, he hummed a few bars of Elgar musical tribute to royalty. "I'll be covering the route of the cortege and I'll be at Windsor. It will be a great show. You don't want to miss it."

"I imagine I'll be seeing it with the Russian delegation. I heard that Grand Duke Michael arrived for the ceremonies."

"He'll have a lot of company. I'll see you when it's all over."

Alexei glimpsed the man who had brushed against him and wondered if he were a pickpocket. He checked the wallet inside his coat, and to his satisfaction it was still there. Checking another pocket, he felt an envelope and pulled it out. Nothing had been written on it, but he could feel a sheet of paper inside. The journalist looked at him quizzically, then glanced at the envelope. Alexei turned about, but the man had vanished.

"I saw him too," said Jones.

"Who is he?"

"I have no idea, but he must know you. You should be careful, these are strange times."

"Do you think he's from here?"

"I doubt it," said the journalist. "He is Asian."

***

Alexei read the note in his hotel room for the third time.

St. James Park, south side of the pond.
Five p.m. February 7. Come alone.

It was not the first time he had received a note requesting that he come to an unusual rendezvous, and he was resolved to be cautious.

A flurry of questions came to mind. Why February seventh, two days after the funeral of Queen Victoria? Was he to meet the man who gave him the envelope? Did it have to do with the Russian legation? Or was Itomo trying to get in touch with him and exercising caution of his own? The words of William-Stuart Jones came back to him: "Be careful, these are strange times."

He wondered if he should tell the count about the note, perhaps even request to be followed by members of the Russian embassy, many of whom were *Okhrana*.

Alexei lay on his bed and considered the possibilities and all the implications. Why five in the afternoon? Vsibility would be limited. The park would be nearly deserted, especially if the weather turned foul. He wondered if he should arm himself, but the only place he could procure a pistol would be at the embassy. There would be questions as to why he would need one, and the use of a firearm in the center of London, especially by a Russian, would be alarming. No, he decided, he would go unarmed. He wished he could talk to Jones, but the journalist had already left for Scotland.

On the morning of the seventh he phoned the Russian embassy and told the receptionist that he would not be in attendance. Then he dressed and walked the streets of London.

The weather had turned nasty and a cold fog had crept in. Impatiently he checked his pocket watch and drew his coat about him. Though people still mourned the loss of Victoria, the capital had returned to its bustling self. Alexei busied himself by wandering through the British Museum. He considered going to the park early but decided against it. The note specified five o'clock and he would adhere to that.

Finally, at four-forty he began walking. He had familiarized himself with the route the day before and was undeterred by the fog that limited visibility to less than ten meters. The grounds were nearly deserted and stillness lay about the park; the treetops disappeared in the gloom. He heard faint footsteps behind him and twice stopped to turn and look, but the hushed sounds also ceased. Alexei continued toward the benches beside the pond, with its thick border of shrubs and wide, flat lily pads floating on the surface. He saw a man emerge from behind a tree, quickly move, then vanish again in the fog. Another figure, bundled against the cold and wearing a large hat, sat on a bench but faced away. He skirted the bench and briefly followed a footpath to see where the man had disappeared.

Standing twenty feet from the bench, he resolved to wait until five-fifteen, then return to his hotel. A soft rain began to fall and he opened his umbrella. He paid no attention to the figure on the bench; if it was his contact, that person would have said something. Perhaps a vagrant, thought Alexei, for despite the splendor of the city there was an unwashed and hungry class of people living a precarious existence.

"Hello, Alexei-san."

He froze, and an electrical sensation shot through him. Turning, he saw a petite woman remove her hat with its black veil. Opening his mouth he simply stared, then in a choked voice said, "Kimi-san."

Instantly his arms were about her. Lifting her off her feet he stared into her green eyes and, to her astonishment, kissed her. She stared back, her eyes searching his, and repeated the words, "Alexei-san, Alexei-san."

Gently he put her down and took her hand in his. "You are here, actually here in England. Are you alone?"

"Yes, I am alone now," she said, glancing about.

"It's cold; we should go someplace else. It is so wonderful to see you, and I have so many questions."

"Alexei, I always hoped to see you again," she said. He had not released her hand; Alexei recalled that only little children hold hands in Japan, but she did not pull away. Again she looked about furtively, and he said, "I do not think it's safe here; I think somebody was following me."

"Then we should go someplace where there are more people."

He had been surprised by her appearance in a fashionable black dress with a narrow waist. It seemed strange, since he had only seen her in a kimono and wearing high *geta* shoes, which made her appear taller. She hurried to keep up with him as they took the footpath beside the pond, past huddling geese and ducks.

Again he heard footsteps, this time running towards them. "This way," he said, leading her off the path. There was a second set of footfalls, this one hurrying over pebbles. A shot rang out just as Alexei and Kimi-san slipped behind a tree. A branch splintered and flew away. Two more pistol shots cracked in the heavy air, followed by a scream.

Kimi-san, terrified, held tightly to Alexei as he listened. His heart pounded at the thought that someone was again trying to kill him. Startled pigeons took flight as another round was expended. Pulling Kimi-san's hand, Alexei cried, "Run!"

CHAPTER 22

London

It was dark when the horse-drawn omnibus rolled to a stop a block beyond the *Rising Sun* tavern. With her hat pulled low and face covered by a veil, Kimi-san drew scant attention from the few passengers on the bus, many of whom were also wearing the black of formal mourning. A gas streetlight issued a dimmed glow as fog swirled down the deserted street.

"This way," said Alexei, holding the key William-Stuart Jones had given him. They climbed the back stairs and heard the raucous laughter of inebriated patrons in the tavern below. No one noticed the couple as Alexei unlocked the door.

"Is this your house?" asked Kimi-san, eyeing the ancient kitchen, parlor and bedroom.

"No, it belongs to a friend, a journalist. He is away."

"Are we safe here?" Kimi-san asked, still shaken by their frantic escape.

"I think we are; I didn't see anyone one in pursuit of us."

They had switched from a horse drawn cab to the omnibus on their convoluted route through the dank streets of London. Sitting close to one another, they had only murmured their fears and tried not to show anxiety each time the coach came to a halt.

Someone had been firing a pistol at them. And what of the scream? Was someone dead? Was someone still chasing them? Questions besieged Alexei's mind. But above all was the inexplicable presence of Kimi-san.

They stood on the uneven floor of the three-room flat. The boards had been worn down by workman's shoes for nearly two hundred and fifty years. The place was Spartan, with only two pictures on the walls: one a print of a very young Queen Victoria, the other a photograph of Jones—tall, with a great twirled mustache, standing beside a Japanese man in samurai leather. Above them were ancient timbers warped by time and weather. For a long moment they stood in silence, relieved to have eluded death and pursuit, but feeling very strange in somebody else's house. It was stranger still, indeed miraculous, thought Alexei, to actually be together after all this time.

Kimi-san shivered, and Alexei hastened to the fireplace and struck a match to the prepared coals. Flame gradually caught and illuminated the room with a warm glow. Peering into the bedroom, he found a blanket, which he gave to Kimi-san and said, "I'll wait out here. You're still wet and you might want to put this around yourself."

Alexei removed his coat and ran his fingers through his hair. Now what? he wondered. The beautiful girl with the oval face and mysterious eyes he had dreamt about was suddenly, mysteriously a few feet away. Nervous, he tried to warm himself by the fireplace.

Had the shots had been intended for him? The question gnawed at him. Who had been the target? Could anyone have any reason for wishing Kimi-san dead? That thought was terrifying. He had no answers to his questions. The only thing he knew was that the girl he loved was with him—and he would do his utmost to protect her from everyone.

Briefly he recalled the note slipped into his pocket. Jones had said that the man who brushed against him was Asian.

Was he Japanese? Was it possible that Kimi-san knew him, had sent him? Or had he followed Alexei to the park? For what purpose? He was still trying to make sense of everything when she stepped out of the bedroom. Her coal black hair was piled atop her head, and the blanket was wrapped about her as if it were a kimono.

She glided to him and bowed. "Alexei-san," she said softly. Then she put her arms about him. "It has been so long. I never thought I would see you again, and yet I prayed each night. I imagined it was you each time my husband took me. I treasured the memory of you."

She seemed so fragile, so vulnerable. The temptation was to carry her to the bedroom and hold her closer than any of his dreams. She looked into his eyes again and he swallowed hard. In all the years since Svetlana he had only lain with two women and had never seen either again. Despite the immediate pleasure of those moments, the lustful sessions had seemed a diversion, a violation of a dream that rooted him to an impossible longing. He had chided himself for his obsession with Kimi-san, for time was passing and he was no longer a young cadet. And there were women, beautiful women, who made every effort to engage him in conversation at the St. Petersburg balls. He had told himself that assessments and realistic decisions had to be made, yet with each possibility her image floated before him like an indelible print nothing could efface.

This moment, he realized, might be the most meaningful of his life. Kimi-san, standing before him, appeared not to search his eyes but rather his soul. For a few precious hours she could be his and his alone. Every other thought, every fear, dissolved. His eyes lingered on her, and he felt as if he were seeing the illumination of a great cathedral. What, he wondered, would she allow herself to do? What would she allow him to do?

He stood stock still, not daring to disturb the stillness. It was she who touched his hand and, again in a whisper, said, "Alexei-san, hold me."

The utter bliss of their coming together did not cease till long past midnight. Endearing, yearning, they gave themselves to every desire, every touch. He marveled at her small but perfect breasts, the suppleness of her body. He breathed in her soft moans and the scent of her hair as it caressed his face. She held him inside of her and, with the subtleness of a whispering breeze, bestowed upon him love he had never known before.

But for the muted glow of the street lamp the room was dark. They lay together, touching with lips and fingertips after their passion had passed. Except for an occasional pedestrian passing below, nothing disturbed the stillness. Kimi-san laid her head upon his chest and sighed. "I do not want to go. I want to stay with you," she said.

"I don't want you to go either."

"What are we to do?"

"I don't know."

He had not wanted to disturb the idyllic moment by asking questions, troubling and perplexing questions. He lay still.

"You want to know, don't you, Alexei-san," she finally said, turning on her stomach. He could feel the warmth of her body and saw a sadness come over her.

"There is so much I don't know, so much I can't begin to comprehend," he said softly.

"Such as why I was waiting for you in the park?"

"And who sent me the note."

"It was Mr. Hiroshi. You must understand, Alexei, I wanted to see you so badly, and they knew it."

"They?"

"Mr. Hiroshi and the *kempetai,* the secret police. They knew that I was in England studying at the London hospital with other girls."

"And Mr. Hiroshi or some Japanese agent in St. Petersburg knew that I would be here, too."

"The *kempetai* knew about our letters and told Mr. Hiroshi that I must meet with you."

"Even if you are married?"

"My marital status does not matter. I was to do it for Japan."

"Do what?" asked Alexei, propped on his elbow.

"Ask you questions. I was to be..."

"A spy? Is that the real reason you're here?" Alexei asked, incredulous. He stared into her eyes.

"No, no! I would never have come into this house if I didn't want to be with you! I loved you from the first day I saw you. You must believe me. I was questioned, interrogated. My father, brother and husband are military officers and the police demanded to know if I was sharing secrets with you. They eventually realized that I know nothing about our military. There was nothing I could reveal, but I know you, and they required me to ask you questions, to get important information."

"Because I'm in the Russian Navy."

"And because your father is still important. Alexei, I am so sorry. I don't want to be a spy."

"What if we weren't chased and had not come here? What if we just stayed in the park and I refused to tell you anything? Just how were you going to get that kind of information? After all, I'm not an agent giving secrets to Japan. Were you going to bribe me with money, or were you going to take me to a hotel?" He immediately regretted the tone, the accusation, but he felt used. Then, he realized, he was not being used by Kimi-san; they were both being used, together.

He did not want to spoil the evening with talk of betrayal. It was certainly not the first time, he thought, as the image of Svetlana's deceit flit through his mind, that the purity, the sanctity of his love for Kimi-san was stained by *real politic*. It seemed a travesty, for she was the one person he truly loved. And none of this was her fault. He wanted nothing to come between them and tried to put it all in perspective.

Kimi-san sank back in the bed, put her hands over her face and sobbed. "I don't know what I would have done. I am so scared of the *kempetai*. They are despicable, and they're everywhere. Yes, I was to take you to a hotel. They told me what I should do."

"Would people from the *kempetai* have been there?"

"I think so, somewhere nearby."

"And they would have questioned you?"

"Yes, absolutely," she said. Alexei felt her shiver.

"But then there was the shooting, and that changed everything," he said, holding her close.

In the growing dawn Alexei could see her nod her head.

"Kimi-san, the shooting may not have been the work of the *Kempetai*. It might have been somebody from my past, or even the Russian secret police."

"Why would they want to shoot you? You are Russian."

"Because they may think I was giving you secrets for the Japanese. Did you see anybody follow you in the park?"

"Nothing I could be sure about. Mr. Hiroshi paused once or twice when he took me to wait for you. I was terribly worried. You came, but at first I couldn't be certain it was you. You have changed; grown older, more mature, and I could not see your face. I was afraid of who might be standing in front of me. Then you turned around and I was relieved."

"And Mr. Hiroshi just left you there. That's strange. He must have heard the footsteps too. And certainly he could not have been the shooter, unless the *Kempetai* wanted him to kill me. But then they would have gained nothing," mused Alexei.

"Then there had to be somebody else on that footpath who was not Japanese," said Kimi-san. She moved to sit on the edge of the bed, her head bowed.

Finally Alexei said, "What are you supposed to ask me?"

"They want to know about the Trans-Siberian railroad. They think you would know because your father is part owner of the lumber mills. They told me to ask you if a second track is being built."

"He was involved years ago, but his mills were bought out. It was a secret; he had to pay everything he had for compensation for what he did to your friend, the *maiko*."

"Her family moved away a month after you left. *Sensei* said that the family came into some money." Kimi-san was quiet for a time, then said, "Alexei, I have to tell the *Kempetai* something. What can I possibly say that they will believe?"

"What happens if you say you learned nothing from me?"

"They will brand me a traitor and tell my husband that I slept with you."

"He doesn't know about all this?"

"No. He is at sea and hasn't been told. He would hurt me if he found out. Even if it was all done for the Emperor. The *Kempetai* threatened me; they said they would tell him I was with you if I didn't comply, and he would believe them. He expects me to be very subservient, and he doesn't like the idea of me learning non-traditional things, especially here in England. He beats me, Alexei, and he would beat me even harder if he learned that I slept with you."

She looked at Alexei with tear-filled eyes and wrapped her arms around him. He took a deep breath and stared at the timbered ceiling. "Tell them that a second track is under consideration, but weather and lack of materials has stopped work. And tell them that there has been much damage from sabotage and more troops may be sent. They will believe that because it's true."

Kimi-san nodded and said, "I do not want to hurt you or your country. Japan is preparing for war; it's all around us. But I pray that war never happens."

"What I wish to know is, how can we be together, Kimi-san? Truly together?"

She kissed him and said, "We can be together in our dreams. We can always dream."

***

The fog and wind had not abated when they silently padded down the stairs and hurried past the Rising Sun tavern. It was early and Alexei was determined to escort Kimi-san to the hospital where her classes would be held. The clop-clop of horse hooves came down the street and a carriage stopped beside them. The door swung open and a short Japanese man stepped out.

"Good morning, Lieutenant Brusilov," said Mr. Hiroshi. "I trust that you and Kimi-san are not hurt."

"We've have not been harmed," said Alexei warily, peering at the soft-spoken man. He was impeccably dressed in the English style and wearing a top-hat. Mr. Hiroshi gave an enigmatic smile. A sudden chill assaulted Alexei, and he noted a bulge in the man's tight-fitting coat. He had been about to say that they'd been shot at, but he quickly changed his mind and pressed his lips shut. There was movement in the carriage and Alexei saw another man behind a water-streaked window.

"Kimi-san will have to come with us."

"Us?"

"With us, *tomodachi* Alexei-san," said Itomo, leaning toward the open door. "I wish we had time to talk, but circumstances dictate otherwise. My sister must return to Japan. Her ship leaves today, as does mine."

"Please let her stay. I will pay for her transportation to Japan, Itomo-san. She wants to finish her medical training."

"She has," Mr. Hiroshi said with a tight smile. "Now she shall enter the carriage, and you should return to your embassy. I'm sure they are concerned about you. Let's not make a scene."

"Will I be able to see her again?" begged Alexei, holding Kimi-san close. Mr. Hiroshi stiffened and said, "That kind of familiarity is inappropriate, Lieutenant. We do not do that in my country, and must you be reminded that she is a married woman?"

Alexei ignored the comment and said, "We are not in your country, and there has been violence. I distinctly heard shots fired and a scream. I think the police would be interested in your activities."

With icy restraint, the man said, "That would not be sensible. It would involve complications that would prove embarrassing to you and your country. Your family has experienced this once before. Now I must insist that this lady return with us."

What hypocrisy, Alexei thought. At that moment, Itomo reached for his sister's hand and pulled her into the carriage.

"Kimi-san, I will see you again, I promise," said Alexei.

"I doubt that very much," Mr. Hiroshi said sternly. "Forget her and go on with your life, Lieutenant Brusilov. I hope it is long and fruitful, but you should not expect to see Mrs. Yoshiharu again."

CHAPTER 23

St. Petersburg
April 1901

The court-martial began a month after Alexei returned to St. Petersburg. Two naval officers, an official from the Russian embassy in London and two members of the *Okhrana*, convened in a sparse room of the Admiralty building. Alexei, standing before them, observed that the only other person in attendance was the count. He wished that admiral Kochenkov could have been there, but he had reported to the fleet months before.

"This court is convened," said the naval captain acting as chief interrogator and judge. There was no defense attorney, although Alexei had requested one.

"Lieutenant Alexei Brusilov, you are charged with an assignation with a foreign agent, giving said agent highly confidential information and attending a clandestine meeting without giving notice to officials of this government."

Alexei knew that an accusation in a Russian court was tantamount to a guilty verdict, but he said, "Excellency, I wish to testify that I did meet with a Japanese lady, not knowing that she had any connection with Japanese military intelligence. She was, in fact, studying medicine in London, and that can be readily ascertained. Nor did I give her any information that could be useful to the Japanese military."

"Incredible! What strange behavior for a Russian naval officer," said a tall, dour member of the *Okhrana*. "And just what prompted you to meet this woman?"

"I received a note from an unknown person. It seemed urgent but mentioned nothing about her."

"Who do you think sent it?" demanded the naval captain.

"I don't know. It could have been from anyone; even one of our own *Okhrana*."

The captain snorted and said, "I think you knew who sent it: the same Mr. Hiroshi the police have been following for years, the same one who had been forwarding your mail and that of Mrs. Yoshiharu. Don't look so surprised, Lieutenant. Our investigators are just as capable of reading illicit dispatches as the Japanese. And as you very well know, Mr. Hiroshi is not an innocent merchant. He is a spy."

"Of this I had no idea," said Alexei.

"And not the slightest suspicion? I question your intelligence as well as your character," said the man from the *Okhrana*, removing his monocle.

"So, we have established that Mr. Hiroshi and Mrs. Yoshiharu are both spies, and spies want secrets. Our secrets. Exactly what did they ask, and what did you tell her? We want the truth," said the embassy official.

Alexei knew this was the end of his naval career. It was entirely conceivable that he would be executed for treason, war or no war. "Of course I would not tell her anything of military value. Mrs. Yoshiharu told me that the Japanese are very interested in the capabilities of our Trans-Siberian railroad. They want to know its carrying capacity. I told her that we were considering the building of a second track. Awareness of such, I assumed, would deter any invasion plans they may have had. They would consider how quickly we could reinforce our regiments in Vladivostok."

There was a brief discussion between the *Okhrana* and the naval officer. Alexei assumed that they were determining the value of what he had said. A moment later the *Okhrana* agent said, "What exactly did you tell her?"

"Only that the railroad's expansion was being considered. I thought that would worry the Japanese. And that we might send more troops; that was all."

There was a pause as the captain again conferred with the *Okhrana* and the embassy official. The *Okhrana* man grunted, turned to Alexei and said, "And this discussion with Mrs. Yoshiharu took place in the flat of Mr. William-Stuart Jones during the night. We are certain of that. We also know that you two ran from the park. It appeared very clandestine."

"It might appear so, but we were being shot at. We didn't know who was shooting, or at whom, or why. We also heard a scream," said Alexei. "Under those circumstances, not being able to see anything due to the fog, we did the only logical thing."

"But your unauthorized presence in the park required one of our agents to follow you. Our only option was to suspect deceit and fraternization with an enemy. Japan, sir, is an enemy. Do you know what happened to our agent, the one tasked to watch your traitorous behavior?" demanded the *Okhrana* agent.

"I have no idea. As I said, we couldn't see anything."

"He was murdered! Yes, his body was found floating in the pond. Shot, then stabbed until dead. *That* is what your illicit tryst, your deceit, resulted in: the execution of a member of our security apparatus. You are an accessory to murder and that is a capital offense!"

A silence engulfed the room. Count Brusilov stood and walked to the dais. Leaning forward with both hands on the table, he spoke to the interrogators in a voice that Alexei could not hear. He handed the judge a telegram. The naval officer read it, listened, and glanced at Alexei.

The count returned to his seat and the judge turned to Alexei. "The court finds you guilty of conspiring with agents of a hostile power. It also finds you complicit in the tragic death of an agent of the Tsar. The appropriate sentence should be execution, but due to the leniency of this court you will be demoted in rank and transported to the village of Chita in Siberia. There you will labor on the Trans-Siberian railroad."

"May I ask how long the sentence will last?" said Alexei.

"Fifteen years. You will leave on tomorrow's troop train. That is all."

***

Count Brusilov turned on Alexei as they walked down the gleaming hall of the Admiralty. "I told you years ago that having anything to do with a Japanese girl was stupid and dangerous! Now you have disgraced the family name and put my career in jeopardy. If it weren't for my position and influence, the court would have had you shot. I care nothing for you; you got what you deserve, but I will not have the family name associated with the execution of a traitor! What an idiot you are to have fallen for a married woman you can never have!"

Furious with the man and the trumped-up proceedings, Alexei, in a seething voice said, "You are the ultimate hypocrite. It is you who destroyed the family and bankrupted us."

"It was my money, not yours. You do not condemn me. You should be thankful I just saved your life," hissed the count, his eyes small and venomous.

Alexei stood silent for a moment, then said, "You haven't saved me. You care only for yourself. To you I'm an expendable pawn on a chess board."

"Now you are off that board. You are a convict, a traitor. I never want to see you again." Count Brusilov turned on his heel to go.

In a loud voice Alexei called after him, "One more thing: I suspect that you knew every aspect of this inquisition before it began. I know that you were required to work for the *Okhrana*. And I suspect you knew the agent who shot at us. Exactly who was he supposed to kill?"

Turning, the count issued a cold smile. "Under the circumstances, it should have been you. But it wasn't. The bullet was meant for the enemy."

"Mr. Hiroshi?"

"Oh no, that would be unprofessional. He's one we enjoy watching. It was meant for the woman, who unfortunately got away. I believe her name was Kimi Karamatsu."

Alexei felt his heart chill in his breast.

***

Kimi, lying on her futon, cradled her son as her mother and Itomo looked on. "Your husband should be here soon," said Kyoko Karamatsu to her anxious daughter.

"His ship docked three hours ago," said Itomo. "A captain has much to tend to before he can get away. But I know he's looking forward to coming back."

Kimi nodded and gently rocked the two-day-old infant. Lieutenant Yoshiharu's voyage took three weeks, and it was two more before he returned from a training cruise. He may have thought it strange that his wife was so willing to accommodate his carnal desires eight-and-a half months before. Though she dutifully performed her conjugal requirements, it was never with obvious pleasure. When he'd finished with her that night, she'd whispered in his ear, "Maybe we will have a baby."

"Yes," he'd said. "A male child will please me. Someday he, too, will serve the Emperor."

"That will be a noble thing," Kimi-san had replied, hoping that too much time had not gone by. But it was not Atsugi she'd thought of when she wrapped her thighs about him and softly moaned as required. Each subsequent night was fraught with worry. She'd tried to tell herself that all would be well, that the baby would look like Atsugi, but now tremors came in waves like a roiling sea.

She heard his stocking feet on the *tatami* mat floor as he entered the tiny bedroom, moving past *shoji* screens and an *ikebana* flower arrangement. "Itomo-san," he said, his face serious as he bowed to Kimi-san's brother before acknowledging his wife and her mother.

"You have a beautiful child," said Kyoko to her son-in-law.

"We have a son, a splendid son," said Kimi-san.

"That is good," said Atsugi, kneeling on the mat to examine the infant. Kimi-san had been rocking the baby and was about to hand the swaddling to her husband when he peered at it closely and knitted his brows.

"What's this?" he said touching the curly brown hair and studying the child's eyes.

"Your son," said Kimi with a tremulous smile and a hint of fear.

Atsugi slowly shook his head and said, "Not Japanese. My hair, your hair is not like this." Then standing he stiffened and said, "This is not my child! What have you done, woman?" Enraged, he shouted, "I know that you were in England. What wretched *geijin* filled you? I will not accept this," he stammered, "this *creature*. No Japanese man would want such a thing. You have defiled my house, insulted me, and brought shame upon yourself!"

Tears ran down Kimi's cheeks and her mother took the child in her arms. "His name is Tadachi in honor of your grandfather," said Kyoko.

"Don't patronize me, and don't insult my grandfather. That," he gestured stiffly at the infant, "is an abomination. I will divorce her," said Atsugi in a cold voice.

"Husband, what color eyes do I have?" asked Kimi-san.

When Atsugi didn't answer, his mother-in-law spoke. "Atsugi-san, I must tell you something that I have mentioned to very few people. The year after the Meiji restoration, when Japan saw the first *geijins,* my mother, a very popular and accomplished *geisha*, entertained a German ship captain. It was said that he loved her, but he was married to a woman in Germany. Weeks after their assignation, he sailed away and never returned. Mother bore me, and to her great relief I inherited no *geijin* characteristics. I never had to tell my husband about my mother's time with the German until Kimi-san was born with my father's green eyes. Now my daughter has given birth to a child inheriting that man's eyes and brown, curly hair. So you see, my daughter has done nothing wrong. It is an inherited trait that may last many generations. And yet, the next child you two have may look as Japanese as you and I."

Atsugi looked from Kyoko to his wife; then, turning to Itomo, he demanded, "Is this true?"

"If my mother says it's true, it is true."

Without another word, Lieutenant Atsugi Yoshiharu bowed to Itomo and walked out of the house.

Kyoko laid the child in her daughter's arms. Kimi rocked her baby and wiped her tears. "Thank you," she said.

Itomo looked at his sister for a long moment, nodded and said, "Alexei-san is my friend. Atsugi is also my friend, and he must never know about your time with Alexei."

"May I not write to Alexei, to tell him about our child?" asked Kimi-san timidly.

Itomo gave his sister a contemplative look, then shook his head. "There is nobody to carry your letters. Mr. Hiroshi is nowhere to be found, and I have no idea what happened to him."

"Oh," said Kimi-san, remembering how he'd interrogated her in the Japanese embassy. He'd not been pleased with her information of questionable worth.

"Alexei should know," Kimi-san said quietly, after her brother left.

"The German captain never knew my name. He did not even know I was born. Some things are just not to be," her mother said, and saw the tears glisten on Kimi-san's cheeks.

CHAPTER 24

Chita, Siberia
October, 1901

Incarceration, following the initial shock, was a numbing experience, like being immersed in freezing water for a very long time. For the first few months Alexei struggled against the isolation and intellectual deadness of internal exile. He was still a naval officer, though now a very junior one, and desired a measure of respectability. But that was in short supply among two hundred military prisoners whose only diversion from stultifying drudgery were a handful of surly, unwashed women who traded their bodies for a few cases of vodka.

Dense birch forests extended to the horizon. The only change was the rumble and screech of troop trains that rarely stopped. There was little reason to. The town of Chita consisted of one store, a supply depot, and a ramshackle saloon next to a dilapidated church with a green onion dome. A few dozen huts were scattered about, one of which was reserved for him and Junior Lieutenant Igor Politovsky. Igor was a minor aristocrat of social revolutionary leanings whose beating of a senior captain had won for him his new abode. He was, according to his own account, a connoisseur of fine women and exotic libation, both of which were non-existent in Chita, thousands of versts from St. Petersburg.

The town lay at the confluence of the Chita and Ingoda Rivers and was bordered by steppes, rugged mountains and occasional stretches of farm land. Beyond that were forest, bears and wolves. Passing river traffic was poled nine hundred kilometers northwest toward Irkusk, only a few days march from Mongolia. Primarily inhabited by people from the steppes of Central Asia, Chita seemed more Asian than European, especially since there was a mixture of clothing as well as language.

"We just repaired the bridge over the Ingoda,"said Politovsky. "It was destroyed by Japanese saboteurs. We caught and executed those who didn't commit suicide."

"We're all prisoners here. I'm surprised that the men were given guns and were willing to fight," said Alexei.

"Why not? They have nothing else to do. So they have guns. Who will they use them on? Each other? Where are they going to go? Into the forest? When they run out of bullets the wolves will get them. And besides, there's damn little to eat out there."

It was late fall, and Politovsky and Alexei were riding their Mongolian ponies across the bridge and high up a mountain trail. From there they could look down on the miniscule town and its fields, now fallow, and foliage long gone though a few crisp brown leaves held stubbornly on. A chill was in the air and Alexei said, "Is winter here like St. Petersburg?"

Igor laughed and said, "Winter in St. Petersburg is like the tropics by comparison. You have never experienced cold until you've been here."

Fifteen winters, thought Alexei. *How does anyone survive?*

"Summer's beauty is short," said Politovsky, waving his hand toward the little huts below. "Flowers erupt like explosions, all frantic to catch the sun, and then it's over and everything freezes. You better find a woman to keep you warm. There aren't many here, so don't be too particular."

"I'm not interested in any of them," said Alexei peering into the valley below.

"Suit yourself, but you'll change your mind. There is one woman looking for a man. She's no beauty, but you're not in high society here. Her husband was a Sergeant, died two months ago fighting the Japanese. I think she likes you—she told me so, but she may just be angling for a new man. Her name's Natasha, in case you come to your senses."

Alexei sighed and said, "I think you should double the guard on the bridge."

"We'll rebuild it if they blow it up. It's been rebuilt three times already. Would you like to hunt bear with me?"

That might not be a bad idea, thought Alexei. Getting killed by a bear would relieve him of fifteen years in a Siberian prison.

***

Alexei was running beside the Neva, whose freezing water rushed madly to the Gulf of Finland. Cherry blossoms, imbedded in chunks of ice, were being thrown at him by Atsugi and Count Brusilov, the latter having only one leg. Alexei was perplexed; he had never seen cherry trees beside the Neva. He was out of breath, and fell on the slick pavement. Across the river, cannon from the fortress of St. Peter and St. Paul were targeting him with shards of ice. He looked back to see Brusilov's twisted face screaming, "Throw harder, Atsugi, you have to hit him!"

"I'm trying," said the Japanese lieutenant, running alongside the count.

Somewhere ahead, Kimi-san shouted above the roar of the wind. "Get up, Alexei, run! You must run!"

Why is Atsugi with Brusilov in St. Petersburg, Alexei wondered, and how could the count, with just one leg, run so fast? None of this made sense. Now Kimi-san was floating above the swirling water. Beside her, a rowboat pitched violently in the current.

"Hurry!" she screamed, her hair askew and her kimono flapping in the wind.

"I'm coming. Don't leave me!" Alexei shouted, leaping over the sea wall and plunging into the icy water. Then, quite inexplicably, she and the boat were gone. Flailing, he frantically waved his arms as he sank and was swept out to sea.

A stream of vodka poured over his face and Politovsky was standing over him. "Damn you, Alexei! This is the third time you woke me with your fucking ravings. Once more and you sleep in the snow."

"Sorry, I guess I was dreaming."

"That was a nightmare, not a dream. And who the hell are Atsugi and Kimi-san? Those are Japanese names."

Alexei rubbed his eyes. "What time is it?"

"Five in the morning. So who are those people?"

"I met them when I was in Japan, years ago."

"This Kimi-san, you keep repeating her name. You must be in love with her."

"I am, or was. It's a complicated story."

"But you still love her," persisted Politovsky.

"She's married, and I'll never see her again."

"There's a lot of things we'll never see again. Get over it. I told that woman Natasha, the one who lost her husband, that she can stay in our hut. Just screw her and drink. It will take your mind off the Japanese girl. I'll have my own woman before winter. Then everything will be cozy and we can forget the world."

"I don't want Natasha or any other of those mammoths," protested Alexei, pulling the blanket over his head.

"Fine. But don't blame me once you've frozen to death," said Politovsky, gulping down the last dregs of vodka.

***

Chita, Siberia
December, 1903

Ice-crusted cap pulled down, the man plodded on, boots sinking into deep snow. His collar was frozen, and fetid breath fouled his balaclava. It was just after dawn when he reached the first dwellings. Three guards slumbered by a fire, but a sergeant, seeing the stranger, stirred and nudged them, then lifted his rifle and wearily stared at the man, an apparition emerging from the fog.

The traveler held aloft a piece of paper and through frost-bitten lips mumbled, "I must see the commanding officer."

The sergeant fingered his weapon and said, "He's still asleep. What do you want?"

"I have to get this signed. I need transport to St. Petersburg," said the man, holding out the stained document.

"Can't read," said the sergeant. "Are you just taking a stroll, or did you escape from prison?"

"Neither. The train I was on broke down twenty versts back. I need this signed so I can take the next one."

"Is that so? Only soldiers can take the train, and you don't look like one."

The man simply shrugged and said, "I'm freezing and these are orders. I'm navy. Can I just get it done?"

The sergeant ignored the paper, snorted and said, "See that hut beside the church? That's where you'll find him. But he won't be sober enough to read anything. If he can still read."

All was quiet in the *izba,* except ragged snoring. The navy man climbed the steps and knocked. He waited a moment, then pushed open the door. A dim, diffused light settled upon four comatose figures; bundles of discarded clothing partially covered their bodies. They lay as still as corpses. A man lay atop a very stout woman. Beside them was a hearth, its embers long dead. The traveler stooped, peered at the slumbering couple, then went to the other heap.

An obese woman with red and purple blotched legs lay naked and sprawled over a nude man, their covers strewn about them. Both snored in unison. Six empty bottles of vodka lay on the floor, and glass shards from another reflected the morning light. The room stank of sweat, sex, scraps of food and alcohol. A mangy yellow dog lay in a corner, its legs raised toward the sagging ceiling. The traveler wondered if it too had been drinking.

One of the men had to be the unit commander, he mused. He took hold of the fat woman. She tried to jerk her arm away, but the man would have none of it and roughly pulled her across the floor. A half moan, half snarl erupted from her toothless mouth as she tried to focus. The light caused her to shield her eyes, then she reached for the blanket to cover her nakedness. The man slapped her and hissed, "Get out!" Rising unsteadily, she spat out a curse; then, tugging at the dog, stumbled into the frigid air. The cur looked back, whined, then unsteadily followed the wench.

The tussle woke the other trollop. Seeing her friend gone, she clutched a threadbare blanket and crawled to the door.

"Cold. Can't do shit," she moaned, peering into the grey dawn. Then, after jamming on a fur cap, she wrapped a blanket around her sagging body and dragged herself out.

The man who had been beneath her rose to his elbows, tried in vain to focus on the stranger standing over him, then fell back with an agonized groan.

"What do you want?" the drunk finally demanded, pulling the remaining blanket over his body.

"I need your signature, if you're the commanding officer."

"Commanding officer?" the drunk said with a lopsided grin. "No, that's his Excellency over there." Picking up a vodka bottle he tossed it at the slumbering lump and hoarsely said, "Alexei, wake up."

"Screw you," said 'his Excellency' and rolled over, praying that night would come without the unnecessary advent of day.

With a combination of impatience, hunger and disgust, the traveler slammed a boot into the man's side.

"Wake up and sign this damn thing!" he shouted.

Alexei moaned and reached for a holstered revolver on a wooden peg, but the traveler grabbed the weapon and tossed it aside. Kneeling, he stared into the drunk's eyes, held up the paper, and in a whisper said, "Sign this, or I'll feed you to the nearest bear."

Alexei propped himself against a wall and, with constricted pupils, stared at the paper. He worked his head back and forth to clear the month-old cobwebs and regarded the frozen but implacable face. Squinting, an inkling of recognition came. Alexei moved closer and put out a hand to touch the man's numbed face. Blinking, he opened his mouth and his pupils suddenly enlarged.

"Sergei? Sergei Ivanovich?" he said, trying to rise.

A puzzled expression came over the traveler's face and he stared hard at the bearded, disheveled drunk. "Alexei? Is that you? What in the hell..." His voice trailed off as he grasped Alexei's arm and dragged him to a chair beside a rickety table.

"Drink," said Alexei, gesturing to a half-drained bottle of vodka. "We must drink to your return," he said, wiping saliva from his lips with the back of his hand.

"You've had enough. I need you to sign this."

"What's this?" said Alexei, staring at the orders. "There's nothing here to write with. Why are you here?" he mumbled, a dizzy spell assaulting him.

"I was released from the camp, a place called Haichentze, a day's train ride from Vladisvostok. The paper, orders, will get me on a train to St. Petersburg. Then I report to the fleet."

Alexei rose, splashed water on his face and looked into a cracked mirror on the wall. He ran his hands over his thick beard, groaned at the sight of himself, and plunked down.

"I was told that you might be here," said Sergei.

Alexei looked at him blankly.

"Tatiana told me." Glancing at Politovsky, who had gone back to sleep, Sergei, said, "Her cell informed her. They know everything. They learned about the court martial and your sentence."

"Fifteen years. I won't live that long."

"Not if you stay married to the vodka. But I doubt you'll be here much longer."

Again a blank look. "What makes you think that?"

"Because you're a trained naval officer. You're needed. There will be war."

Alexei shook his head. "War? You mean your revolution? Nothing changes in Russia. Men have been in this camp for twenty years; most die here."

"Not revolution, not yet; we aren't ready. But things are moving, Alexei. There are new groups, *Menshevicks* and *Bolsheviks*, not just the same old Social Democrats who spout on about gradual change. Factory workers and peasants are fed up. Some have read Marx, and there's a fellow in England named Lenin, a speaker who calls for a rising by the proletariat and the overthrow of capitalism."

"And this proletariat is going to defeat the Tsar's army?" said Alexei with a sneer. "It's going to take a catastrophe to get the peasants to do anything. They worship the Tsar."

Sergei grabbed Alexei's arm and said, "The catastrophe may not be far away. I spoke with Tatiana. The Committee sent her east and she snuck into my prison. She said Japan is fed up with Russia, our troops in Manchuria and Korea. The Japanese are massing armies; they're going to invade. If we lose there will be huge losses, then there will be revolution. It's going to happen."

"Perhaps, but we may not lose. So why are you anxious to get to the fleet?" asked Alexei, rubbing his temples.

"It's part of my sentence, remember? But that's fine with me. The revolution will start with mutiny in the navy."

"And you insist on being there for the revolution," said Alexei, thinking, *This is not a good conversation after five bottles of vodka.*

"I have work to do, Alexei. *We* have work to do. The Russia we've known cannot continue. The revolution will be worldwide, but it must begin with us."

"I told you, Sergei, I'm not a revolutionary. This is your dream, not mine. I'll sign the damn paper, then I just want to forget about everything."

"Sure," Sergei said, looking about the dingy hut. "Who is the woman that was crushing you?"

"Alexei gave a deprecatory wave of his hand. "She's nothing except a warm blanket. You need a warm blanket here."

"Get cleaned up, Alexei. You're going to war. And for Russia's sake, pray that we lose."

***

Sergei boarded the train for St. Petersburg two days later. "I hope to meet Tatiana before I ship out," he said in parting.

"You must be careful, Sergei. You've already been convicted once, and spouting revolution on board ship will get you shot. And that includes anybody working with you."

"I am only a cog in a great wheel, Alexei. The wheel turns with or without me. It's coming, it's inexorable. You might want to be on the right side of history. The revolution will need good naval officers. You can help."

"By losing a war?"

"Nothing will mobilize the masses like defeat. It will be a contagion that will sweep away the Tsar and his sycophants."

"Defeat means dying. What if we die, Sergei? Who leads the revolution then?"

"We will be martyrs, and others will pick up the cause. It's a nation of one hundred and ten million workers and peasants against the aristocracy and the capitalists. Who do you think is going to win?"

CHAPTER 25

Port Arthur, Siberia
February, 1904

The signal officer gave a stiff bow and said, "Captain, we will not be challenged. All is clear."

Itomo Karamatsu nodded. A junior lieutenant entered the bridge and reported that torpedoes were loaded and all guns were in readiness. "Flank speed," ordered Itomo, and through binoculars saw his destroyer-torpedo boat squadron swing into line.

Just as the spies had reported, all the Russian naval units were anchored one behind the other. Ships' officers and most crews were ashore. The lights of the city silhouetted the two enormous battleships, the cruisers and support vessels of the Russian Pacific Fleet.

The lookouts on the ships only stirred when they saw that the bow waves of the incoming vessels were not diminishing. Frantically, skeleton crews raced for the guns, but it was far too late. No steam was up and the ships sat immobile. Gunners watched in horror as Atsugi's speeding vessel, followed by a half-dozen destroyers, launched their net-cutting torpedoes.

Explosions sheared open steel hulls, sheets of flame and debris filled the night sky. Secondary blasts from stores of munitions added to the chaos, and water flooded into holed compartments. Those below crawled toward upper decks, but most drowned or were torn apart by the nine torpedoes that found their mark.

Hundreds on shore rushed to piers and balconies, stunned by the sudden attack. In an instant, the balance of power in the Far East had been irrevocably altered. The Russian Pacific Fleet had been expunged.

As swiftly as they had come, the Japanese squadron turned and steamed away.

***

Only a day before, Itomo and all other captains had been shuttled to the battleship *Mikasa* in Sasebo to hear the diminutive but determined Admiral Tojo announce that diplomatic relations with St. Petersburg were about to end. In a stern but quiet voice he said, "We sail tomorrow, and our enemy flies the Russian flag. Show yourself worthy of the confidence I place in you."

There was no hesitation, no uncertainty in the well-trained and disciplined Japanese fleet. The Emperor had decided that it was time to reduce the Russian navy to burning hulks. With the Tsar's ships eliminated, the invasion of Korea and Manchuria commenced, and the fall of Port Arthur was not far behind.

***

Anger and humiliation coursed through the Admiralty building in St. Petersburg, coupled with disbelief that Japan would have the gall to wage war upon a country with the largest land army in the world. The Tsar, stunned like all other European leaders, declared that the Japanese were "infidels to be wiped off the face of the earth."

Admiral Kochenkov, back from a fleet exercise, ran into Isorovsky, the instructor captain from the Academy.

"The seven battalions the Japanese landed after the Port Arthur attack have been reinforced. They're over-running our forces, and Nicholas won't allow any retreat," said Kochenkov.

"But I've heard that we're sending more troops. The Trans-Siberian tracks can handle reinforcements," said Isorovsky. "Hundreds of thousands will be moving east."

"There's a serious problem," said Kochenkov. "The railroad is serviceable in peace time, but six thousand miles of track under continuous usage? I question its dependability." Taking the captain aside, he said quietly, "I heard that Port Arthur is completely cut off. The Japanese fleet controls the approaches by sea, and their land divisions have surrounded it."

"So our troops can't detrain at Port Arthur?"

"No, they would have to fight their way in."

"Don't we have other naval forces in the Far East?" asked Isorovsky, eyes widening as the direness of the situation dawned on him.

"We have units in Vladivostok, but they are insignificant. Only a few of the ships at Port Arthur are back in commission, and they run to port when the enemy shows up."

"But Admiral Marakov is a brave fellow and very popular with the men. Certainly he will challenge the Japanese."

"Then you didn't hear. He was killed and his ship was sunk. The Tsar is meeting with the Higher Naval Board. I suspect they'll name Admiral Zinovy Rozhestvensky as overall commander of the fleet."

"What fleet?" the captain demanded bitterly.

"The one they're calling the Second Pacific Fleet, the ships at Libau on the Baltic. They will come to the aid of our men and ships at Port Arthur," said the admiral.

"My God, how far would they have to sail?"

"Eighteen thousand miles," said Kochenkov somberly.

"Can it be done? What navy has ever sent an entire fleet so many miles and expected it to fight?"

"None, to answer your question, but it's up to the Emperor. We'll do it if we have to."

The captain stroked his greying beard and said, "So what does the Admiralty have in store for you? A battleship?"

"No. I am to command the cruiser squadron. All of the ships, including the ones that should never sail."

"I don't envy you."

***

The recovery of sobriety and deportment following the appearance of Sergei was not an overnight achievement for lieutenants Alexei and Igor. They took long walks in frigid weather, and abstained from the bottle. Eventually, their heads cleared and a semblance of responsibility returned. Two months later, wearing freshly pressed uniforms, they stood at attention in the Admiralty building before a three-man naval commission.

A captain, the senior officer, gave them a long, hard look and said, "The exigency of the present situation is offering you an opportunity to atone for your crimes against the state. By order of this court you will immediately report for sea duty. You are expected to serve the Tsar and Holy Russia with dedication, honor and courage. Perform your tasks with total devotion and your records will be expunged. Failure to do so will be considered a criminal act. Any questions?"

"Sir, will we be serving together?" asked Politovsky.

The captain glanced at the papers before him and said, "Yes, you will both be replacements on board the cruiser *Mikhail III*. It's an older ship but well-armed. And it's a favorite of the Emperor, since it's named for the first Romanov Tsar, nine hundred years ago."

"May I ask the name of the captain?" said Alexei.

"Captain Anatoly Zotoffka. The cruiser will be the command ship for the squadron and will have a vice admiral on board. He is Grigory Kochenkov. Perhaps you know him, since you attended the Naval Academy."

"I do sir. He is a fine officer" said Alexei.

The captain nodded. Gathering his papers, he said, "Good luck. Do your duty. Dismissed."

***

Having received their orders, Alexei and Politovsky boarded a train for the naval base of Libou on the Black Sea. They were amazed at the frenzied activity at the port. Everywhere people hustled about, a wave of patriotism and the call to arms having energized the populace. Antipathy toward the regime had seemingly disappeared overnight with the Japanese attack on Port Arthur. Widespread support for the Tsar was palpable.

The two lieutenants were surprised that workers as well as members of the elite were eager to shake their hand and wish them well. A band played marching songs as troops boarded trains for the long journey east. Upon seeing Alexei and Igor, the musicians struck up a jaunty navel tune. A chorus of voices shouted, "God save the Tsar" and "Exterminate the Godless Asian monkeys!"

To Alexei's ear the jingoism and boundless confidence was very unsettling. "Asian monkeys," he thought, hardly included Kimi-san, Itomo or their father. Now he was expected to inflict horrible damage upon them and their nation. Though pleased to have been recalled from exile and again be wearing an officer's uniform, he had grave misgivings.

"You seem to know the admiral rather well," said Politovsky as they surveyed the cruiser they were about to board.

"I was supposed to marry his daughter," said Alexei, as he appraised the guns of the warships main batteries.

"You never spoke to me about that before. Apparently, you didn 't marry her."

"She died the day we were to be wed."

I'm sorry. It must have affected you deeply." When Alexei remained silent, Igor said, "On a different subject, you once said that your father is involved with the foreign office. Do you think he'll come to see you off?"

"No, we have no desire to see one another," said Alexei.

"Well he must have influence with the Admiralty. I mean someone got us released. Do you think he had anything to do with that?"

"Absolutely not. Whether I live or die would be of no concern to him, and I'd rather not talk about him. I'm much more concerned about our ship."

"Because it's old?"

"Because it's obsolete. It's an armored cruiser for coastal defense and should never go to sea."

"So we stay in port?"

"You heard what the officer said. We're going to war." Alexei looked out the window, brooding.

***

The jubilation in Tokyo over the destruction of the Russian fleet at Port Arthur was tempered by dismay at the sinking of two Japanese battleships when they struck mines in the waters near Vladivostok. Both the *Hatsuse* and the *Yashima* went down on the same day in May 1904 with a great loss of life. The destruction of two capital ships was a shattering blow, but worse was to come.

Rumors were already circulating when Itomo came to his mother's house after returning from a lengthy patrol. Kyoko bowed as her son removed his shoes, then he accepted the green tea she offered him.

"Your sister and I, as well as the nation, are very proud of your heroic action at Port Arthur," she said in a quiet voice. "And we are pleased that you have been promoted and are safely home."

Itomo nodded and said, "I prayed at the Shrine of *Ise* and we were blessed in our endeavor. Nobody on my ship was injured. I thank you for your concern."

He stared into his *ocha* and said nothing for a long moment.

"Is it true?" Kimi-san said. "About father and..."

Itomo nodded. His mother put her hands to her face, her body bending forward with grief. Stoically Itomo stared into nothingness as Kimi put her arms around her mother.

"Atsugi-san's ship, the *Kinshu Maru,* was sailing toward the coast of Korea, transporting Father and his regiment. Regrettably, the ship had no naval escort. Apparently no one thought that the Russians would have any ships in the area. It was assumed that the remnants of their fleet were all in Port Arthur.

"Survivors said that the officers and crew refused to abandon the ship, even though it was being torn apart by enemy guns. Being a transport, it was only lightly armed and could put up little resistance, but the crews kept firing until the vessel sank. They said that men stood at attention at the railing and cheered for the nation. The survivors, four or five men, did not abandon their post; they were actually blown off the ship and washed ashore."

"And father and my husband?" said Kimi-san.

Itomo bowed his head and said, "They perished bravely. For the Emperor."

"For the Emperor and Japan," said madam Karamatsu quietly, tears in her eyes. She stood, bowed to her son, shuffled into her bedroom, and slid the shoji screen across the entrance. Then Kimi-san and Itomo heard sobs.

***

My husband is dead, Kimi-san said to herself, when only crickets disturbed the night. She lay on her futon with her infant son and came to the realization that she would never see Atsugi or her father again. They had both been military men, autocratic and absolute; but, she reflected, her father had truly cared for her. Her thoughts about Atsugi were terribly conflicted. That he might die in war for the Emperor had always been a possibility—a possibility, which after a particularly harsh beating, she had secretly prayed for. Now she was assailed by guilt. The man, her husband, was at the bottom of the sea.

It would be contemptible, she thought, to assail the memory of the man with recrimination. The beatings and reprimands he had dealt her must be forgotten. She must not sully his character or his bravery with her own resentment. She had been his wife, and if she had not been subservient enough, Japanese enough, it was entirely her fault. He, master of the house, had every right; indeed, it was his duty to punish her for ineptitude or defiance. Kimi-san sighed and thought that she should have the same tears for Atsugi-san as she did for her father. But no tears came.

Her feeling of guilt was compounded by relief. There would be no more beatings, no more ripping of her kimono to satisfy the man's terrifying lust. Now there would be silence. She was an honored war widow, and she would remain one for the rest of her life. What Japanese man would marry a widow with a child who did not look Japanese?

The war had, like the chill of winter, come home. The cherry blossoms of spring, the fanatical excitement of battle against a despised power, had become petals trampled underfoot and grim resolve to continue what the Emperor had begun. She could not imagine what battle must be like. There had been talk of victory, but nothing about carnage. Even now, to speak of losses was tantamount to treason.

She lay still and listened to a cricket. It was soon answered by another. A potential mate? Did the insects express longing, or was it just a biological compulsion to reproduce? The only love she'd ever had, besides for her family, was for a man who'd given her a child, a man her country would kill.

She thought about Alexei each day and night. She hadn't heard from him since she'd left England, and she'd come to the conclusion that she would never see him again. All she would ever have of Alexei was in their child. She must be content with that.

And now there was war. Would he be in it, she wondered? After all, he was a naval officer, and he might be on a Russian ship. For all she knew he might have been at Port Arthur and already dead. Or perhaps he'd been on the Russian ship that sank Atsugi-san's. Did he have something to do with killing her father and her husband? The thought made her shudder. No, that could not be.

Yet, what if Alexei should live? Wars don't last forever, she thought.

CHAPTER 26

Reval, Russia
October 1904

Alexei and Igor Politovsky spent the blustery morning of October ninth standing smartly at the railing, along with hundreds of enlisted bluejackets. The four battleships and several of the cruisers, including the *Mikhail III,* were to receive a visit from Emperor Nicholas II and his uncle, Grand Admiral Alexis, accompanied by officers of the Higher Naval Board, including fleet commander Admiral Zinovi Petrovitch Rozhestvensky and his second in command, Admiral von Felkerzam.

On the main deck, the diminutive, undemonstrative Tsar instructed the officers and crew to take vengeance on the insolent Japanese who had troubled the peace of Holy Russia and to uphold the glory of the Russian Navy. His appearance coincided with an announcement in the Fleet Bulletin that the Empress would create special religious objects for those ships having a chapel. Furthermore, the guns of the main batteries were to be sprinkled with Holy Water prior to engaging the enemy. Great cheers went up following the exhortations of the Tsar; he concluded by wishing the crews a victorious campaign and a happy return to Russia. The admirals were pleased to see that he was impressed by fleet preparations. The bluejacket crew had spent weeks painting and scrubbing each of the dozens of vessels.

That evening, after the Tsar began his return journey to St. Petersburg, there was a banquet on the battleship *Suvoroff* for officers of the fleet. "I hope they save some of the champagne for the voyage," said Igor, sizing up the food-laden tables in the ornate wardroom.

"I'm sure everything will be restocked before we sail," said Alexei. His stomach began to growl as he and others listened to speeches extolling the fighting capabilities of the ships. Then Captain Bukhvostoff of the battleship *Alexander III* took the podium. He waited for the applause to die down and, in a quiet voice, said, "All have stated that our brave sailors will smash the Japanese, but such talk indicates they don't know why we're going to sea. We know that Russia is not a sea power and that public funds on ship construction have been wasted."

Whatever small talk had been going on came to an abrupt halt. Igor looked at Alexei and raised an eyebrow. Some officers were seen to frown, but others nodded in agreement. The captain looked at the surprised audience and continued, "All wish us victory, but we know that there will be no victory. However, there is one thing we do know: we know how to die, and we shall never surrender."

There was a mixture of scattered applause and stunned silence. When he retired from the podium, it took several minutes for the officers to shake off their apprehension and return to the champagne-laden tables.

***

"What did you make of Bukhvostoff's speech?" Igor asked Alexei, as they stood on their ship's fantail later that night.

"I doubt he would have expressed those sentiments if the Tsar had been on board. It was honest of him, I'll give you that."

“It did little to buck up the mood. It was damn depressing and fatalistic, if you ask me,” said Politovsky.

The four battleships of the fleet were lit from stem to stern as bluejackets made final preparations for the next day’s sailing. “See them out there, so low in the water,” said Alexei. “They’re top heavy and can’t open their lower gun decks, not even in even a moderate sea; that reduces their fire power by half. They have ten- and twelve-inch guns, but they’re fired by lanyard, not electrically as in modern navies. Even now engineers are trying to change them over, but the gun crews won’t have time to train. We are well stocked with vodka, champagne, caviar and sturgeon, but we have no extra ammunition for practice firing.”

“I don’t know why you’re so gloomy, Alexei. We have a bigger fleet than the Japanese, and you saw how determined the men are. They’re excited! We’re going to do some real damage, you’ll see,” said Igor puffing on his cheroot. Tall, angular, with thick black hair, he was every inch the imperial officer. Alexei was amazed that the man had maintained his patriotism after five years in a prison camp.

“The men may be excited, but not one in ten is a real sailor. They’re recruited from peasant stock and get only half a year’s training because the Baltic ices up. They have no education or mechanical aptitude. I know this because I ran into my old friend Sergei, whom you met at Chita.”

“He’s on board?”

“Engine room. They made him a petty officer since he was at the Academy. He said that half the crew know nothing, and the others have obsolete knowledge.”

“But they will fight,” Igor persisted.

“I’ll let Sergei tell you about that,” said Alexei, lighting his own cigar. “It won’t be pretty.”

“I suspect it won’t be, but isn’t having Sergei on board a little disturbing?” said Politovsky. “He was and perhaps is still a revolutionary. I have a hard time understanding why the Admiralty put him in such a trusted position. And if we're going into battle..."

"He's older now. I suspect he just wants to get on with life. He's had plenty of time to do damage if he wanted to. But apparently he's proven himself and has been advanced in rank. He is an engineer, after all, and we certainly need men with his training."

"Trained, yes, but I'm still concerned, Alexei. It would be foolish for him to do anything destructive in port where the *Okhrana* is everywhere. But at sea there may be discontent; it has always existed on Russian ships. Given a chance, his old zeal could resurface, and that could mean trouble."

"I think this fleet is full of revolutionaries far more dangerous than Sergei."

"But you trust him?" Politovsky pressed on.

"At this point I have no reason not to; after all, any sabotage or rebellion will endanger this ship and his own life as well. Sergei is a survivor, Igor."

"Survivor, yes. But for whose cause? I, too, have been angry with the system, but I am still loyal. For all our sakes, I hope your friend is, too."

***

Impatient to get to sea, Admiral Rozhestvensky allowed only two weeks of tactical drill, during which many of his obsolete ships suffered breakdowns. One morning, before sunrise, he signaled the fleet to prepare for attack by enemy torpedo boats. "Did you see the signal from the flagship?" asked Politovsky when he encountered Alexei.

"Yes, it's action stations. We have steam up and we will be under way in minutes."

"We should go to our guns," said Igor, starting for the six-pounder armament entrusted to them.

The two officers marshaled their crews and watched for movement in the fleet. There was none. The order from

Admiral Rozhestvensky was signaled again, but no other vessel showed signs of life; not even a single searchlight was turned on.

"Why isn't something happening?" said Igor.

"Because everyone's asleep," replied Alexei, cynically but accurately.

"The entire fleet should be at battle stations by now," said Politovsky with disgust. "This is unbelievable! We'll hear about it later. You know what a disciplinarian Rozhestvensky is."

"Oh, we'll hear about it, all right," said Alexei, directing his men to stand down.

***

Following a severe tongue-lashing by the fleet's commander, coaling and provisioning continued apace; at last, before a delegation of dignitaries, the fleet weighed anchor. Led by the four battleships, the armada began the voyage through the narrow channel at Kronstadt. The *Kniaz Suvoroff,* massing fifteen thousand tons, its decks nearly awash with provisions, was followed by the flagship *Borodino,* then *Alexander III* and the *Oryol,* whose crew hadn't ascertained the channel's depth. The majestic procession was suddenly marred as the *Oryol* plowed into the channel's muddy floor.

"Look what they're doing," laughed Politovsky as the *Mikhail III* passed abeam.

Alexei and Igor were joined by bluejackets as the crew of the battleship ran from starboard to port and leaned against the side in a futile attempt to free the huge ship from the mud. Only the next day did the effort of tugs allow the *Oryol* to sail and rejoin the fleet.

***

"Have you heard the latest?" Politovsky asked. He and Alexei were in the cruiser's wardroom; the fleet was approaching the coast of Denmark. "The Japanese have sent submarines along our route. It's true; they have suicide patrols just waiting for us. European newspapers say that we should expect an attack any day. Everybody is nervous."

"Then we'll have to bed down at the guns," said Alexei. "There won't be much of a warning if it's submarines. But I wonder how they would get here? They're tiny and can't sail more than one or two hundred miles at best."

"They can be carried on battleships, then set into the water at night. One or two torpedoes and we're in trouble. Every ship is on alert," said Igor. "And the crews are more superstitious than ever. Anything will set them off."

The following day the captains were told that on no account must any foreign vessel be allowed to sail amongst the fleet. That evening an alarming message was flashed that Japanese torpedo boats had been spotted. It was further reported that strange, silvery spheres in the night sky were enemy observation balloons studying the formation of the fleet.

That night a heavy fog rolled in, and foghorns blared on every ship. Repeatedly awoken by bellowing sounds, the crews slept fitfully. Word was passed that the supply vessel *Kamchatka* had spotted Japanese destroyers, but there was confusion as to how many there were. Tension increased as the fleet sailed along the Dogger Bank. An hour and a half passed; then across the water bugles and drums sounded and frantic orders were barked on each ship.

Shells were loaded into heavy guns and crew stood anxiously by. Suddenly the battleship *Suvoroff* fired flares and the *Borodino* commenced firing with its main battery. Its cannonade was followed by that of every ship in the fleet. Shells from the heavy guns streamed outward from the massed vessels, narrowly missing other ships in the fleet.

Fearful of being struck by their own guns, captains ordered more steam, thus breaking formation. Sirens blared and signal lights were flashed, but great spouts of water still came dangerously close as excited gunners tried to find the range of enemy combatants.

"Where are they?" cried Alexei, as dozens of search lights illuminated the rolling sea.

"There, there!" pointed Politovsky, in command of the six-incher beside him. "They're all around us, they've penetrated the fleet!" he bellowed above the roar of a battleship's salvo.

Officers and bluejackets were shouting, racing to the guns, loading and firing as fast as they could. Shells streaked into the night, some falling only yards from the *Mikhail III*. There was pandemonium as ships turned to port or starboard, or tore ahead at flank speed. Gunners shouted for more shells when their mounts ran out of ammunition. Machine guns rattled, sending a fusillade of bullets into the night.

Hundreds of searchlights swiveled, their fingers of light crisscrossing one another, finally picking up targets only a thousand yards away.

"There they are!" shouted gunners, who redoubled their efforts. Great blasts of flame were followed by water spurts rising a hundred feet in the air. It seemed that the enemy was everywhere, but the shells began to find their mark. It was reported that Japanese ships had been struck. Now all guns were trained on the enemy, and jubilation swept the Russian fleet.

"We got them!" shouted Politovsky, as he joined in the loading of shells. A cry went up that Japanese cruisers were joining the battle and the gunnery intensified.

Suddenly a single beam from the Suvoroff aimed straight up; the signal to cease fire. Excited gunners could not believe the order; not all the targets had been sunk. Eventually searchlights were turned off and the ships became dark. Giddy with success, gunners proclaimed how many of the enemy ships they had hit during the twenty-minute engagement. The enthusiasm was electric, and the joy of total victory ran through every vessel. Pouring into the wardrooms, the officers toasted their magnificent victory over the Japanese. In ragged formation, the Second Pacific Fleet sailed unscathed into the night, leaving carnage behind.

Two days later, Alexei and Igor left the wardroom, following the posting of orders. "Do you know what concerns me?" said Politovsky.

"Not enough champagne?" said Alexei.

"Well, that could be a problem," Igor grinned. "No, what bothers me is that our ships fired hundreds if not thousands of shells, but we only sank one ship."

Politovsky appeared somber for a moment, then added, "I heard that the Japanese are supposed to be excellent shots, yet we did not lose a single ship. In fact, not one was even hit. Doesn't that surprise you, Alexei?"

***

There was near pandemonium in the St. Petersburg English Club as reporters exchanged notes and scanned European newspapers.

"Impossible! What indescribable stupidity!" bellowed a journalist waving *Le Monde* under the nose of William Stuart Jones. "And they didn't even stop to render assistance. Barbarians!"

"I suspect that they labored under a misapprehension," said Jones. "Not that I'm making excuses for them, old boy. But things can become quite confused in a night action."

"But the entire Russian fleet attacked the Gamecock fleet! Trawlers and fishing boats, for God's sake! They sank a trawler and killed and injured innocent fishermen!"

Another Englishman hurried in and excitedly gestured to a London paper, which referred to the catastrophe as the "Dogger Bank Incident." Shouting for silence he bawled, "Fleet Street says all of the United Kingdom is outraged. The *Standard* reports that the Royal Navy will teach the Russians a lesson. It goes on to say, 'Is this wretched Russian fleet with its inefficient admirals, peasant sailors and blundering navigators to be allowed to proceed?' Gentlemen," the man continued, "England is on the brink of war. Mediterranean and Channel fleets are preparing for battle. Twenty-eight battleships. The Russians may think they're going to fight the Japanese in Asia, but mark my words, they will never get past the English Channel!"

No apology came from Admiral Rozhestvensky; instead, there was an adamant claim that the fleet was most assuredly attacked by Japanese destroyers. Only when they arrived at Vigo on the Spanish coast did the admiral and his captains become aware of how close Britain was to declaring war. British cruisers lay outside the port; Whitehall was demanding a formal apology and the delivery of those responsible before the English fleet would depart.

The Tsar sent the admiral and the fleet a telegram proclaiming his confidence in them, but Rozhestvensky eventually issued a statement of condolence for the death of the fishermen. Demands for war ebbed, but contempt for the Russian fleet did not lessen. What did result was overwhelming British support for Japan and an absolute refusal to assist Russia in its war against a small, greatly maligned nation.

"Who are the men in that boat?" Alexei asked Politovksy, as they supervised the cleaning of their six-pounder guns.

"The sacrificial lambs, the ones to be put on trial for the night action. Three are lieutenants and the other is Captain Klado of the *Suvoroff*. The man is a narcissistic, pernicious fool. A real pain, and I bet the admiral is happy to get rid of him. Klado thinks he knows everything and makes no secret of it. He was in my class at the Artillery school and everyone hated him."

"Well, he's gone for now; but people like that have a habit of turning up again," mused Alexei.

"Perhaps. At least he's out of the fleet and can't do any damage."

"So you say."

CHAPTER 27

St. Petersburg

Countess Olga Brusilov sat at the table with seven other women in Madam Ravitchska's salon. The room was shadowed with heavy drapes, a damask table cloth, and dark wood paneling. A flickering oil lamp sat on the table and an anxious pall engulfed the ladies of the Russian elite. All except Madam Ravitchska held hands; she, her eyes closed, appeared to have fallen into a trance. On occasion she would mumble a few incoherent words or gasp, then submerge again into the whispered mysteries of the oracle.

As minutes passed the women glanced at one another with apprehension, their hands sweating in the close room, thick with the scent of tea and incense. Finally, as if rising to the surface of murky waters, the seer blinked, shook her head slowly and said, "The spirits say worrisome things. Such things as I would not reveal beyond this room."

An hour later, Olga hurried home.

A fervent longing to embrace the souls of the dead had gripped the aristocracy with spellbinding religiosity. Hanging on every word, every nuance, believers listened to prophesies and passed them on with utmost conviction. "I must tell you what she said," blurted the countess, when she saw her husband in the drawing room.

Count Brusilov swirled his cognac and looked at her dispassionately. "What poisonous nonsense did that charlatan prophesize this time?"

"She's hardly a charlatan. All of her predictions have come true. Even members of the court seek her out."

Yevgeny made a face and with an exasperated sigh said, "So what did she say?"

"That we will lose the war, our ships will be sunk, and thousands will drown."

"Really? A great armada of over forty ships will be destroyed by those monkeys? Preposterous. What's more, I would not spread defeatist and alarming rumors. You should know better."

"You are so reprehensible, so pompous. I am afraid for Alexei."

"He chose to be an officer in the Tsar's navy. He will fare as well as all the rest, and you shouldn't worry."

"But I do."

Yevgeny, half under his breath said, "I still can't understand why they reinstated him and put him on board one of our ships." Then he shouted, "In my mind he's still a criminal!"

"Not Alexei. The only criminal is you!"

"Woman, you are disloyal and a disgrace. But you are of no consequence; the Tsar's endeavor is in God's hands."

"And the Japanese are not in God's hands?" Olga retorted.

"They do not have a god; they have senseless myths and our God has forsaken them. It is they who shall bleed. But if you are so worried you should go to St. Isaac's and pray for your dear son. Perhaps the faker Madam Ravitchska is there, too."

But instead of going to St. Isaac's, Olga Brusilov went to her room, lit two candles, said the Shabbat prayers and wept.

***

Determined to mold his ships into a true fighting fleet, Admiral Rozhestvensky scheduled fleet maneuvers whenever possible. Invariably he would be reduced to a fuming, disgusted wreck by day's end, as captains misread his signals or could not properly command their ships. He ordered practice fire, but rarely with live ammunition, since munitions were already depleted and they could not be restocked.

Alexei and Politovsky had been aiming their six-pounders at towed targets when a loud crash and screams came from the deck below.

"Secure the gun," ordered Alexei, then he bolted down the gangway and descended to hell.

Steam billowed from the after boiler room, reddened by a lurid glow, and a wave of intense heat struck Alexei, making him gasp. Scalding water spurted from broken pipes as the ship bucked in a running sea. Pieces of jagged metal had been blown across the compartment, resulting in hideous injuries. Alexei could taste the vaporized blood in the air, and everywhere he looked hideous sights assaulted his senses. The crewmen with severe burns were being lead or carried to the ship's infirmary; two were sobbing from the pain, another seemed dazed, a fourth screamed and thrashed.

Alexei found Sergei pulling stricken men from the boiler room. "What caused it?" he demanded, apprehensive that Sergei may have triggered the explosion himself as an act of sabotage.

"She's old! The boilers are junk, and there's too much pressure. Something had to give. We've been at nine knots for too long. That's what it is, that's *all* it is Alexei, despite what you might think. This tub is a wreck!"

"But she should be able to do twenty," Alexei protested.

"When she was new. You won't get twelve out of her now."

The *Mikhail III* skewed out of line. With only one working boiler she slowed to five knots and wallowed drunkenly in the heavy troughs. Biting back his intense frustration, Captain Zotoffka ordered her back to port.

The following morning the ship's officers were called to the wardroom. The mood was dour; there were no refreshments and little talk. Captain Zotoffka stood impatiently at the front of the wardroom. Not a particularly affable man, he now stood tense and unsmiling, holding a clutch of papers.

"These pages were printed on this ship. They are insidious and violent propaganda inciting insurrection and treason! They were discovered by my flag officer shortly after we sailed. Need I remind you that we are not on some training excursion? We are going to war, and any attempt to dissuade the crew of the righteousness of our mission is contemptible."

There was an undercurrent of voices, some surprised, others less so.

Shredding the papers, Zotoffka shouted, "Such inflammatory filth will not be tolerated! Those responsible for this will be found and punished with utmost severity. Anything that reduces the fighting efficiency of the Pacific Fleet, and specifically this vessel, is an outrage and a strike against Holy Russia and the Tsar. A Russian revolution will not begin on my ship!"

A tall, portly figure entered the wardroom and an ensign abruptly barked, "Attention for the admiral."

Motioning for the meeting to continue, Admiral Kochenkov took a position against the rear bulkhead. After acknowledging his presence, Captain Zotoffka resumed. He was quieter, but white around the lips, and his hands were clenched. "It is the responsibility, no, the absolute duty of every officer to root out and help capture the perpetrators of mutiny. And that is an order, not just from me but from Admiral Rozhestvensky."

Alexei was thankful that the wardroom only admitted officers; Sergei, a noncommissioned officer, was denied entry. But what would Sergei's reaction have been, if he were responsible for the incendiary papers? Certainly Sergei was capable of directing production, but was he actually the printer? It was possible, but there was no proof, thought Alexei, and he wasn't about to make an accusation.

The captain studied his officers and in a less strident voice said, "Many of you might think that the boiler incident was a mishap. 'It's just an old ship, worn out,' some have said. That is not my opinion. It is hardly strange that it coincides with anti-Tsarist propaganda." Raising his voice again, he slammed his hand on the table and declared, "It was deliberate, I tell you! Men could have died and this vessel might have sunk. If such a thing had happened in battle we would have been an easy target, obliterated and sent to the bottom of the sea!"

There was a lengthy pause, then he said, "Fearing insurrection from the beginning, I cabled St. Petersburg for assistance. It was something I did because it had to be done. We have been waiting in port for a man's arrival, and he is now on board."

Captain Zotoffka's eyes met Alexei's and he said, "The officer is waiting outside the wardroom. Lieutenant Brusilov, you will usher him in."

Alexei opened the door, and with a brusque stride a man marched through the assembled officers and stood imperiously beside the captain.

"This is Boris Sokolov, serving the Tsar on behalf of the *Okhrana*. He wears the uniform of a common bluejacket and will appear as a steward, thus giving him access to the wardroom and every other part of this vessel. Though a civilian, you will regard him as an officer. You will not, under any circumstances, reveal his true identity to the crew. We sail immediately. Report to your duty stations. You are dismissed."

Captain Zotoffka left the wardroom, followed by all the officers except the admiral, Alexei, Igor and Boris Sokolov.

Alexei stood stock still; his eyes bored into Boris. Finally, Politovsky tugged on his sleeve and said, "It's time to go."

Boris stood apart and watched the silent departure. Then, approaching Admiral Kochenkov, he said, "Sir, I regret that I never had an opportunity to extend my condolences over the death of—"

"I don't need your condolences. I hold you accountable for her death."

Stunned by the rebuke, Sokolov bristled and said, "I have been accorded an officer's rank and will be treated as such. I work directly for my uncle, the Interior Minister and chief of —"

"I don't give a damn who your uncle is. If you recall, I threw you out of the Academy for lying. Threaten any of my officers or concoct false information, and I will consign you to the brig."

"That would be a violation of—"

But the admiral was already out the door.

Boris stared after him, rage contorting his featured. His right hand gripped a saber that was not there, and then his eyes narrowed.

***

"The Second Pacific Fleet *must* be reinforced," insisted Captain Nicholas Klado, addressing the armchair admirals in St. Petersburg after testifying before the Dogger Bank commission. Furious at being made the sacrificial goat of the

Dogger Bank incident, and carrying weight in the Admiralty due to family connections, he had demanded an audience.

"Reinforced with what ships, and why?" asked senior officers.

"With the remaining ships of the Baltic fleet! Every one of them. It's imperative."

"That's ridiculous," retorted a vice admiral. "The only ships remaining are obsolete. They are defense batteries at best, with ancient, short range guns. You're talking about an eighteen-thousand-mile journey on floating coffins. Why even suggest such a thing?"

"Targets. It's about targets. The more the Japanese have to shoot at, the more dispersed their fire. Gentlemen, we only have four battleships, and as it stands now all the enemy batteries will be directed at them. Our great ships need a diversion, and that means more targets."

"But we would be consigning thousands of sailors to certain death," exclaimed the astonished admiral. "Moreover, the Second Pacific Fleet will have to wait weeks, perhaps months for the Baltic fleet. They will exhaust their supplies holed up somewhere on the African coast. And what if the Japanese attack? It would be a repeat of what Nelson did to the Danish fleet at Copenhagen during the Napoleonic wars: destroy it at anchor."

"The Japanese fleet is patrolling the coast of Korea or standing off Port Arthur. Many, in fact, are being refitted and provisioned in Sasebo. Sir, there is little chance of defeating the Japanese with the Second Pacific Fleet alone. We must send a Baltic reinforcing fleet. Even the editors of the ,*Novoe Vremya* agree."

"But it's suicide," said one of the admirals.

"No, it's murder," another murmured, *sotto voce*. Then he said, "We knew it was from the beginning. So what's the difference? The Tsar will say it was in God's hands and dismiss the whole thing."

Orders were issued. The rusted ships were given new paint, and peasant "sailors" were conscripted, as all the trained ones were already assigned to Rozhestvensky's squadron. With provisions aboard, a dispirited farewell saw the aging vessels put to sea.

***

For reasons unknown to the officers and crew, ports of call were never announced in advance by Admiral Rozhestvensky. The fleet would, after numerous breakdowns and mishaps, arrive in one port or another. Only the colliers with their tons of coal knew where to expect the fleet.

Shadowed and harassed by British cruisers, the fleet crawled past the Straits of Gibraltar to Morocco and entered the port of Tangier.

"This is disgusting," said Politovsky, attempting to brush coal dust off his once immaculate jacket.

"Orders from Rozhestvensky. We must take on every ounce of coal the colliers bring us. You saw the instructions; every bunker, every cabin, every passageway. Everywhere that won't interfere with the operation of the ship," replied Alexei.

"It's inhumane. The dust is choking the crew, and they're falling with heat exhaustion. It's one hundred and twenty degrees and they've been hauling coal since dawn. The men are usually cheerful, or at least indifferent to hard work, but now they're angry, Alexis. Very angry, and some are refusing to work."

"The admiral said he would put the ringleaders in a dingy and set them adrift," said Alexei, as he and Igor moved aside for exhausted bluejackets hauling coal.

"The ships are sitting too low again. Look at the *Suvoroff* and the *Borodino*. Even *Oryol's* main deck is only a foot above the water. We can't fight like this; we'll capsize in even a moderate sea."

"Get used to it. We're the only European power that has no coaling stations. Who knows how far we sail until we're coaled again? We've got to take on everything we can. But I hate it."

The dust permeated food and lungs and fouled the ships. Tempers flared in the heat and drenching humidity. Sailors collapsed, were revived, and ordered to continue on.

With the occasional exception of the French, only Kaiser Wilhelm completely endorsed the Russian efforts. That allowed the Pacific Squadron to anchor in German Southwest Africa. It was the only place to refuel before their voyage around the Cape and across the Indian Ocean to Madagascar.

Boris Sokolov, in his guise as a steward, moved among the men, schooling his arrogant face into impassivity, yet he listened to everything. Again and again he overheard sailors curse the endless sailing, but every time he approached an angry sounding conversation, the voices died to sullen silence; there was something about this bluejacket who no one knew or vouched for that put them on their guard. Perhaps it was the way he stood and walked in a military manner, was a little too arrogant and answered officers in a voice too much like their own. He never spat or made bawdy remarks or used improper language. He was an enigma who appeared and disappeared at will. No order was ever given to him nor any onerous duties.

Those who denounced incompetent officers, would turn away from him, wary and distrusting. But there were others who would stare him down, daring him to say anything.

Sokolov despised the lot of them, foul smelling peasants who would hastily shove a bottle of vodka into a shirt when he approached. Illicit money bet on a card game would be swept off a table, muttering and contemptuous whispers made as he walked past. And more than once came the venomous question, "And just who the hell are you?"

Derision would follow any answer so he retreated into hateful silence. Even bawdy jokes and saturnine melodies on an accordion would abruptly cease. In clusters the crew would lay about the decks, smoking or sleeping off the night's drunkenness. He would be forced to step over them, often slipping in urine or vomit. He knew that these vermin, these peasants, were the antithesis of everything that he stood for as a loyal servant of the *Okhrana*.

A shudder went through him every time he encountered Sergei. The *michman* would nod, smile, even jauntily whistle as if they were both fellow travelers on a summer cruise. And, yet, Sokolov could sense the knife's cold steel plunging into his back. Yes, he thought, the man was plotting and scheming for just the right time. He could so vividly imagine the *michman* slaughtering his way into the officer's wardroom accompanied by dozens of bayonet wielding, demonic revolutionaries.

Assailed by self-righteous indignation, he loathed the unadorned and besotted clothing of the common sailor. His honored position as an investigator of subversion entitled him to wear the uniform of an officer, indeed, one with shoulder boards and a brimmed cap emblazoned with the Tsar's double eagle.

His contempt for everybody around him eventually settled into endless days and nights of dyspeptic melancholy. One stultifying night, alone and wary, he left the ship and began to wander the burgeoning slums of Tangier, ignoring the hundreds of intoxicated bluejackets and officers. He stopped in front of a brothel, its doors flung open and inviting. The smoke-filled interior was crowded and filled with boisterous polluted men and whores ascending and descending a precipitous stair case to rooms above. Their progress was accompanied by encouraging hoots and shouts.

Lascivious grins followed as seamen ascending the stairs lifted the dresses of women to display the prize awaiting them.

A combination of revulsion and envy flooded Sokolov. His eyes scanned the women who laughed and peddled their wares around tables overfilled with half-drained bottles of spirits. Many of the harlots had nested on the laps of bluejackets. Several women had found a table apart where three disheveled ensigns, jackets unbuttoned and hats askew, were caressing breasts that were willingly offered.

Boris Sokolov stared and felt a sudden rampaging need for what he had not had for so long. A woman, not particularly young or attractive, ambled down the stairs rearranging her dress while wiping away an undefinable stain. With sudden lust, Boris pulled a wad of rubbles from a pocket and dashed for the stairs. He had not expected to require money, in fact he agonized over taking it, knowing that so doing would simply encourage temptation. But some intangible hunger demanded it. Now he thrust the rubbles at the woman, clutched her hand and fairly sprinted up the stairs to the door of an open room.

The entire mad, grunting and ravaging event was over within minutes. The woman laughed derisively while stuffing the money into a box and locking if with an ancient iron key. Panting and drained, Sokolov, his body smeared with feculent and odorous corruption, stumbled out of the brothel and into the torpid night. His mind reeled with disgust as he absently wormed his way through crowded streets and back alleys filled with the stink of feces and vomit.

Stumbling, he felt tears welling up. He gagged on the stench and a fetid, bitter taste filled his mouth. Dazed and lunging to the dock he was about to haul himself up the gangplank when he suddenly came to an abrupt halt. Arms crossed, eyes peering at him, a man stood in his way. Sokolov first focused on the man's spotless shoes, then his sharply creased trousers. His eyes moved glacially and warily upwards as one would scan a dangerous precipice. An officer's white jacket came into view and then the face of Alexei Brusilov.

Dully, recognition entered Boris's mind. Involuntarily he heard himself half whisper, "Oh," as if he had incorrectly opened the wrong door, the one leading to purgatory. The figure before him appeared immobile. It evaluated him and judged him, as if to say nothing so venal should be allowed on the Tsar's ship of state.

The eyes bored into him and for a moment Boris considered running away. Then Kochenkov raised his brows, motioned and moved to the side as if to avoid a filthy, petulant child, allowing Sokolov to edge past. At the top of the gangway Boris turned and made an attempt to straighten. Eyes stinging, he saw Alexei slowly shake his head.

"I hate you and I will kill you," said Boris, words hoarse in is throat. Then he turned and entered the dark passageway toward his bunk in the bowels of the *Mikhail III*.

CHAPTER 28

With the coaling completed, the fleet again set out to sea. The voyage was monotonous until the storm hit.

Thick, black smoke roiled from ship's funnels as Admiral Rozhestvensky attempted vainly to organize his ships into line-ahead columns. The wind rose as the sun settled below the horizon, obscured by dense clouds, and by dark enormous swells of water crashing over the fleet. If the ships bows had not been turned into the raging sea, many would have plummeted to the ocean depths.

With search lights blazing and fog horns blaring, the vessels scattered, fearful of colliding with one another. Frantic signals from the *Suvoroff* did nothing to bring the fleet together. On each ship, men were tossed from their bunks and thrown into bulkheads. Others were forced to dodge sacks of coal on tilting decks. Many sacks, ripping open, spewed their contents into passageways, among machinery, and down gangways.

The compartments were a cauldron of humidity and choking dust. Sea water poured in from ventilation funnels until they were sealed, the salt water mixing with the coal to make a terrible smelling soup through which men sloshed and waded. Hatches leaked water as the vessels plunged into troughs, their upper masts and yards barely visible in the driving rain.

"This will go on all night," yelled Politovsky over the storm, observing a bag of coal fly out to sea.

"And perhaps tomorrow," said Alexei as he set out for the engine room, mindful of an additional responsibility which Admiral Kochenkov had assigned him.

"You will be my eyes and ears on this ship," he had said. "I have the utmost contempt for Sokolov, but I must know if there is insurrection. There have been riots on the *Oryol* and that can infect the fleet."

"Why not the flag officer or Lieutenant Politovsky? They outrank me."

"I know you and I trust you. I'm aware of the odds we face against the Japanese, and I don't care to increase them by allowing sedition to go unchecked. Sokolov wants to see men executed; you will tell me quietly if there is trouble, and I may be able to deal with it." He sighed, then added, "I have been entrusted with command of the cruisers and I intend to fight. We may lose, but I must save every man possible. I need your help."

"And you shall have it, sir."

Tons of coal had shifted and the *Mikhail III* was listing four degrees to port. Bluejackets slipped and splashed through ankle-deep water, repositioning sacks to right the list.

His uniform soaked, Alexei found Sergei supervising repairs to valves as the stern rose and fell in the violent sea. Taking him by the shoulder Alexei said, "I must speak with you, it's urgent."

"Can't it wait?"

"No. I can't tell you in front of the men," he said as a team of sailors lurched past.

Motioning with his head, Sergei ushered Alexei into a storage room illuminated by a single overhead bulb.

"You could be in serious danger," Alexei began.

"So? I'm always in danger."

"You must not reveal this to anybody, and I shouldn't be telling you, but Sololov is on board this ship as the captain's spy. He's *Okhrana*, posturing as a steward, and he knows about the revolutionary tracts—the ones being read by the crew. Zotoffka ripped them up in front of us, and the officers are to report any subversion directly to him. It must stop."

"It won't stop. This crew begs for revolution."

"But we're going into battle! If there's mutiny, what chance do we have?"

"What chance have we anyway?" demanded Sergei, exhausted from the intense heat. "I appreciate you telling me, Alexei. You've always been a friend. But it's beyond us. Does anybody else know that you've warned me?"

"No but you're putting me in a terrible bind. Admiral Kochenkov ordered me to be his personal investigator. I'm supposed to report anything suspicious before Boris finds out. Kochenkov is trying to save the men. I'm sure you don't want to see them die. Do you really think the revolution will be advanced if this ship is sent to the bottom by sabotage or mutiny?"

Putting his hands on Sergei's shoulders, Alexei said vehemently, "Damn it, Sergei, village peasants don't give a shit about the navy! For them it's all about bread and land. Most have never seen an ocean, much less a warship. Let these poor souls live."

"The sons and husbands of those village peasants are on this ship. They will care."

"So what do we do when we're being blown to bits by the Japanese?"

"We drown, Alexei. That's what we do. We drown."

Alexei slowly shook his head. "I can't let that happen, Sergei. We may die in battle but the men will prefer that to sabotage. It would at least be honorable."

"So exactly what are you going do?"

"What I have to. I am sorry, but you give me no choice."

***

"The ringleader of the revolutionaries has been identified and this officer is to be commended," said the captain to Kochenkov, while shaking Alexei's hand.

"Is it the one I suspected?" asked the admiral.

"Yes, Sergei Vershinin. I was hoping that it was not him. We are, or should I say, we used to be friends," said Alexei.

"So, you knew him? Asked Zotoffka.

"Yes sir. We were at the Naval Academy together. In fact, we were both on the fencing team."

"Naval Academy? But the man is not an officer, he is a senior enlisted, a *michman*!" said the captain.

"I had him expelled," Kochenkov interjected.

"A matter of character or honor?"

"It was not a matter of honor," said the admiral.

The captain's eyebrows shot up and he tilted his head.

"He was accused of revolutionary activity," said Kochenkov. "But it was never proven. Nevertheless, I was required to expel him."

"And that was his punishment?"

"He spent time in Siberia and the Admiralty Court sentenced him to life on board ship as a common sailor. He'd had a fine education, so naturally rose to petty officer, but I did not know he was on board," said the admiral.

"So I have a revolutionary on my ship in a position of responsibility. Very interesting, and extremely distressful," said Zotoffka. "But now he won't be able to influence anybody else."

The four-by-eight-foot cage was claustrophobic. Sergei sat on a wooden bench and stared at his feet.

"I told you that I had no choice," Alexei said. "This is best, at least for now. You are only suspect but everything is circumstantial. There is nothing directly connecting you to the propaganda," said Alexei.

"And you have stuck me in this God-damned cage," fumed Sergei.

"For your own good. You would be in much greater trouble if Boris found out. Do you remember what he did in St. Petersburg before he had any real power? Now whatever happens on this ship is not your fault," argued Alexei.

"So I should thank you," said Sergei sarcastically.

"Sergei Ivanovich, I'll have you released when we go into battle, as long as you don't sink the ship," Alexei said.

"Don't bother, we'll all die together, martyrs for the revolution," said Sergei. His face lit up with an angelic smile.

***

"Wardroom. Captain's orders!" Politovsky called out. Beckoning Alexei to follow, he hurried up the gangway.

The fleet, its belching stacks staining the clear blue sky, had departed the French port of Sainte Marie off Madagascar. Moments later, the officers assembled before Zotoffka for the second time in three days.

"I just received a message from Admiral Rozhestvensky. Because of its possible effect on morale, the information should not to be disseminated to the crew. This morning one of our reconnaissance vessels returned from the port of Tamatave with dire news. Many of you know of Meter Hill 203, which overlooks the city and harbor of Port Arthur. Our brave army has been fighting the Japanese over that hill for months. Unfortunately, it has fallen to the enemy with great loss of life. French papers indicate that the port itself is within days of falling, and the Pacific Fleet at anchor has been destroyed."

Captain Zotoffka stood silently and watched the mute faces of his officers.

"Sir," asked the flag officer, "our mission was to relieve the port and add to the weight of the Pacific Fleet. Since that is now impossible, are we sailing back to St. Petersburg?"

"No. The Tsar expects us to destroy the Japanese Navy wherever we find it. We will have the additional support of the Baltic Fleet."

There was stunned silence. "But captain, the Baltic Fleet will not join us for months, and it is obsolete, worthless," retorted the flag officer.

"That is apparently of no consequence to the Admiralty. Our rendezvous with the Baltic fleet is not your decision or mine," said Zotoffka abruptly. A short, rotund man with a continuous frown, the captain stared down his flag officer. Then he said, "We have orders from Admiral Rozhestvensky concerning our readiness for action. There will be a final live fire exercise before we meet the Japanese. Our target and that of all battleships and cruisers will be two unoccupied atolls. We shall pass them shortly. The *Mikhail* will be to the port and behind the battleship *Borodino*. Behind her will be the battleship *Oslyabya* and to her starboard will be the cruiser *Svetlana*. We will be making speed, main batteries will concentrate on the atoll to our port side. It is important that we retain our position since the battleship will also be engaged. The six-pounders, for use against close in torpedo boats, will not be firing." Turning to a lieutenant Kirdan, he said, "Listen sharp for commands in steerage. We will be making a five degree turn to starboard as we pass the atolls."

There was sudden movement. Boris Sokolov burst in, shoving his way past startled officers.

"Captain, he is gone!"

Angry at the interruption, Zotoffka said, "Who is gone?"

"The man in the brig. The *michman*, Sergei Vershinin. He escaped!"

"Then find him and chain him to the bars. I don't have time for this," snapped an exasperated Zotoffka. "To action stations. All of you!"

CHAPTER 29

Frantic, Boris rushed from the main deck down the gangway to the engine room. Ignoring the stares of bluejackets, he peered into compartments, peeled away tarpaulins to look beneath them, shouting, "Has anyone seen the *michman*, Sergei Vershinin?

Seamen shook their heads or waved him away. Who was this rating to be running about the ship like an idiot when all were at battle stations?

***

"You said the cell was locked. So how did he get out of the brig?" Kochenkov questioned Alexei.

"I don't know. Either someone slipped him a key or—"

"So now he's loose on the ship," interrupted the admiral.

"He's only one man, and it's only pamphlets. He's—"

"He's not just a printer. He knows the critical machinery on this ship. He could disable more effectively than anyone! You *must* find him."

"Yes, sir. I think I know where he might be," said Alexei, turning to leave the bridge.

"Lieutenant," Kochenkov called after him, "This is not about friendship. Use your pistol if you have to. It's imperative. Take four trusted men and find him."

Four trusted men, thought Alexei. Trusted to fight the Japanese, yes, but who were the revolutionaries and what help would they be? Hurrying past the second of the four smoke stacks he saw Politovsky and made his way over. “The admiral told me to find Sergei. Have you seen him?”

“No. I heard he was in the brig.”

“Not anymore.”

Alexei was heading to the lower gun deck when Politovsky glanced to starboard and said, “The *Borodino* is slowing. At this speed we will be in her firing line.”

“Captain Zotoffka will slow our ship. I have to go below,” said Alexei as he started down the ladder.

“We’re not slowing; we’re turning hard to starboard. We’re crossing the battleship’s stern,” said Igor, frowning.

“He’ll straighten us out.”

“But he’s increased speed, Alexei.”

“Because the *Oslyabya* is behind us. He wants to get out of her way.”

From the bridge, lookouts could see the main battery of the battleships *Suvoroff* and *Oryol* fire on the atoll. The first shells plunged into the water, but then the elevation was corrected and the next rounds exploded upon the outcrop, sending rock and shrapnel skyward. A cheer went up from those who witnessed it, but gunnery practice was not on Alexei’s mind as he dashed to the boiler room. Stokers, bare to the waist in one-hundred-and-twenty-degree heat, shoveled coal into the red-hot furnaces.

Hurrying through, Alexei slammed a water-tight door behind him, escaping the intense heat. He descended another ladder to a catwalk above the steering compartment. His eyes adjusted to the dim light and the rudder machinery below.

From his vantage point, Alexei could see Lieutenant Kirdan in a heated argument with Sergei, who clutched a heavy chain. They were pushing and shoving each other on the narrow platform several feet above gears and pistons.

Then from the shadows, Boris appeared on the opposite end of the catwalk. Seeing the *mishman* he dashed forward, brandishing a heavy pipe.

"Sergei!" Alexei shouted, as Boris swung the piece of steel. Instinctively Sergei took a step to the side, and the pipe slammed into Lieutenant Kirdan. The man clutched his head and fell forward, colliding with Boris. Knocked off balance, Boris grabbed for the safety rail, but he stumbled and pitched over the catwalk, falling heavily into the machinery below. Struggling to his knees, he drew his pistol and fired at Sergei, but the revolutionary ducked, then dashed down the stairs, tossing the chain into the rudder gears. Grinding, then shattering, the connecting cables tore apart, freezing the rudder in a starboard position. As the cruiser continued its hard turn, coal spilled onto the decks, increasing the list.

Boris, thrown off balance, tried to stand. Sergei was nowhere to be seen, but Alexei was still on the catwalk, cradling Lieutenant Kiran, whose blood ran onto the deck below. There was a crack, then another, as Boris fired upward, the rounds piercing pipes above Alexei's head, the echoes of the shots rebounding. When he saw that he'd failed to hit his enemy, Boris struggled to his feet and pulled himself up the gangway.

Three ratings, alarmed by the ship's relentless turn, dashed into the steerage compartment but froze when they saw rudder cables strewn about the deck.

"Up here, help this man," shouted Alexei, as he laid the lieutenant against the bulkhead. Then, after assessing the extent of the damage to cables and rudder, he ran for the gangway leading to the main deck.

Boris, pistol in hand, emerged from below and limped past the stern turret. He looked wild and disheveled in a torn, begrimed bluejacket's uniform, and when he shouted at the seamen to enlist them in his search they ignored him, their attention on what lay directly ahead. Boris aimed his pistol at a horrified sailor and shouted, "I need an officer! Have you seen an officer?"

The man shook his head but pointed to the bridge. Boris looked up, frantically waved an arm to Captain Zotoffka, just visible on the external flying bridge. Not getting any response, he hobbled forward.

Alexei found Politovsky, a worried look on his face as he came from the aft gun.

"I just saw Boris holding a pistol," said Igor.

"He shot at me, but that's not the problem. Sergei sabotaged the ship!"

"Is that why we're still heeling to starboard? Can it be corrected?"

"No, the steering cables are severed and the machinery is broken."

"Look, the *Svetlana* is attempting to turn away, but I do not think she has room!" exclaimed Igor, his face paling.

Alexei's attention was drawn from the *Svetlana,* still in the path of the *Mikhail,* to the bridge where Boris, standing beside the captain, was frantically gesturing astern. The admiral, seeing the *Svetlana* belching smoke and bearing down on them and how the *Mikhail's* continuous turn was putting them in the path of collision, dashed into the bridge housing. The distance between the ships narrowed, and now the stern of the *Svetlana* was only yards away. Sailors, mouths agape, ran in disbelief as sirens blared.

"Move!" shouted Politovsky. He, Alexei, and a dozen bluejackets retreated from the rail. Moving steadily in its ninety-degree turn, the cruiser's yardarms splintered as they raked the *Svetlana's* signal masts. Next there was the terrible sound of the buckling of steel and a shuddering impact as the *Mikhail* slammed into the *Svetlana's* stern. The *Svetlana* spun broadside to the *Mikhail* as the two damaged vessels struggled passed one another. Seamen on both ships staggered with the violent crash, but many on the *Mikhail* turned to gaze at what appeared to be imminent doom.

Alexei, seeing the men's terror, looked between the stacks and cried out, "My God, it's the *Oslyabya*!"

At full speed the great battleship loomed two hundred yards behind the *Mikhail.* Dark smoke roiled from her forward mounts as she fired on the atoll. Moments later her guns ceased and signal flags were run up her masts. Alexei heard the wailing of its sirens as the battleship's bow wave tore through deep blue swells.

"She's going to cut us in two," cried a terrified Politovsky.

But then, heeling hard to port, the great battleship rose from the waves, exposing its protruding steel ram. Alexei glimpsed Sergei, standing transfixed beside a silent gun. For a spellbinding moment nobody moved. Alexei thought it was as if an enormous building was falling and people in utter disbelief could not move their legs. Then the spell broke and men rushed to the bow, ready to jump into the sea.

Sailors on the *Oslyabya* sped aft or frantically ascended gangways. Signals flashed from her, demanding that the *Mikhail* alter course. That captain Zotoffka would endanger his ship as well as others in the fleet was unimaginable! Though vessels of the squadron could rarely form up and minor collisions had occurred, something as potentially catastrophic as this had never happened.

The battleship, with what seemed glacial sluggishness, continued its turn to port, missing the *Mikhail* by ten yards. Crews on the *Oslyabya* stared down on the low-lying cruiser, and those on the *Mikhail* crossed themselves as the battleship, propellers churning, slid past.

Moments later, Boris Sokolov, followed by a dozen sailors with bayoneted rifles, spilled onto the deck. From amidships Alexei saw the men peer around guns, scamper up ladders and prod tarpaulins in search of the saboteur. Accompanied by the flag officer, Boris brandished his revolver as he directed bluejackets to check one possible hiding place after another. Men stood aside and stared at the rating who had masqueraded as a steward. Now there was no need for pretense, and Boris made sure that all recognized his authority.

"Where is he? You know, I'm sure of it!" shouted Boris, striding up to Alexei. Then he saw the pistol in Alexei's hand —it was aimed at him.

"I don't know where he is. But I do know that this is the second time you've tried to kill me. I have every right to shoot you here and now."

"That is a lie!" Boris shouted for all to hear. "I fired at the traitor! You are the one who protected him! He is a murderer, and anyone who aids him is a traitor as well! But I will find him. I promise you that. And then we'll see what happens."

The flag officer, unsure how to proceed, looked first at Alexei, then at Boris, and stepped back. Without another word, Sokolov spun on his heel and hastened from the deck.

***

The ship reversed engines and slowed to a stop two miles behind the fleet. Captain Zotoffka and the admiral inspected the damaged steering equipment and signaled for the supply ship *Zamchatka* to tow them back to port. Repair crews were immediately put to work.

Officers in the wardroom spoke in hushed tones about the near disaster. There was much speculation about how many saboteurs there were and what they might do when the ship encountered the Japanese.

***

The note placed on the carriage of the six-pounder only said, "Bilge, forward." Alexei still held the note as he turned on his flashlight and worked his way to the ship's lowest deck. Ankle-deep water sloshed over his shoes as the ship wallowed in harbor swells. A smell of brine, coal dust and timber permeated the bowels of the cruiser. Silently Alexei moved through a labyrinth of material, the light picking out objects not touched in years.

"Over here," called Sergei in a low voice. He sat behind a generator, a pistol beside him.

"You really intended to sink this ship," said Alexei.

"It will be sunk anyway. Here or there. Sunk here would mean survivors."

"Damn few, and you know it. Exactly how would this be good for the revolution?" inquired Alexei, standing on a box as seawater sloshed around him.

"You throw enough rocks onto a mound and it becomes a hill. Throw more and you have a mountain. It adds up, until there's an avalanche. Then the morass below is swept away."

It's claustrophobic down here, thought Alexei. The air was foul and damp, and his friend's logic, not to mention the analogy, seemed mired in callous arrogance. "It's all in God's hands," the Tsar would say; and nothing, not even the obliteration of his entire navy, would change anything. The futility was obvious; why couldn't Sergei see that?

There was a long interlude and Sergei, seemingly miles away, said, "Alexei, we had a good time fencing all those years ago, didn't we? We were the best at the Academy. Kochenkov thought so. I wish..."

Alexei let out a sigh and said, "Sergei, they're looking for you. I was looking for you. What are you going to do now? They know you tried to destroy the ship."

Sergei gave a hollow laugh and said, “Well, I can slip over the side and swim to shore. It is night, isn’t it? Maybe I can run into the jungle and build a canoe.”

“And go where?”

“Where there’s no firing squad.”

“But you wanted to be a martyr.”

“So what do you recommend? Turn myself in?”

“It would be honorable. Maybe they’ll put you in the brig and take you back to St. Petersburg.”

“That’s not going to happen. Leave me. I’ll do what I’ll do at dawn.”

Alexei turned to go. Sergei looked up and said, “You never did beat me in épée, Alexei.”

“No, I never did. You were a good friend. But none of us deserve to die. Not like this.”

CHAPTER 30

Madagascar
January, 1905

Later that night, Alexei descended to the bilge and found Sergei, resigned to his fate, sitting in the same spot. “Get me some fresh clothes, Alexei. I don’t want to appear a disheveled wreck standing before the admiral and the firing squad. It would not be proper for a petty officer in the Tsar’s Imperial Navy,” he said with a lop-sided smile.

After delivering fresh clothes to Sergei, Alexei went to Admiral Kochenkov.

“Well?” he demanded.

“He has been found. *Michman* Sergei Vershinin requests that you accept his surrender.”

“He should turn himself in to Captain Zotoffka,” said the admiral somberly, his eyes searching Alexei’s face.

“He knows and respects you. I think it has to do with old times.”

“Old times?” said the admiral fiercely. “Old times saw him dismissed from the Academy! I have no sympathy for a traitor.” Kochenkov fell silent, then said, “Very well, let’s get this over with. I’ll receive him, but he’ll be in front of a court-martial within the hour. Three other saboteurs have been identified; they are being held in the brig. They’ll stand trial with him.”

Just at daybreak, Alexei escorted the *mishman* from the bilge to the admiral's quarters. Some of the sailors standing watch knew Sergei and, sympathizing with his revolutionary zeal, gave a slight nod. Others scowled, regarding him as a traitor who had inexcusably endangered them all.

Two guards flanked Sergei outside the admiral's quarters until he was summoned. They were stopped at the door, but Alexei was allowed to enter alongside the disgraced *mishman*. With an expressionless face, Admiral Kochenkov addressed his former student, who stood mute before him.

"I will not and cannot do anything for you. I once admired your skills, but I will not mourn your death. You have committed treason."

It was a very short meeting. At its conclusion Sergei raised his hand to his cap in salute. It remained there for a very long moment while Kochenkov considered the gesture. Finally, he returned the salute. Without anything else said, two ratings appeared with fixed bayonets and led Sergei away.

Attended by Captain Zotoffka, Boris Sokolov, Alexei, and three other officers, the trial of Sergei and his co-conspirators proceeded quickly. None of the defendants offered excuses, none of them pleaded for their lives.

There was nothing Alexei could say that would mitigate his school-mate's offense. Sergei's eyes, meeting those of Alexei, were impassive. What was done was done. The revolution would take place without him. He had tried to put one more nail in the coffin of Tsar Nicholas II and his regime, but outside the fleet no one knew nor cared.

Protocol was observed, even though the verdict was a forgone conclusion. A number of enlisted men were admitted to the proceedings since the trial was instructional, a warning in effect: "This is what happens if you consider insurrection!"

No one was appointed to defend the accused. The list of offenses was read by the judge advocate. He concluded his litany, carefully organized a thin sheath of papers, and looked at Sergei and his accomplices with cold contempt.

All was still and silent, save for the muted sounds of repairs below decks. Like a guillotine with its blade suspended, the four words of the sentence hung over their heads, unspoken, then:

"Death by firing squad," the judge advocate proclaimed, as his gavel came down.

***

The four men were blindfolded and stood at the fantail, hands tied and feet shackled. Five hundred bluejackets were ordered to the stern of the *Mikhail III* to witness the execution. They stood silent behind a dozen riflemen and an officer in his resplendent white uniform. At his command, weapons were raised and the bolts shoved forward.

"Long live the revolu—" Sergei cried out, but his shout was silenced by rounds that blew open his chest. Staggered by the fusillade, the bodies fell to the deck. Many of the bluejackets were dismayed by the sight of their comrades lying in pools of blood. Clenched jaws and an undercurrent of voices arose as friends of the dead seethed at the grisly sight. Worse, it was they who would have to scrub the decks, their hands reddening with the blood of friends slain, not by the enemy, but by their own officers. Officers turned toward the disgruntled men and shot angry looks, and the crew resumed an uneasy silence. They were ordered to resume their tasks and move out, but some of the bluejackets glanced back for a last look.

Boris, petulant at having been robbed of the opportunity to heroically dispatch Sergei, gave Alexei a disdainful glance before repairing to his cabin.

Politovsky joined Alexei, and they looked down at the body of Sergei, blown apart and running with blood. An officer directed crewmen to wrap the bodies for burial at sea, the procedure to be conducted without ceremony. They would be placed on a barge and deposited in deep water beyond the harbor mouth.

"A waste. What did it accomplish?" muttered Politovsky as he and Alexei walked to the wardroom.

"Nothing. But he believed in the revolution. He wanted to change Russia for the better and he thought his way was the only way."

"Only three others were executed, but I wonder how many on board sympathized with his ideals?" said Igor.

They were about to descend the ladder when Politovsky said, "By the way, I heard that Sokolov is banned from the wardroom. Admiral's orders. The word is that, with the mutiny suppressed, Boris has no police function and Kochenkov is refusing him officer's privileges."

"Really? What does the captain say? He's Sokolov's supporter."

"Was. Not any more. Sokolov is under suspicion. Lieutenant Kirdan is recovering, but he told Zotoffka that Boris shot him, then shot at you. Boris insisted he was aiming at the *michman,* but Sergei had already left the catwalk. I'm surprised that you didn't speak up. It was attempted murder, Alexei, and you were the target."

"Kirdan would have been the only witness, and I didn't think he was in any condition to have seen anything."

"Well, he saw it, and I'm sure he would testify."

Half way down the ladder, Politovsky stopped and turned. "Boris has been disgraced and I'm sure he blames you, Alexei. He was trying to kill you even before he was banned from the wardroom. Given the chance, I know he will try again."

Alexei nodded slowly. "Yes, he sees me as his mortal enemy. It is very strange. Everything he lost, he lost because he hated and tried to destroy me. Even Svetlana. I never wanted to marry her. If he had become an officer he could have courted her properly." He shook his head somberly.

***

Three days after repairs were completed, the *Mikhail* steamed into the French port of Nosy Be on the coast of Madagascar. It was a splendid anchorage ringed by lush islands. Young men who had never known any climate but Russia's cold were awed by the warm, clear water that looked like melted turquoise. The fleet was joyfully welcomed by local officials, who saw the arrival of ten thousand sailors as an unexpected boon to the economy.

Word spread quickly, and hundreds of profiteers descended on the town of Hellville, named for the Frenchman who planted his nation's flag at the port. The crews of the ships diligently carried aboard enormous quantities of food and crates of liquor, including the finest champagne for the officer's wardrooms. The few sailors who knew how to swim contrived to fall into the water.

From the railing of the main gun deck, Alexei and Politovsky watched sweating, bare-chested seamen hauling supplies aboard. A heavy, sultry cloud layer had descended upon the harbor, producing a stifling heat. "I'm drenched," said Igor. He plucked irritably at his uniform, which stuck to him. Alexei only grunted and said, "Yes, I'm sure you miss the forty below zero we enjoyed in Siberia. If you wish, I can ask the captain to send us right back. Wouldn't that be wonderful?"

Politosvsky gave Alexei a baleful look and said, "It definitely had some advantages; women, vodka, and—"

"And being frozen in a solid block of ice," said Alexei, abruptly ending the conversation.

A long moment passed and Politovsky said, "I overheard the captain when he was talking to the flag officer. He said that Rozhestvensky wants to leave here as soon as we finish with provisions and coaling, but we're not allowed to sail. We have to wait for the reinforcing fleet."

"That's the fleet Klado convinced the Admiralty to send. There was talk of it in the wardroom," said Alexei. "Well, at least we'll be warm, *tovarich.* And perhaps we can get shore leave and you can meet local women while we wait for the fleet."

"The whole thing is ridiculous. It will take months for the Baltic fleet to get here, and there's nothing to keep the Japanese from attacking us in port. I would imagine that they have already threatened to sink any ships assisting us. That includes the German colliers, and the Germans don't want to send their colliers into a war zone," Igor pointed out.

"Which means that we won't be refueling all the way across the Indian Ocean. Saigon might be the next friendly port—if the French are still supporting us."

"They will as long as they make money and don't offend the British or the Japanese. It's all about profit with them," replied Politovsky, wiping the sweat from his eyes.

"It's hard to blame them. Money is what this war is all about, Isorovsky. Look on the bright side: at least we won't be so low in the water we're unable to fire our guns."

"No, we'll be dead in the water, unable to generate any steam in the boilers."

They watched as a thousand cattle were herded down the street and onto the docks. There was a great lowing as the bullocks angrily pushed against one another and crewmen prodded them with sticks. One beast was gored by another and died, bellowing and scattering blood as it fought frantically to get out of the crush.

"Dinner," said Igor. "How do you like your steak?"

"Cooked," said Alexei as cranes lifted animals onto the decks, while others were put on barges and taken to ships standing in the channels.

"At least we'll have beef and champagne on our way to Valhalla," said Politovsky with a grin. "So what's Rozhestvensky's mood now? I know he throws tantrums when he's frustrated."

"The man's absolutely furious. He'd shoot Klado on the spot if he could. All he wants to do is get to Vladivostok, join whatever we have there and raid Japanese supply ships. That's the best we can hope to do," said Alexei.

***

"This whorehouse is packed. You have to make a reservation," said Igor, peering into the dimly lit environs which exuded the stink of sweat, alcohol and damp, malodorous bedding. "Let's find another!"

"You go on," Alexei said. "I prefer to walk." He did not care for the sights, smells, or sounds that issued forth, and he was very tired of the company of drunkards. This night, he decided, he would walk under the stars. As he moved off, the sounds of debauchery faded, and he could hear the whispers of foliage and the rustles and calls of night creatures. Behind all noises was a deep silence, not the sharp-edged silence of the Siberian winter, but a slow-breathing, velvet quiet. He walked down to the shore, away from the mooring of the ships, and stood where the waves broke, foaming, and ran up nearly to his boots.

Here the night was lovely, tranquil. His heart seemed to expand, and he felt it reaching across the water. Where was Kimi-san? There was no one else he wanted to be with.

That night, like all nights through January and February, saw thousands of sailors stumbling about Hellville in a drunken stupor. Dozens of shanty bars, hastily erected, catered to them. A miasma had infected the fleet: listlessness and defeatism were rampant, and there was a profound desire to enjoy the last moments of life. Signs in French and Russian plastered over bar doors extolled the pleasures offered by "Exotic and Nubile women" while others proclaimed "The Finest Liquor in all of Africa."

The fleet wallowed, rusted, and accumulated barnacles as it waited listlessly beneath a ponderous layer of cloud. Motionless mist hung over the crest of Nossi-Comba, the mountain peak with nearly impenetrable foliage that brooded over the town. The crews brawled, fell drunk in the streets, and caroused day and night. Each morning dozens of men and officers were found sprawled over women or curled up in obscure alleys. Money meant nothing to them, and in the stultifying humidity all discipline evaporated. There began a craze to acquire monkeys, reptiles and multi-colored birds which were brought aboard the warships, where they defecated wherever they wished.

"No one has seen Rozhestvensky for weeks," said Politovsky one day as he oiled his rifle.

"Depression, I hear. They've tried to find him ice for his headaches, but none exists. No one knows what he's thinking," said Alexei, pulling on a pair of hiking boots. "I read a French newspaper that reported the Baltic fleet is still a month away, maybe more. They've had continuous breakdowns."

"How many ships?" asked Igor.

"Maybe ten. None will be any good in a fight," said Alexei. "They're museum pieces."

Igor shrugged and put away his cleaning supplies, then the two set out to meet a half-dozen officers from the *Oryol, Suvoroff* and the *Borodino.*

The surrounding hills and lush jungle were, despite the suffocating heat, a lure for officers wishing to hunt and get out of town. Wild pigs, deer, and a variety of primates populated the emerald green island, and at Igor's prodding Alexei had agreed to join the day's hunt.

"I heard that another group is coming," said Alexei, as they found a trail leading around Nossi-Camba.

"Some of the junior officers on our ship heard of the hunt and got rifles from the armory. I told a sub lieutenant to join us at the ravine on the other side of the peak," Politovsky replied.

The trail devolved into a labyrinth of animal trails and eroded hillsides where vines tangled like mating snakes. Banana leaves sheltered dripping ferns, and trees with convoluted trunks competed with each other for a shaft of light. The tops of the tallest disappeared into the low hanging fog, and the forest floor was a dank morass. Alexei and Igor had come upon the prints of a boar, and Igor, as the more experienced of the two, was leading the way.

"These are dangerous animals," said Politovsky. "They've got those tusks, and when angered they'll come right at you. Keep that rifle handy."

A muffled shot was heard several hundred yards away, then more shots. There were excited voices and something plunged through the undergrowth.

Igor and Alexei came upon a small clearing. Further along, the boar's tracks vanished and the two hunters stopped and peered into a ravine, its tangled undergrowth reaching into a stream one hundred feet below.

"Do you think the pig went down there?" asked Alexei.

"No, it's too smart for that. Slipped into the bush, is my guess," said Politovsky. Then, looking over his shoulder he said, "I think I saw someone. The junior officers must have found us."

There was a snarl and a bullet struck a tree directly behind Alexei.

"Hold fire!" shouted Igor as another round ripped the collar of Alexei's shirt. A third shot rang out, and at the same moment the boar, its tusks stained a greenish brown, burst from the underbrush. Swiftly Alexei raised his rifle and fired, but the shot was high. With the speed of a fencer he twisted away, but the beast slammed into him and he plummeted over the cliff.

"My God!" said Igor, watching Alexei grasp at vines as he tumbled toward the churning current below.

"Help!" Politovsky shouted as he looked back toward the trail. There were no more shots, but a figure, half hidden by the dense foliage, staggered away.

"Damn you, Boris! You bastard! I hope you die!" Politovsky shouted, as his eyes searched for Alexei at the bottom of the ravine.

CHAPTER 31

Madagascar
February, 1905

A tarpaulin covering had been erected over the aft gun and Alexei lay on a cot beneath it. A tight bandage encircled his waist. He was thankful that a breeze had sprung up and a light rain had begun to fall.

"It had to be Boris," said Politovsky sitting beside him. "No one else would have run away when I called for help."

"Is he still in the infirmary?"

"I spoke to the doctor and they removed the bullet. He'll never use his left arm again."

"I was aiming at the boar."

"And you hit a boar, but it had two legs and it deserved to die."

***

The debaucheries in Hellville continued until French officials, alarmed at the occurrences of arson, looting and mayhem, confronted Admiral Rozhestvensky. As if emerging from a trance, he assembled his officers and demanded that they reestablish order. With reports of the approaching Baltic Fleet, strenuous efforts were made to clean the ships and prepare them for sea, all supervised by officers shamed by the admiral. To the dismay of many bluejackets, the animal mascots were taken ashore or simply thrown overboard.

Shore leaves were canceled and work went on at a frantic pace. Monsoon rains soaked the crews and a sullen mood permeated the fleet as it became obvious that there would be little diversion from required drudgery.

It was amid melancholy and fatalism that foreign journals arrived with ominous reports. The news caused morale to plummet even further, and orders were given for all papers to be limited to the senior officers, but within hours the news spread.

"It's centered in St. Petersburg, but also happening in Moscow and in towns and villages all across Russia," Politovsky confided to Alexei, who was still recovering from his injuries. "The Paris papers say that strikes have stopped all production, and the army has been called out. It seems like Sergei's revolution has begun. The Duma was demanding immediate reform, but the Tsar shut it down. The students are in revolt and there have been pogroms everywhere. Plehve has rounded up ten thousand Jewish doctors and sent them off to central Asia."

"Most of the doctors in Russia are Jewish, so that means there's hardly a physician left in St. Petersburg or Moscow," commented Alexei.

"I can already hear the aristocracy's shrill howls when they have a tummy ache or slip and break a leg on the ice. I think the Tsar may have a few questions for Plehve," said Politovsky.

"If the Tsar is even listening. But I haven't been able to get around; tell me, what's happening with the fleet? Are there more revolutionaries?" asked Alexei.

"All suspects on this ship are in the brig. Mostly bluejackets, but also two junior officers! In spite of the admiral's efforts, information is spreading from ship to ship."

"Were they arrested for mutiny?" demanded Alexei.

"What else? I heard that Rozhestvensky will pack them onto the creaking *Malay* and send them home."

"And not shoot them?"

"I don't think the enlisted men would stand for it. There would be mutiny for sure."

The cauldron of disillusionment against the regime simmered without overt acts of insurrection for several days until fresh newspapers arrived. In an effort to get out of the ceaseless rain, Alexei had been helped to the wardroom, where officers spoke in hushed tones.

"Look at this," said Politovsky quietly, handing Alexei the front page of a French newspaper. "If this doesn't start a revolution, nothing will."

"Massacre at the Winter Palace," read the headline. Alexei read the columns, which detailed the worst riots in one hundred years.

> *Many thousands of men, women and children assembled peacefully outside the Winter Palace hoping to petition the Tsar to allocate bread for the hungry masses. Instead, seeing the demonstration as a threat to his regime, the autocrat directed machine gun regiments to open fire on his defenseless subjects.*
>
> *Many dozens lay wounded and dying in the freezing temperature. Not content to have spilt so much blood, the Cossack cavalry, sabers drawn, were ordered to charge the fleeing, stampeding crowd. They trampled screaming petitioners beneath the hoofs of maddened horses.*
>
> *This horrific bloodletting against the Emperor's own subjects has not received any word of remorse or apology from the Tsar. What it has resulted in is a*

great wave of rioting and strikes across Russia. In countless cities and villages hundreds of thousands are in the streets. Seething throngs bravely confront the 'Black Hundreds.' the ruler's thugs, and call for the dissolution of the six-hundred-year-old regime. This massacre outside the Winter Palace, the gilded residence of the pitiless royal family, may well be the beginning of the end for the Romanov Dynasty.

"Do the enlisted men know of this?" demanded Alexei.

"They do now. The news has swept through the ranks. I'm sure it contributed to the mutiny on the *Nakhimoff.*"

"A real mutiny?"

"There was bedlam, and blue jackets were arming themselves. Their captain appealed to Rozhestvensky for help, and the battleship trained its guns on the ship. Fourteen men were rounded up and shot by firing squad. It ended the mutiny on that ship, but others have broken out," said Politovsky.

"How did you hear about the executions?" asked Alexei.

"Captain Zotoffka enthusiastically announced it to everyone in the wardroom. He was positively ecstatic. I think he wanted to pull the triggers himself."

***

With the addition of the Baltic fleet, all ships put to sea, leaving Hellville far behind.

Not a single vessel was sighted during the thirty-five-hundred-mile sail across the Indian Ocean on their way to reinforce Port Arthur. Nevertheless, Admiral Rozhestvensky decided that the fleet's safety required absolute radio silence. Many speculated that he wanted no more interference from St. Petersburg. For three weeks the capital waited in vain to hear of the fleet's progress, but there was no word. No one in the city knew the whereabouts of the Tsar's fleet.

At eight knots the ships, slowed by innumerable breakdowns, sailed slowly across the vast, empty ocean. Once away from the African coast the crews settled into stultifying routines. Boredom, worry and isolation took its toll and suicides became common, as the entire fleet steamed only two knots faster than the average seventeenth century merchantman.

"I've been watching," said Politovsky as he and Alexei stared into the limitless horizon.

"Watching what?"

"Boris. He's terrified and spends almost all of his time sealed up in his cabin. It's funny."

"What's funny, and why is he terrified?" asked Alexei, staring into the waves, his head sunk between his shoulders.

"Because of the way you look at him. You're strange, Alexei. You don't bristle or outwardly threaten him. You certainly haven't beaten him to a pulp, which I would have done. You don't say anything; but a silent threat can be far more menacing than words. He knows that you are just waiting. I can see something in his eyes: failure, futility. Alexei, the man will do something foolish, something desperate."

"There's nothing I can do about that."

"Something must be done. An accident, perhaps."

"There would be too many questions. Things will take care of themselves," said Alexei.

"You must have great faith," said Politovsky, shaking his head.

"Faith is something I haven't thought about for a very long time."

"If I were you, I would consider it," said Politovsky, glancing at the ship's icon of St. Andrew.

***

William-Stuart Jones stood beside Itomo Karamatsu on the dock at Sasebo and gazed at the Japanese naval armada taking on ammunition and supplies. "It was not an easy trip, all the way across Russia, and then talking my way into your lines at Port Arthur. I presume you heard that the Baltic fleet finally caught up to Rozhestvensky? So now they have more twelve-inch guns than your Admiral Tojo commands. Every tactician in Europe is adding up the capabilities of the two navies."

"What is on paper is of no consequence," said Itomo firmly. "Even the Russians call those reinforcements 'galoshes' and 'self-sinkers.'"

"But Japan is concerned. It has protested to France that her neutrality is being violated."

"That is true," said Itomo, "and many in Japan are worried, but I heard that the morale of the Russian sailors is very low and there have been mutinies. Such a thing would be unthinkable in the Japanese navy. A man would rather commit *sepuku* and disembowel himself than defy the emperor or disobey an order. My nation's sailors are a disciplined force of a single mind. I am not afraid of the Russian fleet." He stopped to watch a supply craft sailing toward his destroyer, then asked, "Will you be staying in Tokyo?"

"Heavens, no! I came to see the battle, old boy. I spoke to Admiral Tojo and got his permission to sail with you chaps. The *Times* is expecting a full report."

"That is brave of you," Itomo said gravely. He had a degree of respect for this man who, while only a journalist, had a warrior's spirit and a dedication to his craft that was worthy of a samurai. Nevertheless, he was a *geijin*, and his cheery mannerisms were abrasive. "I assume that you will be sailing on a battleship."

"No, Captain Parkenham will be on the *Asahi* reporting for the Royal Navy. I have no desire to be on a battleship; too far from the eyeball-to-eyeball action, what? I insisted on a destroyer."

"A destroyer? You could be killed."

"Absolutely not. I have the greatest trust in you, Captain."

Itomo looked steadily at William-Stuart Jones. "My ship is small and has no stateroom for a foreign journalist."

"I was a soldier in Her Majesty's Horse Guards and spent many nights sleeping on cold, hard ground. I hardly need a stateroom. A hammock with your crewmen will be just fine."

"Only on one condition will I allow you on my ship. You are not to interfere with my orders or the fighting efficiency of my crew. I will permit you on the bridge and you will have officer status, but you will issue no commands. You are an observer. Just an observer."

"Jolly good, old boy," said the journalist with satisfaction.

One more "Jolly good, old boy," thought Itomo, *and the Brit will swim.*

CHAPTER 32

"Singapore," Alexei sighed. He and Igor gazed ashore as the fleet steam past the British colony. After months at sea, the sight of land made them long to sail into the port.

"Everything we need: provisions, repairs, coal, and time ashore is right there," said Politovsky.

"But we're *persona non grata.* All we can do is look at it," Alexei replied.

"So we tuck our tails beneath our legs and run for Vladivostok. But Alexei, there are a lot of pretty women in Singapore, and the crews desperately need a break. They're very depressed."

"I agree, but there will be other things to occupy their minds."

"Like being sunk?" said Igor grimly. "How long before we approach Japan?"

"About three days, then two more beyond Japan to Vladisvostok. If we can get past Tojo's fleet."

"Hmm," was all Igor said. He was staring hard at the coastline of Singapore.

***

"What do you know about Tojo? You were in Japan; did you ever meet him?" Politovsky asked Alexei later in the evening, when the officers met in the wardroom.

"No, I've only seen photographs. He's quite short and very formal, all decked out in his admiral's uniform with a samurai sword. I do know he went to naval school in England; he even crewed on a British battleship thirty years ago. It is said that he's fearless, a severe disciplinarian and a great tactician. He's fanatically loyal to the Emperor and, like all the rest, willing to die for Japan."

"But I read in a London paper that he's not popular with his crews," said Igor.

"That makes little difference in battle," said Alexei. "They respect him and will do everything he asks. It's that simple."

Talk in the wardroom was subdued. Many talked wistfully of home, wives and girlfriends. Others read or pensively stared into nothingness. All knew that battle was not far off.

An orderly appeared at the door, approached, and handed Alexei a note.

"What's that?" asked Politovsky.

"Admiral Kochenkov wants to see me."

"Maybe he wants you to talk to Tojo, tell him not to worry, that it's all a big mistake and we're going home."

"I'll make an immediate appointment with Tojo, Igor. I'm sure he'll listen to everything I have to say." Alexei rose and quietly departed the wardroom.

"I've fixed you a Scotch; I heard you picked up the taste for it in England," said Kochenkov, filling his own glass with vodka. He motioned for Alexei to sit and, settling into an overstuffed chair, said, "Almost the end of our journey, for better or worse."

Alexei sipped his drink and said, "I wonder how history will regard it; nearly eighteen-thousand miles in mostly obsolete ships with very few friendly ports of call. Storms, mutinies and a constant need for coal."

"I suppose history's regard will depend on whether we win or lose," said the admiral.

Both men stared into their drinks, then Alexei said, "I was thinking about Svetlana this morning. I wanted to tell you how sorry I was, the way it ended for her."

"I thank you. And I owe you an apology, having, along with the count and your mother, forced you into what would have been a dreadful marriage."

"I would have adjusted to it, as most people do. But she was, well, devilishly wild."

"She was always that way. Beautiful, wanton, uncontrollable."

Alexei swirled his scotch and said, "There's something that always bothered me, but I hesitate to ask."

"You might as well. It will likely be the last chance you have."

"Remember the ball at the Winter Palace, after the naval graduation?"

"Of course."

"I suspect she helped set up the attack on me so she could be with Boris. I know that she was complicit. Was I to have been killed?"

The admiral pondered the question, and his possible responses, then said, "I'm surprised that you didn't ask me a long time ago. She came to me while you were still recovering. She had not helped Sokolov set up the attack, of that she was innocent; but she knew what had happened. The girl was terrified."

"Of me dying?"

"Absolutely. Both Svetlana and Boris would have faced murder charges if you had died."

"Why did she come to you?" asked Alexei.

"To use my influence."

"And if that didn't work?"

"To beg me to give her money to flee to America with Boris. I told her I would do neither."

"I doubt they would have hanged her, but they would have executed Boris, unless Plehve intervened."

"Boris was nothing to Plehve except a troublesome sycophant, an embarrassment. Boris would have been hanged."

"And Svetlana?"

"Prison for a few years. Then my wife would have worked the system and got her released. But if it's anything to you, I told Ekaterina that the marriage must be terminated if you did not fully recover, that Svetlana was too dangerous. Your mother would have agreed if she knew all the details. She always cared for you."

"And the count? Did he know?"

"Yes. We agreed to keep a close eye on Svetlana. She would be warned."

"So it went ahead anyway. I was to marry a girl who wanted me incapacitated or even dead."

"No, Alexei, she didn't want that. But..."

"I was in the way. An impediment to her assignations."

"I'm afraid so. And we, that is the count, Ekaterina, Olga and I, were indeed complicit. I am sorry, Alexei. I truly am."

"So except for Boris hiding in his room, that's the end of the story," said Alexei, refilling his drink.

"Not exactly."

"There's more?"

"There's always more." Admiral Kochenkov laughed. "It's the greatest irony, Alexei. Svetlana, my beautiful, flawed daughter, the love of my life, wasn't my daughter at all."

"What?" demanded Alexei, nearly spilling his drink.

"Surprised? Shocked? I thought you would be. Ekaterina could not have children but desperately wanted a baby. It's true. For months we searched the orphanages but found no suitable child. One day we were in Our Lady of Kazan and a woman approached. Quite mysteriously, in fact. She said nothing and ushered us into a room and left. We were mystified and waited, not knowing what to expect. When the woman returned, she put a baby into Ekaterina's arms, a beautiful baby girl'."

"Whose baby was it?" asked Alexei.

"It was all quite secretive, but we insisted on knowing where the child came from. The father was a priest who'd had a relationship with a lay woman of the church. The woman who gave us the child refused to tell us the names of either. The reputation of the birth mother would have been ruined, and the priest excommunicated if exposed. We promised to never divulge their secret; and so the priest continued to do 'God's work' at the cathedral. Only later did I find out the name of the priest. Father Rozinski was screwing a lot of women, and he especially like young, pretty girls. There were rumors, and I followed them."

For a moment Alexei sat immobile. The admiral downed his drink and refilled it. Then Alexei said, "You, Ekaterina and my parents insisted that I wed Svetlana. I was told that marrying into your family would enhance my parent's position. But I always thought you wanted me to marry her to forestall her relationship with Boris."

Leaning forward, the admiral said, "Svetlana was playing a very dangerous game. The last thing we wanted was for her to become pregnant by either Boris or the priest."

"The one at the cathedral? Rozinski, her own father!" Alexei exclaimed.

Admiral Kochenkov nodded grimly and said, "She began to attend Our Lady of Kazan quite frequently. I thought it strange, since she was hardly religious, but somehow she found out about her past—that is, her adoption. And then, apparently, she learned the name of her biological father. I seriously doubt that the man, the priest, knew her real identity, and Svetlana enjoyed nothing more than a great scandal. "

"Undoubtedly, but it would have destroyed her and your family!" blurted Alexei.

"That was the problem; the girl rarely thought about consequences. As I said, I knew about the priest and presented a bishop with all the significant details. I told him that the priest's access to Svetlana must cease immediately. Of course he agreed, and the man was sent off to a monastery. But he never arrived."

"Why not? Did he run away?"

"No. He was murdered."

"By whom?"

"It wasn't by me or Boris or the count. And it wasn't your mother. So who is left?"

Alexei considered, then said, very slowly, "Ekaterina, your wife."

The admiral gave him a wan look but said nothing.

Alexei shook his head and said, "Would you have told me all this if we weren't going to war?"

"Perhaps," said Kochenkov. He let the word hang in the air, then said, "I think you need a refill."

Despite the warmth an involuntary shiver coursed through Alexei. Kochenkov took Alexei's glass and poured the aged scotch. Through a porthole Alexei saw a searchlight scan the horizon. Then the light went out, and except for a battleship's wake, the sea was dark.

"Families have secrets, Alexei. I'm sure that you know at least one, maybe more, concerning your own family."

"I know that my mother is your mistress."

"She has been for a very long time. We were and still are very much in love, but she married Brusilov. She had to."

Alexei raised his eyebrows, and the admiral plunged on. "I guess she saw promise in him, he being a count and all. It was done hastily. He may have loved her at first, but as time went on he had his eye on Ekaterina. He saw her quite often, and under the circumstances, I did not object. I was still in love with your mother."

"But you love your wife."

"A man can have more than one love, especially if everyone knows the rules."

"Rules?"

"Oh yes, there are iron-clad rules. Not a word about any illicit love may be spoken of in public."

"Obviously you know things I don't know."

"And that's what this conversation is leading to. It's why I had you come here."

Kochenkov sipped his vodka and said, almost offhandedly, "You were not aware of it, but I intentionally had you assigned to this ship."

"To be with you?"

"Indeed. I also cabled Count Brusilov before your sentencing and arranged to have you interned in a camp better than most. Of course, you might not have thought so. I did worry about you having sex with those sluts. I received reports, you see."

"But I was to serve fifteen years."

The admiral waved his hand dismissively and said, "You would have been out of there in another six months, war or no war."

"That's encouraging. I wish you could have been at the trial. It was a farce."

"I heard of it but could not be there. I did the next best thing." The admiral sipped his drink, then said, "Olga told you about how she was adopted by my parents, did she not?"

"She did. And that you and she became very good friends."

Kochenkov allowed himself a smile and peered at Alexei. "Yes, we became very good friends." He paused then, as if changing the subject said, “The count only found out about it all after he married your mother.”

“Found out what, that you two were good friends?” said Alexei, wondering why the admiral was being so circumspect.

“Of course he knew that. What he didn’t know was that Olga knew she was pregnant when he married her.”

“Yes, she told me.”

“And I made her pregnant. I am your father.”

Alexei didn’t hear his glass shatter on the deck. He simply stared at the admiral.

“He considered divorcing her,” Kochenkov continued, oblivious to Alexei’s amazement. He was reliving the memory. “He was a gambler back then, and not a very good one. He had inherited a title but was nearly broke. That surprised your mother, who’d thought she was marrying into wealth. At her suggestion I gave him a fairly large sum so he would keep her and take care of you.”

Alexei nodded slowly. It all fell into place.

“Would you have ever told me?” Alexei asked.

“I always wanted to. I should have long ago, but the timing never seemed right. And I didn’t know how it would have affected Yevgeny or your mother. But now it’s out. We’re going into battle and I thought you should know.”

“It is a bit late. Is there anything else I should know?” said Alexei. It came out harsher than he intended, but the shock was severe.

“Not really, Alexei. I hope you are not terribly angry with me.”

“Not angry, not really. I do wish you had told me.”

“And what could you have possibly done? How could it have been different?”

It was Alexei’s turn to sigh. “I don’t know, Father. It was all so complicated.”

"And you still love the Japanese girl?"
"Yes. I love her very much."
"Then pray that you live, Alexei. Pray that we all do."

CHAPTER 33

Tokyo, 1905

Kimi-san gazed out the window and watched her four-year-old son, Tadichi, playing with a kitten in the little garden. The house was a quiet and lonely place since her mother had died of a stroke, six months before. Outside, people spoke of nothing but the advance of the Russian fleet. There was anxiety underlying all the patriotic fervor. "Fifty ships, so many guns," people said in hushed voices. Not since Commodore Perry and the American "Black Fleet" had Japanese worried about a foreign armada so close to the Islands of the Rising Sun.

She had made tea and rice for herself, her child, and Itomo-san, who had told her that he would return before reporting to Sasebo and the Imperial fleet. She sat on a cushion in the empty room and waited. Itomo was the only family member left, and he was going off to war. Only a year ago the house had been filled with the voices of her father, husband and mother. Now there was silence.

Sensei had told her that some people were resettling in Hokkaido, since land there was inexpensive. It had been populated only by Ainu until 1868, when the government forcibly moved in. A cold place, it was said, but Kimi-san thought that she and Tadichi-san might find happiness there. It would not matter where she spent her widowhood.

The kitten jumped out of Tadichi-san's arms and the little boy raced to catch it, his curly brown hair rustled by a morning breeze. He had once asked her why he had brown hair when nobody else did. She'd told him that he was born under a magic spell when the moon danced in the sky and birds flew in circles upside down. He'd laughed, but then became serious, saying that some older boys thought him to be part *geijin.*

"Am I *geijin*?" he'd asked, looking at her.

"Only a little, just like me," she said.

"But you don't look *geijin,*" he persisted. Then he'd spied his kitten and chased it into the garden.

You are very much geijin, she said to herself, thinking of his father—a man so impossibly far away.

The front door opened and closed and she heard Itomo's stocking feet on the bamboo floor.

"I have just made *ocha,* Itomo-san," she said, bowing to her brother.

"Arigato," he replied with a curt nod as he sat on a *tatami* mat by the rice paper window.

"Will you be staying the night?" Kimi-san asked, handing him a cup of tea.

He shook his head and said, "I only have a few hours. Everyone must report to the fleet. Admiral Tojo has scheduled a meeting of all captains for tomorrow."

"Will you be sailing then?"

"I don't know. It's up to him and I couldn't tell you even if I knew."

She sat across from him, her feet tucked under, and said, "I am very proud of you. All of Japan is, especially after your brave attack on Port Arthur."

"It was not dangerous, no matter what the newspapers said." He sipped his tea, then more candidly than she expected, added, "This coming battle will be far more dangerous. Even so, I have no doubt that we will succeed and destroy the Russian fleet. They will suffer the same fate as the Mongols before the *kamikaze* wind."

"*Hai*," said Kimi-san, expressionless. Her one word hung in the air as if it meant, "I hear you," as opposed to, "Of course, their navy will be at the bottom of the sea."

"There will be a *geijin* on my ship; an English journalist wants to record the battle. The admiral says it is necessary for the foreign press to document our victory. I doubt that you remember the man, but you met him at the embassy when he was with Alexei."

"He knows Alexei-san?" Inadvertently she shifted, and her kimono rustled.

"Oh yes, they are good friends, but I—" He stopped himself.

"Itomo-san, do you think that Alexei-san is—"

Itomo held up his hand. "I know what you're going ask me, and I don't know if Alexei is on any of those Russian ships. He was an aide de camp when his father was Ambassador, so he may be in St. Petersburg or Paris or even Berlin."

"But he is a navy lieutenant, isn't he?"

"It doesn't mean that he's at sea."

"But if he is," Kimi-san persisted, "and if you see him in trouble, can you..."

"Can I what?" Itomo said, sitting ramrod straight.

Kimi-san looked down at her hands and said the unimaginable. "Can you save him?"

Itomo simply stared at her. "Dear sister, the man was once my friend, but his country and ours are at war. Thousands of our soldiers have been killed by those barbarians. Alexei is my enemy now, whether he is in Paris or on board a Russian battleship. I dare not even think of aiding our enemy. Not unless he has surrendered, and what ship in modern times surrenders on the high seas? What you are asking is preposterous."

Kimi-san bowed her head and apologized. Then in the softest whisper she said, "Itomo-san, he is the father of my son. I pray each night to see him again."

"What can I possibly do? Maybe his god will help him. There is no way I can."

"I understand," said Kimi-san as she demurely bowed to her brother, the officer who might kill the man she loved.

***

South China Sea

"Prayers are being offered on the main gun deck. Are you coming?" Politovsky asked Alexei.

"Perhaps in a few minutes. The six-pounder has been rolling sluggishly. I want to check it; something's wrong with its track."

"Everyone's going to be there. The priest will sprinkle holy water on the guns."

"You go. I'll say a prayer later."

"It's not the same, but do as you wish."

Alexei fished pebble-size pieces of coal from the track, oiled the wheel bearings and traversed the gun on its half-circular rails. Satisfied that it rolled easily, he sat on a large crate and looked through the gun port to the horizon. On the deck above he heard the crew join in a Gregorian chant, followed by the priest's homily.

He had attended service for years. He had conformed to the expected ritual, adding his voice as required. It was something that afforded comfort, communion and fellowship. It was the religion he had grown up with, the faith of his friends, the faith of complete acceptance. To divert from it would be heresy. He would be considered a traitor to Russian Orthodoxy and Holy Russia as well. The idea had bothered him ever since speaking to his mother on that long ago, memorable Sabbath night. Now he sat in the empty gun compartment and considered joining his comrades in the last religious ceremony before battle.

Ever since the conversation with the admiral a strange thought had been nagging at him. He had heard his real father's confession; it had been a moment of truth. Perhaps Kochenkov was tired of living a convenient falsehood. Maybe it was time for him to do the same.

Alexei stared at the choppy, endless sea. It changed every day, he thought, but it many ways it was always the same; a constant. What was his constant? He had seen his mother tiptoe through the hall with her candles, heard her whispered prayers to a faith that nearly all Russia abhorred. It was, he had been instructed by countless priests, the religion of the anti-Christ. But now, sitting alone with probable death only hours away, he wondered who and what he actually was.

"I am your mother and I am Jewish, and thus you are too," Olga had said. "You may think it a curse; you may wish to deny it. You raise your voice in the cathedral of St. Isaac's to fit in, to become one with Holy Mother Russia, but it is a sham. I know; I do the same to protect us from the scourge of the haters. But it is not who I am, Alexei, and it is not you. Some day you will have to come to terms with that."

What day would that be, he had wondered? How long could he put it off? How long could he deny it?

Slowly he rose and made his way to the officer's sleeping quarters. To his satisfaction, the room was empty. He opened his sea chest and removed its contents. Glued into the corner was a small locked box. Inside was a purple velvet bag with a drawstring.

"Take the scriptures, the *Tanakh,*" his mother had said on the day of his sailing.

"It's too big," he'd protested, gathering up his belongings.

Olga had reflected before replying. "You are right. Instead, I will find something to remind you who you are," she'd said, determination in her voice. She'd left his room. Upon returning, she'd placed the little bag and a black skull cap in his hand and said, "This is all you need."

Only with great reluctance had he accepted. They'd seemed so foreign. But he'd wanted please her. She'd put her head against his chest and said, "May the Lord protect you. Despite everything I have done, I do love you. I love you very much."

Hidden away, the objects sat in the locked box at the bottom of his chest. He stood beside it, wondering what to do next. Whatever it was could not be done here, he told himself.

The lower gun deck. No one would be there until services concluded. From there he would hear the sound of feet after dismissal. He would have time to return to the sleeping quarters.

No one was about; he walked past the main batteries and descended the gangway to the six-pounder deck. He was alone with his thoughts.

From the sack he extracted the *mezuzah*, the small, cylindrical object that contained an Old Testament prayer. Where Judaism was tolerated it would be attached to a door frame and devout Jews would touch it before entering the house. But that would not be prudent in Russia, so Olga had put it inside her closet door. The paper on which the prayer was inscribed was sealed in the brass *mezuzah*. He could not see it but that did not matter; Hebrew was a language he could not read.

He placed the holy object on the breech of the gun, removed his naval officer's cap, extracted the silk *yarmulke* from the bag and placed it on his head. It felt strange, and yet... there was a sense of belonging.

What were the words? A phrase came to his mind, "Hear, O Israe—" he began.

In his peripheral vision he saw the steel pipe spiral toward him. Instinctively he ducked aside, and the metal slammed against the gun's breech, sending the *mezuzah* across the deck.

"Jew!" screamed Boris. "I knew it!" Snatching up the container, he lurched up the gangway and ran toward the bow. Alexei grabbed his naval cap and bolted after him.

The religious services had ended and the crew was returning to their duty stations. Boris looked back and, seeing Alexei, tore past sailors and up the ladder to the interior bridge. Bursting in, he shouted, "I have proof! He's a heretic, a traitor!"

"What? Who's a traitor?" demanded Admiral Kochenkov as he whirled about.

"What are you doing on my bridge?" rasped Captain Zotoffka.

"Him!" shrieked Boris, pointing to Alexei as he ran forward. "He's a Jew! I saw him doing one of those Jew prayers and he had this, this filthy *thing*." He waved the *mezuzah*. In an accusing voice he turned to Kochenkov and spat the words, "You knew he was, didn't you!"

"What do you think you are saying? And who are you to call this officer a traitor? He is the one who alerted us to the sabotage and caught the leader!"

"Captain, that man twice tried to murder me on this voyage. He should be shot," said Alexei, with barely controlled rage.

Fists balled up and shaking with fury, Boris advanced toward Zotoffka. Thrusting his arm at Alexei he screamed, "I will kill this insect! Yes, for the Tsar. He is an enemy of Holy Russia and he will destroy this ship!"

"He will do no such thing," said Zotoffka. "I may not approve of his religion, but I would rather have a thousand of him than one of you. Now get off my bridge!"

"But look!" stormed Boris, spinning and knocking off Alexei's naval cap. "See that?" he cried, snatching the *yarmulke*. He failed to see Alexei's fist, which slammed into his face. Staggering, blood spurting from his nose, he fell back against the tall compass housing. Alexei stepped forward and delivered one more blow, smashing his jaw and knocking him to the floor.

Blood running from his mouth, Boris stared up at Alexei, then at Kochenkov. He tried to speak but choked and spat two teeth onto the deck.

Turning to officers who had hurried onto the bridge, the admiral pointed to Boris and said, "Get that piece of filth to the brig and put a guard on him. We will deal with him when the battle is over."

A moment later, a lookout approached and announced, "Captain, Japanese cruiser off our port quarter, coming on fast."

CHAPTER 34

Tsushima
May 27, 1905

"Now there are three armored cruisers and a battleship. I guess they're just watching us," said Politovsky.

"Out of range of our guns," said Alexei. "If I were Tojo, I would wait until we get through the strait of Tsushima."

"What's Tsushima?" Igor said, hearing a bell ordering the crew aft.

"That's the name of the huge rocks on the peninsula; it means Donkey Ears. What's happening aft?" asked Alexei, nursing bruised knuckles. "What was that bell?"

"Did you forget? It's the anniversary of the coronation of Alexander and the Empress. Every man will get vodka when we raise the flag of St. Andrew."

They could already hear the cheering and repeated cries of "Long Live the Tsar!"

"The stewards have prepared drinks and desserts for all officers," Politovsky said, as they descended the stairs to the wardroom. Laughter and buoyant chatter filled the room. Giddy exuberance overflowed like champagne, but it felt unnatural and reminded Alexei of melting ice on the Neva with rushing water just below. All knew that within hours everything would be decided—for better or worse.

A senior flag officer stood at the front and glasses were raised. In a booming voice he said, "Great good wishes and joy to their Majesties on this glorious day. May God bless and protect our Holy Russia and our fleet. A toast!"

Alexei put his hand to the *mezuzah* that rested inside his naval jacket and hoped that God was listening.

Outside the wardroom, bluejackets energetically prepared for war. Gun sights were checked, passageways cleared of obstructions, ammunitions properly stored, and operating rooms readied for the wounded. Officers barked orders to stokers preparing to shovel tons of coal into furnaces, and sailors were sent to the highest observation platforms to spot the approach of Japanese vessels.

Alexei descended to his gun deck, past determined seamen—anxious, but ready for battle. Gone were the complacency, the boredom and contempt for discipline. The throbbing of engines, the commands, the slap of waves on the sides of the ships, all made a martial music. A sense of purpose transformed the entire crew; deference to officers and cheerful obedience to orders re-established the unity that had eroded. As Alexei approached his six-pounder, his gun crew stood and saluted, and the *michman*, the highest ranking bluejacket, said, "Sir, we are in readiness. You may inspect the gun if you wish."

Alexei returned the salute, looked through the aiming device, checked the swivel tracks and said, "You have all done exceedingly well. I know you will do your duty for Tsar and Mother Russia, and I will be with you."

"Attention!" commanded the *michman,* smartly saluting. Alexei returned the salute and strode toward Politovsky, who was coming down the ladder.

"The whole ship is humming; can you feel it?" said Igor.

"We're as ready as we can be. Let's just hope it is enough."

***

Admiral Tojo's meeting with his captains had concluded, and the officers, having received their special instructions, which included flag signals to be used during the anticipated battle, were departing the *Mikasa*, the admiral's flagship. One small launch bore Captain Itomo Karamatsu back to his ship in Chin-Hei Bay on the eastern coast of Korea. William-Stuart Jones was waiting at the gangplank as Itomo was piped back on board.

With notepad in hand he asked, "Captain, can you tell me what was said?"

"Come with me to the bridge; we will talk there. Remember, all you write will be scrutinized by Japanese officials." Itomo spoke curtly. He had actually been ordered to cooperate with the journalist without compromising any secretive aspects of the deployment, but he wanted to be among his men, not in the company of this annoying *geijin*.

"Of course, but there will not be much to censor if your fleet is victorious," Jones pointed out. "So I wonder if the admiral's Special Boat Squadron has yet found the Russians? Have you received orders?"

"One question at a time. The admiral informed us that Rozhestvensky has decided to pass through the strait between Korea and Japan rather than going west around Honshu. He's trapped, and we know exactly where to strike."

Itomo did not know that luck had lead to that discovery, but he was un der strict orders not to reveal the extent to which the Japanese fleet was employing wireless to speed communications along, so it was convenient to allow the journalist to assume scout boats had been responsible.

With pencil busy, Jones said, "Did he make any comment regarding strategy?"

"There was a samurai sword on the table. He pointed to it and said, 'If your sword is too short, take a step forward.' In other words, don't hesitate to attack."

"Historic, like Nelson's 'England Expects Every Man to Do His Duty.' Trafalgar, 1805. Jolly good copy, old boy!"

Itomo glanced at the water and wondered if the Scot could swim.

***

Throughout the night, heavy fog shrouded the Russian fleet. On occasion, a quarter-moon would peer through, but visibility was near zero. "If this weather holds," Politovsky said hopefully, "We might slip past the entire Japanese fleet."

Standing at the ship's port railing, Alexei and Igor shivered and peered at the long, slow swell. Igor grinned and said, "Do you remember the good times we had in Siberia? The women, the vodka and the summer nights?"

"There's damn little of that place I remember, thanks to the vodka. But I always wondered what you really did to get thrown in that camp. The infraction you told me about was hardly reason enough, considering you were an officer and your father was prominent in aristocratic circles."

"Time for truth, is it, Alexei?"

"Only if you want to divulge your dark secret. You might not have another chance."

"So long as you promise not to tell the Tsar if you happen to run into him."

A light breeze swirled fog around them, and Igor said, "About three years before you arrived I attended a lavish party in Moscow; I was on leave, as my ship was undergoing extensive repairs in the Baltic port. I found myself sitting at a table with an aristocratic and wealthy Russian gentleman and his younger wife. Her name was Isabella. She was Portuguese and extraordinarily beautiful. Needless to say, I immediately fell in love with her, and she smiled at me quite pleasantly."

"An odd combination, Russian and Portuguese," said Alexei.

"Her father sold gems in Moscow and surrounding cities. Anyway, I regaled the couple with stories of naval battles against the Turks and my travels, much of which was true. They were fascinated, invited me to their home, and in short order I was bedding Isabella, since her husband traveled a circuit beyond Moscow."

"I think I see what's coming," said Alexei.

"Unfortunately, I did not. I was quite taken with her. I even suggested that I resign my commission and we would run away together. One day her husband, Stephan, returns while the young lady and I are in a compromising state. He is enraged, grabs a knife and chases me into their field." Igor paused, ruefully shaking his head.

"It was winter, I was naked, no shoes on, and I tripped. We struggled in the snow and I killed him. Simple as that. Except that I was charged with murder and would have hanged if my father hadn't contributed handsomely to the judge's retirement. Ten years was my sentence, but then the war came."

"Fascinating. Did the lady speak Portuguese when you two made love?" asked Alexei wryly.

"She did. It was lyrical."

Igor turned to Alexei and said, "This reminds me of something a little disturbing."

"More than ten years in Siberia?"

"For the present, yes. Isabella received newspapers from home and, knowing that I was a naval officer, once pointed out an article about an invention in Brazil, a country that had been a colony of Portugal."

"I don't see the connection with us here and now."

"Let me finish. It seems that a Brazilian scientist developed an extremely powerful kind of explosive to be used in artillery shells, and the Japanese either bought the invention or the ingredients. The details were somewhat vague, because the Brazilian navy considered it confidential. But somehow a journalist found out about it."

"So much for secrecy," said Alexei.

"But do you see what I'm getting at? The Japanese shells are very likely armed with that explosive. It could be devastating."

"And our Admiralty doesn't know about it?"

"Who at the admiralty reads Portuguese? And what if they did know, would it influence the Tsar? I believe he would have gone to war with Japan anyway. Maybe we should have hidden in the Siberian Forest, Alexei. Better freezing to death than being blown to bits."

"Any death seems better than the one staring you down its gun sights. If you were freezing in Siberia or being mauled by a bear, you would trade your left testicle to be on a battleship. So, what are we fighting for? Personally, I have no quarrel with the Japanese."

Politovsky shrugged and said, "We're naval officers and serve Russia. That is what we do."

"And the Tsar? Is he worth dying for?"

"I thought so at one time. I do not now, not after the Winter Palace massacre, but I will fight for my country against another country." A moment passed before he added, "But I should like to live and see Isabella again."

"Yes, there are people we would like to see again, Igor. But I doubt that we will." Alexei gazed out over the dark waters, wondering....

***

By morning the fog began to break, and each of the Russian ships was clearly visible. The possibility of avoiding action dissipated with the fog. Despite that, the crews were excited, trusting that their superiority in heavy guns would give them the decisive advantage.

"No destroyer-torpedo boats in sight yet; nothing for our-six pounders to shoot at," Politovsky observed as he and Alexei stood on deck.

"Never mind; let's get on the aft bridge so we can see everything," said Alexei.

Sub-lieutenant Veliski joined them aft and said, "Four Japanese cruisers were off our port beam, then scooted away. Others have been all around us, sometimes in range of the battleships guns, but Rozhestvensky hasn't ordered our ships to fire. I don't know why."

"He could send out our fast cruisers, the *Donskoy*, *Svetlana* and *Monomakh*," said Politovsky.

"They can't do much; no firepower. They shouldn't even be here," said Alexei dismissively.

Without warning or signal, the battleship *Oryel* fired its twelve-inch guns at a Japanese cruiser, then others followed suit. Enormous geysers sprouted about the enemy ship, but she turned and, without taking a single hit, sped away. From the admiral's battleship, the *Suvoroff*, came the order to cease fire and conserve ammunition.

"All our guns firing and not one shell found its mark," said Alexei disgustedly. "Is it total ineptness?"

"The crews haven't practiced for months. What do you expect?" said Igor.

"I now expect the worst. I just hope the Japanese can't shoot any better."

"There they are!" said Politovsky, pointing to more cruisers closing the distance.

"Another signal from Rozhestvensky," said the sub-lieutenant. "We're all turning to starboard. First, second and third squadrons. I guess he wants to keep the Japanese from laying mines in front of us."

Minutes passed, and more signal flags were raised. “The battleships are turning nicely, but the second squadron looks confused. They’re coming abeam of the first squadron,” commented Alexei.

“Oh my God,” said Politovsky, “Now they’re all askew; it’s as if they don’t know where to go.”

He lowered his binoculars and glanced down the deck. “Is that Boris? What’s he doing wearing an officer’s jacket?”

Alexei and the sub-lieutenant looked toward the forward turret, and Veliski asked, “How did he get that?”

“He must have stolen it! But he was under guard,” said Politovsky.

“Maybe the guard was called to action station. After all, we’re going into battle,” said Veliski, looking toward the chaos in the fleet.

“Being mistaken for an officer will keep him from being assigned to work details,” said Alexei sardonically.

“Maybe he thinks that if he’s captured he’ll be treated as an officer,” offered Politovsky with disgust.

“Captured? What are the Japanese going to do, board us? This isn’t the eighteenth century,” scoffed Veliski.

Igor turned to Alexei and said, “I saw him earlier. He doesn’t look too pretty after what you did to him. It was about time.”

“He is impersonating an officer, and we are all witnesses. That is an extremely serious offense,” said Alexei. “He could be executed. The captain will deal with him after the battle.”

“I would be happy to shoot him,” said Politovsky.

The cruisers guns swung to starboard and Veliski said, “Battleships! Six of them. About seven thousand yards. We should damn well be able to hit something as big as a battleship!”

The *Mikhail III*, along with two other Russian cruisers, edged closer to the *Suvoroff* as she opened fire on the

Mikasa and the *Shikishima*, the two battleships leading the Japanese fleet. Alexei looked at his pocket watch and saw that it was nearly two o-clock in the afternoon.

"We must be scoring hits. Look, those two cruisers near the battleships; they're hit and they're pulling out of line," said Politovsky excitedly.

The sub-lieutenant consulted an identification book and said, "Those are the *Yakumo* and the *Asuma*. Good shooting; if we keep this up we'll have them. You can hear the lads cheering!"

"But what's happening with their battleships?" asked Politovsky. "We're firing all those shells but I don't see any smoke or flame."

"Our big shells are made to explode after they pierce the hull," Alexei pointed out.

"But nothing is happening! There should be explosions by now," said Veliski, suddenly concerned. "Are they all duds?"

"No, some have hit the *Mikasa*; I can see damage," said Politovsky, pointing toward the distant cruiser.

"But she's not turning or pulling out of line," Alexei replied anxiously.

"They're firing back now," said the sub-lieutenant. "I can actually see their shells. They're concentrating on the *Suvoroff*."

An enormous explosion ripped apart steel plates as four-foot long projectiles tore into the *Suvoroff*. A moment later another explosion burst on the battleship's bridge, sending smoke and flames a hundred feet into the cloudless sky. A stunned silence enveloped those who witnessed it. "My God," Veliski breathed, "Can Rozhestvensky still be alive?"

"The Japanese must be using heavier shells than we have, and theirs explode on contact," said Politovsky, his eyes wide with shock. "They're entire line is turning. What are they doing?"

"It's the 'T'," said Alexei somberly. "They're taking a page from Nelson and crossing the T."

"So *all* their guns are trained on our battleships!" exclaimed Politovsky.

"And our ships are in line ahead and can't return fire," replied Veliski in dawning horror.

"The Suvoroff is listing, I can see fires all along her decks," Politovsky groaned.

Salvos from five hundred guns tore into the Russian ships. Shell after shell found its mark, a testament to British instruction, which the Japanese employed with fanatical dedication, tearing great holes in battleships and cruisers. Turrets, plating, and sailors were blown skyward, smoke and fire erupted throughout the fleet. Steering compartments were destroyed and ships careened on erratic courses, narrowly missing companion vessels. The shelling continued unabated.

Alexei heard the first shells fired from the *Mikhail III,* but they went wide. She began a hard turn to port as an eight-inch shell exploded on the forward gun. The top of the turret was peeled upward, the concussion and fire killing the entire crew. Suddenly everything on the *Mikhail* changed; they were no longer unscathed observers.

"We must get down to our duty stations," shouted Politovsky over the sound of explosions.

Seconds later, another shell struck, blowing the rear funnel overboard. Shards of metal, some like flying daggers and others like ragged spears, flew through the air, killing the closest sailors and wounding a dozen others. Medical crews raced along the deck to collect the injured and transport them to the ship's dressing station.

Several of the bluejackets on the evacuation team slipped in the gore, falling to the deck and dropping stretchers and wounded men. A smell of excrement mixed with blood, vomit, burning oil and gunpowder surged through the passage ways. Nearly blinded by the smoke and choking back bile, the medical teams reloaded the wounded on stretchers and, shaken, struggled to the surgical stations below. Moments later a third projectile struck the observation bridge, bringing down the signal mast.

"That was my duty station!" exclaimed Veliski. "What do I do now?"

"There will be many more casualties if this keeps up. Go help the doctors," yelled Alexei.

It was not supposed to be like this, he thought, as the cruiser shuddered with each successive impact. They had guns that threw heavy shells, but they seemed to have no effect on the Japanese ships, and the *Mikhail* was being systematically torn apart. The stench of smoke and smoldering flesh assaulted his senses. Men had been flung about the deck, and in their agony they screamed and begged for anything that would stop the pain—vodka, morphine. Others pleaded for their comrades to kill them and end their torment.

A sailor, his pants blown away and his legs a mass of shredded flesh and bone, lay at Alexei's feet. The man stared up at him, mouthing the words, "Help me." Sickened and helpless, Alexei backed away, turned and ran. A decapitated head slammed into his back, knocking him to the deck. He lay immobile as another shell burst directly above. Shards of steel rain flayed a half-dozen bluejackets who had emerged from a burning turret. Bile rose in Alexei's throat at the sight of exploding heads; he retched, and a fetid, gelatinous mass spewed from deep within. Breathing heavily he stared at the mess as if he had expelled his very soul. "Oh, Mother," he moaned, "say the prayers. Please say the prayers. Let Him hear me."

Alexei had known fear in the barracks attack, but then he had been able to defend himself, he had been able to fight back; this was different. Now his entire world had turned into utter madness. Rising to his knees, he stared at the head that rolled about at his feet. Only a tuft of hair remained. There were no eyes, only gory sockets. The mouth was open and Alexei gazed into a blackened hole. He felt as if his heart had stopped. The ringing in his ears would not cease and for a moment he wondered if he was still whole.

A demented screech like a siren from Hell shot from a pierced funnel. Alexei slapped his hands over his ears but could not keep out the wailing sound. Out of rage, out of terror, he screamed as a forward magazine exploded, blowing an entire turret into the air.

For what seemed an eternity he remained on his knees. Then slowly, painfully, he rose to his feet. He was shaking uncontrollably and the bile burned in his throat. Gasping and with blurry eyes, he saw smoke and flame rising from dozens of Russian ships. It was an unmitigated disaster. The fleet was made of toys—leaden children's toys, the same he'd played with as a child, he thought. This is what it had all come to, he suddenly understood. All knew that the fleet had its weaknesses, but they should have been able to inflict some damage, at least give a telling and honorable response. Now the fleet was only capable of an apocalyptic finale: a dying wail.

"We know how to die," the admiral had said. *His prophesy has come to pass*, thought Alexei. He rubbed vomit from his face and stared at his once white, immaculate jacket. Blood, spittle, the stain of coal and fragments of human tissue had turned it into a canvas painted by a lunatic.

"Oh God of Israel," he heard himself saying, but the God of Israel, Abraham and Isaac was not there, nor was mercy. Would Olga, if she could see this carnage, be holding her hands to her face? Would she be repeating the holy words she'd beseeched him to utter? "Hear, O Israel..."

Another shell burst aft. Alexei grabbed the railing and watched spell-bound as the bodies of sailors were hurled skyward before plummeting into the sea. A cry of utter despair rose from him. It was all futile, so futile. The swaggering bravado of men going to war, his own pride at being an officer in the Tsar's Navy was rendered senseless as men, in utter terror, sought sanctuary somewhere, anywhere on the flaming, groaning ship. But there was no sanctuary, and they knew it.

Again he sank to his knees and tried to still his hands. He was going to die; they were all going to die, and their deaths would not be heroic, nor noble, nor tranquil. He felt immobilized; dullness like a heavy blanket came over him. He closed his eyes and imagined Kimi-san; he ached to simply hold her again, and he felt tears well in his eyes.

A deafening blast erupted above him. A gun muzzle flashed. The concussion rolled him over and over. There was Politovsky, shouting, reaching for him, but he seemed a blackened specter, a ghostly, disembodied thing. *Why is he doing this? Why is he pulling on me? All we have to do is sit here and wait for the end*, he thought. *Isn't it over?* Igor's mouth was moving but Alexei could hear nothing; all sound was reduced to a silent scream somewhere in his brain.

Slowly he tried to rise. "What? What are you talking about?" he mumbled, certain that his words would be stolen, swallowed by the terrible scream.

"Get up, you have to get up!" bellowed Politovsky, shaking Alexei as if that would bring him back to his senses.

"It's no good, no good," Alexei repeated dully, waving to the carnage about them. Overwhelming fatigue enervated him. All he wanted was to sit down, to hide from it all. A hard slap stung his face and he heard Politovsky say, "Stand! We have to do something! We're officers, men are staring at us."

Alexei squinted through the blurriness and could indeed see numbed, shaken bluejackets looking at them. "Officers," Politovsky had said. The men seemed to be waiting for a command—anything that would motivate them to do something important, something useful. His head was clearing and his hands ceased shaking. He began to comprehend the words as Politovsky let loose of him. He rose, shakily, to his feet.

Both men stared as a great flash erupted a thousand yards away. There was a sudden explosion, and they stood transfixed as the battleship *Oslyabya* blew into fragments that soared a thousand feet into the darkening sky. Moments later came a second sheet of flame, and the great ship rolled over and disappeared from sight.

"She's gone. Just like that," whispered Politovsky in disbelief. Stunned, their attention turned to the *Borodino*, also stricken by enormous shells. Huge pieces of steel blew away and fell, hissing, into the sea. "My God," he said, "Look, I can see men going overboard. They're abandoning ship. That makes three of our biggest."

"The Japanese will be turning their guns on the *Alexander*," said Alexei, finding his voice. "She's our last one."

"So much smoke; it's hard to see," said Politovsky. "There she is, listing and low in the water. Incredible. How can they have destroyed all our capital ships so quickly?"

"I don't know, but it can't last much longer," gasped Alexei. The stench from his clothes was causing the bile in his throat to rise again.

"But her secondary guns are still firing," said Politovsky. "See, she's still fighting, Alexei. It's not over!"

Of course it is, thought Alexei, as a shell exploded off the port bow of the *Mikhail*. Debris and bodies lay all about, but the vessel was still making steam, turning, twisting in a frantic attempt to evade hundreds of guns. Thick, black smoke from downed funnels poured across the aft deck. "See, the *Alexander* is receiving fire now and she's being blown apart just like the others. It's over, Igor."

"Look at me," said Politovsky, as they were drenched by the wave from a near miss. "It's already getting dark and we're still afloat. We still have our guns down below. Maybe we can get away, get to Vladivostok. We have to try, Alexei. We have to!"

"What's the use? Our best ships are gone, what chance have we? Our guns aren't even aimed at the Japanese ships," Alexei said. The stricken cruiser swung drunkenly to starboard and smoke from a funnel's stub spewed over them, adding a layer of black dust to their jackets. Half blinded by the smoke, they stumbled over bodies and sheared metal to a descending gangway. Coughing fits assailed them, but finally Politovsky put his hands on Alexei's shoulders and said, "My friend, I don't know what chance we really have. Probably none; I know that. But dying is not the thing: how we die is, and we must die like men. We must fight if we can. Let's go down to our guns. We can bloody the bastards. Let's do it for the admiral, Alexei, let's run out the guns!"

Alexei's eyes bored into Igor and despite himself he laughed. "You are insane, Igor. You are the most ludicrous idiot I have ever known. But, yes, we'll do that. Let's get to the crews, what's left of them."

"Our battleships are gone and the Japanese destroyers will be coming for us. Maybe we can hold them off with our six-pounders. If we keep steaming we might get through the night, and I damn sure want to kill some of them," said Igor, pointing to the fast ships already bearing toward them.

"Then let's fire the damn guns," said Alexei, "And then we will die."

"Yes, like men," said Politovsky almost joyously. "We will die like men."

CHAPTER 35

A flotilla of four Japanese destroyers sped through the night, their quarry illuminated by the fires coming from the Russian battleship's superstructure and great rents in her hull.

"You're going for the *Suvoroff*?" William- Stuart Jones asked Superior Lieutenant Itomo Karamatsu.

"Her main battery is silenced, but the six-inch guns are still firing. My squadron has been ordered to sink her."

"Her machine guns are also in action," remarked Jones, after a line of bullets stitched its way across the top of the destroyer's observation bridge. A window shattered and a sailor fell, his face lacerated by glass. Sailors immediately carried him to the infirmary below.

"Load all torpedo tubes," Itomo commanded his second lieutenant. The ship increased speed as its forward mount silenced a machine gun on the Russian battleship.

"It was a beautiful ship; it's a shame," said the English journalist as Itomo's machine gunners picked off sailors running along the *Suvoroff's* listing decks.

"They should have considered that before they went to war," said Itomo curtly. "I have no sympathy for them. They killed many of our people in Manchuria. War is not a pleasant thing, Mr. Jones."

The battleship, its ram bow rising from the water, seemed immense as the torpedo destroyer approached. Closing on Admiral Rozhestvensky's flagship, Itomo could see men pointing at his vessel, but the destroyer's torpedoes were already on their way. Moments later, a series of explosions ripped open the warship's hull, blowing many of her sailors overboard. Surviving crew members attempted to launch lifeboats, but most of the small craft fell and capsized into the sea with their occupants or, riddled with holes, quickly sank. One still afloat was machine-gunned. Men screamed as bullets ripped into them; others jumped overboard, only to drown in the night's black sea.

The battleship, like a great dying whale, rolled over, its barnacle-encrusted bottom wallowing. Dozens of men slid over its side. Multiple explosions ripped through her when sea water reached the boilers, throwing steel plates hundreds of feet into the air. Then she was gone: sliding to the bottom was the pride of the Tsar's Navy and a thousand of his men, leaving roiling water and debris floating to the surface.

"Now the cruisers," said Itomo, ordering a new course for his unscathed destroyers.

***

The *Mikhail* was an unrecognizable labyrinth of twisted steel and gaping holes. Smoke and flame poured from fires on lower decks; the air was rent by frantic shouts and screams.

Politovsky and Alexei, arriving at their six-pounders, were amazed to see that the icon of Saint Andrew had not been damaged. "See, Alexei, the saint is still with us. It's a good omen, isn't it?"

Alexei nodded for Igor's sake, but saw that the venerated painting in its glass enclosure was off kilter. The holy water sprinkled on the guns did not make them invincible; the icon, the blessing by the priest provided no miraculous protection from Japanese high explosives. The last act would be played out according to the whims of Fate and Luck; it was as simple as that, he thought.

He noticed that the last life boat on deck was riddled with holes. There would be no way out. Glancing up at the shattered, burning remains of the bridge, it appeared that most if not all of its occupants must be dead. The ship's return fire had become intermittent, and all of the cruiser's main batteries were steel coffins for incinerated crews. A four-foot long *portmanteau* laden with high explosives burst off the *Mikhail's* bow, severing the anchor chains and tumbling the anchors overboard. The cruiser was listing five degrees and only its watertight doors were keeping her afloat.

Below deck acrid smoke and flame filled the corridors, and shrapnel littered the passageways. The stench of burning flesh once again assaulted Alexei as they passed bodies and parts of bodies on their way aft. Some sailors, carrying wounded, picked their way to aid stations further below, but others sat immobile in utter resignation.

"You must go to your duty station," said Politovsky, trying to prod one such bluejacket along. But the man stared at him with a vacant look and refused to move.

"Look at his foot, Igor. It's shattered, he can't walk," said Alexei.

Months ago, the passageways had been jammed with coal, but gradually the stores had been exhausted and the passageways cleared. Now they were like a stygian chambers in Hades, with bare light bulbs flickering on and off illuminating grotesque corpses. Some bulkheads had been blown off their hinges, revealing interior cabins strewn with shattered equipment, their occupants lying in puddles of blood.

"Praise God, you've come," said a sailor when Alexei and Politovsky reached the six-pounders. "We were hoping that we would live long enough to fight," said the *michman*. "Sirs, we had nothing to shoot at, the enemy is so far away. You see what it's like in here. Most of our six-pounders are already scrap metal and the crews..." The man had been speaking rapidly but he stopped and said, "Please excuse me for going on so. Some of the men wanted to go up on deck, but I kept them down here so we could fight."

"That was a good decision," said Igor. "We will have that chance very soon. You are brave men and I will commend you to the admiral when this is over. You shall all be promoted," he said, raising his voice over the inferno beyond.

"See," the *michman* said, turning triumphantly to the eight survivors of the gun crews. "I told you that our officers would come back. They have not forsaken us, lads. Now we will fight gallantly, as we did against the Mongols, the Swedes and the terrible Turks. We will fight for the Tsar, our patron Saint Andrew, and Holy Mother Russia!"

"Down here we haven't been able to see much of the battle," said one of the gunners. "How is the fleet doing? We must have sunk nearly all the enemy by now."

Alexei glanced at Igor, who gave a slight nod. He then looked at the sailor and said, "Our men are doing well; they're fighting bravely and with good heart. The Tsar will be proud of them."

"See, I knew it," said the *michman*. "We'll show those monkeys what cold Russian steel is really like. For the Tsar, our loved ones, and the Motherland!" the man announced, as the ratings slapped each other on the back. Alexei, caught up in the moment, put his arm around Politovsky's shoulder and the *michman,* just as the ship quaked from the impact of another round.

Peering out of the firing port, a gunner shouted, "They're coming! The destroyers are getting closer!"

In the dark it was the torpedo's phosphorescent bow wave that signaled its deadly approach.

"Yes, two of them off the stern quarter, do you see, Alexei?" shouted Politovsky above the din of bursting shells. "Man your gun!" He and his crew rushed to theirs, fifteen feet away.

As a crewman lifted a shell from the storage locker, a sudden blast tore Igor's six-pounder off its carriage. Two crewmen were slammed against a bulkhead. One died with a "Whuff!" as his breastbone was crushed into his spine; the other stared aghast at the stumps that had been legs moments before. Thick smoke enveloped the gun bay as Alexei rushed over.

"Igor, are you alive?" The dry smoldering stench of burnt bone and flesh, the fear of his friend's ghastly death, set his hands shaking again. "This coffin, this damn coffin!" he shouted. But Politovsky emerged, black with soot, jacket ripped and stained. Through a wracking cough he said, "Your gun, Alexei. We must shoot your gun."

Joyous to see his friend, Alexei returned to the weapon and began issuing orders. "Up elevation, compensate for the list, *michman*." The gun was trained on the closest destroyer.

"Yes, I will compensate," said the gunner, anxiously eyeing the enemy ship steaming at them with machine guns blazing. Excitement surged through the crew as a round was shoved into the breech. They would actually be able to hit back, to send fire and steel into a pitiless foe.

Alexei felt an elation he had not expected. A seething desire to impale, to tear asunder glowed on the faces of the men; to scream like savages hurling spears at monsters of the night.

The lead destroyer sheared through the black sea. She was close now, very close, and in the light of the *Mikhail's* fires Alexei could see the Japanese sailors swinging out the torpedo tubes.

"Are you aiming for the bridge?" asked Politovsky, looking over Alexei's shoulder.

"No, we have to get the tubes. Even with the bridge gone she can still sink us," said Alexei.

"I can see their captain," said Igor, raising glasses to his eyes. "He's going to give the order."

"Fire!" shouted Alexei, and the six-pounder belched flame. A second later the torpedo station was obliterated by the incoming shell. There was a blinding flash, and the few survivors, uniforms afire, ran from the conflagration.

"You got him!" shouted Politovsky, slapping Alexei on the back. "Now the bridge."

"She's turning away, we must hurry," yelled a crewman, flinging open the gun's breech.

"Another round," ordered Alexei, his attention turning to a second destroyer coming up fast.

"We need more shells," said Politovsky. Commanding four sailors to follow, he turned and raced toward an ammunition locker across the deck.

Alexei trained the gun on the approaching ship, but the shell exploded prematurely, sending jagged fragments through the gun port. One sailor only had time to scream before collapsing. Everything was frantic now, a blur of activity. The practiced, methodical sequence of loading, aiming, firing and reloading, done so orderly in training, was blindly ignored. Men shouted and rushed about.

"Hurry! It's getting closer. Another round for the second one!" shouted Alexei. A three-inch projectile slammed into the gun port and he was flung across the deck. He shielded his eyes from the inferno that incinerated Politovsky and the gunners. Alexei screamed as his arm was ripped open by hot shards of jagged metal. All about was smoke and fire. A hole appeared in the hull behind him, its steel plates bent outward.

He opened his eyes and crawled to where Politovsky had been, but there were only pools of blood and slips of intestines. "No! You can't die!" Alexei shouted, but he realized that it was all about dying. "We will die like men," Igor had said. Now nothing remained of him. Was there anything left of his being that God would see or pity? Alexei pushed his hands into the mess that had been his friend and in anguish smeared it over his face.

Trembling, he crawled on hands and knees to the remains of his gun and sat beside the splintered metal that reflected the light of flames. Alone, he curled up as a pall of smoke enveloped him. He felt so small, so insignificant. Everyone was dead; he should be dead too. It would not be long now, and then it would be over, he told himself. It was becoming impossible to breathe in the choking smoke.

"Oh Lord," he whispered, "Make it be over. Do it!" he shouted, rage suddenly overwhelming him.

And then it came. The blast sheared open the hull and Alexei spun helplessly into the night.

The water was dark and so terribly cold. Stunned by the shock, he felt himself sinking deeper and deeper. A ship's mast plunged past him, its wires streaming behind like jellyfish tentacles. The torso of a sailor descended not a foot from him; its limp hand momentarily caressed Alexei's face as it made its journey to the bottom of the sea.

At four meters down the sea ceased to churn and, except for muted sounds from the dying ship, there was silence. His air nearly gone, Alexei wondered if he would ever come to the surface. For an instant there was a sense of peace. He would have no more responsibilities; there were no more orders to be given, no more fighting to be done.

Visions rose as the current pulled him away from the *Mikhail*: a tranquil Buddhist temple, a cherry blossom, the face of Kimi-san. Had they been there together, he wondered? He could not remember; it was so long ago. It suddenly occurred to him that she was no more than a hundred miles away.

Sadness came over him; he would never see her again. It was all a dream, distant and unattainable.

What might she think, he wondered, when she heard he was dead? Would she know? Would she pray for his soul? Would she cry and mourn for him? Finally, in death, would he enter her dreams, brush her lips and whisper words of love?

The sense of cold, like an electric jolt, shot through him again. His hands pushed downward and there was illumination above. He shot to the surface, gasping for air. Eyes stinging, he looked about. Everywhere floated bodies and charred pieces of wood. A footlocker bobbed three inches above the surface and he grabbed its handle. The box would keep him afloat, but it was too small to climb onto. He knew that he had to get out of the water before hypothermia killed him. He pushed away the corpse of a bluejacket, its eyes glazed in terror, its mouth open in the rictus of a frozen scream.

Gun flashes bloomed on the horizon and a huge detonation split the *Mikhail* in half. The stern rose perpendicular to the sea, its propellers turning madly. Alexei watched as the jagged bow slid beneath the waves. With a drawn out hiss, the stern followed, the propellers whipping spray across surface. A two-foot wave swelled outward, then there was nothing. Six hundred souls, gasping for the last dregs of air, went plummeting downward.

Still clutching the footlocker, Alexei spied a lifeboat fifty yards ahead. It rose and fell in the troughs as two-dozen bluejackets pulled at its oars. Abandoning the box, he shouted and struck out for it. A man stood up, his hands resting on the shoulders of a sailor for balance. His white officer's jacket was illuminated by oil fires on the water.

The officer focused on an approaching ship, its bow splitting the sea. He barked orders, but some of the rowers reversed oars while others froze in horror as the destroyer charged toward them. The lifeboat swerved and slowed, and Alexei's distance narrowed to a few yards. A sailor shouted encouragement as he gained on the wallowing craft. Grabbing the gunnel he stared up in stunned amazement at the white-jacketed man. A boot slammed down on his hand and Boris screamed, "Die, die!"

Numbed by cold and shocked by the sudden pain, Alexei had no time to evade the kick that followed. His head spun and he was thrown back into the sea. He slipped below the waves as everything went black.

Itomo's destroyer had just torpedoed a supply ship, and now gunners were massacring sailors flailing in the sea. The ocean had become a shooting gallery, and there would be no mercy for the Emperor's foes.

"Rules of war. You can't keep shooting them," protested Jones, as another lifeboat appeared in the water. Itomo looked to where his junior lieutenant pointed. "Take her in," said Itomo, ignoring the Englishman.

Panic seized men in the lifeboat as the destroyer sped closer. Boris, still standing, stared at the hull emerging out of the night. A searchlight swept over him; its glare illuminating the oarsmen pulling frantically as if a few more yards would save them.

"They're helpless, no need to kill them," shouted Jones.

"Silence! They're enemy," replied Itomo.

Alexei was amazed that he actually surfaced again. He felt the throb of the propeller that brought the destroyer close. Looking up, he saw faces of the crew and the machine gun that suddenly ripped open the night.

A stream of bullets riddled the lifeboat. Men, screaming, begging for mercy, were ejected from the craft, their bodies perforated by heavy rounds.

"There, that one, the officer," shouted Itomo. The gun methodically stitched a line across the white jacket Boris had stolen.

Alexei ducked beneath the surface when the searchlight touched him. The machine gun swiveled, the gunners fired a quick burst. Rounds splattered around him, kicking up spurts of water. Gasping, he came back up. Suddenly a man was shouting, "No! Stop, stop!" He kicked the gun, deflecting its aim.

"What are you doing?" yelled Itomo, infuriated that the journalist would dare to interfere.

"In the water, that man!" bawled Jones, as he grabbed a life ring and hurled it overboard.

"You've got to pick him up! You must!"

Itomo looked down at the face in the water that stared back at him. Nearly frozen, the struggling man mouthed the words, "*Please, Itomo-san. Please.*"

The destroyer sped past and heeled to port a half mile on. The man pulled from the water was unconscious, bleeding and barely alive.

CHAPTER 36

Tokyo, 1906

"Easy, old boy. No tally-ho after the fox just yet."

It was, Alexei realized blearily, the voice of William-Stuart Jones.

"Where am I?" Alexei asked, blinking in the bright morning sun.

"In a little village outside Tokyo. Captain Karamatsu got permission to have you moved here."

"Itomo did? How did he...?" Too many questions surged through his mind. He took a breath and asked, "Is this a hospital?"

"Not exactly. More of a *ryokan,* a hostel of sorts. There are no more Russian prisoners in Japanese hospitals. They went home months ago."

Alexei appeared confused and the journalist said, "The war is over, laddie. Count Witte and the Japanese signed all the documents in America. Theodore Roosevelt acted as broker. The Russians got more than they had any right to expect, and the Japanese are quite upset about that. Yes, indeed, the Russians regained control over all their prewar possessions, so the Japanese feel that their sailors and soldiers all died in vain. There was rioting in Tokyo, you know. This was the latest unequal treaty, and trouble will come of it, mark my words."

"I can't remember anything past the *Mikhail* going down."

"Nasty business, what? Lucky for you that I was on Itomo's destroyer. I saw you in the water just before the machine gunners wanted to use you for target practice. I suggested in my most pleasant manner that your old friend pick you up, since he just happened to be passing by. As Wellington said at Waterloo, 'It was a close run thing.'"

"How many others lived?"

"From your ship? One lifeboat got away with a dozen or so. Admiral Kochenkov is alive. Miraculous, really. Nearly everyone else was shot. Bloody unsporting, but the Japanese play by a different set of rules."

"What of the fleet? Did any ships survive?"

"Almost all sunk. Some of the smaller vessels found neutral ports; others were interned by the Japanese. Only three warships actually made it to Vladivostok, but they never left port. It would have been suicide."

It was all so quiet. They were on a low hill and Alexei could see a village and a park below. A soft snow had fallen during the night, coating everything in downy white. It was the snowfall that convinced him of the truth of what he'd heard; many months had indeed passed.

"Rozhestvensky also survived. He was in bad shape, but the crew got him on a Russian destroyer before the *Suvoroff* went down. Tojo met with him and said he was quite brave but had little chance, his ships being old and outgunned. He's also back in St. Petersburg. Had to face an inquiry. The Tsar said that the disaster was in God's hands. Nicholas just wrote it all off. And bye the bye, the Admiralty has lost track of you. There is no record of your survival. They must assume you're dead, along with so many others."

"But I am here. How can there be no record?"

"Any such report was destroyed. On someone's suggestion, dear boy. Rather untoward, but she...." Jones let the sentence trail off.

Alexei looked at him blankly. It was too much to take in.

"But wasn't I with other wounded Russian officers?"

"No, this *ryokan* was just for you. Karamatsu has been promoted to full captain; he can do almost anything he wants. He's a war hero." Jones thought for a moment, then added, "Now that you are back in the world, I thought I should give this to you. It was found in your pocket. I fear its contents did poorly in the water, though."

From his jacket pocket he extracted a small metal object and handed it to Alexei. "Hebrew inscription on it, I surmise."

"A *mezuzah*. My mother gave it to me before the fleet set out. She's Jewish, you know."

"Then so are you. Shalom, shalom," Jones said with a grin. "Who would have thought it?"

"My mother cherished this, and so do I," said Alexei. After a pause he said, "I wonder what it will be like for me in St. Petersburg."

"Well, you won't be too popular in Holy Mother Russia right now. Pogroms and murder. Plehve and his Black Hundreds are expelling thousands of Jews. Does anybody in the Admiralty know your faith?"

"Only my father, my mother and Count Brusilov."

"I thought that Count Brusilov was your father."

"So did I, for a very long time."

"Unless you can keep your religion a secret, I would not advise you to go back. Let things settle down. As I said, they won't be looking for you."

"I have no desire to go back, nor do I intend to remain in the navy."

"There is damn little navy to return to."

Alexei's eyes strayed to a night stand and he focused on a single flower. "What month is this?" he asked, a surge of excitement coursing through him.

"February, my dear boy. You've been in and out of consciousness for some time."

"Winter."

"February is winter in most places. Not all." Then looking at the flower, Jones said, "Ah, yes. A young lady brings one every evening. It is said that she has found a tree that seems immune to the cold. Maybe it's sheltered somehow. Quite unusual, although I must say she is too."

"She must be nearby if she comes every night."

"True, true. She often comes with her brother and Tadichi-san."

"Tadichi-san?"

"Yes, Tadichi-san. Your son."

***

It was midday when he ventured down the hill to the little park with its snow-covered shrine. A breeze lifted the collar of his overcoat and the hand that held the derby shook with nervous strain. The park bench had been cleaned of snow and she sat, her back to him, reading a book. A short distance away a child was scraping up a mound of snow. Hearing footsteps, the boy turned and looked at the man, who smiled at him.

"*Konichiwa*, good afternoon," the man said.

"Oh!" Kimi-san exclaimed, hearing the familiar voice. The mystified boy watched his mother fly into the man's arms.

"Alexei-san, Alexei-san," she murmured. "You've come back to me."

"Yes, I've come back, but in my heart I've never been gone."

Alexei took both his son's hand and Kimi-san's, and they began walking toward the train station.

"We have been staying nearby. I was waiting and hoping you would come today," said Kimi-san.

They passed a tree, its branches nearly bare. A single flower bloomed on it. Alexei carefully picked it and gave it to her.

"*Arigato,*" she said, thanking him with a shy smile. "A cherry blossom. The last one."

"Yes, how remarkable; a cherry blossom in winter."

Contrary to Japanese custom she walked beside him and held his hand.

"It's not far," said Tadichi-san.

"No, it's not far now," said Alexei as they walked from the park.

EPILOGUE

St. Petersburg, 1910

Bare-headed, Alexei felt the cold November rain trickle down his neck. He pulled his scarf closer, but it did little to conserve warmth in the pervading chill. Leaden clouds hung over St. Petersburg in an ominous pall. A powdery snow lay upon the casket. The priest's censer emitted a fragrance of myrrh and his chant floated into the air of the cemetery. It was already long past noon and the light would soon be gone. Alexei, standing beside Admiral Kochenkov and Ekaterina, wondered if his mother, a once beautiful jewel of the court, would have wanted to be here.

"I went to the house hoping to see Olga, but she wasn't there. Where is she staying? Is she well?" Alexei asked quietly.

"When she left here she was frail but in reasonably good health. I was sad to see her go. We had shared so much, and that includes you."

"But you say she's gone away. Where?"

"To New York. She's living with relatives who went there in '06 during the early riots against the Jews. Your mother waited, hoping that you would return, but left a year ago. She didn't want to live in that house anymore. So I have the house back again. I'll sell it. I don't want it either. I wish I could tell you that the count left you an inheritance, but he spent all his money. He even donated some to the war effort."

Alexei stopped and looked at the admiral. "I don't care about the money or any inheritance. I doubt the authorities would let me have it anyway. But I am concerned about my mother, and yes, I feel guilty, terribly guilty for not writing. But I was in a different world, I hope you understand."

"I do; I know what war does to a man's mind. But I don't think she does. She cried after Tsushima, and consoling her was impossible."

"I should have known. I was thoughtless. But New York? She never mentioned—"

"It is not safe here for a Jew, Alexei. Sooner or later she would have been found out. She was always afraid of discovery. And besides, she assumed that you had perished, along with so many others."

"It's my fault," said Alexei, his shoulders slumped. "I should have written. I could have gotten her word of what happened."

"You could have, I suppose. But I assume she's still alive, and you and Kimi-san can sail there. I know the address. At least write to her; she would be so happy to hear from you."

"Of course, I shall write and let her know that we are coming. I had been thinking about America, a place of opportunity. Yes, I think Kimi-san will be happy there."

"I know that for now the Americans still have a love affair with Japan, the small, exotic country that ripped the guts out of the great Russian bear."

"For now?"

"Yes, for now. Japan and America, two Pacific naval powers and only one pond. Political winds are fickle, Alexei, and the Japanese have not forgotten the cost of the treaty that was forced on them—in part by America. That wind may become blustery. What do the Japanese call it, a Great Wind?"

"Divine Wind, *kamikaze*."

"Ah, yes, the wind that destroyed the Mongol invasion. But the Japanese better tread lightly with America. I sailed to America as a cadet, you know."

"I did not know," said Alexei pulling up the collar of his heavy coat.

"They are an energetic and determined people; Manifest Destiny and all that. When angered I suspect they have a terrible resolve. But for now you and your wife will be welcomed there."

"And my sons. We have two now."

Congratulations. I would like to see my grandchildren someday," said the admiral. He reflected a moment then said, "About the count, Alexei. He told me that he hoped to meet you again, to make amends. If that would be possible."

"In a way I was hoping to see him. We might have had convivial words." Then he added, "Perhaps."

Alexei's memories of the man in the coffin, Count Yevgeny Brusilov, were unpleasant and remote, their contentious relationship never softened by time. It had been six years since he had last seen him, six years since he had wanted to see him or any of Russia, for that matter. Had the Trans- Siberian Railway been faster, he might have spoken with the man before the stroke ended his world. Perhaps they might have spoken conciliatory words that would have papered over the great divide. But that was not to be.

The service concluded and the half-dozen mourners tendered their condolences; then, hoping to escape the cold, they hurried through the cemetery gates. Ekaterina laid a flower on the casket.

"You will miss him?" the admiral asked his wife.

"In a way, yes. We had good times and, well, moments that could have been better. We saw little of each other these last years, and he was pleasant those few times we met. Of course, there was no longer any intimacy. Yes, I regret his passing," she said wistfully.

Then, taking Alexei's hand in her own gloved hand, she said, "Do come by before you leave, if you really insist upon leaving."

When she walked away only Alexei and Admiral Kochenkov remained. "I am going to my office. I have dispatches I must look at, but I still have time for lunch. Join me; we have much to discuss, and I know of a nice, quiet restaurant."

They passed a statue of Tsar Alexander III and Kochenkov said, "There are certain things the count wanted me to tell you."

The oil lamps were already being lit along the Neva as they walked past the Winter Palace. "Abandoned since 1905, the Tsar and his family stay at their palace at Tsarskoye Selo," said the admiral. "That is one of the lasting effects of the war. It exacerbated the poverty of Russia and added to the insularity of the Court. And then there's Rasputin, that 'mad monk' who's unassailable and screwing every woman he wants. Or should I say, any woman of high society. He's quite particular that way."

"But not the Tsarina," said Alexei.

"He would not go that far, but he gets all he wants. Women throw themselves at him. It's quite fashionable in our decadent circles. Aristocratic women with their lives centered on balls and ceremonies have little else to do. The Tsarina calls him 'our friend', since he hypnotizes her son every time the lad has a bout of hemophilia."

"What does Tsar Nicholas say about Rasputin?"

"What can he say? He wouldn't argue with his wife. The boy's condition is not much of a secret any more. They panic every time the Tsarevich bumps his knee. "

"We don't get newspapers where we're living; it's a very remote village in Hokkaido. I'm surprised you even found me."

"I wouldn't have, except that I ran into your old friend, William Stuart Jones. But for him we wouldn't have known that you're alive. We assumed that everybody else on the ship was dead: drowned or shot or blown up. The count was astonished to hear that you survived. He wondered why you didn't return after the war."

"I really didn't consider it, after marrying Kimi-san."

"And now?"

Alexei shook his head. "They wouldn't fit in here, and neither would I. To them this would be a hostile and alien land; they would not be welcome here. Besides, I may still be on the books as an officer, and that could be a problem."

"You're worried that not returning after the was will mark you as a deserter?"

"That's why I'm leaving tonight. I'm hoping that I wasn't recognized by the *Okhrana*."

"You weren't. Nobody from the police or the Court attended the funeral, but I'm surprised that you weren't stopped at the port."

"I don't look the same now."

"Still," said Kochenkov remorsefully, "I should have considered the danger and not have asked you to come. Surviving Tsushima and not reporting to the Admiralty... internal security would have serious questions."

"I thought I should come," Alexei replied.

They walked in silence until Alexei remarked, "You said the count wanted to speak with me before he died."

"As I said, he hoped to make amends. He was an ultra-nationalist, like so many of us back then. In the end, Yevgeny regretted the war and all its unfortunate consequences, including sending you to certain death."

"I didn't think sending me was up to him."

"He had influence, and the fleet needed an officer who could speak Japanese," said the admiral.

"So he volunteered my name."

"Yes, but I wanted you on my ship as well. I think I told you that."

"As I recall, I was asking a lot of questions about our lack of preparedness, even before we went to sea. How could the Admiralty fail to foresee the potential for disaster?"

"Minds made up don't want contrary advice. And they argued that improvements were being made for Port Arthur's defense. The count was with the war party back then, and they influenced the Tsar. Nicholas was all for expanding Russian influence in the Far East—and beyond."

Alexei's father sighed deeply, then said, "It was a long time ago, now it's a footnote in history. I'm just glad that we both survived Tsushima. Damn few did. But there are more things to worry about now. I should not be saying this, but we have a dying regime."

"That bad?" said Alexei.

"It's a very unsettled time: revolutionaries and unrest. I might not have thought so before, but there must be changes. Nicholas insists on supreme autocratic power. What are we to do?" The admiral lapsed into silence then said, "Enough of that."

Kochenkov directed Alexei to the Nevsky Prospect, lined with expensive shops, hotels and restaurants. The snow began to fall more thickly, limiting visibility. The wide street was illuminated by gas lamps, backlighting snowflakes with an eerie glow.

"I found this place over twenty years ago," said Kochenkov as he ushered Alexei to a corner table beside a double-paned window. "It's not fancy, but it has the best bread in Russia."

Most of the patrons had scurried home. A scent of dampness pervaded the steamy interior as they removed their heavy coats.

"I used to bring Svetlana here when she was a child. The chef adored her and would give her pastries until she nearly burst. My life is all memories now. My future is a mirror and the only reflection, Alexei, is my dubious past."

The admiral peered through the falling snow to the Neva, now a sheet of blue ice. A few brave souls skated upon it, their bundled forms drifting in and out of the fog.

"Ah, dear, crazed Svetlana; my treasure and my curse. I should have seen it coming—the trouble with her and Boris. There was madness in her from the start. She was uncontrollable; so wild, and she flaunted her beauty—like her mother."

"I was young and could hardly comprehend what was happening," said Alexei. "And there was that pervading fear my mother whispered about."

"Secrets," said Grigory Kochenkov, as he glanced out the window. "Ah, look, another military parade, even in this weather. And is anybody watching?"

"Which unit is that?" asked Alexei.

"The Cossack Konvoi, the Tsar's personal regiment. And it's followed by an infantry company. Freezing to death, poor souls. Alexei, the city has become a stage for one regiment after another, each with its own fancy uniform. You would think we'd had enough of war."

A waitress filled a cup with tea from a samovar and set it on the table, which was festooned with embroidered doilies. The admiral took an appreciative sip and said, "So, does all this look familiar? Do you miss the intrigue of Holy Mother Russia, or the sea? Or has tilling the soil like a peasant settled into your bones?"

"Tolstoy tilled the soil alongside his peasants. I enjoy the tranquility of tilling the soil, and I won't drown in it. There is a beauty in silence, and that's very comforting."

Three well-dressed men in heavy coats entered and cast glances at Alexei and Grigory Kochenkov.

The admiral abruptly tossed a half-dozen kopeks on the table and said, "It's getting stuffy in here. Let's walk."

Once on the street, the admiral said, "I am a loyal servant of the state, but I have my own thoughts. I don't care to share them with the secret police."

"And those men were with the *Okhrana*?"

The admiral looked at Alexei and raised an eyebrow. "I can smell them, the bastards." Then he smirked and said, "Your old friend Sergei would have fit in quite nicely with today's revolutionaries."

Alexei smiled and asked, "What made you think of Sergei?"

"His name just came to mind. He was the finest épée man at the Academy. It seems so long ago... and now they are all gone."

"He was good; I had a dozen rips in my jacket to prove it," agreed Alexei.

"But you were the saber man. Nobody was better. Do you still fence?"

"No. I was fast in my youth, but my arm is too stiff now. The war."

"I only wish that he had gotten a commission. But in the end it made little difference," said the admiral.

Alexei and his father walked to the dock where a Japanese freighter was preparing to sail. "So this is goodbye, at least for now, Lieutenant Alexei Kochenkov of the *Mikhail III*," said his father, smothering him in a bear hug. "I am honored that you have taken my name."

"I will write, and I promise to see you again," said Alexei.

"That's what your admiral expects. Consider it an order. Now as we Russians say, 'Eat salt and speak the truth.' I wish you the best. Journey well."

Alexei saluted his father. The admiral began walking through the falling snow. Half way down the street, Grigory Kochenkov waved, turned a corner and headed for the Admiralty. Alexei, now alone with his thoughts, boarded the freighter and slipped from St. Petersburg to the land of tranquil shrines and the woman and children who awaited his return.

AUTHOR'S NOTE

The Russo-Japanese war was the first major conflict of the Twentieth Century. Like most international wars, it was fraught with gross misunderstanding, over-confidence and xenophobia. As with all writers of historical novels, I have attempted to offer an understanding of the sense of crisis, militaristic jingoism and patriotism that existed in Tsarist Russia and Japan at the start of the last century. I deem it important to bear in mind the fatalism of the Russian navy culminating in the horrific Battle of Tsushima in 1905. That fatalism must be compared to the Bushido spirit, training and quality of ships that favored Japan's outcome in those desperate days.

Many individuals mentioned in the novel did actually exist, including Captain N. Klado; the American boxer, Jim Hercules; politicians V.K. Plehve and Sergei Witte; Admirals Heihachiro Tojo and Zinovy Rozhestvensky; and named members of the royal families.

The Russian cruiser *Mikhail III* is fictitious, but all other naval vessels (including the *Svetlana*) did actually exist, as did all ports of call that harbored the Russian navy.

The incident off Dogger Bank very nearly lead to war between Great Britain and Russia.

The Second Pacific Fleet was required to await the arrival of the decrepit Baltic Fleet, which delayed the sailing of the Russian fleet from the coast of Africa. This delay allowed the Japanese navy time to resupply and reequip their fleet. Had the Russian navy been allowed to proceed without the appendage of the "self-sinkers", it might well have arrived at Port Arthur as originally planned. However, it is questionable that the arrival of the Second Pacific Fleet, combined with the surviving ships of the original Pacific Fleet, would have altered the results of the naval engagement.

The eighteen-thousand-mile journey of the Russian fleet from the Baltic to the Straits of Tsushima, despite breakdowns and bungling, remains one of history's greatest naval exploits.

Admiral Rozhestvensky did survive the war, but only three of his ships evaded destruction by the Japanese fleet and made their way to Vladivostok; several surrendered on the high seas, and others were interned. The horrors of the conflict, though shrugged off by the Tsar, fueled the revolution that ended the Romanov Dynasty in 1917.

Finally, though the war with its hundreds of thousands of casualties remains a footnote in history, the conflict inevitably led to the continued rise of a militaristic Japan, culminating in expansion and Japan's role in World War II.

ABOUT THE AUTHOR

RON SINGERTON

After graduating from California State University at Long Beach in 1965 Ron Singerton joined the U.S. Army Security Agency and spent his overseas time in Asia.

The subsequent twenty-five years were devoted to teaching history and art in Southern California High schools, where he developed a particular love for writing and historical research.

During the early 1980s, he authored a series, *Moments in History,* of some thirty mini books on famous people and events ranging from Columbus to the moon landing. The books were adopted as supplementary teaching material for the State of California and approved by the Los Angeles School board as a teaching aid. Published by Santillana Publishing Company, the original ones are considered collector's items.

An avid horseman and saber fencer with a special interest in the American Civil War, he "heard the bugle and the sound of the drums" and became a re-enactor, riding with the Union cavalry in dozens of engagements from California to Gettysburg, Pennsylvania.

Always interested in an exciting but obscure story, his historical research meandered from the nineteenth and twentieth centuries back to the ancient world. Singerton once said, "Technology of the past often appears elementary to us; the emotions do not." For a writer, the thoughts of peoples long past, as well as civilizations now little more than sand-pitted ruins, still evolve into a pageant of love, intrigue and dire conflict. "It is nothing less than a shadowed mirror of our own world."

Through the writings of Plutarch, Pliny and Julius Caesar he uncovered an epic event that would take him from Rome in the last days of Republic to the Great Wall of China. After years of research the tale became the gist of a two-volume novel: *The Villa of Deceit* and *The Silk and the Sword.*

In his third historical novel, *A Cherry Blossom in Winter*, Singerton turns to the tumultuous opening years of the Twentieth Century with a stirring novel of the Russo Japanese war of 1904.

Ron is also an award winning artist, with artwork in glass, stone, paint and bronze sold and displayed online, in galleries, and numerous art shows.

IF YOU ENJOYED THIS BOOK

Please write a review.
This is important to the author and helps to get the word out to others
Visit

PENMORE PRESS
www.penmorepress.com

Villa of Deceit
BY

Ron Singerton

Action Adventure, Crime, Mystery,

Rome, 70 B.C.E.

A house in turmoil: a controlling father, an adulterous mother, and an angry son made reckless by a forbidden love. Young Gaius defies his father Toronius, fleeing with a slave girl whom he marries, only to see her die in childbirth. Disinherited and grieving, Gaius leaves his infant son Tacitus behind with a trusted aunt and devotes his life to the sword.

On the battle field Gaius is trained and tempered into a hardened veteran of war. His leadership and bravery in campaigns earn him respect and the rank of Senior Centurion. But his greatest challenge is returning home to face his son Tacitus, now grown to a wild, undisciplined youth. Gaius forces the errant boy against his wishes into the army that he may be molded into a man.

Like Gaius before him, Tacitus must fight to become his own man in defiance of his father. But together as Legionnaires, they must survive an invasion mired by betrayal and confront the fury of war.

PENMORE PRESS
www.penmorepress.com

Silk and The Sword
BY

Ron Singerton

Action Adventure, Crime, Mystery, Roman History

Young Tacitus, torn from the girl he loves and accused of defiling his late mother's temple, is dragooned into the Roman army by his father Gaius, a bitter and unbending Centurion. With his father and seven legions, he joins General Marcus Crassus in an ill-fated attack on the sprawling Parthian Empire. After the Roman forces are decimated at the Battle of Carrhae, Tacitus, Gaius, and four hundred survivors venture eastward on the fabled Silk Road to find a river beyond a wall that will lead them back to Rome.Tacitus becomes the soldier he never wanted to be while battling bandits, trekking through frozen mountain passes, and dealing with a formidable foe on the other side of the world. But his greatest challenge is a personal quandary: should he return to Rome for his long-lost love or seek the hand of a princess in the mysterious land beside the Great Wall?

"A tour de force of Roman military survival across a long and arduous trek through the Parthian empire, the silk road, and into the celestial kingdom